美國家庭 (萬用) 英文寫作

從小學到大學，讓你終生受用的親子寫作書！

用英文表達感想
再也不是問題！

給那些為了孩子的「英文寫作能力」而煩惱不已的平凡媽媽們

　　我開始使用親子英文網站 suksuk.com（編註：此網站內容為韓文，是韓國知名親子英文教育網站，懂韓文的讀者可至此網站蒐集大量兒童英文教育資料）已經有六年的時間了。在這裡，我得以和來自全國各地的眾多父母親們結緣，也一路見證了他們的孩子們是如何成長的。原本窩在媽媽懷中聽著英文卡通的孩子，只會聽著播放的 CD 一邊哼歌，可是後來他們竟然也會自動自發的翻起書，甚至開始用英文碎碎唸。看著這樣的他們，我對「親子英文」能提升孩子的英文能力也產生了信心，目前正在努力將親子英文推廣到全國。

　　身為旁觀者的我發現，那些親身實踐親子英文的母親們，內心總有一個角落對英文寫作感到力不從心。因此這一本書不討論「閱讀」，而是以「讓孩子試著以英文寫下自己的想法」這樣的原則出發。為了能夠讓書中內容囊括孩子們會使用到的所有常用句型，本書收錄了邀請親子共同實際創作的英文句型。從 2012 年開始，家長與孩子們同心協力收集撰寫英文文章時常用的句型，直到書籍出版為止，花費的時間一共超過三年。

　　為了讓孩子能夠隨心所欲地寫作，我在英文句型的選擇上的確遇到許多困難。畢竟孩子們的母語和英文能力存在落差，因此要讓他們將母語原封不動地轉換成英文來表達，未免過於困難。再者，如果家長的目標是要讓孩子寫出「漂亮」的英文，這又和孩子們的想法有所出入了。究竟是要讓寫作和平時說話一樣口語化，還是要讓寫作呈現比較文言一點，也著實令我感到苦惱。最後收錄於本書的各種句型，是與幾位教育學者和母語使用者，在經由

無數次討論過、認為不會太過艱澀後而選定的。

　　就算是孩子的母語，寫作的基礎還是在於「閱讀」對吧？相同的道理也可以套用在英文身上。如果擔心孩子的英文寫作能力，不如試著從用英文簡單寫下幾句關於日常生活、或讀過的書的感想開始。寫錯了也沒關係，如果孩子覺得寫作有趣，只要持之以恆，那麼對於英文寫作的恐懼，到了某一天就會被自信給取代。抱持著讓孩子建立寫作自信的企圖心，同時想著是否真能帶來助益，我完成了本書。

　　我想要特別感謝大力協助本書順利問世、來自 suksuk.com 的五位媽媽，她們分別是首爾有石國小金書靜老師、鄭在熙、崔真誠、崔英玉以及文朱利，這一本書也可以算是她們的作品。再來是默默容忍我以各種藉口拖延交稿時間的 Epublic 出版社編輯小組，真心感謝。

suksuk.com 英文教育研究所長

洪賢珠

一同參與本書編寫的
媽媽們的推薦

　　為了編寫出孩子們在寫作上真正會用到的，可以如實表達日常生活大小事和自己想法的英文日記、讀書心得寫作寶典，多年來親自對孩子進行親子英文教育的五位媽媽們也參與了本書的寫作過程。從內容的選定、句型的收集，到英文原文校稿，因為有這五位媽媽們謹慎且辛苦的協助參與，才有本書的誕生。下面是參與本書內容編寫的媽媽們的推薦。

　　雖然我深知指導英文寫作最有效的方法，就是讓學生撰寫英文日記或者英文讀書心得，可是如果真的要指派這項作業給學生，並收回來批改的話，不要說是學生了，就連家長們也會感到困擾。現在有了「美國家庭萬用英文寫作」，就可以輕鬆挑戰這個撰寫英文文章的任務了。特別本書是國內首創的「親子英文寫作書」，書中內容是經過媽媽和孩子們共同參與而編寫出來的，因此所有孩子們想寫的句子都被完整收錄在書裡，我已經開始期待看見孩子們興奮地用英文日記填滿筆記本的模樣了。　　　　　　　- 金書靜（國小英文老師）

　　每次打算寫英文日記的時候，因為不知道該從什麼題材、用什麼方式下筆，結果常常是寫了一兩行就放棄。相信大家都有這種經驗吧？來，從現在開始，如果再遇到這種狀況，就翻開「美國家庭萬用英文寫作」吧！本書內容鉅細靡遺，以英文日記、英文讀書心得寫作的要領當作開始，依照各種情境去分類核心句型和常用表達，而且只挑選孩子們在日常生活中實際會用到的

句子，完整呈現英文日記和英文讀書心得的不同內容和寫作方式。我非常確定，本書將會成為我的孩子，以及其他想要進行親子英文寫作的媽媽們，極為堅強的「英文寫作後盾」。

　　　　　　-鄭在熙（小孩小六生，《幸福英語遊戲百科》（韓文書）作者）

老大開始上小學的時候，我有想過，如果孩子們寫的日記和讀書心得都可以用英文寫的話，那該有多好。不過即使孩子真的用英文寫了，也常常因為不知道寫出來的句子正不正確而感到苦惱。但若想參考市面上的教材，偏偏內容不是偏離了孩子的日常生活，就是僅用幾種簡單的句型而毫無變化，讓我感到非常可惜。所以在編輯本書的時候，我竭盡所能地想把孩子一天的日常生活、意見和感覺等等的題材完整收錄進本書。對於英文寫作感到苦惱或是不知所措的媽媽們，我強烈推薦這本書。

- 崔真誠（小孩小三生和小一生）

繼 2012 年「美國家庭萬用親子英文」後，suksuk 裡的媽媽們為了第二次的全新企劃「美國家庭萬用英文寫作」而齊聚一堂討論。為了要收集孩子們真的會用在英文寫作上的日記和讀書心得內容，媽媽及孩子們於是展開龐大的編撰過程。因為是和孩子們一起進行的企劃，那些大人們想不到的句子，竟如雨後春筍般不停出現。想成為當孩子發出英文寫作的求救信號時，就可以立即親自教學的這種媽媽嗎？這一本書可以讓所有媽媽美夢成真！一句又一句的英文表達累積成了一本親子寫作書，相同的道理，孩子每天練習英文寫作，一句一句地慢慢累積，就能達成寫出完美英文文章的目標。

- 崔英玉（小孩小四生和小一生）

親子英文教學是從孩子幼稚園時期開始的。孩子們鬼靈精怪，喜歡自己編一些好笑的動物故事寫進英文日記裡。字母寫得歪歪斜斜、拼字也很少拼對的孩子們，從高年級開始閱讀英文書籍，也開始會寫讀書心得。如同孩子身高越長越高一般，對於各種英文句型及表達的需求也越發強烈，無奈身為媽媽的我字彙量有限，現在想想，那真是一段令人深感無助的回憶。但在我進行親子英

文寫作教學的期間，因為所有迫切需要的句子都能在本書中找到，使我感到非常開心。特別是《美國家庭萬用英文寫作》不僅只提供單純的範文，內容還包含了許多能夠增廣見聞的多元英文表達，這也是本書的優點之一。不透過補習班或其他課外教學管道，而是由父母親自指導英文寫作是非常困難的一件事。這個時候，就讓《美國家庭萬用英文寫作》來當孩子們最可靠的老師吧！

- 文朱利（小孩國二生）

英文日記寫作，就該這樣教

1 先閱讀「英文童話書」再來談「英文寫作」

所謂的「英文寫作」是指利用英文寫下句子或文章，也就是說孩子必須知道自己要寫些什麼，也知道要如何用英文表達。因此確切地說，要能夠進行英文寫作，必須建立在孩子已經對英文有一定程度了解的基礎之上。

此處的「英文」便是指「英文童話書裡以優美詞句寫成的英文句子」。如果多閱讀那些用優美詞句寫成的英文童話，就可以發現一些雞毛蒜皮的小事也能夠成為寫作題材，也就可以決定文章裡要寫些什麼了。在閱讀了書上出現的單字和句子以後，就可以將它們運用到寫作上。由上述可知，閱讀並試著模仿以優美詞句寫成的英文童話書，是邁向頂尖的英文寫作能力的必經過程。

2 先從零負擔的圖畫日記開始吧！

英文寫作具體來說究竟該從何開始呢？為了要決定「寫作內容」，應該先和孩子好好聊聊一天的生活。不管是用中文還是英文，只要一提到寫作，孩子們常問的問題都是「媽媽，我今天做了什麼？」或者「媽媽，今天要寫什麼？」也就是說，決定「要寫什麼」對於孩子們來說並不是一件簡單的事。

想要開始英文寫作，「英文圖畫日記」將會是個不錯的選擇，對孩子不會有太大負擔。一開始可以先從一天中發生的事件裡任選一件，讓孩子畫出來後，任意寫下

「一個重要的單字」就足夠了。比方說，畫出家人一起外出吃飯的場景，然後在圖畫下方寫下 food、ate/eat、family 這些單字。如果孩子拼字錯誤，就由家長在下方寫上正確的拼法，並且記上日期。另外，如果孩子已經進入可以閱讀完篇幅兩三行的繪本，並可以寫下常見的幾個單字的程度之後，那麼就可以進入下個階段：圖畫下方不再寫上單字，而是以句子來取代。到了這個階段，就算孩子在畫圖上多花了一些時間也不要去催促，因為這時候無法用文字表達的想法正源源不絕地湧現。不僅英文能力提升了，他們也進步到能夠把圖像轉化成文字的全新境界。當寫作的句數逐漸增加，便可以引導他們運用 because 這類的連接詞來加入自己的想法，寫出較長的句子。

3　寫錯了要馬上糾正嗎？

　　孩子從英文日記開始進行寫作的時候，家長因為想幫忙，最常犯的錯就是「改掉錯誤的句子」。用英文寫日記所要達成的目標除了最基本的「表達想法」以外，還必須做到「正確的運用英文句子」這樣的寫作練習。

　　站在孩子的立場來看，用英文寫日記其實是非常不容易的。所以如果媽媽們在孩子好不容易完成的日記上處處指責文法錯誤，孩子會變得不太願意再度提筆寫日記。因此在讓孩子練習英文寫作的時候，「讓孩子自由發揮」與「指導正確的寫作方法」之間需要巧妙的平衡。如果真的想糾正孩子，家長只要在下方寫上正確的句子即可，不需要再讓孩子重新寫過一次，因為讓孩子比較兩個句子的差異也算是一種學習。

　　就算家長沒有糾正錯誤，只要孩子能夠持之以恆，維持寫日記的習慣，寫作能力必定能夠向上提升。經由閱讀英文童話，多多接觸優美的句子，等到要寫英文日記時，那些句子就可以派上用場。不過需要注意的是，每週至少要練習寫 2 到 3 篇英文日記，並且持續一年以上，才可能出現這樣的效果。也許剛開始一兩個月內看不見成效，不過如果拿六個月前所寫的日記和現在寫的來做比較，差異就很明顯了，所以把撰寫日記時的日期記下來也是一個學習的好方法。

4 默寫優美詞句是另外的功課

不要立刻糾正孩子的錯誤，但不代表要放任孩子繼續寫錯誤的句子，也不是說寫日記是為了練出「正確無誤的寫作技巧」。因為比起挑出孩子在英文日記裡的每個錯誤，而讓孩子對於寫作的興趣消失，倒不如選定一本英文童話書去練習「默寫優美詞句」，如此一來會更有成效。

選定英文童話書中圖文並茂的頁面後，從中挑選 2 到 3 句和插畫相關的句子，讓孩子閱讀幾遍後再默寫。孩子默寫過一遍以後，務必記得要和原句做對照，並且讓孩子自行修正錯誤。準備好筆記本，如果每週持續練習默寫兩到三次，那麼他們將學會可以運用在各種生活情境中的句子，並且能夠自然而然地寫進日記裡。

5 孩子的英文日記，把目標放在學會「分段」

當孩子以中文來寫作的篇幅可以超過一頁，並且可以閱讀完沒有附圖、字數較多的英文書時，就可以開始引導孩子寫完整的日記了。以國小生來說，把目標放在學會分段是比較理想的。所謂的段落（paragraph）是由「一個主題句（topic sentence）和能支持主題發展的承接句（supporting sentences）」所構成的。在一篇日記裡，主題句便是一天之中所發生的事和衍生出來的想法。寫完主題句之後，再用幾個句子去詳細說明主題，如此便完成了一個段落。舉個具體的例子來做說明，以下是 The School Field Trip（校外教學）的文章段落。

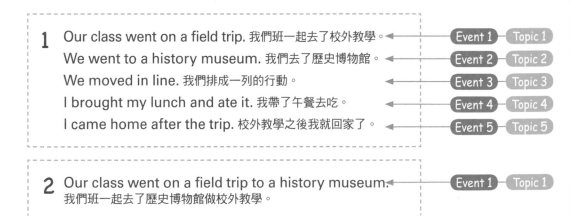

There were lots of things to see in the museum. ← Supporting Detail 1
博物館裡有好多東西可以看。

It was also fun to watch the movie about how we saved old things. ← Supporting Detail 2
我們看的如何保存古老文物的電影也非常有趣。

I learned that we lost so many important things. ← Supporting Detail 3
我學到了我們失去了很多重要的東西。

The trip was fun, and the weather was really beautiful. ← Topic 2
這趟校外教學很好玩，而且天氣非常好。

3 Our class went on a field trip to a history museum. ← Event 1 — Topic 1
我們班一起去了歷史博物館做校外教學。

There were lots of amazing things to see in the museum. ← Supporting Detail 1
博物館裡有好多令人驚奇的東西可以看。

I also watched a movie about how we saved old things. ← Supporting Detail 2
我還看了一部有關如何保存古老文物的電影。

I learned that we have lost many important things so far. ← Supporting Detail 3
我學到了我們到目前為止已經失去了許多重要的東西。

From this trip, I learned we should be proud of our long history. ← Supporting Detail 4
這一趟校外教學讓我知道，我們應該為我們悠久的歷史感到驕傲。

　　1 號文章不過是列出了事件發生的「日誌（time records）」，想要知道文章整體的面貌是比較困難的。2 號文章寫得比較好，可是卻在最後「從校外教學獲得的經驗」中提及與主題句毫無關連的天氣。通常文末的最後一個句子如果不是要展開一個新的段落，那就是要針對這一句的主題提出承接句。而 3 號文章就符合了由「主題＋承接句」延伸成段落的一篇日記。

　　綜上所述，透過和孩子對話來幫助孩子選定寫作主題後，一開始是畫圖加寫一個單字→畫圖加寫一兩個句子→默寫優美詞句等等，這樣循序漸進，就可以幫助孩子發展出以一個主題為中心而延伸出完整段落的日記。切記，要寫出一篇好的日記，不可能僅是寫過幾篇、或是經由一些特殊的教學方法就可以一蹴可及的，孩子一旦開始練習寫作，父母要如何讓孩子持之以恆地繼續練習，這才是關鍵。

洪博士的英文寫作學習法②

英文讀書心得，就該這樣教

1 培養思考與閱讀同時進行的習慣

學英文的過程中，寫作是最困難的一環，因為寫作不單純只是寫出句子，而是要把自己的想法有條不紊地表達出來。而要培養表達自己想法的能力，撰寫讀書心得會是一個很好的方法。但是光是要讓孩子用中文寫讀書心得就不太容易了，更何況是英文。然而孩子們對寫讀書心得覺得困難的原因，正是因為他們沒有培養「思考與閱讀同時進行」的習慣。

以撰寫讀書心得為目的而進行的閱讀，心態上應該和以消遣為目的的閱讀有所區別。也就是說，閱讀的時候不是單純記下書上的內容就好，而是必須培養「一邊閱讀一邊自我提問」的習慣。所謂的提問是指「書名是什麼？」、「主角為什麼會選擇這麼做？」、「接下來會發生什麼事？」或者「這個部分的重點是什麼？」這些問題。找出這些問題的答案，閱讀並整理出自己的想法後，再用英文表達出來，這就是所謂的英文讀書心得。

2 朗讀繪本的同時也別忘了自我提問

思考與閱讀同步進行的習慣，可以從小時候閱讀繪本時開始培養。繪本有一種魔力，可以把孩子的創意思考百寶箱打開。繪本作家透過「文」與「圖」來傳達內容，孩子則以「圖」來表達難以文字化的想法。「單純以圖畫來理解」和「閱讀純文字書後理解」，這兩個過程其實差別不大。因此，在朗讀繪本給孩子聽的時候，家長應該要提出各式各樣的問題去幫助孩子思考，往後當孩子自行閱讀繪本的時候就會漸漸地自我提問。經過這樣的訓練，孩子在寫讀書心得的時候才不會感到茫然。

3 認識英文讀書心得的基本格式

　　雖然英文讀書心得的寫作方式不只一種，不過最基本的讀書心得格式應該是由「引言→本文→結論」所構成。要完成一篇有著引言、本文、結論的完整讀書心得，需要多個階段的練習，因此家長有必要向孩子說明基本的撰寫格式。

引言 (Introduction)

引言是讀書心得的開端，一般會提到書名、作者、插畫家和出版社等背景資料，以及書的主題等等。順道一提，如果可以把選擇該書的動機寫進去會更不錯，像是在引言裡加上「因為朋友的推薦」、「因為是得獎作品」或者「因為是指定作業」等等的理由。

本文 (Body)

不管是由好幾個段落所構成的精彩讀書心得，或是只有寥寥幾行、略嫌空洞的讀書心得，在「本文」的段落內容裡，經常包含以下幾種故事的構成要素（Story Elements）。

● **角色 (Characters)**
描寫主角和配角們之間的關係，或者也可以撰寫登場人物之間的共通點和差異性。

● **背景 (Setting)**
有關故事發生的「時間（Time）」和「地點（Place）」。隨著作品內容的不同及場景的轉換，地點可能有所不同，事件發生的時間點也可能不太明確，不過在讀書心得中只要提及和故事主線較相關的時間和地點就可以了。

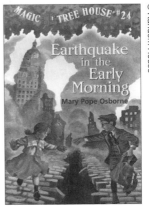

© Random House

● **情節 (Plot)**
故事發展的過程就叫做「情節」。以小說來講，情節即登場人物經歷一連串事件（Events）的過程。描寫情節的時候，「開頭→中段→結尾」的份量分配要得宜，其中最重要的元素「問題→解決辦法」的架構更必須確實掌握。

● 問題 (Problem)

登場人物所經歷的問題（Problem）或也可以稱之為衝突（Conflict）。「問題」並不是說一個事件要多嚴重才能稱得上是問題，凡是可以讓故事變得有趣或有轉折的元素、已發生的事件中的有趣亮點等等，都可以歸類到「問題」裡。在《哈利波特》中主角慘遭惡勢力的攻擊，在《好餓的毛毛蟲》裡毛毛蟲該吃什麼才好，這些都是「問題」之一。因此在閱讀的過程中，要提醒孩子回答「什麼部分最有趣？」、「為什麼主角的處境會變得危險？」和「這個事件會導致什麼後果？」等等的疑問。

● 解決辦法 (Solution)

在一部作品裡，如果出現麻煩，則必定會出現相應的解決之道，可以在讀書心得裡描述一下解決問題的辦法。在故事接近尾聲之前，登場人物們如果遇到了困難，他們一定能從困境中脫身，因此這個部分只要稍稍帶過即可。

● 主題 (Theme)

掌握並敘述作者想要講的故事，並且務必從故事裡找出支持故事主題的部分後寫下「因為～所以我覺得～」這樣的句子。但就算想要跳過此處；直接下結論（Conclusion）也無妨。以國小學童的程度來說，所要求的英文讀書心得寫作並不特別強調這個部分，結尾可以簡單以 I like this story because~ 來收尾就可以了。

結論 (Conclusion)

做為讀書心得結尾的段落，應該綜合該書前述內容，歸納並點出重要的部分，也可以談談自己對這本書所持的正面或反面意見。如果想要推薦此書，還可以另外加上想要推薦的對象，和之所以想要推薦的原因。

4 多加利用組織圖（Graphic Organizer）

讀書心得的撰寫必須依據孩子的程度循序漸進。比較簡單的方式是利用單字或句子填空，等到程度進步後，便可以根據自己的想法進行主題式的寫作。然而學習方法及進度因人而異，這個時候可以多加利用組織圖。所謂的組織圖是指加入圖形、圖畫或者照片等元素的學習單（worksheet），在讓孩子填空的同時，也可以幫助他們學習獨立完成一篇讀書心得的方法。（組織圖學習單的樣式於本書附錄供參考）

● 組織圖的作用

▶ 有助於更聚焦在書的內容

▶ 有助於記憶書籍重點內容

▶ 有助於理解故事中的內容和人物關係

▶ 有助於訓練將想法化為文字的能力

▶ 輕鬆快樂寫文章

5 換作別人來讀會覺得有趣嗎？

最後，寫作的人必須先思考：「別人讀我的文章會覺得有趣嗎？」的問題。一篇文章不是寫出作者的想法就算完成，重點應該在於讓讀者容易理解。因此在寫讀書心得的時候，務必要幫助孩子自我提問以下問題：「如果別人這樣寫我會覺得有趣嗎？」、「看完了這篇讀書心得以後，我的朋友會想去看看這本書嗎？」

如果能夠用英文寫文章的話，就代表孩子已經能夠靈活的運用英文了。可以大聲朗讀（Read Aloud）的話，就要自信地表達出自己的想法（Think Aloud），能夠思考的話，就要好好練習寫作來表達意見（Write Aloud）。能夠達成這三階段的祕訣正是練習撰寫英文讀書心得。與英文日記相同，孩子一旦開始學習英文讀書心得寫作，家長的任務就是監督他們持之以恆，這是非常重要的一點。

孩子的英文寫作SOS！
只要有這本書就不用再煩惱！

▶ 英文寫作能力的基礎正是「英文日記與英文讀書心得寫作」

還在為了如何培養孩子的英文寫作能力而感到苦惱嗎？就像培養中文寫作能力的入門是寫日記和讀書心得，培養英文寫作能力的入門亦是寫「英文日記和讀書心得」。也許孩子寫出來的東西並不完全正確，不過只要每天持續練習，他們的英文寫作能力便會在不知不覺間突飛猛進。當孩子對於寫出來的英文表達方式不太確定、或者好奇是否有更好的表達方式，這種時候就和孩子一起翻開本書，培養他們的英文寫作能力吧！

▶ 孩子們最常用的 5000 個英文表達總整理！

隨著孩子們漸漸長大，經歷的事件、想法和情感表達也越來越五花八門。因此想要用有限的幾個字彙或者句型去表達，簡直就是不可能的任務。本書收錄了超過 5000 個孩子們在撰寫英文日記或是讀書心得時最常用、最想用的英文表達，並詳細分類為 11 個部分、36 個章節與 260 個小主題。現在開始，當孩子在撰寫英文日記或英文讀書心得的時候，就利用本書來幫助他們用英文傳神地表達自己的經驗、想法和情感吧！

▶ 從「核心句型」到「寫作要領」，一本書同時解決所有英文寫作問題！

英文寫作需要透過撰寫英文日記和英文讀書心得來練習。不過市面上的書籍大部分都是針對撰寫「英文日記」而已，不需要擔心！本書除了有傳神又實用的英文日記必備句型，還延伸出多種在寫讀書心得時可能會用到的英文表達。另外，本書亦收錄了用英文寫日記或讀書心得的寫作要領，並依情境將常用英文表達分門別類。相信任何人都能輕鬆打好英文寫作的基礎，成功挑戰英文寫作。從現在開始，這一本書會為你解決培養英文寫作能力的一切疑難雜症！

只要替換單字就可以馬上用的
英文寫作時經常用到的核心句型

本書在英文日記與英文讀書心得的寫作寶典之前，特地整理了進行英文日記和英文讀書心得寫作時最常用到的核心句型，這些都是在日常會話或者英文寫作中經常用到的句型。先抓住基本的寫作句型及要領，試著和孩子一起輕鬆挑戰英文寫作吧！

查閱快速又方便的
英文日記寫作寶典

這部分網羅了從日常生活作息、天氣，甚至學校生活、情緒表現和感興趣的事物，能夠清楚表達孩子們在生活中會經歷的事情、與事件相關的想法和情緒等各種英文表達，一共細分為 8 個部分，30 個章節和超過 220 個小主題，任何人都能輕鬆又快速地查閱想寫的英文表達。

馬上行雲流水
英文讀書心得寫作寶典

本書整理了在撰寫英文讀書心得時最常用的句子，依據書本簡介、登場人物、情節介紹和結論等各主題為中心，分別整理成幾個部分。另外，每個章節都附有精選讀書心得範文，孩子在寫作讀書心得時便可參考利用。

特別收錄

十種組織圖（Graphic Organizer）& 讀書宣言

本書書末特別收錄了培養撰寫讀書心得的能力時可以運用的組織圖。倘若可以活用組織圖，不僅有助於理解書本的核心內容，也可以促進邏輯思考，如此一來培養寫作能力的難度將會大大減低。請試著用 About People、Problem&Solution、The Story Goes...、Story Map 和 KWL 等幾種不同形式的組織圖來增強孩子對於寫英文讀後感的信心，再來也可以利用「讀書宣言」在自家實踐每讀完一本英文書就要寫一篇英文讀書心得的承諾。

目錄大綱

目錄詳細列表

BOOK 1

英文日記寫作寶典

Part 1 日常生活

Part 2 天氣與季節

Part 6 情緒、個性、興趣與煩惱

BOOK 2

英文讀書心得寫作寶典

附錄

● 10 種組織圖 (Graphic Organizer)
● 我的讀書宣言 (My Reading Contract)

BOOK 1

Diary
Expression
英文日記寫作寶典

Intro

英文日記
核心句型50句

50 Useful Patterns for Your Diary

這個部分整理了在進行英文日記寫作時常用的句型，這些「核心句型」是由幾個固定單字組合而成的句型，並依使用情境個別歸納。請各位利用以下的核心句型和例句，試著動手寫寫看自己想寫的句子吧！此外，由於本書重點在於針對孩子的英文寫作打下基礎，因此略過了過於複雜的文法說明，讓孩子能專注在句型使用上。

注意事項

- 句型中動詞的時態雖採用現在式，但亦可視情況替換為過去式。
- 日記中常使用的過去式動詞，將在本書的過去式句型中提及。
- 在「that＋子句」的用法中，that 經常被省略，而本書中不會特別提到不可省略 that 的其他情形。

我很開心～

★ 開心的時候

I am glad/happy (that) ~

在寫句子的時候，雖然有一些事實（fact）只需要如實的表達出來就好，不過如果可以在句子的前面加上 I am glad／happy (that) 的句型，就可以表達「因為～而感到開心」，在語氣上也會比較有禮貌。

- 我很開心 Eric 是我最好的朋友。

  I am glad that Eric is my best friend.

- 我很開心我們班在比賽裡獲得第一名。

  I was glad that our class came in first place in the race.

- 我很開心我們下禮拜要去校外教學。

  I am happy we are going on a field trip next week.

我感到後悔、可惜～

★ 覺得可惜的時候

I am sorry (that) ~

這個句型在 that 的後方加上「自己的事情」就可以用來表示「後悔」，如果是加上「別人的事情」，就可以用來表示可惜。不要一下子就把句子結束，可以試著使用這個句型來把心情表達得更詳細。但是這個句型若解釋成「因為～而感到抱歉」就太過嚴重了。

- 我很後悔我不能堅持到最後。

  I am sorry I could not make it to the end.

- 那位選手在比賽中弄傷了他的鼻子，我覺得很可惜。

  I was sorry that the player broke his nose during the game.

- 我弟弟的身高還不足以搭雲霄飛車，我覺得很可惜。

  I was sorry that my brother was not tall enough to ride the roller coaster.

更進一步！ **I feel bad that~** 雖然也是類似的用法，不過這句有「因此感到難過」的意思。

- 在城鎮裡舉行大型演唱會之後，街道變得髒亂，這讓我感到難過。

  I felt bad that the streets got dirty after the big concert in my town.

Pattern
03 I am afraid/worried (that) ~

我害怕／擔心～　　　　　　　　　　　　★ 擔心或害怕的時候

I am afraid／worried that~ 這個句型通常用在擔心未來可能發生的事情，或是感到猶豫的時候使用。覺得心煩意亂的時候，就可以使用看看這個句型來表達心情。

- 我很擔心 Eric 會把我的綽號告訴全班同學。

  I am afraid that Eric will tell everyone in my class about my nickname.

- 我很怕他們會覺得我在吹噓我的考試成績。

  I was afraid they thought I was bragging about my test score.

- 我很擔心漲潮會讓河水暴漲淹過河岸。

  I was worried that the flood would cause the river to overflow its banks.

更進一步！ that 後面接的子句主詞若和 I 相同，這種情況下就可以替換成較簡單的 **be afraid to** 句型，而不需要用 that 句型。

- 我很擔心我在講英文的時候會講錯。

  I was afraid to make a mistake when I spoke in English.

04 I am thankful/grateful that ~

我很感激～   ★ 表達感謝之意時

在想要說「對於～感到感激」的時候，一般人都會習慣使用「thank＋受詞＋for」，然而在寫作的時候，應該用 be thankful／grateful that~ 會比較好。在這個情況下，也可以省略 that，只不過為了書面體的完整性，還是建議儘可能保留。

- 能夠出生在這個美麗的國家，我覺得很感激。

  I am thankful that I was born in this beautiful country.

- 我很感激警察前來高速公路幫助我們。

  I was grateful that the police came to help us on the highway.

> **更進一步！** 想要表示感激的時候，也可以用 **be thankful／grateful for~**（對～感激）這樣的表達方式。

- 我很感激我的朋友花時間陪我。

  I was thankful for my friends who spent time together with me.

- 我很感激我現在擁有的許多東西。

  I am grateful for many things that I have now.

Pattern
05 I hope (that) ~

我希望～   ★ 說出自己的願望時

用於現在期望未來可能發生的事情。如果期望的內容是為了別人，則有客氣的感覺。因為對別人說 I hope you~ 時，代表希望對方能夠發生好事。

- 我希望我的朋友能夠快點痊癒。

  I hope that my friend feels better soon.

- 我希望天氣能夠放晴，這樣我們就可以去外面玩了。

  I hope the weather gets clear so that we can play outside.

- 我希望能在數學考試上得到滿分。

  I hope I will get a perfect score on the math test.

Pattern 06 真希望～ ★希望困難的願望可以達成時
I wish (that) 主詞＋過去式

I wish 後面接「過去式」以表示假設語氣，而假設語氣通常在希望發生的事情是「難以達成或不可能達成的事情」時使用，包含了因羨慕而迫切渴望的心情，但也帶有嘆息的意味。

- 真希望我能有一個姊姊。

  I wish that I **had** an older sister.

- 真希望我能像我朋友一樣有自己的房間！

  I wish I **could** have my own room like my friends!

- 真希望所有的考試都從世界上消失。

  I wish all kinds of exams **would** disappear from the world.

更進一步！ 在 I wish 的後面使用**過去完成式**（had＋p.p.）則有「對過去的事情感到後悔」的意思。

- 真希望我那個時候有先向 Amy 道歉！

  I wish I **had said** sorry to Amy first!

我覺得～
I think/feel (that) ~

★ 說出自己的想法時

在句子前方加上 I think，就可以用來表達自己的想法。用 I feel 也是差不多的意思，不過語氣稍稍和緩一些。若是使用 guess，則是推論的意思，而 believe 用在相信某事時，寫作的時候不要都只使用 think，可以依據不同情境替換著使用看看。

● 我覺得我們城鎮是很適合居住的地方。

I think that my town is a very good place to live in.

● 我覺得我的主意比 Eric 的更有創意。

I thought my idea was more creative than Eric's.

● 我覺得 Julia 很擅長說英語。

I feel that Julia is very good at speaking English.

我認為我們應該～
I think we should ~

★ 說出自己的主張時

想表達「應該～」的時候，只要在句子中加上 should（應該）就可以了。如果用 must（必須）代替 should，那就表示主張的立場更為強烈。如果在句子前面加上 I think，變成 I think we should~，就可以用來表達自己的主張。

● 我認為我們應該和朋友好好相處。

I think we should get along well with our friends.

● 我認為我們外出的時候應該穿上保暖的衣物。

I think we should wear warm clothes when we go outside.

- 我認為我們必須讓地球不受汙染。

  I think we must keep the Earth clean.

📝 **更進一步！** 用 I 取代 we，也就是 **I think I should**，可用來表示「我覺得自己應該要～」。

- 我覺得在考試的時候，我應該要更小心的看題目。

  I think I should read the questions carefully when I take the exam.

Pattern
09　我寧願～（也不要～）　　　　　　　★ 表達偏好時
I would rather ~ (than ...)

I would rather~ 是用在把某樣事物和其他事物經過比較之後，覺得「這個比較好」的意思。就算沒有提到被比較的對象，但也有一種已經做過比較的感覺。如果想要指出比較的對象，只要在後方加上 than 和被比較的對象就可以了。

- 這種天氣我寧願待在室內。

  I would rather stay inside in this kind of weather.

- 這麼晚了我還是不要傳簡訊比較好。

  I would rather not send texts late at night.

- Jackson 先生說他寧願跟我在一起，也不要跟那些小孩子在一起。

  Mr. Jackson said he **would rather** be with me **than** with those little kids.

📝 **更進一步！** 想給忠告的時候可以用 **had better~**（最好～）。

- 我認為他最好儘快離開。

  I thought that he **had better** leave as soon as possible.

Pattern 10 — 我確定～

I am sure (that) ~

★ 對某事很有把握的時候

I am sure that~ 這個句型可以用在對某些事物很有把握的時候。只要利用這個句型，就算原本聽起來天馬行空的內容也會多了幾分可信度，讓人更容易接受。

● 我很確定我可以馬上就學好游泳。

I am sure that I can learn how to swim well in no time.

● 我很確定如果他再繼續說謊就會惹禍上身。

I am sure that he will get in trouble if he keeps on lying.

● 我很確定數學考卷上的題目我都寫對了。

I was sure I got all the questions right on the math test.

Pattern 11 — 我對～感到驕傲～

I am proud (that) ~

★ 想要表達因某事而自豪的時候

想要表達因某些事物而感到自豪時使用，不過這裡的「驕傲」並不帶有趾高氣昂或是盛氣凌人的感覺。用這個句型來表達他人的長處或成就時，有稱讚的意味在。

● 我對出現在電視上的叔叔感到驕傲。

I am proud that the person on TV is my uncle.

● 我對台灣打進世界棒球 12 強賽感到驕傲。

I am proud that Taiwan has qualified for the Premier 12.

● 我對姊姊獲得北一女中的入學許可感到驕傲。

I was proud that my sister was accepted to Taipei First Girls High school.

更進一步！ I am proud of~（我為～感到驕傲）也可以用來表達因某事而感到自豪。

- 我為在亞運摘下金牌的許淑淨感到驕傲。

  I am proud of Hsu Shu-ching who won a gold medal at the Asian Games.

Pattern
12   我發現～
I found/learned (that) ~   ★ 想要說出新發現時

這個句型比較適合用在「發現」了某些事實的時候，比起 I know（我知道），另外還多了「得到資訊的過程」這樣的感覺。雖然時態是過去式，但是如果想傳達的內容是事實（fact），在 that 之後的動詞可以使用現在式。

- 我發現首爾是世界第四大城市。

  I found that Seoul is ranked as the 4th largest city in the world.

- 我發現穿上足球鞋比較好踢球。

  I found it is easier to kick the ball when I am wearing soccer shoes.

- 我發現如果連我都不相信自己，那也不會有其他人相信我了。

  I learned if I don't believe in myself, no one else will.

更進一步！ I noticed~（我注意到～）和 I realized~（我體會到～）的句型也可以和這個句型一起替換著使用看看。

- 我注意到 Gina 不見了，因為她的座位是空的。

  I noticed Gina was missing because her seat was empty.

- 我體會到我如果不練習，那麼跳繩就不會跳得好。

  I realized that if I don't practice, I can't jump rope well.

13 I know (that) ~

我知道～ ★ 表示自己知道時

用於表示自己清楚某些事物時。想表示「不知道」可以用 I do not know~，想表示「之前不知道」，用 I did not know~ 就可以了。請實際應用看看吧。

- 我知道 Eric 很擅長拉小提琴。

  I know that Eric is good at playing the violin.

- 我就知道 Bill 會再度惹麻煩。

  I knew Bill would get into trouble again.

- 我之前不知道 Eric 是 Amy 的男朋友。

  I did not know Eric was Amy's boyfriend.

Pattern

14 I heard (that) ~

我聽說～ ★ 想說出聽見的內容時

在寫作的時候，很多時候會寫到從別人那裡聽來的事情。如果真要做個比較，本句型和 I found、I learned 其實沒有太大差異，只不過 I heard 多了單純「傳達事實」的感覺。

- 我聽說 Eric 生病了而且沒來上學。

  I heard Eric was sick and missed school.

- 我聽說新老師很嚴格。

  I heard that my new teacher is very strict.

- 我聽說我的奶奶一輩子都奉獻給了她的家人。

  I heard my grandma had lived her whole life only for her family.

● 聽說近來預測天氣變得非常困難。

It is said that predicting the weather is very difficult these days.

Pattern 15 〜告訴我
~ told me (that) ...

★ 想轉述聽見的內容時

在寫作的時候，經常會把別人分享的事情也寫進去對吧？這種時候就可以試著使用這種句型。在提到告訴你事情的人的同時，也可以順便分享聽到的內容。此外，也可以用 said to 替換句型中的 told。

● 老師告訴我應該要準時寫作業。

My teacher **told me that** I should do my homework on time.

● 我不記得是誰告訴了我 Kevin 很笨。

I can't remember who **told me** Kevin was stupid.

● 警察告訴我們今天這條路會被封起來。

The police **said to us that** the road would be blocked today.

更進一步！ 如果想說「我和〜提及〜」，可以用 I talked with~about~ 來表達。

● 我和老師提及了我在回家作業上的問題。

I **talked with** my teacher **about** my homework problem.

我不敢相信～
★ 無法置信的時候
I can't believe (that) ~

用來表示「感到太意外而不敢相信」的狀況，可以用於否定或肯定，如果加上驚嘆號，語氣就會更強烈。不過這個句型的意思和 don't believe（不願意相信）的意思不一樣。

- 我不敢相信我可以進入這間很棒的學校！

  I can't believe that I was accepted to the great school!

- 我不敢相信 Amy 竟然邀請除了我以外的所有人到她家去。

  I can't believe Amy has invited everyone to her house but me.

- 我不敢相信他在比賽中摘下了銀牌。

  I could not believe he was the silver medalist in the race.

更進一步！ **I doubt that~** 的句型很明顯地表示了「質疑」的語氣。

- 我很懷疑樓上的小男孩之前沒有在地板上奔跑。

  I doubt that the little boy upstairs did not run on the floor.

Pattern
17

我懷疑是否～
★ 感到不確定時
I wonder if ~

I wonder if~ 可以用在對某些事物不太確定，或者自言自語表示懷疑的時候，用中文來表達時可能會被翻譯成疑問句，不過以英文來表達時卻沒有疑問句的意思。

- 我懷疑明天是否會放晴。

  I wonder if the weather will clear up tomorrow.

- 我懷疑我明天的數學考試能不能考 100 分。

  I wonder if I can get a 100 on the math test tomorrow.

- 我懷疑爸爸是否能如他之前所承諾的早點回家。

  I wondered if my dad would come home early as he had promised.

更進一步！ I wonder 之後接以「**疑問詞**」**開頭**的句子，則是表達「對該件事感到驚訝、無法理解」。

- 我很好奇這件事是怎麼發生的。

  I wonder how it happened.

Pattern 18 我會再看看～ ★ 表示會再進一步了解時
I will see if ~

帶有「願意花時間觀察結果、進一步了解」的意思，只要是不確定未來事情的發展情形時都可以使用。

- 我會再看看我的大哥是否會遵守他的承諾。

  I will see if my big brother will keep his promise.

- 我會再看看我是否能找到些什麼來幫助那位老先生。

  I will see if I can find anything to help the old man.

- 明天到學校時我會再看看謠言是否是真的。

  I will see if the rumor is true when I go to school tomorrow.

19 as if＋主詞＋過去式動詞／過去完成式

彷彿、就像～ ★與實際狀況不符時

假設語氣 as if 的含意為「就像～一般」，可以用來表示事情並不是真的發生、但卻說得或做得像真的一樣。這裡要注意的是，as if 後面接續的子句所使用的時態必須早於主句。另外，當要使用 be 動詞的時候，was 一律替換成 were。

- Amy 表現得好像她知道所有答案似的。

  Amy acts **as if** she **knew** all the answers.

- 我不懂為什麼叔叔總是講得他好像很有錢似的。

  I don't know why my uncle always speaks **as if** he **were** very rich.

- 我跟弟弟講的一副我看過可怕的怪物一樣。

  I spoke to my baby brother **as if** I **had seen** a scary monster.

20 It seems (that) ~

看來、似乎～ ★無法百分之百確定時

這個句型用在對一件事不太確定的情況下，或者雖然確定該事屬實，但是當下不想把話說死時也很適合使用。在想要避免當下講得振振有詞、日後才發現講錯的時候，就可以活用這個句型。

- 看來學校決定讓假期提前開始了。

  It seems that the school decided to begin vacation earlier.

- 看來 Amy 要轉到台北的大醫院去了。

  It seems that Amy is going to move to a big hospital in Taipei.

- 看來我們班上的每個人都有一支昂貴的手機。

  It seems everyone in my class has an expensive cell phone.

更進一步！ 也可以簡化成 seem(s) to~ 來表達，例如以下的句子。

- 我們的友情好像出了問題，這件事讓我覺得難過。

  I feel bad that our friendship **seems to** be going wrong.

Pattern **21** 結果～ ★ 表達結果的時候

It turned out (that) ~

turn out 有「產生、出現」的意思，經常出現的形式為 It turned out that~。這個句型最常使用在事後回頭看時，才發現和先前所想的結果有出入，或者觀察了一段時間以後發現結果不太一樣的時候。

- 結果那家公司賣出了大量的不良食品。

  It turned out that the company sold a large amount of bad food.

- 結果那位科學家捏造了許多成果。

  It turned out that the scientist had faked many of the results.

- 結果我不能看那部電影，因為我年紀太小了。

  It turned out I could not watch the movie because I was too young.

更進一步！ 也可以利用 turned out to~ 來替換使用。

- 結果那張舊照片是失傳已久的寶藏。

  The old picture **turned out to** be a long-lost treasure.

我無意～   ★ 澄清自己意圖的時候

I did not mean to ~

有時不是故意要這麼做，可是事情就這樣發生了，這時如果想表達自己並不是有意的，便可以使用這個句型。此句型多半用於道歉或解釋，有時候也可以用於辯駁他人意見的時候。

● Mary 哭了，可是事實上我無意取笑她。

Mary burst into tears. Actually, **I did not mean to** tease her.

● 當我說媽媽塊頭大的時候，我其實無意要冒犯她的。

I didn't mean to offend my mother when I said she was big.

● 我無意要散播謠言，但它就是傳出去了。

I didn't mean to pass the rumor along. It just spread.

～起來好像～   ★ 說明感覺時

feel/look/sound/smell like ~

「感官動詞」是指透過身體的感覺器官動作（action）而產生的動詞，有 feel、look、sound、smell 和 taste。在這些動詞後方加上 like，則用來表示「～起來好像～」的意思。

● 那個男人看起來好像是個很重要的人。

The man **looked like** a very important person.

● 麵條太硬了，感覺起來好像橡皮筋。

The noodles were so tough that they **felt like** rubber bands.

- 我覺得那隻鳥的歌聲聽起來好像笛聲。

  I think the bird's song **sounded like** a flute.

更進一步！ 感官動詞後面若連接形容詞，則不加 like，單純以「**感官動詞＋形容詞**」的形式使用。

- 那個男人看起來很有錢，因為他開了一部很大的車。

  The man **looked rich** because he was driving a very big car.

Pattern 24　看見／聽見～　　　　★ 看見或聽見別人的動作時
see/hear＋受詞＋Ving

不同於單純用「see/hear＋受詞」來表達「看見或聽見受詞」，在受詞後面加上 Ving（現在分詞）的句型還能更強調表達受詞的動作，聽起來會更有生動的感覺。

- 我看見我的狗 Mimi 咬著沙發抱枕。

  I **saw** my dog Mimi chew**ing** the sofa cushion.

- 我看見街上的樹正在改變它們的顏色。

  I **saw** the trees on the street chang**ing** their colors.

- 我聽到母親正在和阿姨講電話。

  I **heard** my mom talk**ing** to my aunt on the phone.

更進一步！ 如果在受詞是以被動狀態承受某種動作的情況下，會改用「**being＋過去分詞**」，但這個時候也可以把 being 省略。

- 我看到那個男孩被他的狗舔。

  I **saw** the boy (being) **licked** by his dog.

很難～

★ 表達無法（做）～時

have trouble/difficulty＋Ving

「have trouble＋Ving」和「have difficulty＋Ving」皆是用來表示「做～有難度」的句型。舉例來說，如果想表達「數學不好」，可以換個說法，用「就算念了，還是覺得數學很難」來套入句型。另外，如果替換成 cannot，意思會轉變為「不能～」，在意義上不太一樣。

● 我弟弟很難在課堂上專心。

My brother **has trouble** stay**ing** focused during class.

● 我害怕我很難為自己發聲。

I am afraid that I **have trouble** speak**ing** up for myself.

● 我的阿姨以前常常很難入睡。

My aunt used to **have difficulty** gett**ing** to sleep.

我不知道該如何／～什麼～

★ 不知該如何是好時

I don't know how/what ～

在表達的當下「找不到解決問題的方法、找不到答案」時，就可以應用這個句型，它可以用來表達擔心，或是為了尋求別人的意見而事先說明原由時使用。

● 我不知道該如何處理在學校裡的霸凌事件。

I don't know how I should deal with the bullying at school.

● 我不知道該如何幫助對電玩上癮的朋友。

I don't know how I can help my friend addicted to video games.

- 我之前不知道母親對我有什麼期待。

  I didn't know what my mother wanted from me.

  ✏️**更進一步！** 想表達「不知道當初事情為什麼會演變成後來的結果」時，在 I don't know 後面所
  接的子句的時態將會不同。

- 我不知道我是怎麼加入團體遊戲的。

  I don't know how I **have been** involved with the group game.

Pattern

27 怎麼／為什麼～？
How/Why＋助動詞＋主詞＋動詞？

★ 追究或辯駁時

想要提出問題或是想反駁所遭遇的處境時就可以使用這個句型。利用這種提出疑
問的方式可以加強語氣，看起來也比較有感染力。

- 這怎麼可能是對的？這怎麼可能是真的？

  How can this be true? **How can** this be real?

- 就算我人在那裡好了，怎麼可能沒有人注意到我？

  Let's say I was there. **How could** not the people notice me?

- 如果那不是我的狗，我為什麼要去在意？

  Why should I care about the dog if it is not mine?

Pattern
28　因為～
because ~

★ 說明理由時

這個句型不只在**說明理由**的時候可以使用，甚至找**藉口**時也可以用。另外如果要回答 why 開頭的問題，只要在句子裡加上 because 就可以了。

- 他們長得很像，因為他們是兄妹。

  They both look alike **because** they are brother and sister.

- 因為我不敢相信這個消息，所以我哭了。

  I cried at the news **because** I could not believe it.

- 因為昨晚太熱，所以我沒睡好。

  I could not sleep well last night **because** it was too hot.

🖊 **更進一步！** 寫作的時候，除了 because，也很常用 since。

- 因為連假的關係，公園擠滿了人潮。

  The park was crowded with many people **since** it was a holiday season.

Pattern
29　如此…以致於～
so＋形容詞＋that ~

★ 說明原因和結果時

這個句型用於同時**說明原因與結果**的時候，可以使用這個句型的機會很多，所以請多多練習。除此之外，事情出了差錯想找**藉口**時也可以用這個句型來表達。

- 我的新鞋太硬讓我的腳很痛。

  My new shoes are **so** stiff **that** my feet hurt.

- 我前面的人太高以致於我看不到舞台。

  The person in front of me was **so** tall **that** I could not see the stage.

- 題目太難導致我無法在 30 分鐘內解完。

  The problems were **so** difficult **that** I had trouble solving them within 30 minutes.

  🖊 **更進一步！** 因為某些原因而無法完成某些事的時候，也可以用「too＋形容詞＋to不定詞」（太～以致於不能～）。

- 因為我的新鞋太硬了，以致於我沒辦法走很久。

  My new shoes are **too** stiff **to** walk for a long time.

Pattern
30 would like to ~/want to ~

想要～   ★ 說出想做的事時

「would like to~/want to~」是用來表達「想做～的事」中相當具代表性的句型，不管是寫作或是說話時都常使用。若在句中加上 not 就是「不想～」使用到的機會也相當多。

- 我想要知道這東西在遊戲中是怎麼運作來擊敗對手的。

  I **would like to** know how this thing works to beat the enemy in the game.

- 被問問題的時候，雖然我想回答，可是我太害羞了。

  I **wanted to** speak when I was asked to answer the question, but I was too shy.

- 我不想和表弟一起去遊戲場。

  I **don't want to** go to the playground with my little cousin.

31

很期待～
look forward to+Ving

★ 滿懷期待時

當心中對於某件事物感到期待的時候，就可以使用這個句型。也許看起來有些複雜，可是在日常生活中很常用到，請多加練習。另外，Ving 在文法用語中代表「動名詞」的意思。

● 我很期待開學時能夠認識新同學。

I **look forward to** meet**ing** my new classmates when school begins.

● 我很期待看到你，我的朋友！

I am **looking forward to** see**ing** you, my friend!

● 我很期待聽到搬到台北去的朋友的消息。

I was **looking forward to** hear**ing** from my friend who moved to Taipei.

更進一步！ 因為太過期待而感到焦躁的時候，可以用「can't wait for＋受詞＋to不定詞」（等不及做～）。

● 哦，我等不及暑假趕快來到！

Oh, I **can't wait for** summer vacation **to** come!

32

我打算要～
I am going to ~

★ 說出未來計畫去做的事時

I am going to~ 是用來表示「計畫、預計要做～事」，很常用在日記寫作裡。同樣的情境下也可以使用 I will，只不過使用 I am going to~ 的話，由於已經是計畫好要做的事，所以未來實踐的可能性相當高。

- 我打算這個星期六要踢足球。

  I am going to play soccer this Saturday.

- 我明年要擔任中鋒。

  I am going to play center forward next year.

- 我一週將會朗讀三次英文書。

  I will read aloud English books three times a week.

更進一步！ 將 be 動詞換成過去式的 I was going to~，有「**原本打算～**」的意思。

- 我原本打算要關掉電視。

  I was going to turn off the TV.

Pattern **33** 應該／打算做～ **be supposed to ~** ★用來表達計畫做某事的時候

be supposed to~ 通常用在被他人指派要做某些事，或者有約定好要去做～事時。也許看起來有些複雜，不過在日常生活中很常用到，請多加練習。

- 我明天七點整應該會和 Eric 見面。

  I am supposed to meet Eric at 7 o'clock sharp tomorrow.

- 我原本應該要把書看完的，但是我還沒看完。

  I was supposed to finish reading the book, but I haven't done that yet.

- 我爸爸打給我因為他原本打算在我放學後來接我。

  My dad called me because he **was supposed to** pick me up after school.

Pattern 34　差一點～
almost＋過去式動詞

★ 差一點發生某事時

這個句型用在表達原本打算做某事但沒做，或者明明準備好了可是後來忘了做。另外，因為要說的是過去發生的事，因此該子句的時態要比主要子句的時態來得更早。

- 我差一點就和隔壁同學穿了一樣的外套。

  I **almost wore** the same jacket as my seatmate's.

- 我媽媽在停車的時候差一點撞到牆壁。

  My mom **almost bumped** into the wall when parking her car.

- Amy 說她差一點就忘記把功課帶來。

  Amy said that she **had almost forgotten** to bring her homework.

> **更進一步！** 已經計畫或預計去做某事，不過後來沒做成的狀況下會使用 planned to~ 或者 intended to~ 等表達方式。

- 我們去年計畫要去歐洲。

  We **planned to** go to Europe last year.

Pattern 35　我（原本）應該要～
I should have＋過去分詞

★ 對過去的事情感到惋惜的時候

對過往的事情感到可惜或者難過的時候會使用這個句型。用來表達事後回頭看才覺得應該要做或者不應該做，因此這個句型很常在寫作的時候用到。

- 我應該要更仔細看說明書的。

  I **should have read** the directions more carefully.

- 我之前應該要好好思考，這件事就長遠來看對我有什麼幫助。

  I should have thought about how this would help me in the long run.

- 我不應該對妹妹說這些難聽的話的。

  I should not have used those bad words to my sister.

Pattern 36　如果～

If＋主詞＋現在式動詞, ～

★ 在表達某些條件或前提時

先提出條件，用來表示「達成某條件以後就會做某事」，如果不是胡亂立下條件，這個句型所表達的意義通常會帶來積極正向的效果。這個句型經常使用在日常生活中。

- 如果我存到 5000 元，我就會買新的滑板。

  If I **save** up to 5000 NT dollars, I will buy a new skateboard.

- 如果媽媽願意讓我去學芭蕾舞，我會盡我的全力做到最好。

  If my mom **allows** me to take ballet lessons, I will do my best.

- 如果弟弟把他的玩具借我玩，我也會讓他玩我的。

  If my brother **shares** his toys with me, I will also let him use mine.

> ✏️ 更進一步！　如果 if 出現在整個句子的中間，句中不加上逗號也可以。

- 如果我考試考得好，我會要求爸爸給我獎勵。

  I will ask my dad for a reward **if** I **do** a good job on my exams.

37

如果～

If＋主詞＋過去式／過去完成式

★ 假設與實際不符的時候

當假想或假設的事情與現實不符時，便會使用「假設語氣」。對於現在的假設要使用過去式，而對於過去的假設會使用過去完成式。如同前面所提到的，遇到假設語氣時，be 動詞 was 一律用 were 來取代，這是需要特別留意的地方。

● 如果 Amy 是男孩，她可能會成為一個很棒的足球選手。

If Amy **were** a boy, she could be a great soccer player.

● 如果我的英文說得很好，我就可以更理解 Warren 先生的意思了。

If I **spoke** English well, I could understand Mr. Warren better.

● 如果我有注意到那個污漬，我就不會買那件夾克了。

If I **had noticed** the stain, I would not have bought the jacket.

38

經常做～

tend to ~

★ 有某種傾向時

在提到經常做的事或者發生機率很高的事情時，很適合使用這個句型。如果這個句型被用來引述社會現象，則可以解釋為「有～的傾向」。

● 我經常花大部分的時間在寫學校作業上。

I **tend to** spend most of my time doing my homework for school.

● 當所有人都在家的時候，我們家經常會出去吃。

My family **tends to** eat out when everyone is at home.

● 據說孩子們經常會在假期中發胖。

It is said that children **tend to** gain weight during vacations.

Pattern 39 考量到～
Considering (that) ~

★ 考慮到某件事時

想要提出某些主意的時候，必須先考慮到相關的其他事情。在句子前面加上 Considering~，就可以用來表示正在考慮的事情。

● 考慮到這暖和天氣，我們還是把食物放進冰箱比較好。

Considering that it is warm, we had better put the food in the refrigerator.

● 想到 Amy 人總是這麼好，我不覺得她會那樣做。

Considering Amy is always nice, I don't think she acted like that.

● 考量到我們老師很嚴格，我們決定了要待在教室裡。

Considering our teacher was strict, we decided to stay in the classroom.

✏️ 更進一步！ 想要表達「根據某些理由～」可以用 based on~（依據、根據～）的句型。

● 根據我看的那本書，宇宙裡有超過一億個銀河系。

Based on the book I read, there are more than 100 million galaxies in the universe.

讓…做～

let/have＋受詞＋原形動詞

★ 讓某人做某事時

let、have 表示「使～、讓～」，這兩者被稱作「使役動詞」，通常以「let/have ＋受詞＋原形動詞」的句型來使用，用在促使他人去做某事，句子的重點在於「受詞的意志」而不是主詞的意志。這個句型在日常生活中非常的實用，請多多練習。另外，「don't let/have＋受詞＋原形動詞」則代表「不讓…去做～」的意思。

● 爸爸讓妹妹和我把爬樓梯當作運動。

My dad **lets** my sister and me **take** the stairs for exercise.

● 校長不讓我們在禮堂裡大聲說話。

The principal would not **let** us **talk** aloud in the hall.

● 別擔心，我會讓我的狗在適合的地方尿尿。

Don't worry. I will **have** my dog **pee** in the right place.

更進一步！ get、tell、force 也都是類似的動詞，不過差別在於這些動詞的受詞之後不用原形動詞，而要加「to不定詞」。

● 我哥哥叫我離開他的房間。

My brother **told** me **to get** out of his room.

● 我爸爸強迫我每天走路 30 分鐘。

My dad **forces** me **to walk** for 30 minutes every day.

雖然～／儘管～
Though/Although ~,

★ 克服問題或困難時

在進行某件事情的時候出現了問題或困難，或者想表達「即便是～還是～」的意思，都可以利用這兩個連接詞造句。

● 雖然我是最後一個，但我還是奮力跑向終點。

Though I came in last, I ran hard to the finish line.

● 雖然 Amy 看起來不太舒服，她還是積極的參與報告。

Though Amy looked sick, she actively participated in the presentation.

● 雖然我妹妹還不知道怎麼看書，可是她很喜歡書。

Although my little sister does not know how to read, she likes books.

📝 **更進一步！** despite 也有「即便是這樣～還是要」的意思，**不過後面不接子句，接的是名詞**，因此在使用上和 though 的句型不太一樣。

● 儘管天氣很糟，我們還是按原先計畫去校外教學。

Despite the bad weather, we went on the field trip as it was scheduled.

Pattern 42

曾經～

主詞＋have＋過去分詞

★ 想要分享經驗時

在英文裡，在描述過去的經驗時會使用「現在完成式（have＋過去分詞）」的句型，像是 have seen（曾經看過）、have heard（曾經聽過），試著在 have 後面加上過去分詞來表達經驗吧！

● 我之前曾經看過食蟻獸，而且昨天又看到了一隻。

I **have seen** an anteater before, and I saw one again yesterday.

● 我曾聽說過 Bob Dylan 是美國的一位傳奇歌手。

I **have heard** Bob Dylan is a legendary singer in America.

● Amy 曾經去過倫敦兩次去看她的祖父母。

Amy **has been** to London twice to visit her grandparents.

✎ 更進一步！ 在經過某個過程後，想要說出**剛剛才完成的事情**，也是使用現在完成式來表達。

● 我很開心我把《哈利波特》系列全部看完了。

I am glad I **have finished** reading the entire *Harry Potter* series.

Pattern 43

碰巧～

happened to＋動詞

★ 偶然發生的事情

描述偶然經歷的事情時使用。只要先選擇適合該情境下使用的動詞，並在動詞的前面加上 happened to 就可以了。

● 我上個星期天碰巧在百貨公司遇到 Amy。

I **happened to** meet Amy at the department store last Sunday.

- 我偶然告訴了媽媽 Philip 是怎麼變成惡霸的。

  I **happened to** tell my mom about how Phillip had been a bully.

- 他們碰巧在市場附近找到了那隻失蹤的狗。

  They **happened to** find the missing dog near the market.

Pattern
44

最～

the most ~/-est＋名詞

★描述程度最～的

在寫作的時候會經常提到最喜歡的、或者最討厭的事物或人物，這個時候就會用
「形容詞最高級」來描述。形容詞最高級用來搭配名詞，前面一定要記得加上
the。the worst 用來表示「最壞的」。

- 我爸爸說我是世界上最漂亮的女孩。

  My dad said I am **the prettiest girl** in the world.

- 最有趣的就是他們兩個不再吵架了。

  The most interesting fact was that the two did not fight anymore.

- 在八月初去海邊是最糟糕的度假計畫了。

  Going to the beach in early August was **the worst vacation plan**.

更進一步！ **副詞最高級**也可以用在同樣的情況下。

- 在所有的運動裡面，我最喜歡足球。

  Of all sports, I love soccer **the most / the best**.

Pattern

45

更～

more ~/-er than ...

★ 在做比較時

在比較過人或物品的外觀、性質和特徵後，可以使用這個句型來描述。如果想要寫出更棒的句子，可以學習更多的形容詞，然後運用在這個句型中，就可以寫出更多精彩的句子囉！

- 在科學實驗課上 Eric 比我更興奮。

  Eric was **more excited than** I in the science lab class.

- 我喜歡這個沙發，因為它比椅子更舒服。

  I love the sofa because it is **more comfortable than** the chair.

- 女生在排隊的時候比男生還要有耐心。

  The girls were **more patient than** the boys when they waited in line.

更進一步！ 也可以用**副詞**來當比較級。

- 我喜歡到室外玩勝過待在室內。

  I like playing outside **better than** staying indoors.

Pattern

46

～的人／事物

名詞＋to不定詞

★ 想要單純修飾名詞時

通常人或事物都會用形容詞來修飾，不過把 to不定詞（to＋原形動詞）加在名詞後方也有一樣的效果，而所謂的「修飾」是指描述該名詞的狀態、外觀、作用等等。

- 在一口氣爬到五樓以後，我需要一些喝的東西。

  I needed **something to drink** after walking all the way up to the 5th floor.

- 即使我們有很多的作業要做，Kevin 還是要求繼續玩。

  Kevin asked to play more even though we had a lot of **homework to do.**

- 沒有圖書館員可以幫我找到正確的那本書。

  There were no **librarians to help** me find the right book.

Pattern 47　～的人／事物
名詞＋that/who ~

★ 想要描述名詞時

前面已經學過了如何以「to不定詞」來修飾名詞，另外還有一個方法可以更清楚的描述名詞，也就是以 that、who 等關係代名詞來修飾前面的名詞。

- 這是我看過的書中最有趣的一本了。

  It is the most interesting **book that** I have ever read.

- 事實上，還有一些事是我沒有告訴媽媽的。

  Actually, there is **something that** I did not tell to my mother.

- 我們和原本應該要帶我們去機場的那個男子碰面了。

  We met **the man who** was supposed to take us to the airport.

時間／地點 ★ 更進一步描述時間和地點時

時間名詞＋when ～／地點名詞＋where ～

需要詳加描述名詞的時間或地點時，可以用「when / where＋子句」來進一步表示更詳細的資訊。在這種情境下，可以想成是在提供資訊，而不是在修飾前面的名詞。

- 我很期待夏天的到來，那個時候我有長假可放。

  I look forward to **summer when** I can have a long vacation.

- 我希望爺爺記得我們曾經快樂的待在一起的那個時候。

  I hope my grandpa remembers **the moment when** we were happy together.

- 我們必須找到一個可以搭帳篷的地點。

  We had to find **a place where** we could set up our tent.

📝 更進一步！ 「when＋子句」用來表示「～的時候」，也可以放在句首使用。

- 當我們去露營的時候，我們必須找到一個地方搭帳篷。

  We had to find a place for our tent **when** we went camping.
  When we went camping, we had to find a place for our tent.

就是～ ★ 用來加強語氣時

It is ～ that …

在 It is 和 that 之間加入敘述句的某個部分，就可以用來加強強調那個部分的語氣。只要在 It is 和 that 之間加入想強調的部分就可以了。也就是說，如果把 It is~ that 去掉，就會回復到一般句子的型態。

- 我媽媽總會確認我放學後人在哪裡。

  My mom always checks where I am after school.　　[一般句子]

- 總會確認我放學後人在哪裡的人**是我媽媽**。

  It is my mom **that** always checks where I am after school.　　[強調主詞]

- **在放學後**，我媽媽總會確認我人在哪裡。

  It is after school **that** my mom always checks where I am.　　[強調時間]

Pattern
50

有趣的結論
疑問句／感嘆句／祈使句／強調動詞

★ 寫出有趣的結論

把很多個事件（events）展開，就可以串成一篇文章了。一篇好的日記，除了能夠以有趣的句子做為開頭，寫出有力的結論也是必要的。嘗試練習照樣造句吧！

[疑問句]

- Julie 依然如她之前所說的那樣是我最好的朋友嗎？

  Is Julie still my best friend as she said before?

[感嘆句]

- 媽媽為我煮了這麼好吃的食物，真是太棒了！

  How wonderful my mom is to cook this great food for me!

[祈使句]

- 就讓我們把這個忘掉，然後重新開始吧！

  Let's just forget about it and start all over again!

[強調動詞]

- 我真的很想躺著然後什麼事都不做！

  I **do want** to enjoy lying around and doing nothing!

Part

1

日常生活

一天的感想

It Is Not Fair!

Wednesday, September 18, Sunny

I was depressed all day because I got scolded by my mother. My younger brother and I had fought, but she got angry only at me. Actually, it was he that hit me first. Should I be patient all the time just because I am a big brother? It is not fair! I guess my mom favors my brother over me.

這不公平！　9 月 18 日星期三，晴天

我今天一整天都很沮喪，因為我被媽媽罵了。我和弟弟打架，可是媽媽卻只對我生氣。但事實上是他先打我的。難道就因為我是哥哥，所以我應該要無時無刻都有耐心嗎？這不公平！我想媽媽比較偏心弟弟。

‧depressed （心情）沮喪的　**get scolded** 被罵了　**patient** 有耐心的　**favor** 偏愛

刺激的一天 ★ An Exciting Day

- 今天是很刺激的一天。

  Today was a very exciting day.

- 我跟朋友玩了一整天。

  I played with my friends for the entire day.
  / I played with my friends all day long.
  • entire 整個／全體　　一整天

- 我今天在遊樂園裡過了很刺激的時光。

  Today, I had an exciting time at the amusement park. 遊樂園

- 我玩得太開心了，以致於我完全沒有注意到時間過得有多快。

  I had so much fun that I didn't even know how fast time flew by
  （時間）過得很快

- 我很高興今天考了一百分。

  I am so happy that I received a 100 on my exam.
  • receive 得到

- 媽媽買了一些樂高積木給我，所以我覺得很開心。

  My mom bought me some Lego, so I felt great.

- 我希望每天都可以過得像今天一樣。

  I wish every day were like today.

- 爺爺奶奶能來真的是太棒了。

  It was so good that my grandparents came by.
  （短時間）到訪、過來

- 爸爸一直稱讚我，所以我很開心。／我很開心能得到爸爸的稱讚。

  Dad praised me a lot, so I felt very good. / I felt so great to have received praise from my father.
  • praise 稱讚

- 在圖書館看了很多我最喜歡的書讓我很開心。

  I was so happy to have read a lot of my favorite books at the library.

- 我吃了很多美食。

  I enjoyed a lot of good food.

- 吃東西的時候，我覺得我是世界上最快樂的人。

  When I eat, I feel like the happiest person in the world.

  覺得

沮喪的一天 ★ A Depressing Day

- 我一整天都很沮喪，因為我和朋友吵架了。

  I was depressed all day long because I had fought with my friend.

  • depressed 憂鬱的、沮喪的

- 應該要怪的人是我弟，可是我媽卻只對我發脾氣，我覺得很難過。

  My brother was to blame, but my mom got angry only at me. I felt very upset.

  • be to blame 該受責備的／該負責的

- 哥哥一直打我讓我覺得很煩。

  I feel so irritated because my brother keeps on hitting me.

  • irritated 煩躁的   一直做～

- 我隔壁的同學一直發出噪音，可是老師卻罵我。

  My seatmate was making noise, but I got in trouble with the teacher.

  • 一起做某事的對象稱作 partner（夥伴），坐在隔壁的同學就稱為 seatmate。

- 這太不公平了，因為我根本就沒有講話。

  It is so unfair because I didn't talk at all.

  • unfair 不公平　not ~ at all 完全沒有

- 我覺得很難過，因為我最好的朋友 Amy 要搬家了。

  最好的朋友

  I feel so sad because my best friend Amy is moving.

- 我想買支手機，可是爸爸不讓我買，所以我覺得難過。

  I want to get a cellular phone, but my dad doesn't let me, so I feel upset.

  手機／行動電話 (= cell phone, mobile phone)

- 我的數學考得很爛，所以我覺得情緒很低落。

  I did poorly on my math exam, so I felt down.

  情緒低落

  • poorly 很糟的

- 我希望我在學校的成績可以更好。 | I wish I could get better grades at school.
  - grade 成績

- 生活好無聊，因為我沒有親近的朋友。 | Life is so boring because I don't have any close friends.
  - boring 無聊的、沒意思的　close 親近的

平凡的一天 ★ A Usual Day

- 今天和平常的日子沒有差別。 | Today was just like every other day.

- 我今天一整天都無所事事，所以我的日記裡沒什麼東西可以寫。 | I just loafed around the entire day, so I have nothing to write in my diary.
  > 遊手好閒、無所事事

- 雖然今天是星期天，但我一整天都只待在家裡，真是無聊透頂。 | Even though it was Sunday, I just stayed home all day long. It was such a drag.
  > 雖然～
  > 非常～
  - drag 令人厭倦的人事物

- 我就只是整天在家什麼都沒做。 | I just goofed around the house all day long.
  > 虛度光陰

- 因為我好無聊，所以我讀了一本書。 | I read a book because I was so bored.

- 今天好無聊，因為姊姊不在我身邊。 | It was a boring day because my older sister wasn't around.

- 能夠休息一整天的感覺很棒。 | It was such a great feeling to relax the entire day.
  - relax 放鬆、休息

- 我最喜歡星期四，因為那天我完全沒事。 | I like Thursdays the best because I am totally free.
  - totally 完全地、完整地

- 我很開心週末可以休息，因為平日我都很忙。

I am glad I am able to rest on weekends because I am very busy during the weekdays.

• weekend 週末

- 每天都過得很普通真的好嗎？我喜歡每天都有一些特別的事情發生。

Is it really good for us to have an average day? I like it if something special happens every day.

• average 一般的，普通的

忙碌的一天 ★ A Busy Day

- 我今天忙了一整天。

I had a busy day today.

• have a ~ day 過了～的一天

- 我今天真的很忙碌。

I was so busy today.

- 我甚至沒有時間可以休息一下。

I didn't even have time to take a short break.

• take a break 休息

- 在一整天的奔波之後，我感到非常疲倦。

After spending the day moving around, I was extremely tired.

• spend＋時間＋Ving 花時間做～　extremely 非常地

- 在運動會練習結束後，我好累。

After practicing for sports day, I am tired.

運動會

- 我在星期三最忙。

I am busiest on Wednesdays.

- 忙碌比無聊要來得好。

It is better to be busy than to be bored.

晨間活動

Late Again!

Tuesday, April 5, Cloudy

I overslept again! I skipped breakfast and ran to school. I got scolded by my teacher for being late. It is hard for me to wake up early in the morning. My parents tell me to go to bed at 10:00 p.m., but I usually fall asleep at 11:00 p.m.. So things always get messy in the morning. Starting tomorrow, I will go to sleep early and wake up early.

又遲到了！ 4月5日星期二，多雲

我又睡過頭了！我沒吃早餐就跑去學校了。我因為遲到而被老師罵。早起對我來說真的很困難。爸媽告訴我要在晚上10點上床睡覺，但我通常要到晚上11點才會睡著，所以早上通常是一團混亂。從明天開始，我會早睡早起。

· oversleep (oversleep-overslept-overslept) 睡過頭　skip 跳過　fall asleep 睡覺　messy 混亂的

起床 ★ Getting up

- 我通常在七點起床。

  I usually wake up at 7 o'clock. /
  I usually get up at 7.　　校外教學、體驗活動

- 今天我為了去校外教學而早起。

  Today, I got up early to go on a field trip.

- 我早上總是很早起。

  I tend to wake up early in the morning.
  〜總是

- 早起對我來說很困難。

  It is hard for me to wake up early in the
  morning.

- 我不是個早起的人。

  I am not a morning person.
  早起的人

- 不知道為什麼，我今天很早就
  醒了。

  For some reason, I woke up early today.
  因為某些不知名的原因

- 週末的時候我常常早起。

  On weekends, I tend to wake up earlier.

- 媽媽用親吻叫醒我。

  My mother woke me up with a kiss.

- 外面天色還是暗的。

  It was still dark outside.

- 外面天色已經亮了。

  It was already bright outside.

- 我很早就醒了，因為我昨晚沒把
  作業全部寫完。

  I woke up early since I didn't finish up all
  of my homework last night.

  • since 因為

- 全家都睡著了。

  My whole family was asleep.

  • asleep 睡著

- 早起的鳥兒有蟲吃。

  The early bird gets the worm.
  早起的人

鬧鐘／睡過頭 ★ Alarm/Oversleeping

- 我今天早上睡過頭了。

  I overslept this morning.
  - oversleep 睡過頭

- 我醒來之後又睡著了。

  I **fell asleep** again after waking up.
  （睡著）

- 我昨天晚上不知道為什麼無法入睡，所以到很晚才睡著。

  For some reason last night, I wasn't able to sleep, so I fell asleep late.

- 喔，我今天睡過頭，然後上學又遲到了。

  Oh, I overslept and was late for school again today.

- 我沒有聽見鬧鐘的聲音。

  I didn't hear my alarm clock.

- 我的鬧鐘沒有響。

  My alarm didn't **go off**.
  （鬧鐘等）響起

- 我忘記設鬧鐘了。

  I forgot to set my alarm.

- 媽媽今天很晚才叫醒我。

  My mother woke me up late today.

- 我昨晚寫作業寫到很晚，所以很晚才去睡，而且早上睡過頭了。

  I was doing my homework late last night. So I went to bed late and overslept this morning.

- 我弟弟總是睡過頭。

  My younger brother always oversleeps.

- 我很羨慕我弟弟可以睡過頭。

  I envy my younger brother, who can oversleep.
  - envy 羨慕

- 星期天可以晚點起床的感覺真是太好了。

  It feels good to be able to wake up late on Sundays.

- 我希望週末可以快點來。

  I wish the weekend would come sooner.

- 我從今天開始應該早點上床睡覺。

  I should go to sleep early starting from today.

早餐 ★ Breakfast Time

- 我早上都會吃早餐。

  I always eat/have breakfast in the morning

- 如果我早上不吃東西，就會沒有精神。

  If I don't eat in the morning, I have no energy.

- 我在早上不想吃東西。

  I don't feel like eating in the morning.

  • feel like +Ving 想做～

- 我在早上沒有食慾。

  I have no appetite in the morning.

  • appetite 食慾、胃口

- 我早餐通常吃得很簡單。

  I usually have a simple breakfast.

- 媽媽告訴我早上一定要吃早餐。

  My mother tells me I must eat breakfast in the morning.

- 媽媽總是為我精心準備早餐。

  My mother always serves a nicely prepared breakfast.

  精心準備的

  • serve 準備、提供（食物）

- 我早餐吃麥片。

  I had cereal for breakfast.

- 媽媽很晚起床，所以我必須吃麵包來代替白飯。

  My mother got up late, so I had to eat bread instead of rice.

  代替～

- 僅有的菜只有培根和炒蛋。

  The only dishes were bacon and fried eggs.

  • dish 料理、盤子

- 唉，吃早餐真的很困難。

  Oh, it is so hard to have breakfast.

- 我太晚起床所以沒能吃早餐。

  I woke up so late that I couldn't have breakfast.

  • so＋形容詞＋that＋主詞＋動詞 如此…以至於～

- 我下次應該早點起床吃早餐。

  I should wake up early and eat breakfast next time.

- 如果我沒吃早餐，那我在學校裡很容易就累了。

  If I don't have breakfast, then I get worn out easily at school.

  疲倦

洗臉／刷牙 ★ Washing My Face / Brushing My Teeth

- 我試圖藉著洗臉來讓自己清醒。

  I tried to wake myself up by washing my face.

  • by + Ving 藉由～

- 儘管我洗了臉，我還是無法讓自己清醒。

  Even though I washed my face, I couldn't wake myself up.

- 我洗了臉，可是眼睛裡還是有眼屎。

  I washed my face, but there was still sleep in my eyes.

  • sleep 眼屎

- 我洗完臉，然後擦了一些乳液。

  I washed my face and then put on some lotion on it.

  擦、塗抹

- 乳液的香味真的很好聞。

  The fragrance of the lotion was really good.

  • fragrance 香味

- 妹妹胡亂洗臉的樣子很滑稽。

  It is funny how my younger sister roughly washes her face.

  • roughly 粗暴地、粗略地

- 我每天都淋浴。

  I take a shower every day.

- 我每兩天淋浴一次。

  I take a shower once every two days.

  • once every two/other~ 每兩～做一次

- 我每天洗頭。

  I wash my hair every day.

- 我必須早起洗頭和吹頭髮。

  I have to wake up early to wash and dry my hair.

- 我晚上洗頭。

  I wash my hair in the evening.

- 我用吹風機把頭髮弄乾。

  I dried my hair with a hair dryer.

  → 吹風機

- 我家只有一間浴室。

  My house has only one bathroom.

- 我姊姊只要進了浴室就不出來了。

  If my older sister goes in the bathroom, then she never comes out.

- 因為我哥哥淋浴淋了很久，他差一點上學遲到。

  Since my older brother took a shower for such a long time, he was nearly late for school.

  • nearly 差一點

- 我一天刷三次牙。

  I brush my teeth three times a day.

- 刷牙真是件麻煩事。

  It is such a hassle to brush my teeth.

  • hassle 麻煩、討厭的情況／事情

- 刷完牙之後，我覺得好清爽。

  After brushing my teeth, I felt so refreshed

  • refreshed 清爽的

- 牙刷壞了，我應該要去買支新的。

  The toothbrush is worn out. I should get a new one.

  → 磨損到無法使用

- 我把牙膏用完了。

  I ran out of toothpaste.

  → 用完～

- 電動牙刷用起來舒服又有效。

  Using the electric toothbrush felt so comfortable and good.

  • electric 電動的　comfortable 舒服的、舒適的

- 我在刷牙的時候發現牙齦在流血。
  While brushing my teeth, I found my gums bleeding.
  • gum 牙齦 bleed 流血

- 我在洗臉的時候突然流了鼻血。
  (All of a sudden), I got a bloody nose while washing my face.
  突然
  • bloody 流血的

- 舌頭上的潰瘍讓刷牙變得很痛苦。
  It was really hard to brush my teeth because of the sore on my tongue.
  • sore 瘡、潰瘍 tongue 舌頭

- 我的嘴巴很臭，因為我沒有刷牙。／我有口臭，因為我忘了刷牙。
  My breath smelled bad because I did not brush my teeth. / I had (bad breath) because I forgot to brush my teeth.
  口臭
  • breath 氣息、呼吸

穿衣服 ★ Putting on My Clothes

- 我換了衣服去上學。
  I changed my clothes for school.
  • change 換（衣服）

- 我脫掉睡衣，然後換上洋裝。
  I (took off) my pajamas and changed into my dress.
  脫掉（衣服）
  • pajamas 睡衣

- 我被媽媽罵了，因為我把睡衣丟在地上。
  I got in trouble with my mom because I left my pajamas on the floor.
  • get in trouble 被罵、惹上麻煩

- 媽媽說那條褲子和那件 T 恤不搭。
  My mother said that the pants did not match the T-shirt.
  • match （顏色、花紋、款式）很搭

- 媽媽說那條褲子和那件T恤不適合我。

My mother said that the pants and the T-shirt did not suit me.
- suit 適合

- 媽媽幫我挑衣服。

My mother (picked out) my clothes.
挑選

- 我想要穿褲子，可是媽媽一直叫我穿裙子。

I want to wear pants, but my mother keeps telling me to wear a skirt.
- keep +Ving 一直做～

- 當我穿著漂亮的衣服去上學時，我覺得心情很好。

I feel good on my way to school when I wear pretty clothes.
- on one's way to 在去～的路上

- 我無法不去看有誰穿著漂亮的衣服。

I can't stop looking at others to see who is wearing pretty clothes.

- 我想要自己挑衣服穿。

I want to pick out my clothes for myself.
- for oneself 親自

- 去年穿的洋裝現在對我來說已經太小了。／我發現我去年穿的洋裝已經不能穿了。

The dress I wore last year is too small for me. / I found I had outgrown the dress I wore last year.
- outgrow 長大了便不再適用

- 新的褲子穿起來很不舒服。

The new pants feel too uncomfortable.
- uncomfortable 不舒服

- 條紋洋裝是我最喜歡的衣服。

The striped dress is my favorite outfit.
- striped 條紋的　outfit 服裝、衣服

- 我的衣服好皺。

My clothes were wrinkled.
- wrinkled 皺的、有皺紋的

- 媽媽幫我燙襯衫。

My mom ironed my shirt. / My mom had my shirt ironed.
- iron 熨燙、熨斗

- 天氣變熱了。我從現在開始應該要穿短袖襯衫了。

The weather has gotten hotter. From now on, I should wear short-sleeved shirts.
從現在開始　短袖的

- 天氣變冷了。我從現在開始應該要穿衛生衣了。

The weather has gotten colder. From now on, I should wear long johns.
衛生衣

- 因為我穿的衣服太薄了，我覺得好冷。

Since I wore thin clothes, I was really cold.
• thin 薄的

- 在衣服裡面穿衛生衣讓我活動起來不舒服。

Wearing long johns under my outfit made it uncomfortable for me to move.

- 我因為沒有合適的衣服可以穿而覺得心煩。

I am so upset because I have nothing appropriate to wear.
• appropriate 合適的

- 我希望媽媽可以買些新衣服給我。

I wish my mother would buy me some new clothes.

- 我因為在找運動服而上課遲到。

I was late for class because I was looking for my gym clothes.
運動服

- 因為今天有體育課，所以我穿了運動鞋。

Today I had P.E., so I wore my sneakers.
• P.E. 體育(= physical exercise)　sneakers 運動鞋

- 我想要買一雙新鞋子。

I want to buy a new pair of shoes.

- 我已經選好了野餐要穿的衣服了。

I already chose the clothes that I'm going to wear at the picnic.

- 媽媽把我想穿的衣服拿去洗了。

My mother washed the clothes that I wanted to wear.

- 昨天媽媽洗了我的 T 恤，可是還沒全乾。

Yesterday, my mother washed my T-shirt, but it hasn't dried all the way.
完全

- 我把衣服穿反了。

  I wore my outfit (inside out).
  （裡外）穿反

- 我穿襯衫的時候穿太快，把扣子扣錯了。

  Putting on my shirt quickly, I put the button in the wrong hole.
  • hole 洞

- 我的其中一隻襪子破了一個洞。

  One of my socks had a hole in it.

- 我想要跟哥哥一樣穿學校制服。

  I want to wear a (school uniform) just like my older brother.
  學校制服

梳頭髮 ★ Combing My Hair

- 我用扁梳梳頭髮。

  I combed my hair with a comb.
  • comb 扁梳

- 我的頭髮打結了，所以沒辦法好好地梳開。

  My hair got (tangled up), so I couldn't comb it well.
  打結了、糾結

- 媽媽把我的頭髮綁得很漂亮。

  My mother tied my hair beautifully.
  • tie 綁

- 媽媽把我的頭髮綁太緊了。

  My mom tied my hair too tight.

- 我把頭髮綁成一條辮子。

  I tied my hair into one braid.
  • braid 辮子

- 我把頭髮綁成兩條辮子。

  I tied my hair in two braids.

- 我把頭髮綁成一條側邊辮。

  I tied my hair in one braid on the side.

- 起床以後我的頭髮亂翹了。

  My hair was (sticking up) after I woke up.
  突起、豎起

- 我去上學的時候沒綁頭髮。

  I let my hair down when I went to school.
  - let A down 讓 A 垂下

- 我喜歡把頭髮放下來。

  I like my hair hanging down.
  垂下

- 我不喜歡戴髮箍。

  I don't like putting on a headband.
  - headband 髮箍

- 如果我戴髮箍，我會頭痛。

  If I put on a headband, my head hurts.

- 媽媽買了一個漂亮的髮圈給我。

  My mother bought me a pretty hair tie.
  髮圈

- 我的瀏海快要擋住眼睛了。

  My bangs are getting in the way of my eyes.
  遮住、妨礙
  - bang 瀏海

- 我應該要去剪頭髮。

  I should have my hair cut.

- 因為我留了一頭短髮，我就只要梳頭髮就可以了。

  Since I have short hair, all I have to do is just comb it.

在早上念書 ★ Studying in the Morning

- 我每天早上六點半起床讀書。

  Every day, I wake up at 6:30 a.m. and study.

- 我起床後的第一件事就是寫習作本裡的數學題。

  The first thing I do when I wake up is solving the math questions in my workbook.
  - workbook 習作本

- 如果我在早上念書，我就可以很順利地解題。

  If I study in the morning, I can solve the questions pretty well.

- 我在早上可以非常專心。　　　　I can concentrate very well in the morning.
  - concentrate 專心

- 每天早上我都會看英文的 DVD。　　Every morning, I watch a DVD in English.

- 每天早上我都會聽英文童話故事。　Every morning, I listen to English storybooks.

- 早上去上學之前，我必須要寫完四　Before I go to school in the morning, I
  頁數學習作。　　　　　　　　　have to complete 4 pages in my math workbook.
  - complete 完成

- 早上我匆忙地把作業趕完，因為我　趕著做～
  昨天沒有寫。　　　　　　　　　I hurried through my homework in the morning because I did not do it yesterday.

- 因為我都在早上讀書，早起已經變　Waking up early in the morning has
  成一種習慣。　　　　　　　　　become a habit because I study in the morning.

- 我感到非常疲倦，因為我在早上讀　I am very tired because I study in the
  書。／在早上讀書讓我覺得非常疲　morning. / Studying in the morning has
  累。　　　　　　　　　　　　　caused me to be very tired.

上學 ★ Going to School

- 我在早上八點二十分左右去上學。　I go to school at around 8:20 a.m.

- 從我家到學校大概需要二十分鐘。　It takes me about 20 minutes to go from my house to school.
  - take＋時間＋to不定詞 花費～時間做～

- 我走路上學。　　　　　　　　　I go to school on foot. /
  I walk to school.　　用走的

- 我希望我家能離學校更近一點。

  I wish my house were closer to the school.

  我希望～就好了

- 因為電梯壞了,所以我用走的到一樓。

  Since the elevator was broken, I walked down all the way to the first floor.

  • broken 壞掉

- 媽媽每天早上送我到學校。

  Every morning, my mother takes me to school.

- 因為我錯過校車了,所以媽媽載我到學校。

  Since I missed the school bus, my mother drove me to school.

  • miss 錯過 drive A to 載 A 去～

- 爸爸上班的時候順便載我一程。

  My dad gave me a ride on his way to work.

  • give A a ride 用車載 A on one's way to 某人前往～的途中

- 以前我喜歡媽媽送我,不過現在我喜歡跟朋友一起上學。

  I liked my mother taking me before, but now I enjoy going with my friends.

- 我在上學途中遇到 Amy。

  On my way to school, I met Amy.

- 我在上學途中去了一間文具店買了直笛。

  On my way to school, I stopped by the stationery store and bought a recorder.

  路過、順便去～
  文具店

- 我在上學途中必須穿過一個有紅綠燈的馬路。

  On my way to school, I have to cross one street at the stoplight.

  • stoplight 紅綠燈、交通號誌燈

- 我忘記帶功課了,所以必須回家去拿。

  I forgot my homework, so I had to go back home to get them.

- 我今天必須在八點前到校,因為我要做一些晨間運動。

  I had to get to school by 8 o'clock today since I had to do some morning exercises.

- 為了不要遲到,我用最快的速度跑到學校,我幸運地沒有遲到。

  I ran to school as fast as I could for not to be late. Fortunately, I was not tardy.

  • as fast as one can 以最快的速度做～ tardy 緩慢的

- 我睡過頭而且上學遲到了。

  I overslept and was late for school.

- 我因為遲到而被老師處罰和斥責。

  I was punished and scolded by my teacher since I was late/tardy.

  • be punished 被處罰　be scolded 被責罵

- 我今天不想去上學，因為我有個考試。

  Today, I didn't feel like going to school since I had an exam.

- 因為我把作業忘在家裡，所以媽媽幫我送來學校。

  Since I left my homework at home, my mother brought it over to school.

- 因為我們學校有個小山坡，所以不是很好走。

  Since my school has a hill, it is very difficult to walk to.

- 我因為遲到而被記過。

  Since I was late/tardy, I got a demerit.

  • demerit 記過

- 我從現在開始應該要快一點做好上學的準備。

  From now on, I should get ready for school a lot faster.

放學後

I Love Soccer!

Monday, October 13, Sunny

After school finished, my friends and I played soccer in the schoolyard. We had a match with some boys from other classes. We won by the score of 2 to 1. I scored one goal. Hooray! It was so fun that we didn't even know how fast time flew by. I wish I could play with my friends more often.

我喜歡足球！　10 月 13 日星期一，晴天

在放學之後，我跟朋友一起在操場踢足球。我們跟其他班的男生一起比了一場，最後以二比一的成績獲得勝利。我踢進了一球，萬歲！比賽太有趣了，所以我們完全沒有注意到時間過得有多快。我希望我可以更常和朋友一起玩。

·schoolyard 操場　match 比賽　score 分數、得分　fly by （時間）過得飛快

- 我今天上了五堂課。

  Today, I had 5 classes.

- 在下課以後，我大概在兩點左右到家。

  When school is finished, I arrive at home at around 2 o'clock.

- 我比較晚到家，是因為我比較晚才打掃完。

  I came back home late because I finished cleaning up late.

- 當我從學校回到家裡，我做的第一件事就是洗手。

  The first thing I do when I come home from school is wash my hands.

- 洗完手之後我吃了點心。

  I ate/had a snack after I washed my hands.

  • snack 點心

- 我因為幫老師跑腿，所以上安親班遲到了。

  跑腿

  I was running an errand for my teacher, so I was late for my after-school class.

  安親班

- 我在安親班上電腦課。

  I am taking a computer course at an after-school class.

- 我在星期二和星期四上電腦課。

  I have a computer class on Tuesdays and Thursdays.

- 我喜歡上課，因為我和我的朋友 Amy 一起上課。

  I like it since I take the class with my friend Amy.

- 在下課之後，我會去圖書館等著上安親班。

  After school ends, I go to the library and wait for my after-school class to begin.

- 我在回家途中跟朋友一起在小吃店吃了薯條。

  On my way home, my friends and I ate French fries at a snack house.

- 放學後，我和朋友在學校前面的文具店買了一個陀螺。

  My friends and I bought a top at the stationery store in front of our school after school was over.

  在～前面

  • over 結束

和朋友一起玩耍 ★Hanging out with My Friends

- 放學以後，我和朋友一起在操場上玩。

  After school finished, I played with my friends on the schoolyard/field.

  • schoolyard（學校）操場　field 運動場

- 我踢了足球，而且玩得非常愉快。

  I played soccer and had a very good time.

- 我在操場上玩了剪刀石頭布。

  剪刀石頭布

  I played a game of rock-paper-scissors at the playground.

  • playground 操場

- 我在學校操場上玩了捉迷藏。

  學校操場

  At the school field, I played a game of hide-and-seek.

  捉迷藏

- 我放學以後去了 Eric 家玩。

  After school, I went to hang out at Eric's house.

  一起玩樂

- 我去了朋友家一起寫作業。

  I went to my friend's house, and we did our homework together.

- 時間在我們寫作業和玩遊戲的時候過得飛快。

  Time flew by while we were doing our homework and playing games.

- Eric 的媽媽給了我們好吃的點心。

  Eric's mother gave us a delicious snack.

- 我放學以後和 Amy 一起在我家玩。

  After school, I hung out with Amy at my house.

- 我媽媽說我可以邀請朋友來家裡一起玩。

  My mother said that I could invite my friends over and play with them.

  • invite A over 邀請 A 來家裡

- Amy 邀我放學後一起去玩。

  Amy asked me to hang out after school.

- 我用 Amy 的手機打給媽媽，想得到她的同意。

  I used Amy's cell phone to call my mom and to ask for her permission.
  - permission 同意

- 我問了媽媽，她說我不可以這樣做。／我問了媽媽，但是沒有得到她的同意。

  I asked my mother, and she said that I couldn't do it. / I asked my mother but did not get her approval.
  - approval 贊成、同意

- 我必須馬上去補習班，所以不能一起去玩。

  I had to go to cram school right away, so I couldn't hang out. ── 馬上
  - 「補習班」在英文裡還可以用 academy、private institute 來表達。

- 我是唯一一個不能去玩的人，因為我必須去補習班，這讓我覺得很難過。

  I felt bad that I was the only one who could not play because I had to go to cram school.

- 在和朋友玩的時候，我錯過了校車。

  While playing with my friend, I missed the school bus.

- 我媽媽因為我蹺了補習班的課去和朋友玩而罵我。

  My mother scolded me because I skipped cram school to play with my friends.
  - scold 責罵 skip 跳過、略過

- 我希望我每天都可以這樣玩。

  I wish I could play like this every day.

 閱讀 ★ Reading Books

- 我喜歡看書。

  I like reading books.

- 我沒有那麼喜歡看書。

  I don't like reading books that much.

- 當我看書的時候，我不會注意到時間流逝。

When I read books, I lose track of time.
　　　　　　　不知道時間流逝

- 我希望我可以只看書，而不需要做其他的事情。

I wish I could just read books and do nothing else.

- 我喜歡奇幻小說。

I like fantasy novels.

• fantasy 幻想、想像　novel 小說

- 我今天到書店買了我想要的書。

Today, I went to the bookstore and bought the book that I wanted.
　　　　　　　借（書等等）、確認

- 我從學校圖書館借了《老鼠記者》。

I checked out the book *Geronimo Stilton* from the school library.

- Eric 覺得那本書很有趣，所以推薦給我。

Eric recommended it to me because he thought it was interesting.

• recommend 推薦

- 我今天借的書都很好看。

The books I checked out today were all great.

- 我借了一本數學故事書，可是內容太難了。

I checked out a math storybook, but the content was too difficult.

• content 內容

- 《哈利波特》是一系列很有趣的書。

Harry Potter is a very interesting series of books.

- 在讀完《賣火柴的小女孩》以後，我難過到流下眼淚。

After I read the book *The Little Match Girl*, I was so sad that I was in tears.
　　　　　　　哭、流下眼淚

- 今天我和媽媽一起去圖書館。

Today, I went to the library with my mother.

- 一張借書證最多可以借五本書。

With one library card, I can check out up to 5 books.

• up to 最多

- 我忘了還《39 條線索》這本書了。

  I forgot to return the book *39 Clues*.
  - return 歸還

- 它已經過期一個禮拜了。

  It is one week overdue.
  - overdue 過期

- 我不能再借任何書了，因為我有一本書過期還沒還。

  I could not check out any books because I had an overdue book.

- 朋友借我《39 條線索》這本書。

  My friend lent me the book *39 Clues*.
  - lent (lend – lent – lent) 借出

- 媽媽叫我不要再看漫畫了。

  My mother tells me to stop reading comic books.
  - comic book 漫畫書

- 很多漫畫裡都有有用的知識。

  There are many comic books that have useful knowledge.
  - knowledge 知識

- 我希望媽媽可以買一本漫畫給我。

  I wish my mother would buy me a comic book.

- 我一定要看這本書來準備明天的圖書測驗。

  I must read this book to prepare for the book quiz tomorrow.

- 因為我看了很多書，所以我獲得了一個獎品。

  Since I read a lot of books, I received a prize.
  - prize 獎、獎品

- 媽媽答應我，如果我讀完一百本英文書就會買腳踏車給我。

  Mom promised to buy me a bicycle if I read 100 English books.

- 我很喜歡看書，可是寫讀書心得很討人厭。

  I enjoy reading books, but writing (book reports) is a (pain in the neck).

  讀書心得　　　討厭的事情、棘手的事情

寫作業 ★ Doing My Homework

- 今天我有好多學校作業。

  Today, I had lots of school homework.

- 我一回家就開始寫作業。

  I began to do my homework (as soon as) I got back home.

  ─～就～

- 媽媽告訴我要先寫功課才能玩。

  My mother tells me to do my homework first and then play.

- 我的老師是出了名的愛出作業。

  My teacher is famous for giving out lots of homework.

- 我們班的作業不太多。

  My class doesn't have much homework.

- 我今天的回家作業是寫一篇日記和讀書心得。

  My homework for today is to write a (diary entry) and a book report.

  日記

- 我寫完功課之後已經是晚上了。

  After I finished my homework, it was night.

- 我真的很討厭算數。

  I really hate arithmetic.

  • arithmetic 算數、演算

- 我的習作本進度落後。

  I am really behind with my workbook.

  • be behind with 延遲、落後

- 當我寫完所有的學校作業之後，我還要寫課外學習的作業。

  When I finish all of my schoolwork, then I have to do the homework for my (private lesson). 課外學習

  • schoolwork 學校作業

- 我羨慕不用寫任何作業的大人們。

  I envy adults, who don't have to do any homework.

- 我希望住在一個沒有回家作業的世界。

  I want to live in a world where we don't have any homework.

- 我不能寫作業，因為我的電腦壞了。

  I couldn't do my homework because my computer was broken.

  • broken 壞掉

- 我必須把作業印出來，可是印表機的墨水用完了。

  I have to print my homework, but the printer has no ink.

- 我今天自修教材的進度嚴重落後，所以我不能看任何電視了。

  I was so (far behind) with my (homeschool materials) that I couldn't watch any television today.

  遠遠落後
  自修教材

- 我忘記有作業了。

  I forgot about my homework.

- 每次我試著要寫功課時就會覺得想睡，讓我不想再寫了。

  Every time I try to do my homework, I get so sleepy that I don't want to do it anymore.

- 我決定明天早上要早起寫作業。

  I decided to get up early tomorrow morning to do my homework.

- 我必須先寫完功課才會覺得比較輕鬆。／在做任何事之前先把功課寫完，會讓我覺得比較輕鬆。

  I must do my homework first to feel better. / I feel better when I do my homework first before anything else.

- 從明天開始，我應該要先寫完作業再玩。

  Starting tomorrow, I should do my homework first and then play.

- 我忙著寫回家作業和看書。

  I am totally busy doing my homework and reading books.

幫忙做家事 ★ Helping out with the Household Chores

- 今天我幫媽媽做家事。

  Today, I helped out my mother with the household chores.
  家事

- 我幫忙摺衣服。

  I helped out by folding the laundry.

  • fold 摺疊　laundry 洗好的衣物

- 我幫媽媽打掃。

  I helped my mother clean up.

- 爸爸很會幫忙做家事。

  My dad does a very good job of helping out with the chores.

  • do a good job 擅長做（某事）

- 因為媽媽生病了，我負責煮飯。

  I prepared food because my mother was sick.

- 我負責做資源回收。／我是我們家裡應該做資源回收的人。

  負責
  I'm in charge of recycling. / I am supposed to do the recycling in my house.

  • recycling 回收　be supposed to 應該

- 在整理完桌面以後，我覺得煥然一新。

  I feel so refreshed after organizing my desk. / I feel so refreshed after tidying up my desk.
  清理乾淨

  • organize 整理

- 在洗完碗以後，我被媽媽稱讚了。

  I was praised by my mother after doing the dishes.

  • be/get praised 被稱讚　do the dishes 洗碗

- 媽媽很感謝我的幫忙。

  My mom was very thankful for my help.

- 爸爸給了我一些錢當作獎勵，因為我幫他把鞋子擦亮了。

My dad gave me some money as a reward because I polished and shined his shoes.
  - reward 補償、獎賞　polish/shine 擦亮

- 從今天開始，我應該要自己打掃房間。

From today, I should clean up my room by myself.
  - by oneself 親自、自己

- 我被稱讚了覺得好開心。

I felt so happy getting praised.

- 每天都要做家事的話很煩人，不過偶爾幫忙的話還可以。

It is a hassle doing the household chores every day. Helping out from time to time is okay, though.
  — 偶爾、有時
  - hassle 討厭的事情

晚間活動

Dad Came Home Early! Friday, January 20, Freezing

My father came home early from work today. After dinner, we played a board game together. I won in the last round. My dad often works overtime at night. I was so happy that my dad came home early and played with me. It would be very good if this happened every day.

爸爸提早回家！ 1 月 20 日星期五，非常冷

今天爸爸提早下班回家。吃過晚餐以後，我們一起玩了桌遊。我贏了最後一場。爸爸晚上常常加班。我很開心爸爸提早回家陪我玩。如果每天都可以這樣，那就太好了。

·round 一局、一回合　work overtime 加班

家人回家了 ★ Family Returning Home

- 今天爸爸很早到家。

  Today, my father arrived home early.

- 因為爸爸很早下班回家，所以他陪我們玩。

  Since my father got back home from work early, he played with us. 回家

- 爸爸常常很晚回家。／
  爸爸通常很晚才下班回家。

  常常、傾向做～

  My father tends to come back home late. / My dad usually comes home late from work.

- 爸爸晚上經常加班。

  My father works overtime at night a lot.

  加班

- 爸爸通常在八點左右回家。

  My father usually returns home at around 8 o'clock.

- 妹妹大概三點從幼稚園回家。

  My younger sister comes back home from kindergarten at around 3 o'clock.

  • kindergarten 幼稚園

- 我每個星期一、三、五從英文課下課回到家的時間大概是六點。

  When I come back home from my English lessons on Mondays, Wednesdays, and Fridays, it is around 6 o'clock.

- 補習班下課以後，我五點鐘回到家。

  After I finish cram school, I arrive at my house at 5 o'clock.

- 媽媽很晚下班。

  My mom leaves work late.

  下班

- 我希望媽媽可以早一點下班。

  I wish my mom could leave work a little earlier.

- 媽媽因為和同事一起吃晚餐而很晚回家。

  Because my mom had dinner with her co-workers, she came home late.

  • co-worker 同事

- 提早回家的是爸爸而不是媽媽。

  Instead of my mom, my dad came home early.

- 當爸爸提早回家的時候，我很開心。

  I am very happy when my father comes home early.

- 如果爸爸可以每天都提早回家的話，那就太好了。

  It would be so good if my dad could come home early every day.

晚餐 ★ Dinner Time

- 我們家在七點吃晚餐。

  In my house, we have dinner at 7 o'clock.

- 我比較早吃晚餐。

  I had an early dinner.

- 今天晚上我們喝了蘿蔔湯。

  Tonight, we had radish soup.

  • radish 蘿蔔

- 我幫媽媽擺餐具。

  I helped my mother set the table.
  擺餐具

- 我們晚餐訂了比薩。

  We ordered pizza for dinner.

- 因為我生日，所以我們出去吃。

  We ate out since it was my birthday.
  出外用餐

- 我們晚餐吃豬排。

  We had pork cutlet for dinner.
  豬排

- 我最喜歡的食物是香腸和雞肉。

  My favorite foods are sausage and chicken.

- 因為我們配了些好吃的菜，所以我吃了兩碗飯。

  Since we had some delicious dishes, I had two bowls of rice.

  • bowl 碗

- 我覺得我晚餐吃太多了。

  I think I had too much for supper.

- 我不喜歡（吃）魚和蘑菇。

  I dislike fish and mushrooms.

- 媽媽說我不可以挑食。

  My mother said I should not be picky.

  • picky 挑剔的

- 因為爸爸提早回家，所以我們全家一起吃晚餐。

  Since my dad came home early, we all had dinner together.

- 吃完晚餐以後，我們外出散步。

  After eating dinner, we went out for a walk.

  外出散步

- 我太早吃晚餐以致於晚上又餓了，所以我吃了泡麵。

  I ate dinner so early that I became hungry at night, so I had instant noodles.

- 晚餐的味道讓我覺得心情很好。

  The smell of dinner made me feel happy.

洗澡 ★ Washing and Bathing

- 我一星期泡兩次澡。

  I take a bath twice a week.

  • twice 兩次

- 吃完晚餐以後，我泡了澡。

  After having dinner, I took a bath.

- 踢完足球以後我的身體黏黏的，所以我沖了澡。

  My body felt sticky after playing soccer, so I took a shower.

  • sticky 黏黏的

- 今天天氣很熱，所以我沖了兩次澡。

  The weather today was hot, so I took a shower two times.

- 我在沒有媽媽的幫忙下自己淋浴。

I took a shower by myself without the help of my mother.
- without the help of 沒有～的幫助

- 我和弟弟一起在浴缸泡澡。

I took a bath in the bathtub with my younger brother.
- bathtub 浴缸

- 浴室的地板滑滑的。

The bathroom floor was slippery.
- slippery 滑的

- 我在浴室滑倒。

I slipped in the bathroom.
- slip 滑倒

- 我把身上的汙垢都洗掉了。

I washed off the dirt from my body. / I scrubbed off the dirt from my body.
- dirt 灰塵、汙垢　　搓揉掉～

- 很多汙垢從我皮膚上脫落。

A lot of dirt came off my skin.

- 我兩天洗一次頭。

I wash my hair once every two days.
每兩天、隔一天

- 洗髮精跑進我的眼睛裡了，讓我的眼睛有刺痛感。

The shampoo got into my eyes and stung them.
- sting (sting-stung-stung) 刺痛、扎

- 洗髮精用完了。

We ran out of shampoo.

- 我用乾淨的水洗頭。

I rinsed my hair with clean water.
- rinse 沖洗

- 我忘記洗腳了。

I forgot to wash my feet.

- 我用毛巾把身體擦乾。

I dried my body with a towel.

- 洗完澡以後，我在身上擦了一些乳液。

After taking a bath, I rubbed some lotion on my body.
- rub 塗抹、擦

• 媽媽在我的背上擦了一些乳液。	My mother rubbed some lotion onto my back.
• 洗完澡以後，我換上了睡衣。	After washing up, I changed into my pajamas.
• 我在洗完臉和刷完牙後準備好睡覺了。	I got ready to sleep after washing my face and brushing my teeth.

睡覺 ★ Sleeping

• 我在十點睡覺。	I go to sleep at 10 o'clock.
• 我九點睡覺、七點起床。	I go to sleep at 9 o'clock and get up at 7 o'clock.
• 我一天大約睡九個小時。	I sleep around 9 hours a day.
• 我躺下以後馬上就睡著了。	When I lie down, I fall asleep right away. • lie down (lie-lay-lain) 躺下　　馬上、立刻
• 昨天我累到一躺下來就睡著了。	Yesterday, I was so tired that I fell asleep as soon as I lay down.
• 昨晚我沒睡好。	Last night, I couldn't sleep very well.
• 我晚上想要再多玩一下，所以不喜歡太早去睡。	I want to play more at night, so I don't like going to sleep early.
• 聽說如果太晚睡會長不高。	It is said that if you go to sleep late, you won't grow taller.
• 我家的人都睡在一起。	My family sleeps all together.
• 我一個人睡在自己的房間裡。	I sleep alone in my room.

- 爸爸睡覺的時候會打鼾。

My father snores when he sleeps.
- snore 打鼾

- Amy 睡覺的時候會磨牙。

Amy grinds her teeth when she sleeps.
- grind one's teeth 磨牙

- 媽媽在我睡覺前唸書給我聽。

Before I went to sleep, my mom read a book to me.

- 我睡覺的時候做了惡夢而醒了過來。

While I was sleeping, I had a bad dream and woke up.

- 我因為要上廁所而醒來。

I woke up because I had to go to the bathroom.

- 妹妹睡覺的時候不能沒有她的娃娃。

When my younger sister sleeps, she cannot sleep without her doll.

- 如果沒有我的毯子，我就完全睡不著。

If I don't have my own blanket, I cannot sleep at all.

- 我睡覺的時候從床上摔了下來。

As I was sleeping, I fell off the bed.
從～摔下

- 昨晚我做了惡夢。

I had a nightmare last night.
- nightmare 惡夢

- 我做了一個夢，但當我醒來的時候，我什麼都不記得了。

I had a dream, but when I woke up, I couldn't remember it.

- 當我醒來的時候，我發現媽媽就睡在我身旁。

When I woke up, I found my mother was sleeping right beside me.

- 我的脖子不太能轉動，因為我睡覺的姿勢不對。

I can't turn my neck properly because I slept the wrong way.
- properly 正確地、恰當地

Part 2

天氣與季節

天氣

What a Fine Weather!

Thursday, June 1, Sunny

The sky was very clear without a single cloud. The weather has been really nice for the past few days. It was so good that I wanted to go out to play somewhere. I will ask my mom to take me to the park this weekend. Hopefully, this good weather lasts through the weekend.

天氣真好！　6月1日星期四，晴天

天空非常晴朗，連一朵雲都沒有。過去幾天的天氣都非常好。天氣太好了讓我很想出去外面玩。這個週末我會請媽媽帶我去公園玩。但願好天氣會持續到週末。

·past 過去的　somewhere 某處　last 持續、繼續　through 透過、在…期間

晴天 ★ Fair Weather

- 今天天氣真好。

  The weather was nice today. /
  The weather was good today.

- 今天是晴朗的好天氣。

  It was a bright sunny day.

- 過去幾天的天氣都非常好。

  The weather has been really nice for the past few days.

  • past 過去的

- 天空很晴朗，連一朵雲都沒有。

  The sky was clear without any clouds.

- 陽光很溫暖。

  The sun was warm.

- 陽光非常燦爛。

  The sun was shining brilliantly.

  • shine 閃耀 brilliantly 一閃一閃地、燦爛地

- 天空好漂亮！

  The sky was so beautiful!

- 天空放晴了。

  The sky cleared up. / 放晴
  The rain went away.
  消失

- 我和弟弟一起在操場玩，因為天氣很好。

  I played with my younger brother on the playground because the weather was so nice.

- 氣象預報說會下雨，但幸好天氣很好。

  根據 天氣預報
  According to the weather forecast, it was going to rain. Fortunately, the weather was pretty good.

  • fortunately 幸好

- 因為天氣很好，我想出去玩！

  Since the weather is so nice, I want to go somewhere!

  • since 因為～

陰天 ★ Cloudy Weather

- 今天是陰天。

  It's a cloudy day. 心情不好

- 因為天氣陰陰的,所以我也覺得心情不好。

  Since the weather is gloomy, I feel down, too.

  • gloomy 灰暗的、陰暗的

- 這幾天都是陰天。

  It has been cloudy for a few days.

- 今天一整天都是沒有下雨的陰天。

  It has been cloudy without any rainfall all day.

  • rainfall 雨、降雨

- 早上天空還很晴朗,但到了下午就突然變成陰天了。

  The sky was clear in the morning, but it suddenly became cloudy in the afternoon.

- 天空滿是雲朵。

  The sky is full of clouds. 充滿

- 我覺得明天應該會下雨,因為今天一整天都是陰天。

  I think it's going to rain tomorrow since it has been cloudy all day.

- 從早上開始就是陰天,所以我有帶傘出門。

  It was cloudy since morning, so I left home with an umbrella.

- 陰陰的天氣讓我覺得憂鬱。

  The gloomy weather is making me feel depressed.

  • depressed 憂鬱的

- 我因為一直都是陰天所以心情不好。

  I'm down because of this never-ending gloomy weather.

  • never-ending 不停的

- 我希望可以盡快放晴。

  I hope a sunny day comes as soon as possible. 盡快

- 沙塵暴嚴重到天空好灰暗。

  The yellow dust was so heavy that the sky was dark.
  沙塵暴

- 沙塵暴的預警已經發布了。

  A yellow dust precaution has been issued.

  • precaution 預警、預防措施　issue 發布

- 因為嚴重的沙塵暴，我上學的時候戴著口罩。

  Because of the heavy yellow dust, I wore a mask when going to school.

下雨天 ★ Rainy Day

- 一整天都在下雨。

  It rained all day.

- 從早上開始，天空就灰濛濛的。到了下午就開始下雨了。

  In the morning, the sky was unclear. By the afternoon, it started to rain.

- 從早上就開始下毛毛雨。

  It has been drizzling since morning.

  • drizzle 下毛毛雨

- 傾盆大雨下了好幾天了。

  It has been pouring for days.

  • pour 倒、灌注

- 我希望可以不要再下雨了。

  I wish it would stop raining.

- 一場小小的雷陣雨過後，天空很快放晴了。

  After a light shower, the sky quickly cleared.

  • light 輕微的　shower 雷陣雨

- 伴隨著打雷和閃電，雨下了一整晚，所以我完全睡不著。／因為大雷雨，我整個晚上睡不著。

  It rained with thunder and lightning all night. So I couldn't sleep at all. / I couldn't sleep all night because of the thunderstorm.

  • lightning 閃電　thunderstorm 大雷雨

- 我在操場上玩的時候，突然就下起雨了。

  I was playing on the playground when it suddenly started to rain.

- 下了傾盆大雨。

  The rain poured down.

  傾盆而下

- 我很害怕，因為又打雷又閃電。

  I was scared because there were thunder and lightning.

- 風大到讓我覺得好害怕。

  The wind was blowing so hard that it scared me.

- 因為上學途中下雨了，我所有的衣服都被雨淋得溼透了。

  Because it rained on my way to school, all of my clothes were soaked by the rain.

  • soak 濕透

- 因為大雨，我的襪子都濕了。

  Because of the heavy rain, my socks were soaked.

- 因為我沒帶傘，所以我必須要淋雨走路回家。

  Because I hadn't brought any umbrella, I had to walk home in the rain.

- 因為我淋雨走路回家，所以感冒了。

  Since I walked home in the rain, I caught a cold.

  感冒

- Alice 撐傘送我走路回家。

  Alice walked me home with her umbrella.

- 我跟 Alice 一起撐傘。

  I shared my umbrella with Alice.

- 大雨下得彷彿天空破了洞似的。

  It has been pouring as if the heavens opened.

  彷彿

- 因為在下雨，所以我穿雨鞋和雨衣去上學。

  I wore rain boots and a rain coat when I went to school because it was raining.

- 因為在下雨，我整天都待在家。

  I stayed home all day because it was raining.

- 因為在下雨，校外教學延期了。

  The field trip has been postponed because of the rain.
  - postpone 延期

- 因為強風把雨傘吹到開花，我被雨淋得濕透了。

  I got soaked in the rain because the fierce wind had turned my umbrella inside out.
  - fierce 強烈的、強的

  裡朝外地

- 媽媽說今天下雨我最好不要出門，因為下的是酸雨。

  My mother said that I shouldn't go out in the rain today because it is acid rain.
  - acid 酸的

天氣預報 ★ The Weather Forecast

- 我每天早上都會看電視上的天氣預報。

  I check the weather forecast on TV every morning.

- 如果沒有看天氣預報，我就會感到不安。

  If I don't watch the weather forecast, I get anxious.
  - anxious 不安的

- 天氣預報說明天會下雨。

  The weather forecast said that it will rain tomorrow.

- 氣象預報說明天會下雪。

  The weather forecast said that it will snow tomorrow.

- 氣象預報說週末會下一些雨。

  According to the weather forecast, there will be some rain during the weekend.

- 氣象預報說明天會是晴天。

  The weather forecast said that it will be sunny tomorrow.

- 我出門有帶雨傘，因為天氣預報說會下雨。

  I left home with an umbrella because the weather forecast said that it's going to rain.

- 我今天早上沒有看氣象預報，結果很不幸地下雨了。

  I didn't watch the weather forecast this morning. Sadly, it rained.

- 天氣預報總是預測錯誤。

  The weather forecast is always wrong.

- 最近天氣預報非常的準確。

  These days, the weather forecast is really accurate.

  • accurate 準確的

- 從現在開始，我一定會看氣象預報。

  From now on, I'll make sure that I watch the weather forecast.　確實、一定要

春、夏

Hot Summer Nights

Wednesday, August 25, Hot

It was so hot last night that I couldn't sleep at all. I turned on the fan, but it was no use. The news said that it will be hot again tonight. I think this summer is especially hot. I am waiting for this summer to end and for autumn to come.

炎熱的夏夜　　8月25日星期三，大熱天

昨晚太熱害我完全睡不著覺。我打開電風扇，可是一點用處也沒有。新聞說今天晚上一樣會很熱。我覺得這個夏天好像特別熱。我在等著這個夏天的結束，迎接秋天的到來。

·**turn on** 打開（電源）　**no use** 沒有用　**especially** 尤其、特別地

春天 ★ Spring

- 因為春天來了，天氣變暖和了。

It got warmer because spring came. / Spring came around, and it became warmer.
　　　　　　　　回來
• get + 比較級 變得～

- 春天是旅遊的季節。

Spring is the season of trips.

- 我希望春天可以快點來。

I hope spring comes soon.

- 春天太短暫了。

Spring is too short.

- 春天是我最喜歡的季節。／在所有的季節之中，我最喜歡春天。

Spring is my favorite season. / Among the seasons, spring is my favorite.

- 我等不及要迎接春假了。

I can't wait for spring break.
　　　　　　　　春假

- 當春假結束，我回到了學校。

When spring break ended, I went back to school.

- 我們去公園春遊。

We went to the park for a spring field trip.

- 下了春雨。

Spring rain fell.

- 最後一波的強烈寒流還沒走。

寒流
The last fierce cold snap is still here.
• fierce 強烈的、猛烈的

- 我聽說最後一波寒流今天會來，感覺好像冬天又回來了。

I heard that the last cold snap would be here today. It really felt as if winter had come back.

- 今天是我家的春季大掃除日。

Today was my family's spring cleaning day.

- 我把冬天的衣服都收了起來，拿出了春天的衣服。

  I put away all of my winter clothes and took out the ones for spring.

  收、放入 / 拿出

- 因為春天很乾燥，經常會發生森林大火。

  Because it is dry during spring, forest fires often take place.

  森林大火 / 發生、引起

- 艾草、薺菜、山蒜都是代表性的春天蔬菜。

  Mugworts, shepherd's purses, and wild chives are typical spring greens.

  • mugwort 艾草　shepherd's purse 薺菜　wild chive 山蒜
    typical 代表性的、典型的　greens 蔬菜

- 今天的晚餐餐桌上滿是春天的蔬菜。

  Today's dinner table was full of spring greens.

- 換季的時候，我的過敏性鼻炎就會變嚴重。

  When the seasons change, my nasal allergies / rhinitis get worse.

  過敏性鼻炎 / 惡化

  • rhinitis 鼻炎

繁花盛開的春天 ★ Spring Flowers

- 櫻花在公園裡開得好漂亮。

  Cherry blossoms bloomed beautifully at the park.

  • cherry blossom 櫻花　bloom 開花

- 盛開的櫻花十分美麗。

  The fully opened cherry blossoms were so beautiful.

- 我和祖父母一起去賞花。

  I have been to see flowers with my grandparents.

- 賞花之旅是很棒的春季活動。

  Going on a trip to see flowers is a perfect spring activity.

- 櫻花飄落的時候看起來好美。

When cherry blossoms flutter, they look so beautiful.

• flutter 飄動、搖晃

- 我和家人一起到日本賞櫻。

I went to Japan with my family to see the cherry blossoms.

- 這一週是賞櫻的高峰期。

This week is the (peak time) for cherry blossoms.
└ 高峰期、全盛期

- 今年櫻花會比較慢開。

This year, the cherry blossoms will bloom later.

- 我拿出了春天穿的外套，因為天氣變暖和了。

I took out my spring jacket because the weather became warmer.

- 葉芽從樹上冒出，因為春天到了。

Buds are (shooting out) from the trees since it is spring.
└ 冒出（芽）

• bud 葉芽、花苞

- 櫻花和杜鵑花是典型的春季花朵。

Cherry blossoms and azaleas are typical spring flowers.

• azalea 杜鵑花

- 我在上學途中四處張望，我看見櫻花開了。

As I looked around on my way to school, I could see the cherry blossoms blooming.

- 我猜春天來了，因為杜鵑花開了。

I guess spring has come since the azaleas are blooming.

- 我在週末去爬山，看到了春天的花朵盛開。

I went to a mountain on the weekend and saw the spring flowers (in full bloom).
└ 盛開、全開

- 櫻花凋謝了。

The cherry blossoms are gone.

- 因為花粉四處亂飛，我的過敏變嚴重了。

  Because of the blowing pollen, my allergies got worse.
  - pollen 花粉

- 我有花粉症。

  I have hay fever.
  - hay fever 花粉症

- 我因為花粉開始狂打噴嚏，而且眼睛也覺得好癢。

  Because of the pollen, I am sneezing a lot. My eyes itch as well.
  - sneeze 打噴嚏　itch 發癢　而且

夏天 ★ Summer

- 炎熱的夏天開始了。

  The hot summer has begun.

- 我覺得夏天真的來了。

  I think summer is really here.

- 我覺得是時候穿上短袖了。

  I think it's time to wear short sleeves.

- 在夏天裡，我覺得好像再怎麼玩也沒關係。

  In the summer, I feel as if it is okay to play as much as I want.
  覺得好像

- 今年夏天特別熱。

  This year's summer is especially hot.

- 整個世界充滿綠意，蟲兒大聲鳴叫著。

  The world was filled with green. Bugs were chirping loudly.
  充滿
  - chirp 昆蟲發出唧唧聲

- 我整個晚上都睡不著，因為蟬叫得非常大聲了。

  I couldn't sleep all night because the cicadas were chirping so loudly.
  - cicada 蟬

- 我因為吃了太多冰淇淋而肚子痛。

  I had a stomachache from eating too much ice cream.
  - stomachache 腹痛

- 比起寒冷的冬天，我更喜歡炎熱的夏天。 I like hot summer more than cold winter.

- 我喜歡夏天，因為我們有暑假！ I like summer because we have summer vacation!

- 我在等待這個夏天過去，並迎接涼爽的秋天到來。 I am waiting for this summer to pass and for the cool autumn to come.

炎熱的天氣 ★ Hot Weather

- 天氣變熱了。 It's getting hot.

- 今天天氣超級熱。 Today was boiling. /
It was scorching today.
  - scorching 炎熱

- 我因為高溫而覺得筋疲力盡。 I'm exhausted because of the heat.
  - exhausted 筋疲力盡的　heat 高溫

- 我覺得很虛弱，就好像生病了一樣。 I feel weak as if I'm sick.

- 當我抬頭看天空，天空晴朗的連一朵雲也沒有。 When I looked up at the sky, it was clear without any clouds.

- 從今天早上開始就很悶熱。 It has been sweltering since this morning.
  - sweltering 悶熱的

- 今天一整天都很悶熱。 It has been sweltering all day.

- 陽光非常炎熱。 The sun was extremely hot.
  - extremely 非常地

- 天氣熱得讓人覺得好痛苦。

It is painfully hot.
  - painfully 痛苦地

- 因為天氣太炎熱，我流了好多汗。

I was sweating a lot because of the sizzling heat.
  - sweat 流汗、汗　sizzling 炎熱的

- 高溫似乎讓我越來越煩躁。

使煩躁、難受

The heat seems to be getting to me.

- 昨晚很熱而且潮濕。

Last night was very hot and humid.
  - humid 潮濕的

- 因為熱帶夜，所以整晚都很熱。

Because of the tropical night, it was hot all night long.
  - tropical 熱帶地區的
  - 註：熱帶夜指夜間的最低氣溫在攝氏25度以上。

- 天氣太熱讓我完全睡不著。

It was so hot that I couldn't sleep at all.

- 陽光太強，所以我戴上了帽子。

The sunlight was so strong that I put on a hat.
  - sunlight 陽光

- 媽媽幫我撐陽傘。

My mother put her parasol over me.
  - parasol 洋傘

- 我擦了防曬油來保護皮膚。

塗抹、擦

To protect my skin, I put on sunscreen.
  - protect 保護　sunscreen 防曬油

- 我忘記擦防曬油了。

I forgot to put on sunscreen.

- 今天的不適指數很高。

The discomfort index was high today.
  - discomfort index 不適指數（discomfort 不適、不舒服）

- 我受不了這種高溫了。

I can't stand the heat.
  - stand 承受

- 我流了很多汗。

I sweat a lot.

- 天氣熱讓我很容易煩躁。

  I got annoyed so easily because of the heat.
  - annoyed 煩躁

- 天氣熱的時候，沒有比玩水更棒的事了。

  There's nothing better than playing in the water when it's hot.

- 當我站在陽光底下，真的很熱。不過到陰影下就變涼爽了。

  When I stand in the sun, it's really hot. But in the shade, it's cool.
  - shade 陰影

- 沖澡的效果只能撐一陣子。

  A shower works only for a short time.
  - work 有效果、產生影響

- 就算我什麼都不做也會流汗。

  Even though I was not doing anything, I was sweating.

梅雨 ★ Rainy Season

- 梅雨季來了。

  The rainy season has come.

  雨季、梅雨季 (= rainy spell)

- 今年的梅雨季似乎很長。

  This year's rainy spell seems so long.

- 因為現在是梅雨季，天氣很潮濕。

  Because it is the rainy season, it was so humid.

- 梅雨季讓天氣很潮濕。

  The rainy season made the weather so damp.
  - damp 潮濕的、有濕氣的

- 因為現在是梅雨季，衣服很難乾。

  It is hard to dry the laundry because it is the rainy season.

- 下了整天的雨，因為梅雨季開始了。

  It has been raining all day because the rainy season has started.

- 雨季應該開始了，可是竟然沒下什麼雨。

  It is supposed to be the rainy season, but it hardly ever rains.

  • be supposed to 應該要～　hardly 幾乎沒有

- 我希望梅雨季能夠快點結束。

  I hope the rainy season ends soon.

- 梅雨季終於結束了。

  The rainy season is finally over.

- 我沒來由的感到煩躁。我猜是因為潮濕的天氣吧。

  I feel so annoyed without any reason. I guess it is due to the humid weather.

  ——因為～

電扇／冷氣 ★ Fans / Air Conditioners

- 就算我開了電風扇，還是很熱。

  Even if I turn on the fan, it's still hot.

  • turn on/off 開／關（電源）

- 就連電風扇吹出來的風也是暖風。

  Even the wind from the fan is warm.

  • warm 溫暖的

- 我設定了電風扇的定時器。

  I set the timer of the fan.

- 我在把電風扇調成轉動之後就去睡了。

  I slept after setting the fan to spin.

- 我打開了冷氣，不過還是好熱。

  I turned on the air conditioner, but it was still hot.

  ——:冷氣

- 當我打開冷氣，我就覺得冷。可是當我關掉冷氣，我又覺得熱。

  When I turn on the air conditioner, it's cold. But when I turn it off, it's hot.

- 我們家沒有冷氣。

  We don't have an air conditioner in our house.

- 就連圖書館的冷氣都不夠冷。

  Even the library's air conditioner wasn't cold enough.

- 最近公共機關都把冷氣開得很弱。

  These days, (public institutions) turn their air conditioners on low. 公共機關

- 我聽說冷氣會消耗大量的電力。

  I heard that air conditioners consume large amounts of electricity.

  • consume 消耗、消費　electricity 電力

- 媽媽很擔心電費會很貴。

  My mother is so worried about the high cost of our electricity bill.

  • cost 費用　bill 帳單

- 因為冷氣吹太久，我頭痛了。

  I got a headache from spending too much time under the air conditioner.

- 我感冒了，因為我開著冷氣睡覺。

  I (caught a cold) because I slept with the air conditioner on. 感冒

- 教室的冷氣壞了。

  The classroom's air conditioner broke.

蚊子 ★ Mosquitoes

- 我被蚊子叮了三個包！

  I have three mosquito bites!

  • bite (bite-bit-bitten) （蚊蟲）叮咬

- 全身上下這麼多個地方，蚊子偏偏叮了我的臉。

  Of all the body parts, the mosquito bit my face.

- 弟弟因為被蚊子咬，所以眼睛腫了。

  My younger brother's eye was puffy because of a mosquito bite.

  • puffy 腫

- 蚊帳被掀開了。

  The screen had been opened.

  • screen 蚊帳

- 家裡有一隻蚊子，可是我打不到。

  There was a mosquito in the house, but I couldn't catch it.

- 我點了蚊香，因為家裡有蚊子。

  I burned a mosquito coil because mosquitoes were in my house.

  • mosquito coil 蚊香

- 我睡在蚊帳裡面。／在架好蚊帳之後，我在裡面睡覺。

  I slept under a mosquito net. / After putting up a mosquito net, I slept underneath it.

  裝設好　蚊帳

  • underneath 在～之下

- 我在房間裡噴了防蚊液。

  I used mosquito spray in my room.

  防蚊液

- 雖然夏天已經過完了，還是有一些蚊子。

  Although summer is already over, there are still some mosquitoes.

- 我躺下準備睡覺後，就聽到蚊子在嗡嗡叫。

  I heard a mosquito buzzing after I lay down to sleep.

  • buzz 嗡嗡叫

- 被蚊子叮的包好癢。

  The mosquito bite was so itchy.

  • itchy 癢的

- 我癢到受不了。

  I can't stand the itchiness.

  • itchiness 癢

- 我抓了蚊子叮的包，所以開始流血了。

  I scratched the mosquito bite, so it started to bleed.

  • scratch 抓　bleed 流血

- 我常常被蚊子叮。

  I get bitten by mosquitoes very often.

- 每當我聽到蚊子的聲音，我就覺得很害怕。

  Whenever I hear a mosquito, I feel horrified.

  • horrified 害怕、恐懼

夏季水果／夏季飲食 ★ Summer Fruits / Summer Dishes

● 夏天是西瓜的季節！

Summer is watermelon season!

● 西瓜是我最喜歡的水果。

Watermelon is my favorite fruit.

● 媽媽從市場買了一顆西瓜。

My mother brought a watermelon from the market.

● 這是我在夏天吃到的第一顆西瓜。

It was my first watermelon of the summer.

● 晚餐以後我吃了西瓜當點心。

I had watermelon for dessert after dinner.

● 西瓜很甜很好吃。

The watermelon was so sweet and delicious.

● 吃起來就像蜂蜜。／真好吃。

It tasted like honey. /
It tasted so good.

● 這顆西瓜還沒熟透。

The watermelon is not ripe.

• ripe 熟的

● 這顆西瓜太熟了。

The watermelon is overripe.

• overripe 過熟

● 比起香瓜，我更喜歡西瓜。

I like watermelons more than oriental melons. / I prefer watermelons to oriental melons.

• (oriental) melon 香瓜

● 我不吃西瓜的籽。

I don't eat the seeds in watermelons.

• seed 籽

● 現在是葡萄盛產期。

It is grape season. /
Grapes are in season.

當季

- 葡萄好酸。

  The grapes were sour.

  • sour（味道）酸

- 我吃葡萄會連籽一起吃下去。

  I eat grapes with seeds.

- 我吃葡萄會把籽拿掉後才吃。

  I eat grapes after taking out seeds.

- 葡萄好甜，所以我吃完了整整一串。

  The grapes were so sweet that I finished the whole bunch.

  • bunch 一串

- 媽媽煮了一些玉米當點心。

  My mom boiled some corn for a snack.

  • boil 煮、滾

- 這是一些美味的玉米！

  It was some delicious corn!

- 我妹妹很喜歡吃玉米。

  My younger sister loves corn.

- 今天的午餐我吃了涼麵。

  For today's lunch, I had cold noodles.

  • noodle 麵條

- Amy 的媽媽買了紅豆冰淇淋給我吃。

  Amy's mother bought me some red bean ice cream.

- 因為天氣非常熱，我吃了三支冰淇淋甜筒！

  Because of the extreme heat, I had three ice cream cones!

  • extreme 極度地、非常地

- 我吃了太多冰冷的食物，結果肚子痛。

  I got a stomachache from eating too much cold food.

夏天的活動 ★ Summer Activities

- 我用捕蟲網抓了一隻蟬。

  I caught a cicada with a (butterfly net).
  捕蟲網

- 今天，我抓了五隻蟬。

  Today, I caught five cicadas.

- 我把蟬放生了。

  I set the cicadas free.
  • set A free 把 A 放走、放生 A

- 蟬死掉了，因為我把它關在了昆蟲箱裡。

  The cicada died because I left it inside the insect box.

- 我跟朋友們在遊樂場玩水槍大戰。

  My friends and I had a (water gun) fight at the playground.
  水槍

- 我在山谷的溪流裡玩水。

  I played in the valley stream.
  • valley 山谷 stream 溪流

- 我跟朋友一起去了游泳池。

  I went to the (swimming pool) with my friends.
  游泳池

- 週末我去了水上樂園，我玩得很開心。

  I went to the water park on the weekend and had a wonderful time.

- 我的臉曬黑了。

  My face got tanned.
  • tanned 曬黑

- 我喜歡夏天，因為有很多有趣的事情可以做！

  I like summer because there are so many fun things to do!

Chapter 07

秋、冬

Yellow Gingko Leaves

Friday, October 20, Windy

On my way to school, I found that the ginkgo leaves had turned yellow. Autumn has come! Of all the seasons, I love autumn the most because it is neither hot nor cold. I wish this season would last longer.

金黃銀杏葉　10 月 20 日星期五，大風

在我上學的途中，我發現銀杏葉都已經變黃了。秋天來了！在所有的季節裡，我最喜歡秋天，因為既不熱也不冷。我希望這個季節可以持續久一點。

·ginkgo 銀杏　on one's way to 在～途中　neither A nor B 不是 A 也不是 B　last 持續

秋天 ★ Autumn

- 秋天就要來了。

  Autumn is just around the corner.

  即將到來的、臨近的

- 秋天來了。

  Autumn has come.

- 我最喜歡秋天。

  I like autumn the most.

- 秋天是我最喜歡的季節。

  Autumn is my favorite season.

- 我喜歡秋天，因為它既不熱也不冷。

  I love autumn because it is neither hot nor cold.

  • neither A nor B 不是 A 也不是 B

- 秋天是閱讀的季節。

  Autumn is the season for reading books.

- 早晚都變得比較涼了。

  It is becoming cooler in the morning and evening.

- 早上天氣挺涼的。

  It is quite chilly in the morning.

  • chilly 涼的、冷的

- 不過白天的時候還是很熱。

  But it is still hot during the day.

- 秋天太短暫了。

  Autumn is too short.

- 秋天的微風很清涼。

  The autumn breeze is very refreshing.

  • breeze 微風　refreshing 清涼的

- 當我抬頭看天空，天空非常漂亮。

  When I looked up at the sky, it was so beautiful.

- 天空好高又好藍。

  The sky was so high and blue.

- 秋天一定是來了，我覺得穿這件短袖襯衫有點冷。

  It must be autumn now. I feel cold in this short-sleeved shirt.

- 新學期在秋天開始，我一定要用功讀書。

  A new semester begins in autumn, and I must study hard.

  • semester 學期

- 下了一場秋雨。

  An autumn rain fell.

- 這場雨代表寒冷的季節要來了。

  This rain means that the cold season is coming.

楓葉／落葉 ★ Fall Leaves / Fallen Leaves

- 銀杏葉已經變黃了。

  The ginkgo leaves have turned yellow.

  • ginkgo 銀杏（樹）

- 楓葉已經變紅了。

  The maple leaves have turned red.

  • maple 楓樹　turn 變成～

- 楓葉讓遠處的山變了顏色。

  The fall leaves（楓葉）have changed the color of the mountain in the distance.

- 街道旁的樹也變成了美麗的紅色。

  The trees along the streets have turned into a beautiful red color.

- 染上不同顏色的樹看起來好美麗。

  The trees tinted with（染上）different colors looked so beautiful.

- 我們週末去了賞楓之旅。

  We went on a trip to see the fall leaves on the weekend.

- 今天好漫長，因為有太多人都來賞楓。

  It was a long day（漫長的一天、疲憊的一天）because there were too many people who came to see the fall leaves.

- 陽明山的楓葉正處於高峰期。

  The fall leaves were at their peak at Mt. Yangming.

- 陽明山的樹葉還沒有變色。

  The leaves haven't changed colors yet at Mt. Yangming.

- 陽明山是賞楓最佳勝地。

  Mt. Yangming is the best place to enjoy the fall leaves.

- 街上的落葉已經堆成了高高的落葉堆。

  On the streets, the fallen leaves have been piled up into tall stacks.

  落葉

  堆積

  • stack 堆

- 我拾起一片落葉，然後將它夾在書頁之間。

  I picked up a fallen leaf and then placed it between the pages of a book.

  • place 放置

- 我應該要撿起一片落葉，然後把它夾在書頁之間乾燥。

  I should pick up one of the fallen leaves and dry it up by putting it between the pages of a book.

- 我想工友打掃落葉時應該會很辛苦。

  I think the janitor will have a hard time sweeping the fallen leaves.

  • janitor 警衛、工友　sweep 掃

 冬天 ★ Winter

- 冬天來了。

  Winter has come.

- 很快就會是冬天了。

  It will soon be winter.

- 冬天已經來了。

  It is already winter.

- 比起夏天，我更喜歡冬天。

  I like winter more than summer. / I prefer winter to summer.

- 雖然冬天很冷，卻也讓人精神為之一振。

  Although winter is cold, it is also refreshing.

- 我討厭冬天，因為很冷。

  I hate winter because it is cold.

- 我的寒假從今天開始。

  My winter vacation starts today.

- 我想這個冬天甚至會更冷。

  I think this winter is even colder. /
  I think this winter is even more freezing.

  • even、much、a lot 加在比較級形容詞的前面，用來表示強調「更加」的意思。

- 我希望春天能夠快點到來。

  I hope spring will come soon.

寒冷的天氣 ★ Cold Weather

- 今天天氣真的好冷。

  It was really freezing today.

  • freezing 極冷的

- 今天一整天都好冷。

  It has been freezing all day.

- 今天溫度下降到十度。

  The temperature dropped to ten today.

  • temperature 溫度

- 今天是十度。

  Today was 10 degrees.

- 今天是一年之中最冷的。

  It is the coldest day of the year.

- 據說這是十年來最冷的一天了。

  It is said that it was the coldest day in last 10 years.

- 風寒效應會讓人覺得比實際溫度更冷。

  風寒效應

  It felt colder than the actual temperature because of the wind chill factor.

  • 註：風寒效應指皮膚暴露在風中時，會感受到比當時氣溫更冷的效應。

- 我覺得臉好像要凍僵了，因為風太大了。

  I felt as if my face was going to freeze because the wind was blowing too hard.

  • freeze 凍結

- 早上我一點都不想起床，因為太冷了。

  In the morning, I don't want to wake up because it is too cold.

- 天氣變冷的時候我不想去上學。

  When it gets cold, I don't want to go to school.

- 教室好冷。

  The classroom was freezing.

- 暖氣壞了，所以我上課的時候都在發抖。

  The heater was broken, so I was shivering during my classes.

  • shiver （身體）發抖

- 雖然我穿著室內鞋，可是我的腳還是覺得好冷。

  Although I was wearing classroom shoes, my feet still felt cold.

  • 在教室裡穿的「室內鞋」用 classroom shoes 來表達就可以了。

- 我的手差點凍傷，因為我忘了戴上手套。

  My hands almost got frostbite because I forgot to put on gloves.

  • frostbite 凍傷

- 我整天都待在家裡，因為天氣好冷。

  I stayed home all day because it was cold.

- 我無法忍受寒冷！

  I can't stand the cold!

- 我明天一定要穿更暖和的衣服。

  確實地做～、一定要

  I will make sure that I wear warmer clothes tomorrow.

雪 ★ Snow

- 今天下了今年的第一場雪。

  Today we had the first snow of the year.

- 雪下得很大。

  It snowed heavily.

  • heavily 很嚴重地、強烈地

- 大片的雪花落下，堆滿了整條街。

  Large snowflakes came down and piled up on the streets.

  • snowflake 雪花　pile up 堆積

- 雪沒有堆積起來，全部融化了。

  The snow didn't pile up. It all melted.

  • melt 融化

- 當我今天早上起床的時候，窗外的世界已成了一片冬日仙境。

  When I woke up this morning, the world outside the window had turned into a winter wonderland.

  • winter wonderland 描寫被雪覆蓋的冬日情景。

- 整晚都在下雪。

  It has been snowing all night.

- 在窗外，大片的雪花飄落。

  Outside the window, large snowflakes were coming down.

- 我和弟弟到外面一起堆了個雪人。

  I went outside with my younger brother. We built a snowman together.

- 做雪球好困難。

  It was hard to make a snowball.

  • snowball 雪球

- 我和朋友一起在學校操場打雪仗。

  I had a snowball fight with my friends in the schoolyard.　雪仗

- 結成冰的雪讓路面變得很滑。

  The road was slippery from the frozen snow.

  • slippery 滑的

- 我要小心不要滑倒，因為整條街都很滑。

  I had to be careful not to slip because the streets were slippery.

  • slip 滑倒

- 我走路的時候摔倒了，因為街上很滑。

  I (fell down) while walking because the street was slippery.

  摔倒

- 下雪讓交通變得壅塞。

  There was (heavy traffic) because of the snow.

  交通壅塞、交通混亂

- 雪下得太大了，讓我的腳一直陷進雪裡。

  It snowed so heavily that my feet sank deep under the snow.

  • sink (sink-sank-sunk) 下沉

- 氯化鈣被灑在路面上來融雪。

  (Calcium chloride) was sprayed on the road to melt the snow.

  氯化鈣

- 結成冰柱了。

  Icicles formed.

  • icicle 冰柱

- 北方地區正為雪崩所苦。

  The northern region is (suffering from) avalanches.

  為～所苦

  • avalanche 雪崩

禦寒用品 ★ Winter Goods and Clothes

- 我聽說今天會很冷，所以我拿出了衛生衣來穿。

  I heard that today was going to be freezing, so I took out my (long johns) and wore them.

  衛生衣

- 我一點也不覺得冷，我覺得可能是因為我穿了衛生衣。

  I didn't feel cold at all. I think it was probably due to my long johns.

- 因為我沒有穿衛生衣，我覺得要冷死了。

  I was freezing because I wasn't wearing my long johns.

- 從現在開始我一定要穿衛生衣。

  I will make sure that I wear long johns from now on.

- 因為我衣服穿太少了，所以我快要冷死了。

  I was freezing because I dressed lightly.

  • dress 穿衣服　lightly 薄地

- 雖然我穿了很多衣服，可是我還是覺得冷。

  I still felt cold though I was wearing piles of clothes.

  很多、成堆的

- 媽媽買了新的冬季外套給我。

  My mother bought me a new winter jacket.

- 因為這件是鴨絨大衣，我覺得好暖和。

  Because it is a duck down parka, I feel so warm.

  鴨絨

- 我的手凍僵了，因為我忘了戴手套。

  My hands were freezing because I forgot to put on my gloves.

- 我一點都不覺得冷，因為我穿上了靴子。

  I didn't feel cold at all because I was wearing my boots.

- 我一定是把其中一隻手套掉在某個地方了。

  I must have left one of my gloves somewhere.

  • must have＋過去分詞 一定是做了～

- 我因為把手套弄丟而挨了罵。

  I got into trouble for losing my gloves.

- 我一點也不覺得冷，因為我帶了暖暖包。

  I didn't feel cold at all because I had put on hot packs.

- 我一點也不覺得冷，因為我戴了面罩和圍巾。

  I didn't feel cold at all because I had put on a face mask and a scarf.

  • mask 一般指醫療用或普通的口罩。我們常見的防寒面罩因為沒有相應的詞彙，所以用 face mask 來表達就可以了。

- 當我戴上面罩，我就覺得好像快要窒息了。

  When I wear a face mask, I feel like I am suffocating.

  • suffocating 窒息的

- 當我戴上耳罩，我覺得很溫暖。

  When I wear earmuffs, I feel so warm.
  - earmuff 耳罩

- 我睡在電熱毯上，所以我一點也不覺得冷。

  I slept on the electric pad, so I didn't feel cold at all.
  - 電熱毯的英文也可以叫做 electric blanket。

冬季飲食 ★ Winter Food

- 冬天是烤地瓜的季節。

  Winter is the season for baked sweet potatoes.
  - baked 烤的   sweet potato 地瓜

- 這是特選地瓜，所以非常好吃。

  It was a selected sweet potato.
  That's why it was so delicious.

- 比起用蒸的，我比較喜歡烤地瓜。

  I like baked sweet potatoes more than steamed ones. / I prefer baked sweet potatoes to steamed ones.
  - steamed 蒸的

- 今天是冬至，所以我吃了一些湯圓。

  Today was the Winter Solstice, so I ate some tangyuan.

- 奶奶買了一些烤栗子給我。

  My grandmother bought me some roasted chestnuts.
  - roasted 烤的   chestnut 栗子

- 媽媽煮了地瓜粥給我。

  My mother cooked me sweet potato porridge.

- 我吃了一顆很甜的紅柿子當點心。

  I ate a really sweet red persimmon as a snack.
  - persimmon 柿子

冬天的橘子最好吃了。

Tangerines are the best in winter.

• tangerine 橘子

我吃了十顆橘子！

I had ten tangerines!

橘子酸酸甜甜的，真的很好吃！

Tangerines are both sweet and sour. They are so delicious!

無庸置疑，冬天還是吃火鍋最棒了。

There is no doubt that eating hot pot is best in winter. *無庸置疑地*

• hot pot 火鍋

媽媽買了鯛魚燒給我吃。

My mother bought me a fish-shaped sweet cake.

• shaped ～形狀的

因為街上買得到烤栗子了，所以我猜冬天來了。

Since roasted chestnuts are available on the streets, I guess winter has come.

• available 買得到／可用的

我們在桌上邊煮火鍋邊吃。

We ate hot pot while boiling it on the table.

• boil 煮

我們冬天的時候一定要吃湯餃。

In winter, we definitely eat dumpling soup.

• dumpling 水餃

Chapter
08

自然災害

A Winter Wonderland   Monday, December 18, Snowy

When I woke up this morning, the world outside the window had turned into a winter wonderland. I realized we had had a sudden snowfall overnight. All schools are closed because of the heavy snow. I went outside and made a snowman with my brother. I wonder if I can go to school tomorrow.

冬日仙境　12 月 18 日星期一，下雪

今天早上起床的時候，窗外的世界已成了一片冬日仙境。我才發現昨天晚上突然下了一場雪。因為大雪，所有的學校都關閉了。我和弟弟一起到外面堆了個雪人。我很懷疑我明天能不能去上學。

·turn into 變成　sudden 突然　overnight 前一天晚上的　wonder if 好奇、懷疑～

暴風雨／颱風 ★ Storms

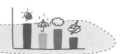

- 因為暴風雨，今天下了一整天的大雨。

  It has been pouring all day because of the storm.

  •pour 倒、注　storm 暴風雨、颱風（颱風也叫做 typhoon）

- 我聽說暴風雨要來了。

  I heard that a storm is approaching.

  •approach 靠近

- 我聽說要來的颱風會是超級颱風。

  I heard that the coming typhoon will be a super typhoon.

- 因為颱風，所有的學校都關閉了。

  Because of the typhoon, all schools are closed today.

- 因為颱風，課程都被延後了。

  Because of the typhoon, classes have been delayed.

  •delay 延遲、拖延

- 因為強風，樹木都倒光了。

  Because of the strong winds, trees have fallen down.

- 暴風雨把操場上的一棵樹完全吹倒了。

  The storm completely blew away a tree in the schoolyard. 吹倒

  •completely 完全地

- 風把我的雨傘吹到開花。

  The wind turned my umbrella inside out.

- 因為打雷和閃電都沒有停過，所以我很害怕。

  Because the thunder and lightning didn't stop, I was terrified.

  •terrified 害怕

- 強風把窗戶吹得咯咯作響。

  The windows rattled because of the strong wind.

  •rattle 咯咯作響

- 颱風穿過了台灣。

  The typhoon has passed through Taiwan.

- 台北是這次颱風受害最嚴重的地方。 | Taipei suffered the most from the typhoon.

- 爸爸買了一些杯麵回來當作緊急糧食。 | My father brought some cup noodles for our (emergency food supply).
緊急糧食
  - cup noodle 杯麵

淹水／豪雨／大雪 ★ Floods / Heavy Rain / Heavy Snow

- 下了傾盆大雨。 | Rain was pouring down.

- 豪雨讓淡水河的水溢了出來。 | The (heavy rain) caused the Tamsui River to overflow.
豪雨
  - overflow 溢出

- 橋樑倒塌讓某些地方成了孤島。 | Some places are isolated because a bridge has collapsed.
  - isolated 被孤立　collapse 倒塌

- 大雨一直下個不停，難怪有一些地方會淹水。 | It has been pouring rain. No wonder some places are flooded.
  - flood 淹水

- 路上塞車是因為突然下了一場大雪。 | The roads are jammed with traffic because of the sudden (heavy snowfall).
大雪
  - be jammed with 壅塞

- 豪雨造成花蓮地區山崩。 | The heavy rain caused landslides in Hualien.
  - landslide 山崩

- 高溫／暴風雪／寒流特報發布了。 | A heat wave warning / blizzard watch / cold wave watch has been issued.
  - heat wave warning 高溫特報　blizzard watch 暴風雪特報
    cold wave watch 寒流特報　issue 發布

地震／海嘯 ★ Earthquakes/Tsunamis

- 我在新聞上看到日本被地震襲擊。

  I saw on the news that Japan was hit by an earthquake.

  • hit 襲擊　earthquake 地震

- 新聞說在中國有很多人因為地震而受傷。

  The news said that a lot of people were injured by the earthquake in China.

  • injured 受傷

- 這是芮氏規模七的強烈地震。

  It was a powerful earthquake that rated 7.0 on the Richter scale.

  • rate 分級　　芮氏規模

- 當地震發生時，我們應該躲在桌子底下。

  When an earthquake takes place, we should hide under a desk.　發生

- 我希望台灣不要發生地震。地震真的很可怕。

  I hope no earthquakes hit Taiwan. They're really scary.

- 在印尼有很多人因為海嘯而死。

  A lot of people were killed in Indonesia because of a tsunami.

  • tsunami 海嘯　　全球暖化

- 因為全球暖化，自然災害比以前更常發生了。

  Because of global warming, natural disasters are taking place more often than before. 自然災害

- 今天早上霧很濃。

  It was very foggy this morning.
  - foggy 有霧的

- 因為霧很濃，所以我看不太清楚。

  I couldn't see clearly because of the dense fog.
  - dense 濃的

- 能見度很低。

  There is low visibility.
  - visibility 能見度

- 突然間下起了冰雹。

  突然間
  All of a sudden, hail started to fall.
  - hail 冰雹

- 今天一片灰濛濛的，因為懸浮微粒過多。

  The day was gloomy because of the heavy fine dust.
  懸浮微粒
  - gloomy 灰濛濛的

- 整個世界都因為沙塵暴而變得陰陰的。

  The whole world is cloudy because of the yellow dust.
  沙塵暴

- 沙塵暴和懸浮微粒都是環境汙染造成的結果。

  Both yellow dust and fine dust are the results of environmental pollution.
  - environmental 環境的   pollution 汙染

Part

3

家人與朋友

家人

My Little Sister

Sunday, February 4, Foggy

I have a little sister. She is two years younger than I. Sometimes it is annoying to take care of her. But it is better to have her because we have fun playing together. I will try to get along with her all the time.

我的妹妹 2月4日星期日，有霧

我有一個妹妹，她比我小兩歲。照顧她有時候是一件很煩的事。不過我覺得還是有她比較好，因為我們一起玩的時候很開心。我會試著一直好好和她相處。

· **take care of** 照顧　**get along with** 和～好好相處

家人 ★ Family

- 我家有三個人。 — There are three people in my family.

- 我家有四個人，包括媽媽、爸爸、弟弟和我。 — There are four people in my family including mother, father, younger brother and me.
  - including 包括

- 我的家庭成員分別是爺爺、奶奶、媽媽、爸爸、哥哥和我。 — My family members are my grandfather, grandmother, mother, father, older brother, and me.

- 在我家裡有兩個男孩和一個女孩，我是最小的。 — Of the two boys and one girl in my family, I'm the youngest.

- 我是家裡最大的小孩。 — I am the oldest child in my family.

- 我是家裡最小的小孩。 — I am the youngest in my family.

- 我是唯一的小孩。 — I am an only child.

- 我是獨生女／子。 — I am the only girl/boy.

- 我沒有任何兄弟姊妹。 — I don't have any siblings.
  - sibling 兄弟姊妹

- 我希望我有弟弟或妹妹。 — I wish I had a younger sibling. / I want to have a younger sibling.

- 我很羨慕有很多兄弟姊妹的朋友。 — I really envy my friends who have a lot of brothers and sisters.
  - envy 羨慕

- 有妹妹很好，因為我們可以一起玩。 — It is nice to have a younger sister because we can play together.

- 我不想當最大的小孩。

  I don't like being the eldest child.

  • eldest 最年長的

- 我必須要照顧我的弟弟／妹妹，因為我是最大的。

  I have to take care of my siblings because I am the oldest. / I have to babysit my little brothers/sisters because I am the oldest.

  照顧

  • babysit 照顧

- 我很開心我有哥哥。

  I am really happy to have an older brother.

- 我是排行中間的小孩。

  I am the middle child.

- 我有一個大家庭。

  I have a big family.

- 很難找到三代同堂的家庭。

  It is hard to find a home where three generations live together.

  • generation 世代

- 我很開心能和爺爺奶奶一起住。

  I'm really happy about living together with my grandparents.

- 我沒有媽媽。

  I don't have a mother.

- 媽媽在我五歲的時候過世了。

  My mother passed away when I was five.

  過世、逝世

- 我的爸媽離婚了，所以我和爸爸一起住。

  My parents got divorced, so I live with my father.

  離婚

- 雖然我的爸媽離婚了，但他們還是很愛我。

  Although my parents are divorced, they still love me.

- 媽媽和爸爸彼此很相愛。

  My mother and father love each other very much.

- 我在充滿愛和關懷的家庭中成長。

  I live in a loving, caring family.

  • loving 愛的

- 我住在一個充滿愛的家裡。／我家充滿了愛。

  I live in a house full of love. / My home is full of love.

- 我的家人們全都比較安靜。

  All of my family members are rather quiet.
  • rather 比較、有點

- 我的家人都很活潑。

  Everyone in my family is very active.

- 我們家很喜歡去旅行。

  My family loves to travel.

我的爸爸 ★ My Father

- 我的爸爸很貼心。／我有很貼心的爸爸。

  My father is really sweet and caring. / I have such a caring dad.
  • sweet 貼心的　caring 體貼的、貼心的

- 爸爸常常花時間陪我們玩。

  My father spends time playing with us often.

- 我爸爸長得很帥。

  My father is really handsome.

- 每個人都說他很帥。

  Everyone says that he is handsome.

- 我爸爸幫忙做很多家事。

  My father helps a lot with the housework.

- 我爸爸現在四十幾歲了。

  My father is in his forties.

- 我爸爸的肚子很大。

  My father has a big stomach.

- 我爸爸有一點白頭髮。

  My father has a little bit of gray hair.

- 我爸爸是警察。

  My father is a policeman.

- 我爸爸在資訊公司上班。

  My father works at an IT company.

- 我爸爸的家鄉在高雄。

  My father's hometown is Kaohsiung.
  • hometown 家鄉

- 我爸爸有一點嚴格。

My father is kind of strict.
- strict 嚴格   有一點

- 我爸爸是保守派。

My father is conservative.
- conservative 保守的

- 我爸爸非常沉默寡言。

My father is so inexpressive.
- inexpressive 話不多的、木訥的

- 我爸爸常講好笑的笑話。

My father often makes funny jokes.
- make jokes 講笑話

- 爸爸總是對我們惡作劇。

My father plays tricks on us all the time.
      惡作劇

- 我爸爸很幽默又聰明。

My father is humorous and smart.

- 爸爸很了解我。

My father understands me very well.

- 爸爸和我的關係很好。

My father and I have a perfect connection. /
My father and I connect with each other
well.
- connection 關係   connect 連結

- 我喜歡爸爸多過於媽媽。

I like my dad more than my mom.

- 我爸爸每天都很忙。他早上很早就出門上班，然後很晚才回家。

My father is busy every day. He leaves for work early in the morning and then comes home very late.

- 假日的時候，爸爸就只是整天睡覺。

When there is a holiday, my father just sleeps all day.

- 爸爸休假的時候就只是整天在睡覺。

When my father is off duty, he just sleeps all day.
      休假

- 我希望爸爸可以多陪我玩。

I wish my father would play with me more.

• 我很驕傲我有一個很棒的爸爸。	I am very proud of my wonderful father.
	• be proud of 以～為傲

我的媽媽 ★ My Mother

• 我媽媽很漂亮。	My mother is really pretty.
• 我媽媽有在上班。	My mother has a job.
• 我希望媽媽可以和其他的媽媽一樣待在家裡。	I wish my mother could stay home just like other mothers.
• 我媽媽是家庭主婦。	My mother is a housewife.
• 我媽媽很苗條。	My mother is slim/slender.
	• slim/slender 纖細的、苗條的
• 我媽媽有點肉肉的。	My mother is kind of chubby.
	• chubby 肉肉的
• 媽媽很愛乾淨。	My mother is very neat.
	• neat 整潔的、乾淨的
• 媽媽出生於 1980 年。	My mother was born in 1980.
• 我媽媽年紀有一點大。	My mother is kind of old.
• 我媽媽煮菜很好吃。	My mother is very good at cooking.
	• be good at 擅長、很會做～
• 我媽媽煮的每樣東西都很好吃。	Everything that my mother cooks is very delicious.
• 我媽媽不太了解孩子的感受。	My mother doesn't really understand how children feel.

- 媽媽常常對我嘮叨。

My mother nags me all the time

• nag 嘮叨　　經常

- 媽媽老是跟我說只要讀書就好。

My mother always tells me just to study.

- 媽媽生氣的時候真的很可怕。

My mother is really scary when she's angry.

- 我媽媽仍然是我在這世界上最愛的人。

Still, my mother is the person that I love the most in the world.

- 我希望我長大也可以當一個像我媽媽一樣完美的媽媽。

I wish I could be a perfect mom like my mother when I grow up.

- 我媽媽很容易忘東忘西。

My mother easily forgets things.

- 我媽媽是一個能幹的職業婦女。

My mother is a competent career woman.

• competent 能幹的　career 職業的

- 我媽媽可以把每件事都做得很好，這讓我覺得很驕傲。

I am very proud that my mother can manage everything well.

• manage 管理、做到～

姊姊／哥哥 ★ My Sister / Brother

- 我有一個哥哥和一個姊姊。

I have an older brother and an older sister.

- 我哥哥和我差很多歲。

My older brother and I have a big age gap.

• gap 差距

- 我姊姊比我大三歲。

My sister is three years older than me.

- 我哥哥跟我差一歲。

My brother and I are a year apart.

• apart 距離

- 我哥哥跟我是雙胞胎。

  My brother and I are twins.

  • twins 雙胞胎

- 我希望我有一個姊姊。

  I wish I had an older sister.

- 我哥哥是國中生。

  My older brother is a middle school student.

- 我哥哥正值青春期。

  My older brother is in his adolescence.

  • adolescence 青春期

- 我哥哥對我真的很好。

  My older brother is really nice to me.

- 我姊姊常常陪我玩。

  My older sister plays with me a lot.

- 我哥哥幾乎不陪我玩。

  My older brother hardly ever plays with me.

- 因為我哥哥必須讀書。

  Because my older brother has to study.

- 我哥哥擅長所有事。

  My older brother is good at everything.

- 我姊姊真的很聰明。

  My older sister is really smart.

- 我哥哥在學校表現很好。

  My older brother does well at school.

  在學校表現很好

- 我很為我哥哥感到驕傲。

  I am really proud of my older brother.

- 我哥哥跟我相處的很融洽。

  My brother and I get along really well.

  相處融洽、很合拍

- 我哥哥常常生氣。

  My older brother gets angry all the time.

- 我姊姊跟我長得很像。

  My older sister and I look alike.

  • alike 相似地

- 我的鄰居說我姊姊跟我看起來一模一樣。

  My neighbors say that my older sister and I look exactly the same.

- 因為我跟哥哥吵架，所以我被媽媽罵了。／媽媽因為我和哥哥吵架而責備我。

I got into trouble with my mom for fighting with my older brother. /
My mom scolded me for fighting with my older brother.

挨罵

• scold 責備

- 哥哥的個性真的很差。

My older brother is really mean.

• mean 個性很差

- 我哥哥經常打我。

My older brother hits me all the time.

- 我媽媽只關心我的哥哥。

My mother only cares about my older brother.

關心、在乎

- 我不想穿姊姊留下來的衣服。

I don't want to wear passed-down clothes from my sister.

• passed-down 傳承下來的

- 姊姊總叫我幫她做事。／姊姊每天都叫我幫她跑腿。

My older sister always asks me to do things for her. / My older sister asks me to run some errands for her every day.

• run an errand 跑腿

- 姊姊跟我的品味完全相反。

My older sister and I have completely opposite tastes.

• opposite 相反的　taste 品味

- 我哥哥從不讓我進他房間。

My older brother never lets me into his room.

- 我很羨慕有姊姊的朋友們。

I really envy my friends who have older sisters.

- 我希望哥哥可以不要再打我了。

I wish my older brother would stop hitting me.

- 我哥哥因為他的幽默感而很受歡迎。

  My older brother is popular because of his (sense of humor).
  ⌐ 幽默感

- 我希望姊姊可以多花一點時間陪我。

  I wish my older sister would spend more time with me.

弟弟／妹妹 ★ My Little Brother/Sister

- 我有一個弟弟。

  I have a younger brother.

- 我弟弟五歲。

  My younger brother is 5 years old.

- 我弟弟跟我差兩歲。

  My younger brother and I are 2 years apart.

- 我弟弟在上幼稚園。

  My younger brother goes to kindergarten.

- 我希望我有一個很可愛的妹妹。

  I wish I had a really cute baby sister.

- 我妹妹很可愛！

  My younger sister is so cute!

- 我妹妹很愛我。

  My younger sister loves me.

- 我妹妹很聽我的話。

  My younger sister listens carefully to me.

- 我很會跟弟弟玩。

  I am good at playing with my younger brother.

- 我弟弟常常來煩我。／我弟弟是個討厭鬼。

  My younger brother bothers bugs me all the time. / My younger brother is (a pain in the neck).

  • bother 打擾　bug 折磨 ⌐ 討厭的人

- 我弟弟很喜歡學我。／我弟弟是個學人精。

  My younger brother does everything I do. / My younger brother is a copycat.
  - copycat 模仿貓、學人精

- 我妹妹很調皮。

  My younger sister is really naughty.
  - naughty 調皮搗蛋的

- 我妹妹是個愛哭鬼。她動不動就會哭。

  My younger sister is such a crybaby. She cries over nothing.
  - crybaby 愛哭鬼

- 如果不順妹妹的意，她就會哭。

  My younger sister cries if she doesn't get her way. 順～的意

- 當我妹妹一哭，我就無論如何得讓她。

  When my younger sister cries, I have to give up no matter what. 無論如何
  讓步

- 我總是因為我弟而被罵。

  It is I that always get in trouble because of my younger brother.

- 我媽媽只喜歡弟弟。

  My mother only likes my younger brother.

- 我媽媽總是叫我要讓步。

  My mother always tells me to give in.

- 就算是弟弟的錯，媽媽也只罵我。

  Even if it is my younger brother's fault, my mother only scolds me.

- 弟弟太小了。

  My younger brother is too young.

- 因為妹妹年紀比我小，所以我必須要多多照顧她。

  Because my sister is younger than me, I have to take care of her a lot.

- 當個哥哥是很累的工作。

  Being an older brother is a very tiring job.
  - tiring 很累的

- 我希望妹妹可以快點變成小學生。

  I wish my younger sister would become an elementary school student soon.
  國小

- 我希望我妹妹可以不要再碰我的東西了。

  I hope my younger sister stops touching my things.

- 我會試著對妹妹好一點。

  I will try to treat my sister more nicely.

- 我妹妹很受歡迎，因為她對每個人都很溫柔。

  My younger sister is popular because she is sweet to everyone.

  • sweet 和藹的、溫柔的

- 一旦妹妹開始發脾氣，就沒人可以阻止她。

  Once my younger sister throws fits, no one can stop her.

  發脾氣

爺爺／奶奶 ★ My Grandparents

- 我爺爺很親切。

  My grandfather is really kind.

- 我爺爺很嚴格。

  My grandfather is really strict.

- 我奶奶很體貼。

  My grandmother is very thoughtful.

  • thoughtful 體貼的、親切的

- 奶奶永遠站在我這邊。

  My grandmother is always on my side.

  站在～邊

- 奶奶很疼愛我。

  My grandmother adores me so much.

  • adore 疼愛

- 奶奶說我是這個世界上最棒的。

  My grandmother says that I'm the most wonderful thing in the world.

- 奶奶叫我「狗狗」。

  My grandmother calls me "puppy."

- 曾祖母只喜歡我哥哥。

  My great-grandmother only loves my older brother.

- 奶奶在我出生以前就去世了。

  My grandmother passed away before I was born.

- 爺爺和奶奶都在我很小的時候就過世了。

  Both my grandfather and grandmother passed away when I was young.

- 我很羨慕那些爺爺和奶奶都還健在的朋友。

  I envy my friends whose grandmother and grandfather are still alive.

- 我的祖父母和外祖父母都還健在。

  My grandparents on both sides of my family are still alive.

- 我奶奶住在台北。

  My grandmother lives in Taipei.

- 我奶奶的家在台北。

  My grandmother's home is in Taipei.

- 我們通常每兩週去探望奶奶一次。

  We usually visit my grandmother's house once every two weeks.

- 因為我媽媽要上班，所以由奶奶來照顧我們。

  Because my mother has to work, my grandmother takes care of us.

- 我奶奶很會煮菜。

  My grandmother is a great cook.

  • cook 廚師

- 我的祖父母對我有求必應。

  My grandparents do everything I ask them.

- 當我去探望奶奶的時候，她會煮美味的食物給我們吃。她還會給我們零用錢。

  When I visit my grandmother, she cooks delicious food for us. She also gives us pocket money.
  零用錢

- 當爺爺奶奶在場，就算我不讀書，媽媽也不會罵我。

  When my grandparents are here, my mom doesn't scold me even if I don't study.

- 爺爺給了我一些零用錢，因為我幫他按摩肩膀。

  Grandpa gave me some pocket money because I massaged his shoulder.

  • massage 按摩

- 奶奶和爺爺是我在這世上最喜歡的人。 Grandma and Grandpa are my favorite people in the world.

- 我喜歡外婆多過於奶奶。 I like my grandma on my mother's side more than my grandma on my father's side.
  • on one's side ～的那一邊

- 爺爺的聽力不太好。 My grandfather can't hear well. / My grandfather has a hearing problem.

- 爺爺有戴助聽器。 My grandfather wears hearing aids.
  助聽器

- 奶奶有戴假牙，所以她不能吃硬的食物。 My grandmother wears dentures, so she can't eat hard food.
  • denture 假牙

- 奶奶說她沒有辦法看清楚小字。 My grandmother says she can't see small letters clearly.

- 奶奶年紀很大了，可是她還是很健康。 My grandmother is very old, but she's really healthy.

- 我希望奶奶可以一直健康下去，這樣她就可以和我們在一起久一點。 I hope my grandmother stays healthy so that she can stay with us for a long time.

親戚 ★ Relatives

- 我們家有很多親戚。 We have a lot of relatives in our family.
  • relative 親戚

- 我爸爸是長男，所以很多親戚會聚在我家。 My father is the oldest son, so many relatives gather in my house.
  • gather 聚集

- 我有很多堂／表兄弟姊妹。

I have a lot of cousins.
  - cousin 堂（表）兄弟姊妹

- 我們沒有很多親戚。

We don't have a lot of relatives.

- 我很羨慕那些有很多親戚的朋友。

I really envy my friends who have a lot of relatives.

- 今天是爺爺的忌日，所以親戚們來到我家。

Today is my grandfather's memorial service day, so my relatives came to my house. 忌日

- 我有兩個叔叔。

I have two uncles.
  - 在英文裡面，伯伯、姨丈、姑丈、舅舅都稱作 uncle。

- 我有一個阿姨。

I have one aunt.
  - 在英文裡面，嬸嬸、姑姑、阿姨、伯母都稱作 aunt。

- 我只有叔叔，所以我很羨慕有阿姨的朋友。

I only have uncles, so I envy my friends who have aunts.

- 我舅舅還沒有結婚。

My uncle is not yet married.

- 我舅舅常常給我一些零用錢。

My uncle often gives me some pocket money.

- 我舅舅給了我一些零用錢。

My uncle gave me some pocket money.

- 我去叔叔家慶祝爺爺的生日，還得到了 500 元的零用錢。

I visited my uncle's house for grandfather's birthday and got 500 NT dollars in pocket money.

- 放假了，所以我去了叔叔在花蓮的家。

It was my vacation, so I went to my uncle's house in Hualien.

- 我的阿姨很疼我。

My aunt adores me.
  - adore 非常喜歡、疼愛

- 姑姑稱讚我看起來變漂亮了。

My aunt complimented me on how I look prettier.
• compliment 稱讚

- 我姑姑買了一個娃娃給我當生日禮物。

My aunt bought me a doll for my birthday present.

- 今天姑姑一家人來探望我們。

Today, my aunt's family came to visit us.

- 我們和姑姑一家人一起去了濟州島。

We went to Jeju Island together with my aunt's family.

- 我姑姑住在我家附近。

My aunt lives near my house.

- 我堂哥很會讀書，運動也很厲害。

My cousin is good at studying and playing sports.
• 堂（表）兄弟姊妹都叫做 cousin。

- 我阿姨生了一個很漂亮的孩子。

My aunt gave birth to a really pretty baby.
　　　　　　　生下

- 我堂哥／堂姊很喜歡我。

My cousin brother/sister really likes me.

- 我的堂哥 Eric 和我讀同年級。

My cousin Eric is in the same grade as me.
• grade 年級

- 我堂姊比我大兩歲。

My cousin is two years older than me.

- 我跟堂弟一起玩到很晚。

I played with my cousins until late at night.

- 和堂妹一起玩真的很開心。

Hanging out with my cousins is really fun.
　　　　　一起玩樂

- 我一開始沒有認出堂哥，因為他變了好多。

I didn't recognize my cousin at first because he had changed so much.
• recognize 認出

- 我很喜歡所有親戚齊聚一堂的假日。

I love holidays when all of my relatives get together.
　　　　　　　團聚

朋友

My Best Friend, Adam   Wednesday, March 19, Rainy

I moved to this town a year ago, so I didn't know the kids here. I met Adam then. I learned we both like to play video games and to read comic books. Since then, he and I have always been together. Adam is truly my best friend.

我最好的朋友 Adam   3 月 19 日星期三,雨天

我是在一年前搬來這個城鎮的,所以我並不認識這裡的孩子。後來我認識了 Adam。我發現我們都喜歡玩電動遊戲和看漫畫。從那個時候開始,他跟我總是形影不離。Adam 真的是我最好的朋友。

·comic book 漫畫   since 從~開始   truly 真的

交朋友 ★ Making Friends

- 我有很多朋友。

  I have a lot of friends.

- 我很開心我有很多朋友。

  I'm happy that I have a lot of friends.

- 我沒有很多要好的朋友。

  I don't have many close friends.

- 我沒有很多朋友，因為我二年級才
  轉學到這間學校。

  I don't have many friends because I
  transferred to this school in the 2nd grade.
  • transfer 轉移、轉學

- 我一年前才搬到這個城鎮，所以我
  不太認識這裡的孩子。

  I moved to this town a year ago, so I don't
  really know the kids in here.

- 交朋友對我來說很容易。／
  交新朋友對我來說相對容易。

  I make friends easily. /
  It is rather easy for me to make new
  friends.
  • rather 反而、相當地

- 我很難交到朋友。

  很難～

  I (have a hard time) making friends.

- 我不敢跟第一次見面的人說話，因
  為我很害羞。／我沒有辦法開啟對
  話，因為我太害羞了。

  I can't talk to someone new because I'm
  too shy. / I can't really start a conversation
  because I'm too shy.

- 我很羨慕 Adam 善於交際的個性。

  I envy Adam's sociable personality.
  • sociable 善於交際的　personality 個性

- 我想和 Amy 當朋友。

  I want to be friends with Amy.

- 今天我和 Amy 成為了朋友。

  Today, I became friends with Amy.

- Amy 跟我有很多相似的地方。

  Amy and I have a lot (in common).

  共通地

- Amy 跟我很聊得來。

  Amy and I have a perfect connection.

- Eric 和我是在操場一起玩的時候變熟的。

  Eric and I got close (親近) while hanging out (玩樂) together on the playground.

- Eric 跟我會變熟，是因為我們上同一堂跆拳道課。

  Eric and I got close because we are in the same taekwondo class.

- 因為我沒有補習，所以沒有可以陪我玩的朋友。

  Because I don't go to a cram school, I don't have friends to play with.

- 我上很多個不同的補習班，所以我沒有時間跟朋友玩。

  I go to so many different cram school that I don't have any time for friends.

- 和別人做朋友的時候，我不想太過挑剔。／我想和不同類型的人做朋友。

  I don't want to be picky when making friends with others. / I am interested in being friends with many different people.

  • picky 挑剔的

好朋友 ★ Close Friends

- Adam 是我最親近的朋友。

  Adam is my closest friend.

- Amy 是我最要好的朋友。

  Amy is my best friend. /
  Amy is my bestie.

- 我和 Adam 從一年級開始就是朋友了。

  Adam and I have been friends since we were in the 1st grade.

- 我們上同一間幼稚園。

  We went to the same kindergarten.

- 我們在踢足球的時候變成好朋友。

  We became best friends while playing soccer together.

- 我們每天見面，並一起回家。

  Everyday, we meet and come home together.

- 我們的爸媽也很熟。

  Our parents are close as well.
  ㄝ～

- 我希望我們的友誼能夠長存。

  I hope our friendship lasts forever.
  • last 持續、繼續

- 我很難過，因為我最好的朋友和我在不同班。

  I'm so sad because my best friend is in a different class.

- 我很難過，因為我的好朋友要轉到其他學校去了。

  I'm so sad because my close friend is transferring to another school.

和朋友出去玩 ★ Hanging out with Friends

- 和她一起出去很好玩。

  It's really fun to hang out with her.

- 每當我和他一起出去，我們最後總是會吵架。

  Whenever I hang out with him, we end up fighting.
  結果變成～

- 今天 Amy 來我家玩。

  Today, Amy came to play at my house.

- 我和朋友一起寫功課。

  I did my homework together with my friends.

- 在去補習班之前，我和朋友一起在操場玩。

  I played with my friend on the playground before going to the cram school.

- 和朋友一起玩的時候最快樂了。

  I feel happiest when playing with my friends.

- 我的朋友們比較喜歡去外面玩。／ 我的朋友們喜歡戶外活動。

  My friends prefer playing outside. / My friends enjoy (outdoor activities).

  戶外活動

- Amy 喜歡在家裡玩。

  Amy likes to play at home.

- 最近女孩們只和其他女孩做朋友。

  These days, girls are only close with other girls.

- 我和好朋友們組成了一個祕密社團。

  I made a secret club with my close friends.

朋友的優缺點 ★ The Strengths and Weaknesses of My Friends

- Adam 真的很善良。

  Adam is really kind.

- Adam 很體貼。／ Adam 總是禮讓別人。

  Adam is considerate. / Adam always lets others go before him.

  • considerate 體貼　let A ＋動詞原形 讓 A～

- Adam 踢足球踢得很好。

  Adam plays soccer very well.

- Amy 是個會念書的漂亮女孩。

  Amy is a pretty girl who also studies well.

- Amy 又高又有運動神經。

  Amy is tall and athletic.

  • athletic 運動神經發達的

- Amy 在她的朋友之間很受歡迎。

  Amy is popular with her friends.

- 由於 Amy 的領導能力很強，所以她總是當班長。

  由於

  (Thanks to) her great leadership, Amy is always the class president.

- Amy 很友善，所以每個人都很喜歡她。

  Amy is so friendly that everyone likes her.

- Alice 很固執又有點自私。

  Alice is stubborn and a bit selfish.
  • stubborn 固執的　selfish 自私的

- Alice 很容易就生氣。

  Alice gets upset easily.

- 雖然我和 Alice 一起玩，可是我不是真的很喜歡她。

  I hang out with Alice, but I don't really like her.

- 當 Alice 心情一不好，她就很難平復心情。

  Once she's upset, Alice doesn't get over it quickly.
  恢復

- Adam 總是很任性。

  Adam always tries to get his way.
  隨心所欲

- Adam 總是很強勢。／
  Adam 態度很強硬。／
  Adam 總是對別人頤指氣使。

  Adam has a strong voice. /
  Adam is very bossy. /
  Adam is always bossing others around.
  • bossy 強勢的、自作主張的　boss around 頤指氣使

- 雖然 Adam 看起來很冷淡，可是他還是我重要的朋友。

  Although Adam seems to act cold, he is still my dear friend.

和朋友吵架了 ★ Fights with Friends

- 今天我在學校和 Adam 吵架了。

  Today, I fought with Adam at school.

- Adam 嘲笑我很胖。

  Adam made fun of me by calling me fat.

- 今天 Adam 和 Eric 大吵一架。

  Today, Adam and Eric had a big fight.

- 我和他們兩個都很要好，所以我被尷尬的夾在中間。

  Both of them are really close to me, so I was awkwardly caught in the middle.
  • awkwardly 尷尬地

- 我現在覺得很為難，因為我不能偏袒任何一方。

  I am in trouble now because I can't take anyone's side.

- 今天 Chris 和我大打出手。

  Today, Chris and I beat each other up.

  • beat up 打

- Chris 先打我的。

  Chris hit me first.

- 因為我嘲笑了他，所以我也有錯。

  I made fun of him, so it was partly my fault.

  • partly 部分地

- 但我覺得打我打得很用力的 Chris 更過分。

  But I think Chris is guiltier because he hit me hard.

  • guilty 有罪的

- 我不打算再和 Chris 玩，除非他先道歉。

  I'm not going to play with Chris unless he apologizes first.

  • apologize 道歉

- 這個叫 Chris 的男孩一直來煩我。

  This boy named Chris constantly bugs me.

  • bug 煩擾、折磨

- Chris 今天對我罵髒話。

  Chris swore at me today.

  • swear 罵髒話

- 他一直嘲笑我，還來煩我。

  He kept teasing and annoying me.

  • tease 嘲笑

- 我聽到 Lisa 在我背後說我壞話。

  I heard that Lisa is talking about me behind my back.

  • talk behind one's back 在～背後說壞話

- Lisa 一直霸凌我。

  Lisa keeps bullying me.

  • bully 排擠、折磨、惡霸

- 我很受傷，因為我的朋友們一直取笑我的頭很大。

  I am hurt because my friends keep on teasing me about having a big head.

- 我們班上的女生好像惡霸。

  The girls in my class act like bullies.

- 當我們在一起玩的時候，Lisa 生氣了。

  While we were playing together, Lisa became sulky.

  • sulky 生氣的、生悶氣的

- 我不知道為什麼 Lisa 生氣了。

  I don't know why Lisa was angry.

- 仔細想想，那沒有什麼好吵的。

  Come to think of it, it was nothing to fight over. ── 仔細想想

- 我應該要更有耐心一點。

  I should have been more patient.

  • patient 有耐心的

- 我想要儘快和 Lisa 和好。

  I want to make up with Lisa as soon as possible. ── 和解

- 我明天應該要先道歉。

  I should apologize first tomorrow.

- 我希望 Chris 和 Lisa 可以快點和好。

  I hope Chris and Lisa make up soon.

和朋友和好 ★ Making up with My Friends

- 今天我先向 Chris 道歉了。

  Today, I apologized to Chris first.

- 我說我很抱歉，他說他也是。

  I said I was sorry, and he said he was sorry, too.

- 那個男生從來不道歉。

  That boy never says sorry.

- 我寫了一封道歉信給我朋友。

  I gave a letter of apology to my friend.

  • apology 道歉

- 我傳了一封簡訊跟她道歉，所以她回傳了說她也很抱歉。 回覆、回答

  I texted her a message to apologize, so she replied back that she was sorry.
  • text a message 傳簡訊　apologize 道歉

- 當我和朋友吵架的時候，我通常是先道歉的那一個。

  When I fight with my friends, I'm usually the first one to say sorry.

- 在和朋友吵完架並和好後，我覺得我們更親近了。

  After fighting and making up with my friends, I think we get even closer.

- 因為我們吵了架卻絕不道歉，所以我們漸行漸遠。

  Because we had a fight and never apologized, we drifted apart. 漸行漸遠

- 我很容易生氣，但是我也很快氣消。

  I tend to get angry easily, but I get over it quickly, too. 克服、恢復

- 雖然我們和好了，可是我們之間還是很尷尬。

  We made up, but things are still awkward between us. 和好
  • awkward 尷尬的

- 在和朋友和好以後，我覺得很棒。

  I feel so good after making up with my friends.

- 我覺得先讓步的人就贏了。

  I think you win when you give in first. 讓步

- 我說了我很抱歉，但是我並不是真的覺得抱歉。

  I said I was sorry, but I didn't really mean it.

- 因為爸媽叫我道歉，所以我傳了簡訊給他。

  Because my parents told me to apologize, I sent a text message to him. 簡訊

霸凌 ★ Bullying

- 我們班沒有被排擠的人。

  There are no outcasts in my class.
  • outcast 被排擠的人

- 我覺得我的同學們在偷偷孤立 Sam。

  I think my classmates are secretly isolating Sam.
  • isolate 孤立、排擠

- 每個班上總是會發生霸凌事件。

  There are always bullies in every class.

- 如果有一群人想要霸凌我／找我麻煩，我會受到很大的打擊。

  If a group of kids ever bullied /picked on me, I would be devastated.　找麻煩、找碴
  • devastated 受到很大的打擊

- 我覺得被排擠的孩子很可憐。

  I feel so bad for the outcast.

- 沒有人和他說話。

  No one talks to him.

- 我勇敢的站出來為班上被排擠的人發聲。

  I bravely stood up for the outcast in my class.　站出來、支持

- 我想要幫他，可是我怕我會像他一樣被排擠。

  I want to help him, but I'm afraid of becoming an outcast like him.

- 我應該告訴老師他／她被排擠了。

  I should tell my teacher that he/she is being bullied.

- 我受到很大的打擊，因為我覺得好像被排擠了。

  I feel devastated because I feel like an outcast.

- 班上同學從不和我說話，而且每次都在我經過的時候大笑。

  My classmates never talk to me and laugh whenever I pass by.

- 如果他們再繼續這樣做，我就要告訴老師這件事了。

  If they keep on doing that, I'm going to tell the teacher about it.

- 當霸凌事件發生時，老師說我們必須要伸出援手。

  My teacher says we have to help when there is bullying going on.

睡衣派對 ★ Pajama Party

- 我請求媽媽在我們家裡辦睡衣派對。

  I begged my mother to have a pajama party at our house.

  • beg 哀求、請求

- 這個週末在我家有一場睡衣派對。

  There will be a pajama party at my house this weekend.

- 我不知道應該要邀誰。

  I wonder who I should invite.

- 昨天 Alice 家有一場睡衣派對。

  Yesterday, there was a pajama party at Alice's house.

- 朋友和我聊了一整晚。

  My friends and I talked all night long.

  整晚

- 我們玩了捉迷藏、桌遊和電腦遊戲。

  We played hide-and-seek, board games, and computer games.

- 因為我們玩到凌晨，所以隔天大家都睡到很晚。

  Because we played till dawn, we all slept in the next day.

  • dawn 凌晨　sleep in 睡到很晚才起床

- 睡衣派對真的好好玩！

  Pajama parties are really fun!

- 如果我可以常常辦睡衣派對的話，那該有多好啊！

  How nice would it be if I could often have pajama parties?

- 雖然我們只是聊天聊了整個晚上，但還是很好玩。

  Although all we did was talk all night long, it was still very fun.

- 大人叫我們去睡覺，可是我們一點也不想睡。
  The adults told us to sleep, but we were not sleepy at all.

朋友的生日派對 ★ Friends' Birthday Parties

- 今天是 Amy 的生日派對。
  Amy's birthday party was today.

- 我不知道該送什麼給我朋友當作生日禮物。
  I don't know what to give to my friend for her birthday.

- 我想要買生日禮物給朋友，可是我錢不夠。
  I am trying to buy a birthday present for my friend, but I am short of cash.
  • cash 現金　　　不夠

- 我買了一支自動傘當禮物。
  I bought an automatic umbrella as a present.
  • automatic 自動的

- 我沒有受邀參加朋友的生日派對。
  I didn't get invited to my friend's birthday party.

- 我不能參加朋友的生日派對，因為我得了流感病倒了。
  I couldn't go to my friend's birthday party because I had come down with the flu.
  • flu 流行性感冒　　　病倒

- 因為我真的很想去，所以我很沮喪。
  I really wanted to go, so I am very disappointed.
  • disappointed 沮喪的

- 我吃了很多好吃的食物，也玩了遊戲，真的很好玩。
  I ate plenty of delicious food and played games. It was really fun.

- 我想和 Alex 一起出去。

  I want to (go out with) Alex.

  一起出去

- 有傳言說她和 Alex 一起出去，我覺得好受傷。

  There is a rumor that she is going out with Alex. It's hurting me.

  • rumor 謠言　hurt 心痛

- Alex 告訴那個女孩說他喜歡她。

  Alex told the girl that he liked her.

- Alex 約他喜歡的人出去約會，可是被拒絕了。

  Alex asked his crush out on a date but got rejected.

  • crush 喜歡的對象　ask... out on a date 邀…出去約會　reject 拒絕

- 我傳簡訊告訴 Alex 說我喜歡他。

  I told Alex that I liked him by texting him.

- 我決定要和 Alex 交往。

  I have decided to (go steady with) Alex.

  和～交往

- 我打算情人節的時候要告訴他／她，我喜歡他／她。

  I'm going to tell him/her that I like him/her on Valentine's Day.

- Alex 和我是很特別的朋友。

  Alex and I are very special friends.

- Alex 是我的男朋友。

  Alex is my boyfriend.

- Amy 是我的女朋友。

  Amy is my girlfriend.

- 我們一起到學校上課，然後去同一個補習班。

  We commute to school together and then go to the same academy.

  • commute 通勤　academy 補習班

- 當我們一起出去玩的時候，有些朋友會開我們的玩笑。

  Some friends tease us when we hang out together.

寵物

Mimi and Eddie

Saturday, July 8, Humid

There are two puppies in my house. Their names are Mimi and
Eddie. Taking care of them is my responsibility. Looking after pets
is difficult. But I love being with them because they are very cute.

咪咪和艾迪　　7月8日星期六，潮濕的天氣

我家有兩隻小狗。牠們的名字分別叫 Mimi 和 Eddie。照顧牠們是我的責任。照顧寵物很難，可是我很喜歡
和牠們在一起，因為牠們非常可愛。

· responsibility 責任、義務　look after 照顧 (= take care of)

寵物 ★ Pets

- 我們家養了一隻寵物貓。

  Our family has a pet cat.

- 我真的想要一隻狗狗，可是我媽媽不願意買給我。

  I really want a puppy, but my mother will not buy me one.

- 我家有兩隻狗。

  There are two dogs in my house.

- 爸爸買了一隻貓給我當生日禮物。

  My father bought me a cat for my birthday.

- 媽媽終於同意讓我養寵物。

  My mom finally allowed me to have a pet.

- 我們的貓叫做 Momo。

  Our cat's name is Momo.

- Momo 是母貓。

  Momo is a female cat.
  - female 母的、女性的

- Jerry 是公貓。

  Jerry is a male cat.
  - male 公的、男性的

- 媽媽說我們不能養寵物，因為 Amy 有異位性皮膚炎。

  My mother says that we can't have pets because of Amy's atopic eczema.
  異位性皮膚炎

- 我希望妹妹可以快點好起來，這樣我們才可以養狗。

  I hope my younger sister gets well soon so that we can have a pet dog.
  痊癒

- 媽媽說她很怕貓。

  My mother says she is scared of cats.
  害怕

照顧寵物 ★ Taking Care of Pets

• 我負責餵貓。

Feeding the cat is my responsibility.

• feed 餵食　responsibility 責任

• Mimi 把我的回家作業咬爛了。

Mimi chewed up my homework.
咬爛、毀壞

• 貓抓傷了我的手臂。

A cat scratched my arm.

• scratch 抓傷

• 我的貓有受過上廁所訓練。

受過上廁所訓練的
My cat is toilet-trained.

• 我的狗狗還需要更多上廁所的訓練。

My puppy still needs more toilet training.
上廁所訓練

• 因為牠到處尿尿和便便，這讓我覺得很煩躁。

Because he pees and poops everywhere, it annoys me.

• pee 尿尿、尿液　poop 便便、大便

• Mimi 在我的床上尿尿。

Mimi peed on my bed.

• 媽媽叫我要跟在貓後面清理。

My mother told me to clean up after my cat.
跟在～後面清理

• 媽媽告訴我，照顧貓是我的責任。

My mother told me that it is my responsibility to take care of the cat.

• 照顧寵物是一件很困難的工作。

Taking care of pets is a really difficult job.

• 我帶寵物去動物醫院打預防針。

I took my pet to the animal hospital for a vaccination. / I brought my pet to the vet for a vaccination.

• vaccination 預防針　vet 獸醫

- 我的狗懷孕了。

  My dog is pregnant.
  - pregnant 懷孕的

- 我的狗 Mimi 今天生產。

  My dog Mimi gave birth today.
  ‎生產

- 每當我看著狗狗們的時候，因為牠們實在太可愛了，導致我忘了時間。

  Every time I look at the puppies, they are so cute that I lose track of time.
  ‎錯過～

- Mimi 病得很重。

  Mimi is very sick.

- 流浪狗好可憐。

  Stray dogs are so pitiful.
  - stray 無主的、迷路的　pitiful 可憐的

- 我希望我的狗狗可以活很久。

  I hope my puppy lives for a long time.

- 我的狗狗太胖了。

  My puppy is obese/overweight.
  - obese 肥胖的　overweight 過重的

- 我的貓很討厭洗澡。

  My cat really hates baths.

- 因為養了寵物，所以我家有一股很怪的味道。

  Because we have a pet, my house smells funny.

各種寵物 ★ Kinds of Pets

- 我養的兔子叫做 Bunny。

  My pet rabbit's name is Bunny.

- 我的朋友 Adam 養了鸚鵡當寵物。

  My friend Adam has a pet parrot.
  - parrot 鸚鵡

- 我養了兩隻刺蝟當寵物。

  I have two pet hedgehogs.
  - hedgehog 刺蝟

- Sam 拿給我他養的倉鼠。

  Sam gave me his hamster.

- 我去 Lisa 的家裡看她養的倉鼠。

  I went to Lisa's home to see her hamsters.

- 倉鼠在晚上很活躍。

  Hamsters are active at night.

- 朋友把他的小魚分給我。

  My friend shared his baby fish with me.

- 我買了一個魚缸來養魚。

  I bought an aquarium to raise fish.

  • aquarium 魚缸

- 我幫魚缸換了水。

  I changed the water in the aquarium.

- 我的小丑魚產卵了。

  My clown fish laid eggs.

  • clown fish 小丑魚（電影《海底總動員》的主角魚）

- 我的烏龜從牠的籠子裡逃跑了。

  My turtle escaped from its cage.

  • escape 逃跑   cage 籠子

- 我的鄰居養了寵物蛇。

  My neighbor has a pet snake.

  • neighbor 鄰居

Part 4

學校生活與讀書

Jump Rope Is Hard!

Monday, April 14, Windy

I played jump rope in P.E. Jump rope was actually harder than I had thought. I got really tired after jumping only 20 times. However, it seems like a great way to exercise. From now on, my goal is to jump rope 100 times.

跳繩很難！ 4月14日星期一，風很大

體育課的時候我跳了跳繩。跳繩事實上比我之前所想的還要難。我才跳了 20 下就累壞了。不過跳繩似乎是一個不錯的運動方式。從現在開始，我的目標是跳繩 100 下。

·jump rope 跳繩　P.E. 體育課 (= physical exercise)　goal 目標

學校／年級／班級介紹 ★ Introducing My School/Grade/Class

- 我上納拉國民小學。

  I go to Nara Elementary School.

- 我的學校是納拉國小。

  My school is Nara Elementary School.

- 我現在是二年級。

  I am in the 2nd grade now.

  • grade 學年

- 我在一年三班。

  I am in class 3 in grade 1.

- 一年級有五個班。

  Grade 1 has 5 classes.

- 我的教室在二樓。

  My classroom is in the 2nd floor.

- 我們班有 25 個學生。

  There are 25 students in my class.

- 我們班的男生比女生多三個。

  There are 3 more boys than girls in our class.

- 我們班有 16 個男生和 16 個女生，一共 32 個學生。

  My class has a total of 32 students with 16 boys and 16 girls.　　總計

- 我是班上第十高的。／根據我的身高，我在班上排第十。

  I am the tenth tallest student in my class. / I got assigned the number 10 according to height in my class.　被任命為～、被指定為～

  • height 身高

- 我的座位在教室的最後面。

  My seat is at the very back of the classroom.

- 我的座位在第一行的第一排。

  My seat is in the front row of the first column.

  • row 橫排　column 行、直排

- 因為我坐在後面，所以我看不清楚黑板。

  Because I sit in the back, I can't see the blackboard clearly.

  • blackboard 黑板

- 我可以從教室看到操場。

  I can see the schoolyard from my classroom.

- 我的座位靠近走廊。

  My seat is on the hallway side.

  • hallway 走廊

 導師 ★ Homeroom Teacher

- 我的導師是李老師。

  My homeroom teacher is Ms. Lee.
  導師

- 我的老師人很善良又親切。

  My teacher is really nice and kind.

- 我的老師很親切。

  My teacher is really kind.

- 我的老師很嚴格。

  My teacher is really strict.

  • strict 嚴格的

- 我的老師很可怕。

  My teacher is so scary.

- 我的老師很幽默。

  My teacher is really humorous.

- 我的老師年紀很大。

  My teacher is old.

- 我的老師因為出很多作業而有名。

  My teacher is known for giving a lot of homework.
  因～而出名

- 我的老師很喜歡我。

  My teacher likes me very much.

- 我的老師只喜歡女生。／
  我的老師似乎偏愛女生。

  My teacher only likes the girls. /
  My teacher seems to favor the girls.

  • favor 偏愛、鍾愛

- 老師常常罵我。

  My teacher scolds me very often.

- 我的老師很時尚。

My teacher is very fashionable.
- fashionable 時尚的、流行的

- 我的老師像個熱心的老奶奶。

My teacher is like a warm-hearted grandmother.
- warm-hearted 熱心的、友好的

隔壁同學／團體 ★My Seatmate/Group

- 今天是換座位的日子。

Today was the day we changed seatmates. / Today, we were supposed to switch seatmates.
- seatmate 隔壁同學　switch 交換

- 今天在學校換了位子。

Today at school, we changed seatmates.

- 我們班每個月會換座位。

In my class, we change partners every month.

- 我們用抽籤來換位子。

We changed seats by (drawing lots).
抽籤

- Adam 變成了坐我隔壁的同學。／
Adam 和我坐在一起。

Adam became my seatmate. /
Adam and I will sit together.

- 可以和我最好的朋友坐在一起真是
太興奮了。

I am thrilled to have my best friend as my seatmate.
- thrilled 興奮的

- 我最討厭的小孩在今天變成我的隔
壁同學。

Today, the kid that I hate the most became my seatmate.

- 我很不高興，因為班上最調皮的男
生換來坐我旁邊。

I am so upset because the naughtiest boy in my class came to sit (next to) me.
- naughty 調皮的
在旁邊

- 坐我隔壁的同學人很好。

  My seatmate is really nice.

- 坐我隔壁的同學一直來煩我。

  My seatmate keeps bothering me.
  • bother 煩擾、讓人傷腦筋

- 我因為和旁邊同學聊天而被老師罵了。

  I got into trouble with the teacher for chatting with my seatmate.
  • chat 聊天

- 我很生氣，因為坐我隔壁的同學一直作弄我。

  I was so angry because my seatmate kept teasing me.

- 坐我隔壁的同學和我住在同一個公寓裡。

  My seatmate and I live in the same apartment.

- 我隔壁的同學在一年前才轉來我們學校。

  My seatmate transferred to my school just a year ago.

- 今天我們這組得到第一名。

  Today, my group came in first.
  └ 得第一名

- 今天我們這組得到最後一名。

  Today, my group came in last.
  └ 得最後一名

- 我們這組裡面有很多聰明的人。

  There are a lot of smart students in my group.

- 我們組裡面有很多調皮的人。

  There are many naughty students in my group.

- 別組有六個人，不過我們這組只有五個人。

  There are six students in other groups, but my group has five students.

- 我們組長是 Sam。

  Our group's leader is Sam.

- 我也想當組長。

  I wanted to be the group leader, too.

- 我很喜歡我的組員。

  I really like my group members.

- 今天我們有四堂課。

  Today, we had 4 periods.
  • period 期間、（一堂）課

- 今天上的課是社會、國語、數學和自然。

  Today's classes were social studies, Chinese, math, and science. 社會

- 今天有五堂課。

  Today, we have five periods.

- 我們在星期二和星期四有五堂課。

  On Tuesdays and Thursdays, we have 5 periods.

- 我在早自習讀了《芙蘭妮》。

  In the morning study hall, I read *Franny*. 自習時間、自習室

- 我喜歡星期三，因為學校很早放學。

  I like Wednesdays because school ends early.

- 今天的國語課我學到了詩。

  In today's Chinese class, I learned about poetry.
  • poetry 詩

- 今天的數學課我學到了圖形。

  In math class today, I learned about shapes.
  • shape 圖形

- 老師要我們在明天以前把九九乘法表背起來。

  The teacher told us to memorize the multiplication table by tomorrow.
  • memorize 背　九九乘法表

- 我今天在體育課跳了跳繩。

  In today's P.E. class, I played jump rope.
  • P.E. (= physical education) 體育課

- 因為下雨，所以我們在禮堂上體育課。

  We had P.E. class in the auditorium because of the rain.
  • auditorium 禮堂

- 美術課的時候，我們畫了我們想像中因為科技而發展得很好的未來。

  In art class, we drew pictures of our imaginary future that is (well-developed) by science.　發展的很好的
  - imaginary 只存在於想像的、假想的

- 美術課的時候，我們用水彩畫畫。

  In art class, we painted with watercolors.
  - watercolor 水彩

- 今天的音樂課，我們學了叫做《布穀鳥》的歌。

  Today in music class, we learned a song called *Cuckoo*.

- 今天我在實驗室裡做了一個實驗。

  Today, I did an experiment in the lab.
  - experiment 實驗　lab (= laboratory) 實驗室、研究室

- 我最喜歡的課是體育課。

  My favorite class is P.E.

- 我最不喜歡的科目是數學。

  My least favorite subject is math.
  - subject 科目

- 學校的英文課很簡單。

  The English classes at school are very easy.

- 因為我在補習班已經上過數學了，所以數學課對我來說很容易。

  Because I have already studied math at a cram school, math class is very easy.

- 數學很有趣。

  Math is fun.

- 對我來說，社會是最難的科目。

  (Social studies) is the most difficult subject for me.　社會

- 社會科有好多東西要背。

  There are so many things to memorize for social studies.

- 我不太擅長需要背誦的科目。

  I am not really good at subjects requiring memorization.
  - require 需要　memorization 背誦、記憶

- 今天的體育課很有趣。

  Today's P.E. class was really fun.

- 今天很無聊，因為我們今天有兩堂數學課。

  Today was so boring because we had two periods of math at school.

- 我喜歡自然課，特別是做實驗的時候。

  I like science class, especially when we do an experiment.

- 我不知道為什麼在上數學課的時候，時間會過得這麼慢。

  I don't know why time passes this slowly when I am in math class.

課堂參與 ★ Participating in Class

- 我在課堂參與上表現得很好。

  I participate well in class.

  • participate 參與（包括上課時認真聽，或是在報告或討論的時候發言）

- 我不太參與課堂討論。

  I don't really participate in class discussions.

  • discussion 討論

- 我真的很討厭在課堂討論上發言。

  I really hate speaking in class discussions.

- 當我必須要講話的時候，我就會覺得很緊張。

  Whenever I have to speak, I am so nervous.

  • nervous 緊張不安的

- 當我在討論時發言，我的聲音就會變啞。

  Whenever I speak in a discussion, my voice cracks.

  • crack （聲音）變啞

- 上社會課的時候，我在全班同學面前做報告。我覺得好緊張。

  In my social studies class, I did a presentation in front of the entire class. I was so nervous.

  • presentation 報告　entire 整個

- 我應該要練習在表達想法的時候，講話講得大聲一點。

  I should practice speaking loudly when presenting my ideas.

  • present 表達

- 我舉了手，可是老師沒有叫我。

  I raised my hand, but the teacher didn't call on me.
  > 點、叫

- 我應該要多多參與。

  I should participate more.

- 從現在開始，我會更積極參與。

  From now on, I will actively participate.
  - actively 積極地

- 因為我今天很認真參與，所以得到了一些獎勵貼紙。

  Because I participated well today, I got some praise stickers.
  - praise 獎勵

- 每當我在課堂上發言，我就會臉紅且感到不好意思。

  Whenever I speak in class, I blush and feel shy.
  - blush 臉紅

- 我很擔心如果我講錯了也許會被同學嘲笑。

  I am worried that my classmates might laugh if I said something wrong.

營養午餐 ★ School Lunch

- 今天的午餐是咖哩飯。

  Today's lunch was curry and rice.

- 今天的午餐是我最喜歡的豬排。

  Today's lunch was my favorite food, pork cutlet.
  > 豬排

- 今天午餐有我最討厭的蘑菇。

  For today's lunch, there were mushrooms, which I hate the most.

- 我喜歡星期三，因為有好多好吃的食物可以吃。

  I like Wednesdays because there are so many delicious foods to eat.

- 肉的料理總是很快就被吃光了。

  We always run out of meat dishes quickly.
  > 用完、耗盡

- 今天的菜不夠，所以我到學校的自助餐廳去拿更多的食物。

Because there weren't enough dishes, I went to the school cafeteria to get more food.
  - cafeteria 自助餐廳

- 我先排隊的，可是 Adam 插了隊。

I lined up first, but Adam cut in line.
  - 排隊　　　　　　　　插隊

- 因為我沒有帶湯匙，所以我用了免洗湯匙。

Because I didn't bring my spoon, I used a disposable one.
  - disposable 拋棄式的

- 學校的餐點很可怕。

The school meals are horrible.
  - horrible 可怕的

- 今天的菜單都是我討厭的菜。

Today's menu was full of the food that I hate.

- 可是我不應該把食物丟掉，所以我還是吃完了。

But I shouldn't throw away the food, so I ate it all.
  - 丟掉

- 學校的湯總是很淡。

The soup at school is always bland.
  - bland 淡的

- 我是最後一個吃午餐的人。

I was the last one to eat lunch.

- 因為我沒有把任何食物倒掉，所以得到了一張好寶寶貼紙。

Because I didn't throw away any food, I received a good-job sticker.

- 我在家很挑食，可是在學校不會。

I am a picky eater at home, but at school I am not.
  - picky 挑剔的

- 因為我什麼都吃，所以我最喜歡午餐時間了。

Because I can eat anything, I love lunch time the most.

幫忙打菜 ★ The Lunch Helper

- 今天輪到我們這組幫忙打菜了。

  Today was our group's turn to help serve lunch.

  • turn 順序、值班

- 有些人常常要求要吃更多的菜。

  Someone kept asking for more food.

  要求

- 今天媽媽來幫忙打菜。

  Today, my mother came as a lunch helper.

- 我很開心可以看到媽媽在午餐時間來幫我們班。

  I was so happy to see my mother coming to help my class during lunch time.

- 奶奶代替媽媽來幫忙打菜。

  Instead of my mother, my grandmother came as a meal helper.

下課活動 ★ Out-of-Class Activities

- 每當下課時間，我們會坐在走廊玩撲克牌。

  休息時間

  Whenever we have break time, we sit in the hallway and play cards.

  • hallway 走廊

- 在玩撲克牌時，最困難的是橋牌。

  Bridge is the hardest one when playing cards.

- 最近翻花繩在我們班很流行。

  These days, Cat's Cradle is a popular game in my class.

  翻花繩

- 我和朋友們一起在操場玩鬼抓人。

  I played tag with my friends in the schoolyard.

  玩鬼抓人

- 在午休的時候，我和同學一起玩打紙牌遊戲。

  During lunch break, I played the (slap-match game) with my classmates.

  打紙牌遊戲

- 在午休的時候，我和朋友們一起玩跳房子。

  During lunch break, I played hopscotch with my friends.

  • hopscotch 跳房子

- 午餐過後，我和朋友們在教室後面玩德國心臟病。

  After lunch, I played Halli Galli with my friends at the back of the classroom.

- 在午餐時間，我去學校圖書館借了一本書。

  During lunchtime, I went to the school library and borrowed a book.

- 我很快地吃完午餐，然後跑到操場去玩。

  I quickly finished my lunch and then went out to the schoolyard and played there.

- 因為 Amy 吃午餐吃很久，所以我們沒有很多時間可以玩。

  Because Amy took a long time to finish her lunch, we didn't have much time to play.

- 因為我在和朋友玩，所以沒聽到鐘聲。

  Because I was playing with my friends, I didn't hear the bell.

- 在放學之後，我在回家之前和朋友們在操場上玩了一個小時。

  After school, I played with my friends on the playground for an hour before coming home.

- 因為放學後我和朋友踢了足球，所以補習遲到了。

  Because I played soccer with my friends after school, I was late for cram school.

- 因為我在和朋友玩，我忘了要上安親班。

  Because of playing with my friends, I forgot to go to my after-school classes.

- 我希望下課時間可以長一點。

  I wish break time were longer.

- 在下課時間，就算我不特別做些什麼，還是很有趣。

  Even if I don't do anything special during recess, it is still fun.

  • recess 下課時間

打掃時間 ★ Cleaning up the Classroom

- 我們組這週負責打掃。

My group is the cleaning team this week. / My group is in charge of cleaning this week.
負責

- 今天是大掃除日。

Today was the big cleaning day.

- 在打掃時間，老師分配給每一個人不同的任務。

During cleaning time, the teacher gave each of us different duties.

• duty 責任、該做的事

- 我用濕抹布擦桌子。

I wiped the desks with wet rags.

• wipe 擦

- 我用吸塵器打掃教室。

I vacuumed the classroom.

• vacuum 用吸塵器打掃

- 我用拖把打掃走廊。

I cleaned the hallway with a mop.

• mop 拖地

- Sam 和我用掃把掃樓梯。

Sam and I swept the staircase with brooms.

• sweep (sweep-swept-swept) 掃　staircase 樓梯
　broom 掃把

- 我負責洗抹布。

I was the washer for wet rags.

- 洗拖把不容易。

It is really hard to wash the mop.

- 我們三個一起出去幫花園澆水。

Three of us went out together to water the garden.

• water 澆水

- 我必須把資源回收箱搬到一樓，它很重。

I had to carry the recycling box to the first floor. It was very heavy.

• recycling 回收用的

- 資源回收很難做。

  Recycling is really hard to do.

- 因為我擦過窗戶了，所以玻璃閃閃發亮。

  Because I cleaned the window, the glass was shining.

- Eric 在打掃時間無所事事，不去做他的工作。

  Eric kept on (fooling around) and didn't do his job during cleaning time.

  遊手好閒、無所事事

- 我在課堂上講話的懲罰是打掃教室。

  As punishment for talking in class, I had to clean the classroom.

  • punishment 懲罰

- 因為我在打掃，所以上英文課遲到了。

  Because I was cleaning, I was late for my English class.

- 在體育課和打掃教室以後，我覺得有點累了。

  After having P.E. and cleaning up the classroom, I got a little tired.

- 我連自己的房間都不打掃，可是我竟然要打掃教室！

  I don't even clean my own room, but I cleaned up the classroom!

- 灰塵好多，這讓我很討厭打掃教室。

  It's so dusty that I hate cleaning the classroom.

  • dusty 滿是灰塵的

課後活動 ★ After-School Classes

- 我的課後活動報名了西洋棋和美術課。

  For the after-school program, I signed up for the chess and art classes.

  • sign up for 報名、申請

- 在課後活動裡的實驗課已經被登記額滿了。

  The lab class in the after-school program is already fully booked.

  • booked 被預約、被登記

- 我發現學生是依照先後順序報名的。

  I found that students signed up on a first-come, first-served basis.
  按先後順序

- 因為烹飪課和科學實驗課都很熱門，所以上課學生是用抽籤決定的。

  Because the cooking class and the science lab experiment class are very popular, the students are selected by drawing lots.
  • select 選擇
  抽籤

- 課後活動我本來想上烹飪課，可是我沒選到。

  I was going to take a cooking class in the after-school program, but I failed to get into it.

- 今天是課後活動報名的最後一天，可是我把報名表忘在家裡了。

  Today was the last day to sign up for the after-school program, but I left the sign-up slip at home.
  報名表

- 每週一、三、五的課後活動我都去上英文課。

  On Mondays, Wednesdays, and Fridays, I go to the English class in the after-school program.

- 課後活動的美術課在下午 2:30 開始。

  The art class in the after-school program starts at 2:30 p.m.

- 我很開心 Eric 會跟我一起上美術課。

  I am so happy that Eric will be in the art class with me.

- 在上課後活動之前，我到圖書館看了一些書。

  Until it was time for the after-school program, I went to the library and read some books.

- 課後活動比學校課程還要有趣多了。

  There are more fun things in the after-school program than in my school classes.

- 我在課後活動學吹長笛。

  I am learning how to play the flute in the after-school program.

- 我在週末的學校課程學跳舞。 | I am learning to dance in the weekend school program.

- 我在準備電腦課的 Word 的檢定考試。 | I am preparing for the certificate exam for Word in my computer class.
  - certificate 證書

- 我在機器人課上做的機器人很快就要被展出了。 | Soon, the robot that I made in my robot class will be exhibited/displayed.
  - exhibit/display 展示

- 我希望課後活動裡可以有戲劇課。 | I hope there is a drama class in the after-school program.
  - drama 戲劇

聯絡簿 ★ School Planner

- 我把聯絡簿放在學校裡了。 | I left my school planner at school.
  - 英文裡面沒有和「聯絡簿」相對應的單字。就記錄日程和注意事項的功能來說，school planner 應該最為接近，不過不一樣的是老師不會特別叫學生填寫。

- 因為我把聯絡簿放在家裡，所以我沒辦法抄下要寫什麼作業。 | Because I left my school planner at home, I couldn't write down my homework list.

- 我沒有把聯絡簿寫完。 | I didn't finish completing my planner.
  - complete 完成

- 因為媽媽沒有簽聯絡簿，所以我不能拿到獎勵貼紙。 | Because my mother didn't sign my school planner, I couldn't get a praise sticker.

- 因為我把聯絡簿放在學校，所以我打電話給 Eric 問有什麼回家作業。 | Because I left my school planner at school, I called Eric to ask him about the homework.

作業和成績

I Messed up My Exam

Tuesday, May 10, Sunny

Today, I took midterm exams. It was a long day because I had four tests. I did a good job on the Chinese and social studies exams, but I got three wrong on the math exam. I thought I had studied hard, but maybe I did not study enough. I am afraid to see my report card next week.

我考爛了　5月10日星期二，晴天

今天我考了期中考。因為我考了四科，所以今天非常難熬。國語和社會我考得很好，可是數學我錯了三題。我覺得我已經很認真讀書了，不過也許我讀得還不夠。我很害怕下週看到我的成績單。

· midterm exam 期中考　do a good job 表現良好　report card 成績單

作業 ★ Homework

- 我今天唯一的作業就是寫日記。

  The only homework I have today is to write in my diary.

- 今天的回家作業是寫讀書心得和訂正數學習題。

  讀書心得

  Today's homework is to write a (book report) and to correct the wrong answers for math problems.

  • correct 訂正

- 今天的回家作業是幫父母按摩。

  Today's homework is to give a massage to my parents.

- 社會作業星期三要交。

  My social studies homework is due on Wednesday.

  • due 到期、預計要做的

- 我今天有好多作業。

  I have a lot of homework today.

- 老師給我們太多功課了。

  My teacher gave us too much homework.

- 我們班的功課總是太多。

  There is always too much homework in my class.

- 我們班的功課沒有很多。

  There is not much homework in my class.

- 我們聚在 Amy 家寫國語課的團體作業。

  We gathered at Amy's house and did group homework for Chinese class.

- 為了要寫團體作業，我們分配了角色。

  To do the group homework, we chose our roles.

- 在話劇裡面，我演老虎。

  In the play, I have the role of Tiger.

- 我為社會作業做了 PowerPoint 報告。

  I made a PowerPoint presentation for my social studies homework.

- 我必須要寫作業,可是我忘了把自然課本帶回家。

  I have to do my homework, but I forgot to bring my science textbook from school.
  • textbook 教科書

- 因為我的功課太多,所以我必須要寫到很晚。

  Because I had too much homework, I had to do it until late at night.

- 在我寫完作業後,已經是晚上 10 點了。

  After I finished my homework, it was already 10 o'clock at night.

- 我已經寫完其他所有功課了,除了日記還沒寫。

  I have finished all of my homework except for writing in my diary.
  └ 除了

- 我明天會早起把剩下的作業寫完。

  I will wake up early tomorrow to do the rest of my homework.
  • rest 剩下的

- 我必須要寫作業,可是我的電腦壞了。

  I have to do my homework, but my computer broke.

- 我必須把作業列印出來,可是印表機的墨水沒了。

  I have to print my homework, but there is no ink in my printer. / I have to print my homework, but my printer ran out of ink.

- 因為要寫補習班的作業,我沒辦法寫學校作業。

  Because of cram school homework, I couldn't do my school homework.

- 我沒辦法寫作業,因為這個週末我去拜訪了外公。

  I couldn't do my homework because I visited my grandfather this weekend.

- 老師檢查了我們的作業。

  The teacher checked our homework.

- 我把作業忘在家裡了。

  I forgot to bring my homework from home.
  └ 挨罵

- 我被老師罵了,因為我沒有寫作業。

  I got into trouble with my teacher because I didn't do my homework.

- 我想要住在一個沒有作業的世界裡。

  I want to live in a world where there is no homework.

- 我們在學校已經學過了，為什麼我們還要寫作業？

  We learned everything at school. Why do we still have to do homework?

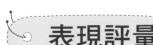 表現評量 ★ Performance Evaluations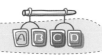

- 老師要求我們種一些豆子當作回家作業。

  The teacher told us to grow some beans for our homework.

- 種豆子也被列入評量的範圍。

  Growing beans is included in the assessment.

  • assessment 評量

- 明天我要考跳繩，所以我和弟弟一起練習。

  Tomorrow, I have a jump-rope test, so I practiced it with my younger brother.

- 今天有體育測驗，不過我因為腳踝受傷而無法練習。

  —— 表現評量

  There was a P.E. performance evaluation today, but I couldn't practice because of my ankle injury.

  • injury 受傷

- 調查鎮裡的商店是我的作業，這被列入了表現評量裡。

  Doing research on the stores in my town is my homework. It is included in my performance evaluation.

  • research 調查

- 今天的英文評量要考口說測驗。

  Today, we had a speaking test for the English assessment.

- 我很難過，因為英文口說考試我考爛了。

  I am so upset because I messed up on my English speaking test.

  • mess up 弄亂、弄糟

- 星期三有一場美術測驗，但因為我那天沒來，所以我今天必須要考。

  There was an art test on Wednesday. But I was absent that day, so I had to take it today.

- 我在整體表現評量得到的分數比一般考試高。

  I get better scores on my overall performance evaluations than on my general tests.

  • score 分數　general 普通的、一般的

誇獎／處罰 ★ Compliments / Punishments

- 老師在國語課上誇獎我，因為我寫了一首好詩。

  My teacher praised me during Chinese class because I wrote a good poem.

  • praise 誇獎　poem 詩

- 在美術課上，我畫了一個朋友的臉。老師說我畫得很好。

  In art class, I had to draw a friend's face. The teacher said that my drawing was good.

- 今天我們組被稱讚團隊合作得很好。

  Today, my group received a compliment for working together well. / Today, my group received a compliment for cooperating well.

  • compliment 稱讚　cooperate 合作

- 我很開心被老師稱讚。

  I was so happy to get a compliment from the teacher.

- 從現在開始，我會更聽老師的話。

  From now on, I will be more obedient to my teacher. / From now on, I will listen to my teacher even better.

  • obedient 順從的、聽話的

- 當學生表現良好的時候，老師會發獎勵貼紙。

  My teacher gives out praise stickers when students do well.

- 今天收到很多好寶寶貼紙，我很開心。

  I was really happy that I received many good-job stickers today.

- 今天我得到兩張獎勵貼紙。

  Today, I got two reward stickers.
  • reward 獎賞

- 我得到一張好寶寶貼紙，因為我在午餐時間沒有丟掉任何食物。

  I got a good-job sticker for not throwing away any food during lunchtime.

- Tom 是我們班上收集到最多貼紙的人。

  Tom has collected the most stickers in my class.
  • collect 收集

- 因為 Amy 太調皮了，所以她是班上貼紙最少的人。

  Because Amy is too playful, she has the lowest number of stickers in my class.
  • playful 調皮的

- 因為我收集到 20 張貼紙，所以我拿到了一張「換座位卡」當作獎品。

  Because I have collected twenty stickers, I received a "changing seatmate card" as a prize.

- 我會更努力的再收集 10 張貼紙，這樣我就可以得到「不用寫作業卡」了。

  I will work to get ten more so that I can earn the "homework pass card."

- 因為我們組表現得最好，所以每個人都可以得到三個獎勵章。

  Because my group was the best one, each of us received three praise stamps.
  • stamp 印章

- 我很確定我會是班上有最多貼紙的人！

  I am sure I will be the one with the most stickers in my class!

- 我今天被老師罵了，因為我在課堂上聊天。

  Today, I was told off by my teacher for chatting during class.

  (被～罵)

- 因為我忘了帶作業，所以被處罰打掃教室。

  Because I had forgotten to bring my homework, I had to clean up the classroom as punishment.

- 因為我今天上學遲到，所以我被罰站在教室後面。

  Because I was late for class today, I had to stand in the back of the classroom as punishment.

- 沒有帶課本的同學被要求到教室後面罰站。

  The students who didn't bring their textbooks were sent to the back of the classroom and had to stand there.

- 當我們和朋友吵架，我們必須要面壁思過。

  When we fight with a friend, we have to stand facing the wall.

  • face 面對

- 因為我和朋友吵架了，老師叫我要寫道歉信。

  Because I had fought with my friend, the teacher told me to write a letter of apology.

  道歉信

- 上課的時候我被老師抓到在看手機。

  I got caught looking at my cell phone by my teacher during class.

  被抓到

- 上課的時候我拿了一些彈珠在手裡，所以彈珠被老師沒收了。

  I was holding some marbles (in my hands) during class, so the teacher took them away.

  • marbles 彈珠

- 老師因為我在走廊奔跑而罵我。

  The teacher scolded me for running in the hallway.

- 當我被處罰的時候，我整天都覺得心情不好。

  When I get punished, I feel bad all day long.

考試 ★ Exams

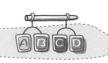

- 老師說明天自然要考單元小考。

  The teacher said that we have a chapter test in science tomorrow.

  單元小考

- 我讀了數學，因為明天有一個考試。

  I studied math because there is a test tomorrow.

- 今天我要期中考／期末考。

  Today, I had a midterm/final.
  • midterm (exam) 期中考　final (exam) 期末考

- 期中考／期末考明天開始。

  Midterms/Finals start tomorrow.

- 今天在國語課考了第三課的小考。

  Today, we had a quiz for lesson 3 in the Chinese class.

- 我們學校不考期中考也沒有期末考。

  My school doesn't have midterms and finals.

- 今天我們考了國語和數學。

  Today, we had tests in Chinese and math.

- 今天好漫長，因為我考了四個考試。

  It was a long day for me because I had four exams.

- 每當要考試，我就會緊張。

  Whenever I take a test, I am nervous.

- 因為昨天參加家族聚會，所以我沒能好好準備考試。

  Because I had a (family gathering) yesterday, I couldn't study very much for my test.　家族聚會

- 爸爸答應我，如果我考 100 分就要買新手機給我。

  My dad (promised to) get me a new cell phone if I get a 100 on my exam.　答應

- 考試比我想像中的簡單。

  The test was easier than I had expected.

- 這一次數學考得很難。

  This time, the math test was really difficult.

- 因為考卷出太難，所以我寫不完。

  Because the test was too hard, I ran out of time before I could finish it.

- 我每一題都寫了，可是沒有時間再檢查一遍。

  I answered all of the questions, but I didn't have time to check them over.
  • check over 檢查

- 自從升上四年級以後，考試就變難了。

  自從～

  (Ever since) I became a 4th grader, the exams have become harder.

- 我考試的時候好想去上廁所。

  I really wanted to go to the bathroom while taking the test.

- 因為考完了，我和朋友一起玩。

  I played with my friends because the exam was over.

- 我覺得好放鬆，因為考完了。

  輕鬆、興奮的心情

  I (feel like flying) because the exam is over. / I felt very relieved when the exam was over.

  • relieved 放鬆的、安心的

- 我希望可以住在一個沒有考試的世界！

  I wish I could live in a world where there are no exams!

- 我很沮喪，因為考了一題沒有預期到的題目。

  I was disappointed because there was an unexpected question on the test.

  • disappointed 沮喪　unexpected 無預期的

- 我的考試雖然寫得很順，可是我還是有點擔心。

  I didn't have any difficulty taking the test, but somehow I am anxious.

  • anxious 不安的、擔心的

成績　★ Grades

- 我在拼字測驗考了 100 分。

  I got a 100 on my spelling test.

- 期末考的所有科目我都拿到了滿分。

  On my finals, I got perfect grades in all of the subjects.

  • grade 分數、成績

- 我和隔壁同學交換考卷互相改。

I exchanged test papers with my seatmate, and then we marked each other's paper.
- exchange 交換　mark 批改

- 自然考試沒有人考到滿分。

There was no one who got a (perfect score) on the science exam.
└── 滿分

- 我們班的國語考試只有兩個人拿到 100 分。

There were only 2 students who got a 100 on the Chinese test in my class.

- 數學考試我只錯了一題。

I made only one mistake on my math exam.

- 我覺得很難過，因為我答錯了我會的題目。

I feel bad that I missed the question that I knew the answer to.

- 困難的題目我都答對了，可是簡單的反而寫錯了。

I got all of the difficult questions right, but I got the easy one wrong.
- get ~ right 寫對　get ~ wrong 寫錯

- 我寫錯是因為我誤解了題目。

I got it wrong because I misunderstood the question.
- misunderstand 誤解、理解錯誤

- 因為粗心錯了兩題，我很難過。

I am distressed about getting two questions wrong (by mistake).
- distressed 難過
└── 粗心

- 我在最後一刻改的答案反而是錯的。

The one that I changed the answer to (at the last moment) is the one that I got wrong.
└── 最後一刻

- 第 12 題我是用猜的，但是我猜對了。

I guessed at question number 12, but I got it right.

- Emily 一邊哭一邊說她沒有考好。

Emily cried and said that she didn't do well on her test.

- 媽媽買了一些炸雞獎勵我考了好成績。

  My mother bought me some fried chicken for doing well on my exam.

- 我的分數比上次考試進步了 20 分。

  My score went up by 20 points from the last time.

  • go up 上升

- 媽媽因為我沒有考好而罵我。

  My mother scolded me for not doing well on my exam.

- 媽媽叫我要小心看題目。

  My mother told me to read the questions carefully.

- 希望下次我可以考好一點。

  I hope my grades get better next time.

- 下次考試我真的很希望可以考一百分。

  I really want to get a 100 on my next exam.

- 我會努力確保在下次考試拿到一百分。

  I will try hard to make sure that I get a 100 on my next exam.

  確保

- 從現在開始我會檢查我的答案。

  I will review my answers from now on.

  • review 檢查

- 這個考試竟然可以讓我又哭又笑，真是太好笑了！

  It is so funny that the exam makes me laugh and cry!

校內比賽／得獎 ★ School Competitions / Prizes

- 我報名了學校的英文演講比賽。

  報名、登記

  I signed up for the English Speaking Contest in my school.

- 我決定要參加學校的歌唱比賽。

  I have decided to participate in the school's singing competition.

  • competition 競賽

- 媽媽建議我去參加看看，來累積經驗。

My mother suggested that I give it a try to get experience.
嘗試
• suggest 建議

- 明天我們有閱讀測驗。

Tomorrow, we have a reading quiz.

- 英文演講比賽的預賽在下個星期三。

The preliminary for the English Speaking Contest is next Wednesday.
• preliminary 預賽、預備的

- 從今天開始我會認真練習。

I will practice hard from today.

- 我在年級閱讀測驗比賽中拿到了銀牌。

I received the silver medal in the reading quiz competition in my grade.

- 我在繪畫比賽中以科幻畫作得獎。

I won the prize in the drawing contest for sci-fi pictures.
• sci-fi (= science fiction) 科幻

- 我得到了好寶寶獎，這個獎是由班上同學投票決定的。

I received the good behavior award, which is a prize given to a person voted on by his or her classmates.
• behavior 行為　award 獎　vote 投票

- 因為我的分數進步了很多，我得到了學業進步獎。

Because my grades have improved a lot, I received the academic enhancement award.
• improve 進步　academic 學業的　enhancement 進步

- 數學競賽我得到了第二名。

I came in second in the math competition.

- 我們班有一個同學得銀牌，還有三個同學拿銅牌。

One student from my class got the silver medal while three others got the bronze.
• bronze 銅牌

- 我們班上沒有人得金牌。

There were no gold medal winners in my class.

- 很遺憾地，我們班沒有人得獎。

Sadly, there was no one in my class who won a prize.

- 我在學校的作文比賽拿到銅牌。

I won the bronze medal in the school essay contest.

- 在英文演講比賽預賽的時候，我被選作班級代表。

In the preliminary for the English Speaking Contest, I was selected as my class representative.

• representative 代表

- 我在英文演講比賽得到鼓勵獎。

I received the encouragement award at the English Speaking Contest.

• encouragement 鼓勵、獎勵

- 進入決賽的人都能得到獎項。

Prizes were given to everyone who participated in the finals.

• final(s) 決賽

- 參加決賽的時候，我因為其他優秀的參賽者而感到氣餒。

When I went to the finals, I was discouraged by the other excellent participants.

• discouraged 氣餒的　participant 參賽者

- 當我站在舞台上，我覺得好緊張。

When I stood up on the stage, I was so nervous.

- 我參加了兒童歌唱大賽，但沒能通過預賽。

I participated in the singing competition for children, but I didn't pass the preliminary.

- 因為我通過了預賽，所以可以進到決賽。這讓我既興奮又緊張。

通過

Since I made it through the preliminary, I can go to the finals. It is making me both excited and nervous.

- 四重唱的夥伴們和我一起做了我們的制服。

My quartet members and I made uniforms for ourselves.

• quartet 四重唱團、四重奏團

- 今天我得到了一個獎來獎勵我讀了很多書。

  Today, I received an award for reading a lot of books.

- 我很羨慕我得獎的朋友們。

  I was so envious of my friends who got awards.

  • envious 羨慕

- 雖然我沒有得到任何一個獎，可是我認為這是一次珍貴的經驗。

  Although I didn't win any award, I think it was a valuable experience.

  • valuable 珍貴的、貴重的

- 我下次會更努力，這樣才可以得獎。

  I will try harder the next time so that I can get an award.

- 天啊！我不敢相信！我得到了第一名！

  Oh, my gosh! I can't believe it! I came in first place!

  第一名

新學期活動

She Is a Schoolgirl Now! Monday, March 2, Chilly

Today, there was a school entrance ceremony for my little sister.
I attended it with my parents. My grandparents also came to
celebrate her being a student. After the ceremony, we went to a
Chinese restaurant. I can't believe my little sister is a schoolgirl
now.

她現在是學生了！　3月2日星期一，涼爽

今天是妹妹的入學典禮。我和爸媽一起參加，爺爺奶奶也一起來慶祝妹妹當學生了。在典禮結束以後，我們一起去吃中華料理。我不敢相信妹妹現在是學生了。

·entrance ceremony 入學典禮　attend 參加　celebrate 慶祝

入學典禮 ★ Entrance Ceremonies

● 我從今年開始上小學。

Starting this year, I am attending elementary school.

● 一想到要變成小學生，我就覺得好興奮。

Thinking about becoming an elementary school student excites me. /
Thinking about becoming an elementary school student makes me feel excited.

• excite 使興奮　excited 刺激的、興奮的

● 阿姨買了一個背包給我當作上學禮物。

My aunt bought me a backpack for a present because I go to school.

• backpack 背包、書包

● 叔叔給了我一些零用錢當作禮物，因為我要開始上學了。

My uncle gave me some pocket money for a present because I start going to school.

● 我被分到一年 5 班。

I was assigned to class 5 in grade 1.
　　被分配

● 今天有入學典禮。

There was a school entrance ceremony today.
　　　入學典禮

● 我沒來由的感到害怕和擔心。

I was scared and worried for no reason.
　　　沒來由的

● 弟弟今天進入小學就讀。

My younger brother enrolled in elementary school today.

• enroll 登錄、入學

● 入學典禮在學校禮堂舉行。

　　　　　　　　　　舉辦
The entrance ceremony was held in the school auditorium.

• auditorium 禮堂

● 老師看起來人非常親切。

The teacher looked very kind.

- 爺爺和奶奶都來參加我的入學典禮。

  My grandfather and grandmother came to my entrance ceremony.

- 媽媽買了一些花給我。

  My mom brought some flowers for me.

- 我手上捧著花和家人一起照相。

  I held the flowers in my hand and took a picture with my family.

  照相

- 在去參加妹妹的入學典禮的路上，我在學校前面買了一些花。

  On my way to my younger sister's entrance ceremony, I bought some flowers in front of the school.

  • on one's way ～途中

- 在入學典禮之後，家人和我一起去了家庭餐廳。

  After the entrance ceremony, my family and I went to a family restaurant.

- 一些可愛的小朋友入學了。

  Some cute little ones enrolled as new students.

- 我不敢相信就在幾年前我也是他們其中的一員。

  I can't believe I was one of those new students just a few years ago.

- 弟弟的入學典禮讓我們有像參加派對的感覺。

  My younger brother's entrance ceremony made us feel in a party mood.

畢業典禮／升國中 ★ Graduation Ceremonies / Going to Middle School

- 今天我從國小畢業了。

  Today, I graduated from elementary school.

  從～畢業

- 今天有畢業典禮。

  There was a graduation ceremony today.

  畢業典禮

- 今天我去參加姊姊的畢業典禮。

  Today, I went to my sister's graduation ceremony.

- 爸爸休了一天假來參加我的畢業典禮。

My father took a day off from work and came to my graduation ceremony.

休假一天

- 爸爸因為出差而不能來參加我的畢業典禮。

My father couldn't make it to my graduation because of his business trip.

來～、到達

出差

- 我代表全體畢業生領獎。

I received an award as the representative of the graduating students.

• representative 代表

- 我送了老師一些花，然後我們一起照了張相。

I gave some flowers to my teacher, and we took a picture together.

- 遞給我畢業證書的時候，她緊緊的抱了我。

While handing me the diploma, she hugged me tightly.

• hand 遞給　diploma 畢業證書　hug 擁抱　tightly 緊緊地

- 一想到要離開我摯愛的學校就覺得很難過。

I was so sad at the thought of leaving my beloved school.

• beloved 摯愛的

- 一想到要和朋友分開我就哭了。

I cried at the thought of parting from my friends.

• part 分開

- 在畢業典禮的時候，我看到朋友們哭成一團。

I could see my friends crying here and there during the graduation ceremony.

- 我被分到台北國中就讀。

I was assigned to Taipei Middle School.

被分配

- 我們大部分都要去念台北國中。

Most of us are going to Taipei Middle School.

- Eric 和 Ted 會去信木國中就讀。

Eric and Ted will go to Shinmoo Middle School.

- 我很難過，因為我的好朋友和我會去不同的學校念書。

  I am so sad because my close friends and I will be going to different schools.

- 畢業典禮後，我和家人一起到外面吃飯。

  After graduation, I went out to eat with my family.

- 我不敢相信我現在是一個國中生了。

  I can't believe that I am a middle school student now.

- 畢業了很開心，但是我也有點害怕要變成國中生了。

  Graduating makes me happy, but I am also a bit scared of becoming a middle school student.

- 我和朋友一起拍了很多照片。

  I took a lot of photos with my friends.

開學 ★ Starting School

- 學校明天開學。

  School starts tomorrow.

- 今天開學了。

  Today, school started.

- 今天是開學的第一天，所以我見到了很久不見的朋友們。

  Today was the first day of school, so I met my friends after a long time.

- 因為我很久沒見到他們了，所以看到他們很開心。

  Because I hadn't seen them for a long time, I was so happy to see them.

- 早起上學對我來說很難。

  It was hard for me to wake up early to go to school.

- 有些朋友在放假期間長高了很多。

  Some of my friends grew much taller during vacation.

- 我的同學們全都曬黑了。

  All of my classmates were tanned.

  • tanned 曬黑

- 我昨天寫假期作業寫到很晚。

  I had to do my vacation homework until late last night.

- 我小心翼翼地把假期報告帶到學校。

  I carefully carried my vacation project to school.

- 我不小心把假期作業忘在家裡。

  I left my vacation homework at home by mistake.

- 只有 5 個學生交了假期作業。

  There were only 5 students who submitted their vacation homework.

  • submit 繳交

- 在放假過後的第一天看到老師，我發現她換了髮型。

  When I saw my teacher on the first day after vacation, I noticed that her hairstyle had changed.

  • notice 注意到

- 媽媽很開心我要回學校上課了。

  My mother is so happy that I'm going back to school.

- 為什麼假期總是這麼快結束？

  I wonder why vacations end so quickly.

- 隨著開學日期越來越近，我越來越不開心。

  As the school starting date is coming, I am becoming more depressed.

  • depressed 憂鬱的

新學年 ★The New School Year

- 因為暑假已經結束，所以新的學年開始了。

  Summer vacation has ended, so the new school year has begun.

- 從今天開始，我就是三年級生了。

  Starting today, I am a 3rd grader.

  • grader ～年級的學生

- 我不敢相信我已經四年級了。

  I can't believe that I am already in the 4th grade.

- 因為我現在已經升上更高年級了，所以我的態度也改變了。

  I found my attitude has changed (now that) I am in a higher grade.　既然、因為
  - attitude 態度、心態

- Eric 和我在同一班讓我覺得鬆一口氣。

  I feel relieved that Eric and I are in the same class.
  - relieved 放心的、安心的

- 要和好朋友分開真的很難過。

  I am really depressed about (parting ways) with my close friends.　分開

- 我希望新的導師是個好人。

  I hope my new (homeroom teacher) is a nice person.　導師

- 我很擔心，因為我的導師是以可怕出名的。

  I am worried because I have a homeroom teacher who is famous for being scary.

- 新的導師是我們學校裡唯一的男老師。

  The new homeroom teacher is the one and only male teacher at my school.
  - one and only 唯一的　male 男性的

- 老師從華中國小轉來我們學校任教。

  My teacher has transferred to my school from Hwajung Elementary School.

- 老師比我預期的還親切。

  The teacher was kinder than I had expected.

- 我今年的目標是交到很多朋友。

  My goal for this year is to make a lot of friends.

- 我會更用功讀書，因為我升上五年級了。

  I will study harder since I am in the 5th grade.

- 每當我升上了更高的年級，媽媽就會告訴我說我長大了。

  Whenever I go up to a higher grade, my mother tells me that I am all grown up.

- 新學年開始的好處就是我可以買新的學校用品了。

  A good thing about having the new school year is that I can buy new school supplies.
  └─ 學校用品

轉學生 ★Transferred Students

- 今天有一個新同學來到我們班上。

  Today, a new student came to my class.

- 新轉來的同學叫作 Tony。

  The newly transferred student's name is Tony.

- 新同學很外向，所以他很受歡迎。

  The new student is outgoing, so he is popular.
  • outgoing 外向的　popular 受歡迎的

- 新同學很有禮貌，也很安靜。

  The new student is very well-mannered and quiet.
  • well-mannered 有禮貌的

- 老師要求我幫助新同學。

  My teacher asked me to help out the new student.

- 我會幫助新同學適應我們學校。

  I will help the new student to fit well into our school.
  └─ 適應、適合

- 我想和新同學當朋友。

  I want to be friends with the new student.

- Tony 轉到另外一間學校了。

  Tony transferred to another school.

- 因為 Tony 轉到另一間學校了，所以我覺得很孤單。

  Because Tony transferred to another school, I am lonely.

- 明天我要轉學到另一間學校。

  I am transferring to another school tomorrow.

- 因為我即將要去新學校，我覺得既興奮又緊張。

  Now that I am going to a new school, I am both excited and nervous.

- 因為我搬家了，所以也轉學到新學校了。

  Because I moved, I also transferred to a new school.

- 我的新學校叫作民生國小。

  My new school's name is Minsheng Elementary School.

- 班上同學都很親切。

  All of my classmates are very kind.

- 今天我和一個叫作 Amy 的女孩變熟了。

  Today, I got close with a girl called Amy.
  變熟

- 因為我在這裡沒有很多朋友，我覺得有點孤單。

  Because I don't really have many friends here, I feel a bit lonely.
  • lonely 孤單的　有點

- 我想盡快和班上同學變成好朋友。

  I want to be good friends with my classmates as soon as possible.
  盡快

- 新學校的操場比之前學校的還大。

  My new school has a bigger schoolyard than my previous school.
  • previous 之前的

- 因為這間新的學校在幾年前才剛成立，所以它的設備都非常好。

  Because the new school was founded only a few years ago, its facilities are very good.
  • found 設立、成立　facility 設備

- 我的新學校的設備太過老舊，所以用起來非常不方便。

  老舊的
  My new school's facilities are so worn out that they are very inconvenient to use.
  • inconvenient 不方便的

- 我想念以前學校的朋友們。

  I miss my friends from my old school.

選班級幹部 ★ Class Elections

• 明天要選班級幹部。

There will be a class election tomorrow.
• election 選舉

• 今天要選班長。

Today, there was an election for
class president.
└─ 班長

• 我們學校允許二年級到六年級的班級選級長。

My school allows the classes from grade 2 to grade 6 to have presidents.

• 我想當班長。

I want to be the class president.

• 這是我第一次出來競選，所以我很緊張。

It is my first time to run in an election, so I am nervous.
└─ 競選

• 我不知道演講稿該寫些什麼。

I don't know what to write for my speech.
• speech 演講（稿）

• 很受歡迎的同學通常都會被選為第一學期的班長。

Usually, the popular kids are chosen as the 1st semester presidents.
└─ 被選擇、被選上
• semester 學期

• 因為 Sam 很受歡迎，所以他總是被選作班長。

Because Sam is popular, he is always elected president.
• elect （選舉）選上、選出

• Sam 是我最大的競爭對手。

Sam is my biggest competitor.
• competitor 競爭對手

• 我朋友推薦我當班長候選人。

My friend recommended me as a presidential candidate.
• recommend 推薦　candidate 候選人

- 我說如果我當上班長，我會讓我們班變成學校裡最有趣的班級。

  I said that if I become the class president, I will make my class the most fun class in the school.

- 我在講競選班長的理由的時候在發抖。

  As I was saying my reasons for running for president, I was shaking. 競選

- Sam 是男生的班長，Amy 則是女生的班長。

  Sam became the male president, and Amy was the female one.
  • female 女性的、女性

- 我覺得很多同學投給 Amy 的原因是因為她很善良。

  I think a lot of my classmates voted for Amy because she is very nice.

- 我聽說 Sam 當上了二班的班長。

  I heard that Sam became the president of class 2.

- 剛轉來的同學被選為班長。

  A student who just transferred was elected the president.

- 班長選舉我只輸了二票，不過我還是很開心可以以第二名擔任副班長。

  選班長
  I only lost the presidential election by 2 votes. But I am still glad to become the vice president as the runner up.
  副班長 • vote（選舉）票、投票 亞軍、第二名

- 今天我出來競選班級幹部，可是沒選上。

  I ran in the class election today, but I lost.

- 我只差兩票而就選上班長了。

  I lost the presidential election by just two votes.

- Adam 在選舉中只拿到三票。

  Adam only got three votes in the election.

- Alice 在選副班長的時候自動棄選。

  Alice withdrew from the vice presidential election.
  • withdraw (withdraw-withdrew-withdrawn) 退出

- 我通常會在第二學期當班長。

  I usually become the class president in the 2nd semester.

- 媽媽說當第二學期的班長比較好做事。

  Mom says that being the 2nd semester's president is easier to work.

- 我真希望可以當上第二學期的班長。

  I really hope that I become the president in the 2nd semester.

- 我會盡我所能的當好第一學期的班長。

  I will do my best as the class president for the 1st semester.

- 老師的鼓勵讓我更加下定決心了。

  I became more determined because of my teacher's encouragement.

  • determined 下定決心的　encouragement 鼓勵、支持

選學生會長 ★ Student Council Leader Elections

- 明天要選學生會長。

  There will be the election for the student body president tomorrow. /
  There will be an election for the president of the student council tomorrow.

  • student body/council 學生會

- 我和朋友們一起在家準備選舉活動要用的宣傳資料。

  I made some promotional materials for the election campaign at home with my friends.

  宣傳資料　選舉活動

- 我每天早上在校門口都會看到正在進行的選舉活動。

  Every morning, I see the election campaigns going on at the school entrance.

  • entrance 入口、門

- 候選人為了選舉活動而忙碌的在學校裡到處穿梭。

  The candidates are busy campaigning for the elections around the school.

  • campaign 活動

- 學生會長是從六年級中選出來的，不過兩個副會長是從五年級和六年級學生中選出的。

  A student council leader is elected from among the 6th graders while two vice presidents are elected from both the 5th and 6th graders.

- 我很好奇誰會選上學生會長。

  I am really curious as to who will become the student president.

- Amy 的姊姊出來競選學生會長。

  Amy's older sister is running for president of the student council.

- 第一位候選人的演說是最令人印象深刻的。

  The first candidate's speech was the most memorable one.

  • memorable 令人印象深刻的

- 我投給第二個候選人。

  I voted for the 2nd candidate.

- 當我升上六年級的時候，我想要競選學生會長。

  I want to run for student council leader when I become a 6th grader.

- 我今天登記為候選人了，所以從現在開始我會忙著做競選活動。

  I registered as a candidate today, and I will be busy with my campaign from now on.

  • register 登記

- 我的朋友們幫忙做海報和牌子。

  My friends offered to help by making posters and pickets.

  • offer 提供～　picket 牌子

- 我當上學生會長了！

  I became the president of the student body!

家長會/家長觀摩教學/家長會談
★ PTA / Open Class / Parent-Teacher Conference

- 學校今天提早放學，因為要舉行家長會會議。

  School ended early today because there was a PTA meeting.
  • PTA (Parent-Teacher Association) 家長會

- 媽媽從家長會回來了。

  My mom came back from the PTA.

- 每次要開家長會會議的時候，媽媽都比我還要緊張。

  Whenever there is a PTA meeting, my mother gets more nervous than me.

- 因為我是班長，所以媽媽成了家長會代表。

  Because I am the class president, my mom became the Class Mom.
  家長會代表

- 今天有觀摩教學。

  We had an open class today.
  觀摩教學

- 媽媽今天來學校參加觀摩教學。

  My mother came to school today because there was an open class.

- 我在報告的時候非常緊張，因為爸媽都在場。

  I was really nervous during my presentation with my parents there.
  • presentation 成果發表

- 這一週有家長會談。

  This week, there is a parent-teacher conference.
  家長會談

- 我很好奇媽媽和老師談了些什麼。

  I wonder what my mother and teacher talked about.

- 媽媽從會談回來後，告訴我說老師說了很多有關於我的好話。

  My mother came back from the meeting, and she told me that teacher had said a lot of nice things about me.

- 我很開心，因為我聽到老師稱讚了我。

  I felt really happy because I heard that my teacher had complimented me.
  • compliment 稱讚

學期中活動與放假

Field Trip Day

Thursday, April 28, Sunny

I went to the Chiang Kai-shek Memorial Hall on a field trip yesterday. It is a famous attraction in Taipei, but it is not fascinating to me anymore because I have been there a lot with my mom. But I enjoyed playing and picnicking with my classmates. I hope we can go to a theme park for our next field trip.

校外教學　4月28日星期四，晴天

我昨天校外教學去了中正紀念堂。它是台北的知名景點，不過它對我來說已經再也沒有吸引力了，因為我已經和媽媽一起去過很多次了。但是我很享受和同學一起玩樂和野餐。我希望下次我們的校外教學能去主題公園。

·field trip 校外教學　attraction 景點　fascinating 極好的、迷人的

校外教學／營隊 ★ Field Trips / Retreats

- 明天是校外教學日。

  Tomorrow is a field trip day.

- 明天終於是校外教學的日子了。

  Tomorrow is finally the day we go on a field trip.

- 校外教學我去了故宮。

  I have been to the National Palace Museum on a field trip.

- 媽媽幫我打包了炸雞當午餐。

  My mother packed me fried chicken for lunch.

  • pack 打包

- 在巴士上我和 Amy 坐在一起。

  I sat with Amy in the bus.

- 因為巴士要搭很久，所以我吃了一些暈車藥避免想吐。

  Because of the long bus ride, I took some motion-sickness pills for nausea.

  • nausea 作嘔、想吐　暈車

- 我和朋友在巴士上玩遊戲玩得很開心。

  My friends and I had a fun time playing games on the bus.

- 我們到的時候已經到了午餐時間。我們坐在一起吃午餐。

  When we arrived there, it was already lunchtime. We sat together and ate lunch.

- 媽媽幫我帶了橘子和餅乾當點心。

  My mother packed tangerines and chips for snacks.

- 我很喜歡這次的校外教學，因為自由活動的時間很多。

  I really liked this field trip because we had a lot of free time.

- 我喜歡校外教學，因為我可以盡情的大吃點心。

  I love field trips because I can eat as many snacks as I want to.

- 在回家途中，我們全部的人都累到在巴士上睡著。

  On our way home, all of us were so tired that we fell asleep on the bus.

- 星期五我到花蓮參加童軍營隊。

On Friday, I went to Hualien for a Cub Scout retreat.

• retreat 靜修、營隊

- 我去了兩天一夜的學生代表營隊。／我和其他學生會成員一起去了兩天一夜的營隊。

I went to an overnight retreat for student representatives. /　學生代表
I went to an overnight camp with the other members of the student council.

• overnight 過夜的、一夜之間

- 我到花蓮三天參加校外教學。

I went to Hualien for 3 days on a school trip.

- 迎新活動說實在的有點無聊。

The orientation was actually a bit boring.

- 講師好可怕。

The instructor was really scary.

• instructor 講師

- Adam 在才藝表演的時候跳舞跳得很棒。

During the talent show, Adam danced wonderfully.　才藝表演

- 我最喜歡營火了。

I enjoyed the campfire the most.

- 因為在和朋友玩，所以我很晚才睡。／我和朋友一起玩到很晚才睡。

I didn't go to sleep until late at night because I was playing with my friends. / I stayed awake to play with my friends until late at night.

- 老師叫我們馬上去睡覺。

Our teacher told us to go to sleep right away.

- 營隊真的太好玩了。

The retreat was so much fun.

- 在學校的活動之中，校外教學是最有趣的。

Among the school events, a school trip is the most fun activity.

- 當我去校外教學的時候，比起學習些什麼東西，我更喜歡和朋友一起玩樂。

Whenever I go on a field trip, I enjoy playing with my friends far more than learning something.

才藝表演／成果發表會 ★ Talent Shows

- 下星期三學校有一場才藝表演。

There will be a school talent show next Wednesday.

才藝表演、成果發表會

- 我們在第三和第四節課的時候練習學校的才藝表演。

During 3rd and 4th periods, we practiced for the school talent show.

- 我們聚在 Adam 家裡練習。

We gathered at Adam's home and practiced.

- 我們班已經決定好要演《羅密歐與茱麗葉》了。

My class has decided to perform the play *Romeo and Juliet*.

• perform 表演　play 戲劇

- 我朋友和我會在才藝表演上跳舞。

My friends and I will dance in the talent show.

- 四班要表演真的很有趣的短劇。

Class 4 is performing a skit, and it is really funny.

• skit 短劇

- 我們決定上衣要穿白色，下半身穿黑色。

We decided to wear white for our tops and black for our bottoms.

• top 上衣　bottom 下著

- 我們班決定要借戲服。

My class decided to rent costumes.

• rent 借　costume 戲服

- 我們班的男生要示範表演跆拳道。

The boys from my class put on a taekwondo performance demonstration.

• performance 表演　demonstration 示範

- 我忙著練習學校的歌唱比賽。

I am very busy practicing for the school singing/choir competition.

• choir 合唱

- 我每天都在練習學校的演奏會。

  I am practicing for the school concert every day.

- 演出非常成功！

  The performance was a big success!

- 我們得到非常熱烈的掌聲。

  We got a huge round of applause.

  • huge 很大的、巨大的　a round of applause 一輪掌聲

- 我覺得我們班最棒。

  I think my class was the best.

- 媽媽在獻花給我的時候說我很棒。

  Mom said I was wonderful while handing me some flowers. / My mother said I did a good job and gave me some flowers.

  • hand 遞給　　做得很好

- 爸爸稱讚我說我是最棒的。

  Dad complimented me by saying I was the best one.

- 表演完以後，老師買了一些好吃的漢堡給我們班。

  After the performance, my teacher bought some delicious hamburgers for my class.

- 表演順利進行讓我如釋重負。

  I am so relieved that the performance went well.

  • relieved 安心的、輕鬆的　go well 進行順利

- 我覺得下次才藝表演我可以做得更好。

  I think I can do better at the next talent show.

- 媽媽錄下了完整的演出，所以我可以在家看。

  My mother videotaped the entire performance, so I could watch it at home.

  • videotape 錄影

運動會 ★ Field Days

- 今天在學校有運動會。

  We had a field day at my school today.

  運動會 (= sports day)

- 終於，今天就是我非常期待的運動會了。

  Finally, today was the field day that I had been waiting for so badly.

  • badly 非常地

- 我因為氣象預報說今天會下雨而很擔心，但是天氣非常好。

  I was worried because the weather forecast said that it would rain today. But the weather was very good.

  • weather forecast 氣象預報

- 運動會因為下雨而延期到下週。

  The field day has been postponed until next week because of rain.

  • postpone 延期

- 我被分到藍隊，而我妹妹在白隊。

  I was on Team Blue while my younger sister was on Team White.

- 我在教室把表演要穿的戲服換上了。

  I changed into my costume for the performance in the classroom.

  換成

  • costume 戲服

- 一年級表演了玩偶舞。

  Grade 1 performed a puppet dance.

  • puppet 木偶、玩偶　perform 表演

- 三年級表演了扇子舞。

  Grade 3 performed a fan dance.

- 五年級表演了民俗舞蹈。

  Grade 5 performed a folk dance.

- 丟沙包是最好玩的遊戲了。

  Throwing the beanbag was the most fun game.

  • beanbag 沙包

- 白隊以二比一贏得了拔河比賽。

  Team White won tug of war by a score of 2 to 1.

  拔河

- 賽跑我得了第二名。

  I came in 2nd place in the race.

- 我跑步的時候跌倒了。

  I fell down while running.

- 我被選做大隊接力的班級代表。

  I was chosen as the class representative for the relay.

  • representative 代表　relay 接力賽

- 藍隊贏了接力賽。

  Team Blue won the relay.

- 我們班在啦啦隊比賽得到最高分。

  My class received the highest score in the cheering competition.

  • cheer 加油

- 白隊是運動會的冠軍。

  Team White was the winner of the field day.

- 學弟妹們跑來跑去、滾著大球的時候看起來好可愛。

  The young ones looked so cute when they were running around, rolling the big balls.

- 二年級的座位正對陽光，所以我的眼睛好痛。

  The 2nd graders' seats were directly facing the sun, so my eyes hurt.

  • directly 直接地　face 面對

- 我午餐吃了媽媽做的炒飯。

  I ate fried rice that my mom made for lunch.

- 因為是運動會，所以提供了很多種好吃的食物當作午餐。

  Since it was field day, many delicious foods were provided for lunch.

  • provide 提供

- 跑了一整個早上似乎讓我覺得午餐特別好吃。

  Running around all morning seemed to make me think that lunch tasted especially good.

- 我喜歡運動會，因為不用上課！

  I like field day because there are no classes!

- 每當運動會結束，我們一家就會出去吃飯。

  Whenever field day is over, my family goes out to eat.

- 難怪運動會甚至比校外教學還要好玩！

  No wonder field day is even more fun than a field trip!

提早放學／停課／校慶

★ Early Dismissal / Temporary Closing of the School / School Foundation Day

- 因為明天有才藝表演，所以今天提早放學了。

  Because there is a talent show tomorrow, the school hours were shortened today.

  • shorten 縮短、變短

- 今天學校第四節就放學了。

  Today, school was dismissed after 4th period.

  • dismiss 解散、使離開　period 期間、一堂課

- 畢業典禮結束之前都會提早放學。

  School will get out early until the graduation ceremony of school is over.

- 學校暫時因為長假而關閉，明天不用上學。

  There is no school tomorrow because the school will be temporarily closed for long holidays.

  • 經政府下令停課的上課日，多半是因為和假日連成長假，所以決定放假。

- 今天是我們學校的校慶。

  Today is my school's foundation day.
  校慶

- 我今天因為校慶而沒去上學。

  I didn't go to school today because it is my school's foundation day.

- 因為奶奶生日，所以我提交了請假單並回老家去。

  Because of my grandmother's birthday, I turned in an excused absence form and went back to my hometown.
  提交　請假

  • form 申請表

- 我提交了請假單，然後到台北家族旅行了三天。

  I turned in an excused absence form and went on a family trip to Taipei for 3 days.

- 我交了請假單，然後和阿姨一家人一起去了台北。

  I turned in an excused absence form to go to Taipei together with my aunt's family.

志願服務 ★ Volunteer Work

- 我做的志願服務是幫一年級打菜。

  For my volunteer work, I helped serve lunch to 1st graders.

  （志願服務）

- 我在志願服務網站登記當義工。

  I signed up to be a volunteer on the volunteer work website.

  （申請、登記）

  • volunteer 志工、義工

- 沒有很多志願服務的機會可以提供給國小學生參與。

  There are not many volunteer opportunities that elementary students can participate in.

  • participate 參與

- 我每年必須當兩小時的志工。

  I have to do 2 hours of volunteer work per year.

- 我參加過一個身心障礙者計畫，可以了解身心障礙者的經驗。

  I have been to a disability program designed for understanding the experience of people with disability.

  • disability 障礙

- 我做的志願服務是在公園打掃步道。

  I cleaned up the trails at the park for my volunteer work.

  • trail 步道

- 我今天的志願服務是在學校附近撿垃圾。

  Today, I picked up trash around the school area for my volunteer work.

- 雖然天氣很冷，可是看到打掃完的公園，我覺得心情很好。

  Although it was cold, I felt good after seeing the cleaned-up park.

  （打掃完的）

- 今天我們合唱團一起到養老院去做義工。

  Our choir went to a nursing home to do some volunteer work today.

  （養老院）

- 我們在長者的面前唱歌。

We sang in front of the elderly.
> 有年紀的人、老年人

- 那些像是我們的爺爺奶奶的長者，他們全心全意的歡迎我們到來。

The elderly, who are like our grandparents, wholeheartedly welcomed us.
• wholeheartedly 全心全意地

- 志願服務並不容易，可是辛苦得很值得。

Volunteer work is hard, but it is still worth it.

- 我希望參與各式各樣的志願服務。

I would like to participate in various types of volunteer work.

- 我爸媽一直都在做志工，現在我也在跟他們一起做志願服務。

My parents have always been volunteer workers, and now I am doing volunteer work together with them.

- 我剛好和姊姊做一樣的志願服務。

I just happen to do the same volunteer work as my sister does.
> 剛好

放假 ★ Vacation

- 距離放假只剩一個星期了。

There is only a week left before vacation starts.

- 我等不及要放假了，希望假期快點來！

I can't wait for vacation. I hope it comes soon!

- 今天我的暑假／寒假開始了。

Today my summer/winter vacation started.

- 學校今天提早放學，因為我們只需要參加休業式。

School finished early today because we only had the end of semester assembly.
• assembly 集會
> 休業式

- 我做了一個放假的生活計畫表。 I made a (daily schedule) for vacation.
  生活計畫表、日程表

- 我喜歡放假，因為可以睡很晚。 I like vacation because I can sleep in late.

- 我決定放假要去學游泳。 I've decided to learn how to swim during vacation.

- 我放假必須去上加強班。 I have to take some intensive courses during vacation.
  • intensive 加強的

- 我答應媽媽說我放假時會看很多書。 I promised my mom that I would read many books during vacation.

- Adam 說他放假會出國旅行。 Adam said he is traveling abroad during the vacation.
  • abroad 到國外

- 這次放假，我會到菲律賓學英文。 This vacation, I will be going to the Philippines to learn English.

- 因為我放假了，所以我去了花蓮的奶奶家。 Since I am on vacation, I visited my grandmother's house in Hualien.

- 在學校放假的時候，我和阿姨一家人一起去了花蓮。 I went to Hualien with my aunt's family during my school vacation.

- 因為我放假了，我和家人一起到中國去家族旅行。 Since I am on vacation, I went to China on a family trip.

- 我不敢相信假期只剩一半了。 I can't believe that only half of my vacation is left.

- 因為我放假還去補習，所以完全沒有假期的感覺。 Since I go to cram schools during vacation, it doesn't feel like a holiday at all.

- 我比較喜歡放暑假，因為暑假比寒假還長。

  I prefer summer vacation because it is longer than winter vacation.

- 放假的時候，時間過得比平常還要快。

  During vacation, time passes faster than other days.

- 我因為假期太短暫而覺得難過。

  I am sad because vacation is too short.

- 只要想到假期就讓我很開心。

  Just thinking of vacation makes me feel happy.

- 雖然要放假了，可是我還是連休息一下都不行，因為我必須去補習。

  Though it is time for vacation, I can't even get any rest because I have to go to cram school.

假期作業 ★ Vacation Homework

- 我的假期作業是寫日記、讀書心得和跳跳繩。

  My vacation homework is to write in my diary, to write a book report, and to jump rope.

- 日記最少一週要寫兩次。

  I have to write in my diary at least two times a week.

- 假期作業中必須要寫五篇讀書心得。

  I have to write five book reports for vacation homework.

- 我們班放假都要寫很多作業。

  My class is always given a lot of homework for vacation.

- 為了完成寫一封信給親戚的作業，我寫了一封信給爺爺。

  I wrote a letter to my grandfather (in order to) do my homework of writing a letter to a relative. 為了

  • relative 親戚

- 我今天參觀了故宮，因為假期作業要求參觀一間博物館。

  I visited the National Palace Museum today because I had to visit a museum for my vacation homework.

- 我為了假期作業去參觀了美術館。

  I visited an art museum for my vacation homework.

- 新學期在下週開始，可是我還沒完成任何假期作業。

  The new semester will start next week, but I haven't finished any of my vacation homework yet.

- 從今天開始我真的必須認真寫假期作業了。

  I really have to work hard on my vacation homework starting today.

- 昨天我寫假期作業寫到很晚。

  Yesterday, I did my vacation assignment until late at night.

  • assignment 作業

- 從下次開始，我會提早開始寫假期作業。

  Starting next time, I will do my vacation homework beforehand.

  • beforehand 事先、提前

- 放假就是要休息！為什麼要有這些作業？

  Vacations are for resting! What's all this homework for?

- 多希望有一個長官出現，許我們一個零作業的假期！

  I wish we had a superintendent who would give us a homework-free vacation!

  • superintendent 管理者、監督者　-free 沒有～的

上補習班

Life Tied up with Cram School Friday, June 5, Cloudy

I go to an English cram school on Mondays, Wednesdays, and Fridays and to a math cram school on Tuesdays and Thursdays. I study better by going to the cram schools than by studying alone at home. But the large amount of homework for my cram schools does not allow me to play. I am afraid that I might fall behind at school if I don't go to my cram schools, though.

被補習班綁住的生活　　6月5日星期五，陰天

我每週一、三、五上英文補習班，週二、四上數學班。比起自己在家裡念書，我到補習班可以念得更好，可是大量的補習班作業讓我沒有時間可以玩。即便如此，我害怕如果不去補習班的話，我在學校的成績就可能會落後其他人。

· (be) tied up with 忙著～、被綁住　**amount** 份量、數量　**fall behind** 落後

上補習班 ★ Going to a cram school

- 我一週上三次跆拳道。
  I go to a taekwondo studio three times a week.

- 我沒有補很多習。
  I don't go to many cram schools.

- 我連一家補習班也沒上。
  I don't even go to a single cram school.

- 我只有補英文。
  I only go to an English cram school.

- 我在平日總是必須補習。
  I always have to go to my cram school on weekdays.

- Adam 和我上同一間補習班。
  Adam and I go to the same cram school.

- 比起自己在家裡念書，我到補習班可以念得更好。
  I study better by going to the cram school than by studying alone at home.

- 比起補習，我比較喜歡在家念書。
  I prefer studying at home than going to a cram school.

- 星期二很累，因為我要上數學和英文課。
  Tuesdays are so tiring because I have math and English lessons.
  • tiring 累人的、疲倦的

- 上星期六我考了補習班的分級考。
  I took a level test for a cram school last Saturday.

- 星期四我很有空，因為我只需要上鋼琴課。
  I am pretty free on Thursdays because I only have a piano lesson.

- 星期五不用補習。
  Friday is a no-cram-school day.

- 我轉到台北英文補習班上課了。
  I transferred to Taipei English.

- 我在補習班上高級班。
  I am in the high level at my cram school.

- 因為我星期三沒去補自然，所以我今天必須去補課。

  Because I missed my science class on Wednesday, I had to attend a makeup class today.

  補課

- 因為要上跆拳道，我把寫作課從星期二挪到星期三。

  Because of my taekwondo classes, I changed my writing class from Tuesdays to Wednesdays.

- 我把鋼琴課從一週三次減少到一週兩次了。

  I cut my piano lessons from three times a week to two times.

- 補習班的接駁車在整個鎮裡繞太久了。

  My cram school shuttle bus goes around the whole town too much.

- 因為我錯過了巴士，所以媽媽開車載我去。

  Because I missed the bus, my mother drove me.

- 我這整個星期都無法去補習班，因為我病得很嚴重。

  I couldn't go to my cram school for this whole week because I was very sick.

- 我因為在朋友家玩而補習遲到，所以媽媽責罵我。

  My mom scolded me because I was late for my cram school while playing at my friend's house.

- 這個月之後我就不上寫作課了。

  I will stop going to my writing classes after this month.

- 我想要繼續上鋼琴課。

  I want to continue my piano lessons.

  • continue 繼續

英文／英文補習班 ★ English / English Lessons

- 我不補英文。

  I don't go to an English cram school. /
  I don't take any English private lessons.

- 我透過寫寄來我家的學習單來學英文。

  I study English by doing the worksheets delivered to me at my home.

  • worksheet 學習單　delivered 寄送

- 我用網路視訊學英文。

  I study English by the web conferencing system. （視訊系統）

- 我在學校的課後輔導學英文。

  I learn English in the after-school program at school.

- 我星期一、三、五上英文補習班。

  I go to an English cram school on Mondays, Wednesdays, and Fridays.

- 我的程度很好。

  My level is high.

- 我在英文補習班學自然發音。

  I am learning phonics at my English cram school.

- 我們補習班以作業超多而出名。

  My Cram school is famous for giving out tons of homework. （非常多的）

- 每天我都有線上作業。

  Every day, I have online homework.

- 我每天都必須背 30 個單字。

  I have to memorize 30 words per day.

  • memorize 背誦

- 我因為作業而要寫英文日記。

  I have to keep an English diary for my homework.

- 我因為英文補習班的作業太多而很痛苦。

  I am having a hard time because I have too much homework for English cram school.

- 我的讀書心得被選為本月最佳讀書心得。

  My book report was selected as the book report of the month.

  • select 挑選

- 我聽不懂外籍老師在講什麼。

  I don't understand the native English teacher.

- 我的外籍老師是從澳洲來的。 　　My native teacher is from Australia.

- 我的老師是台籍美國人，所以他的中文說得很好。 　　My teacher is Taiwanese-American, so he speaks Chinese very well.

  • Taiwanese-American 台籍美國人

數學習作／數學補習班 ★ Math Workbooks/Math Cram School

- 我每天早上都會練習一張計算題。 　　I practice an arithmetic worksheet every morning.

  • arithmetic 算數的、演算的

- 我每天都會寫四頁數學習作。 　　I do 4 pages in my math workbook each day.

  • workbook 習作、練習本

- 我昨天沒有寫完學習單。 　　I didn't finish my worksheets yesterday.

- 我被媽媽罵了，因為我習作的進度落後。 　　I got into trouble with my mother because I was behind schedule in doing my workbook.

  進度落後

- 我星期二、四會去補數學。 　　I go to my math cram school on Tuesdays and Thursdays.

- 我有一個數學家教。 　　I have a math tutor.

  • tutor 家教

- 我和朋友一起讀書的時候會更認真。 　　I study harder when I study with my friends.

- 我通常是一個人在家解練習本的題目來念數學。 　　For math, I study alone at home by solving problems in a practice book.

  • solve 解決、解題　　　練習本

- 我用線上課程學數學。 　　I study math through an online class.

  線上課程

- 我檢討了錯的答案，然後在我的筆記本上重新解題。

  I reviewed the wrong answers and resolved them in my notebook.
  • review 檢討　resolve 解決

- 我在學校學的數學對我來說很簡單。

  The math I learn at school is easy for me.

- 因為我現在升上了五年級，數學變得更難了。

  Math has gotten harder now that I am in the 5th grade.

- 我覺得我必須去補數學。

  I think I have to go to a math cram school.

- 我每個學期都會寫完三本數學習作。

  I complete 3 math workbooks per semester.

- 數學補習班老師出太多作業了。

  My math cram school teacher gives out too much homework.

- 幾何是我的弱點。

  Geometry is my weak spot.
  • geometry 幾何、圖形　弱點

- 我去上了新的數學補習班。

  I moved to a new math cram school.

- 很多學生在補習班學更進階的數學。

  A lot of students learn more advanced math at cram schools.
  • advanced 進階的

- 我的數學成績在我開始上數學補習班以後進步很多。

  My math grade improved a lot after I started taking math lessons at a cram school.
  • improve 進步

鋼琴／小提琴／長笛課 ★ Piano/Violin/Flute Lessons

- 今天我第一次去上鋼琴課。

  Today, I went to the piano class for the first time.

- 我每天都去上鋼琴。

  I take piano lessons every day.

- 我從七歲就開始上鋼琴課。

  I have been taking the piano lessons since I was seven.

- 我每週上兩次鋼琴家教課。

  I have piano class from a visiting tutor twice a week.

- 我最近在學拜爾的樂譜。

  Currently I am learning Beyer sheet music.

  • currently 最近、現在

- 我終於進階到徹爾尼的 100 首樂譜了。

  I finally got to the Czerny 100 sheet music.

- 在所有補習課程之中，我最喜歡的就是鋼琴課了。

  Among the classes that I am attending, I like piano classes the most.

- 鋼琴老師說我對鋼琴很有天分。

  My piano teacher said that I am talented in piano.

  • talented 有天分的

- 我的夢想是成為鋼琴家。

  My dream is to be a pianist.

- 我再也不想上鋼琴課了。

  I don't want to take piano lessons anymore.

- 這個星期四的鋼琴課上有一場成果發表會。

  There is a recital for my piano lessons this Thursday.

  • recital 成果發表會

- 我在發表會上要彈的曲名叫做《筷子進行曲》。

  The title I am going to play at the recital is "Chopsticks."

- 我還沒有背下整首曲子。

  I haven't memorized the whole piece yet.

  • piece （美術、音樂等）作品

- 今天的鋼琴課有一場發表會。

  Today there was a recital for my piano class.

- 我在鋼琴課努力練習，因為下週有比賽。

  I practiced very hard in the piano class because of the competition next week.

  • competition 比賽

- 我參加了鋼琴比賽然後得到了金獎。

I competed in the piano competition and won the Gold Prize.

・compete 比賽、競爭

- 因為我升上了三年級，所以我開始學拉小提琴。

I started learning to play the violin now that I am 3rd grader.

- 媽媽問我想不想學小提琴。

My mother asked me if I want to learn to play the violin.

- Amy 小提琴拉得非常好。

Amy plays the violin very well.

- 學小提琴需要大量的練習。

It takes a lot of practice to learn to play the violin.

- 我在學校的管弦樂隊拉小提琴。

I play the violin in the school orchestra.

- 因為我才剛開始學小提琴，會拉的曲子還沒幾首。

Because I just started learning to play the violin, there are not many musical pieces that I can play.

樂曲

- 小提琴課的老師很嚴格。

My violin teacher is very strict.

- 我想要學長笛。

I want to learn to play the flute.

- 我開始學吹長笛。

I started learning how to play the flute.

- 長笛的聲音很美妙。

The flute has a very beautiful sound.

- 我一週上一次長笛課。

I have a flute class once a week.

美術班 ★ Art Class

- 我每個星期四上美術班。

I go to art class every Thursday.

- 我有時候會沒去上其他補習班，可是我絕不會錯過美術班。

I sometimes skip other cram schools, but I never miss art class.

・skip 略過、跳過 miss 錯過

- 今天我在美術班做了一個聖誕花圈。

  Today I made a Christmas wreath in my art class.

  • wreath 花圈

- 今天我在美術班用陶土捏了人偶。

  Today I made a human figure with clay in my art class.

  • figure 形狀

- 老師叫我們畫一幅有關暑假的畫。

  My teacher told us to draw a picture about summer vacation.

- 比起畫畫，我更喜歡做手工藝。

  I prefer crafting to drawing.

  • craft 製作手工藝品、工藝品

- 我和一些年紀比我大的三年級學生同班。

  I am in the same class with the 3rd graders, who are older than me.

- 當我畫畫的時候，壓力全都消失了。

  When I draw, all my stress disappears.

  • disappear 消失

- 我喜歡上美術班，因為不用寫作業。

  I like the art class because there is no homework.

- 上美術班的時候有很多東西要帶。

  There are a lot of things to bring when going to the art class.

- 做為假期作業，我交了一件我在美術班做的作品。

  As a vacation project, I turned in the piece that I made in my art class.

  提交、繳交

跆拳道／跳繩／游泳 ★ Taekwondo/Jump Rope/Swimming

- 我在三點上跆拳道。

  I go to taekwondo class at 3 o'clock.

- 我七歲開始學跆拳道。

  I started to learn taekwondo when I was seven.

- 我現在是綠帶。

  I am in the green belt level.

- 今天跆拳道課有分級測試。

  Today there was a belt test in my taekwondo class.

- 我在今天的分級測驗得到了黑帶。

  I got black belt in today's belt test.

- 我參加跳繩班。

  I attend jump rope class.

- 今天我跳繩跳了 300 下。

  Today I did jump rope for 300 times.

- 今天我跳繩跳了 10 次二連跳。

  Today I did double skipping for 10 times.

  （跳繩）二連跳

- 我還是不會跳交叉跳。

  I still can't do the cross jump.

- 跳繩的時候我都會流很多汗，可是我覺得很神清氣爽。

  When I do jump rope, I sweat a lot but it feels refreshing.

  • refreshing 神清氣爽的、消除疲勞的

- 在跳繩課裡面，就屬星期四的課最有趣了。

  Among the jump rope lessons, Thursday one is the most fun.

- 我不會游泳。

  I can't swim.

- 我很怕水。

  I am afraid of water.

- 我開始學游泳，因為夏天到了。

  I started to learn swimming because it is summer.

- 今天的游泳課我學了仰式。

  Today in the swimming class, I learned backstroke.

  • backstroke 仰式

- 蛙式比自由式來得舒服。

  Breaststroke is more comfortable than free stroke.

  • breaststroke 蛙式　free stroke 自由式

- Eric 會游蝶式。

  Eric can do butterfly.

  • butterfly 蝶式

- 每當我游完泳，我都覺得很餓。 — Whenever I finish swimming, I feel hungry.

- 游泳很有趣，可是我非常討厭游泳的時候水跑進鼻子裡。 — Swimming is fun, but I really hate getting water in the nose while swimming.

- 我很怕水，可是在學了游泳以後我的恐懼就一掃而空了。 — I was afraid of water, but my fear disappeared after learning swimming.

電腦 ★ Computer

- 我報名了課後電腦班。 — I signed up for the after-school computer class.

- 我報名了電腦班的程式設計課程。 — I signed up for programming lessons at the computer class.

- 我想學 Photoshop，可是媽媽要我報名 PowerPoint 班。 — I wanted to learn Photoshop but Mom told me to sign up for PowerPoint class.

- 我一分鐘可以打 30 個字。 — I can type 30 characters per minute.
  • character 字體、符號

- Sam 是我們班打字速度最快的同學。 — Sam types at the fastest rate in my class.
  • rate 速度

- 他一分鐘可以打 100 個英文字母。 — He can type about 100 English letters per minute.

- 我必須多多練習打字。 — I have to practice typing hard.

- PowerPoint 班很有趣。 — The PowerPoint class is very fun.

- 我報名了 Microsoft Office 考試。 — I registered for the Microsoft Office test.
  • register 報名

- 我下週要考 PowerPoint。
  I have a PowerPoint test next week.

- 我拿到了一張 Excel 的證書。
  I earned a certificate for Excel.
  • earn 取得（資格）　certificate 證書

- 自從我去上電腦班以後，我打字比以前快了。
  Since I went to the computer class, I can type faster than before.

- 我報名了一堂課來拿到 Microsoft Word 的證照。
  報名
  I enrolled in a class to earn a Microsoft word certificate.

芭蕾／舞蹈 ★ Ballet / Dance

- 我每週二和週四會去芭蕾舞班。
  I go to a ballet class on Tuesdays and Thursdays.

- 芭蕾舞班上有很多苗條又漂亮的女孩。
  There are a lot of skinny and pretty girls in the ballet class.
  • skinny 瘦的

- 在跳芭蕾之前，我們會先做伸展運動。
  Before doing the ballet, we do stretching first.
  • stretch 伸展、舒展肢體

- 我筋骨很軟／硬。
  I am flexible/stiff.
  • flexible 有彈性的　stiff 僵硬的

- 今天有一場芭蕾舞表演。
  There was a ballet performance today.

- 我真的很喜歡穿著芭蕾舞衣在觀眾面前表演。
  芭蕾舞衣
  I really like wearing ballet suits and performing in front of audience.
  • audience 觀眾

- 我的夢想是當芭蕾舞者。
  My dream is to be a ballerina.

- 我的芭蕾舞鞋在芭蕾舞班不見了。
  I lost my toe shoes in my ballet class today.

- 當我從芭蕾舞班下課回家的時候，我的腳好痛。

  When I come home after the ballet class, my legs hurt so much.

- 從這個月開始，我就要開始學跳舞了。

  From this month on, I will be learning dancing.

- 今天是第一堂課。

  Today was the first class.

- 要跟上舞步好困難。

  It's hard to follow the moves.
  • move 動作、移動

- 跳舞可以幫助我紓壓。

  Dancing helps me to release my stress.
  • release 紓解、解放

歷史／寫作／自然 ★ History / Essay Writing / Science

- 每個星期六，我都會去上內容包括參觀歷史遺跡的歷史課程。

  Every Saturday, I attend a history program that includes visiting (historical sites).
  歷史遺跡

- 歷史課的時候，我參觀了國立歷史博物館。

  I went to the National Museum of History in the history class.

- 今天我在 Adam 家裡一起進行了團體寫作課程。

  Today I had a private essay group lesson in Adam's house.

- 因為是討論課，所以真的很好玩。

  It was a discussion class so it was really fun.
  • discussion 討論

- 我們在自然補習班裡做實驗和寫實驗報告。

  In my science class, we do experiments and make lab reports.
  • experiment 實驗

- 我的目標是要成為科學家，所以我去補了自然。

  My goal is to be a scientist, so I go to science class.

Part

5

節慶、假日與家族活動

節慶與假日

Lunar New Year's Day   Tuesday, January 28, Cold

My family went to my grandparents' house for Lunar New Year's Day. My sister and I dressed up in new clothes and gave new year greeting to my grandparents. My grandpa gave me 1,000 for New Year's money. I love Lunar New Year's Day because I can get money by giving new year greeting. This year, I earned 10,000. Yeah!

農曆新年　　1 月 28 日星期二，寒冷

我們全家一起到爺爺奶奶家慶祝農曆新年。姊姊和我穿著新衣服向祖父母拜年。爺爺給了我一千元的壓歲錢。我好喜歡農曆新年，因為拜年我就可以拿壓歲錢。今年我拿到了一萬元。耶！

·**Lunar New Year's Day** 農曆新年　　**dress up** 穿上（衣服等）　　**earn** 賺到（錢）

新年 ★ New Year / New Year's Day

- 新的一年開始了。
  A new year has begun.

- 現在是新的一年。
  Now it's a new year.

- 新的一年開始,我現在十歲了。
  I am 10 now that a new year has begun.

- 今年是龍年。
  It is the year of the dragon.

- 根據農曆,今天是新年的第一天。
  Today is the first day of the new year according to the lunar calendar.
  根據 ── according to   農曆 ── lunar calendar

- 今年的春節假期很長。
  The lunar new year holiday is long this year.

- 新年我去了奶奶家。
  I went to my grandma's house for New Year's Day.

- 塞車很嚴重,讓我們花了 7 個小時才到達奶奶家。
  到達
  The traffic was so heavy that it took us 7 hours to get to my grandma's house.
  • traffic 交通   heavy (量比起平常)還要多、嚴重

- 因為是新年,所以有很多好吃的食物。／在新年的時候會準備很多食物。
  There is a lot of delicious food since it is New Year's Day. / A lot of food is served on New Year's Day.
  • serve (食物)上菜

- 媽媽準備了一些食物。
  My mother prepared some food.
  • prepare 準備

- 爸爸和我炸了一些雞肉。
  My father and I fried some chicken.

- 因為是新年,我吃了水餃。
  I ate dumplings because it was New Year's Day.

- 媽媽做的水餃總是如此美味。

  My mother's dumplings are always so delicious.

- 我一直吃個不停，肚子快要爆炸了。

  My stomach is about to explode from eating constantly. / My stomach (is about to) burst because I kept eating.

  將要～

  • explode 爆炸　constantly 持續地　burst 破裂

- 我吃了年糕，又長了一歲。

  I ate rice cake and aged a year.

- 我很早起床參加祭祖。

  I woke up early and participated in the (memorial service).

  祭祀、祭祖

- 祭祖結束後，我去了祖先的墓地。

  After the memorial service, I visited my ancestors' graves.

  • ancestor 祖先　grave 墳墓

新年家族聚會 ★ Family Gatherings on New Year's Day

- 在新年那天，我起得很早去了叔叔家。

  On New Year's Day, I woke up early and went to my uncle's house.

- 因為是新年假期，爺爺奶奶來了。

  My grandparents came for the new year holiday.

- 爸爸是長子，所以全部的親戚都來到我們家了。

  My father is the eldest son, so all of the relatives come to my house.

- 所有的親戚在新年齊聚一堂。

  All of my relatives (are gathered) together on New Year's Day.

  （因為活動等）聚集

- 當我們放假的時候，我所有的親戚就會聚集到爺爺家。

  When we have holidays, all of my relatives gather at my grandfather's house.

- 我們家和親戚們聚在一起打麻將。

  My family and relatives gathered together and played mahjong.

- 我聽說明天我們會去一些親戚家拜年。

  I heard that we will be visiting some of my relatives' homes to make new year's visits tomorrow.

  • make a visit 拜訪

- 我很開心叔叔一家人熱情地迎接我們。／我覺得高興，因為我叔叔一家人很開心見到我們。

  I was glad that my uncle's family welcomed us warmly. / I felt good because my uncle's family was very happy to see us.

- 表哥和我玩得很開心。

  My cousin plays well with me.

- 照顧比我年紀還小的堂弟妹讓我好累。

  I was so tired from (looking after) my cousins who are younger than me.

  照顧

- 我們家放假的時候哪裡也不去。

  My family doesn't go anywhere on holidays.

- 因為我沒有很多親戚，所以放假的時候覺得好無聊。

  Because I don't have a lot of relatives, I feel bored on holidays.

- 我覺得姑姑和媽媽都好可憐，因為她們做事好辛苦。

  I feel bad for my aunt and mother because they work too much.

- 我喜歡新年因為可以和親戚見面！

  I love New Year's Day because I get to meet my relatives!

- 因為是新年，我穿了新衣服。

  I dressed up in a new clothes because it was New Year's Day.

- 我去年穿的衣服已經太小了，所以我買了一件新的。／我買了新的衣服，因為我去年的衣服已經穿不下了。

  The clothes that I wore last year was too small for me, so I bought a new one. / I had new clothes because I outgrew the one that I wore last year.

  • outgrow（身體長大使得衣服尺寸）變得不合

- 我去年穿的褲子今年已經太短了。

  The pants that I used to wear last year are too short for me now.

- 我穿了新衣向爺爺奶奶拜年，祝他們新年快樂。

  I dressed up in new clothes, made New Year's greeting to my grandparents, and wished them a happy new year.

- 在向父母拜年之後，我收到了紅包。

  I received New Year's money 壓歲錢 after giving New Year's greeting 拜年 to my parents.

- 爸爸給了我一千元壓歲錢。

  My dad gave me 1,000 for my new year's money.

- 我喜歡新年，因為可以領壓歲錢。

  I love New Year's Day because I can get New Year's money.

- 我不能領很多壓歲錢，因為我的親戚很少。

  I can't get a lot of New Year's money because I have only a few relatives.

- 今年我領了一萬元壓歲錢。

  This year, I got 10,000 for my New Year's money.

- Amy 說她拿了 2 萬元的壓歲錢。

  Amy said she got 20,000 for her New Year's money.

- 我會用這筆錢買我想要的東西。

  I will buy what I want with this money.

- 我把壓歲錢存到儲蓄帳戶裡面。

  I put the new year's money into my savings account. 儲蓄帳戶

- 我用壓歲錢買了一些漫畫。

  With the New Year's money, I bought some comic books.

新年新希望 ★ New Year's Resolutions

- 我們全家人聚在一起，許下他們的新年新希望。

  Everyone in my family gathered and decided on their new year's resolutions.

  • resolution 決心

- 媽媽說她要減肥。

  My mom said she will lose some weight.

  • lose weight 減肥

- 爸爸說他要戒菸。

  My dad said he will quit smoking.

- 今年我要和朋友們好好相處，並且更用功讀書。

  This year, I will get along with my friends and study harder. 好好相處

- 新的一年我會看更多書。

  In the new year, I will read more.

- 今年我想要交更多朋友。

  This year, I want to make more friends.

- 今年我要更認真念數學。

  I will study math harder this year.

中秋節 ★ Mid-Autumn Festival

- 今天是中秋節。

  Today is Mid-autumn Festival.

- 中秋節是農曆 8 月 15 號。

  Mid-autumn Festival is August 15 on the lunar calendar.

- 今天在去奶奶家的路上塞車塞得很嚴重。

  There was heavy traffic on our way to my grandmother's house.
  在～途中

- 我們在休息站吃午餐。

  We ate lunch at the rest area.
  休息站

- 因為短暫的中秋假日，交通變得更擁擠了。

  The traffic was even heavier because of the short Mid-autumn Festival holiday.

- 因為是中秋節，親戚們在我家團聚。

  Since it is Mid-autumn Festival, our relatives gathered at my house.

- 親戚因為中秋節而來訪，所以我家非常擁擠。

  My relatives came for Mid-autumn Festival, so my house was packed/crowded.
  • packed 擁擠的　crowded 擁擠的

- 夜晚時，滿月高掛空中閃耀。

  At night, the full moon was shining up in the sky.
  滿月
  • shine 發光

- 我可以清楚地看見滿月，因為天氣很好。

  I could see the full moon clearly because the weather was good.
  • clearly 清晰地

- 因為天氣陰陰的，所以我看不見滿月。

  Because of the gloomy weather, I couldn't see the full moon.
  • gloomy 陰鬱的、陰天的

- 我向滿月許了願。　　　I made a wish to the full moon.
　　　　　　　　　　　　許願

中秋節飲食 ★ Mid-autumn Festival Foods

- 中秋節的代表食物是月餅。

    Mooncakes are the food that represents Mid-autumn Festival.

- 市場有很多剛收成的水果。

    There were a lot of newly harvested fruits at the market.

    • newly 新的　harvested 收穫的、收成的

- 我喜歡中秋節因為有很多好吃的食物可以吃。

    I love Mid-autumn Festival because there are so many delicious foods to eat.

- 媽媽從烘焙坊買了一些月餅。

    My mother bought some mooncakes from the bakery.

- 今年我們自己在家做月餅。

    We made mooncakes at home this year.

- 我們全家聚在一起做月餅。

    Everyone in my family gathered and made mooncakes.

- 我喜歡吃內餡是芝麻的月餅，所以我在每個月餅裡放了很多芝麻。

    I love mooncakes with sesame filling, so I put a lot of sesame seeds inside each mooncakes.

    • sesame (seed) 芝麻　filling （食物的）內餡

- 整個家裡都是月餅的味道。

    The entire house was filled with the smell of mooncakes.

- 我吃了好多月餅，肚子好飽。

    I was full from eating too many mooncakes.

- 弟弟和我剝了栗子來吃。

  My younger brother and I peeled chestnuts and ate them.

  • peel 剝（皮）　chestnut 栗子

- 我們家很喜歡吃栗子。

  My family loves chestnuts.

- 奶奶做了我最喜歡的柚子醬。

  My grandmother made my favorite pomelo sauce.

- 奶奶做的柚子醬最好吃了。

  My grandmother's pomelo sauce is the best ever.

國定假日 ★ National Holidays

- 因為國慶日，所以我今天不用去上學。

  Because of National Day, I don't need to go to school today. 國慶日

- 我今天和爸爸一起出去看國慶遊行。遊行樂隊和表演真的很棒！

  I went out with my dad to watch National Day parade today. The marching band and the performances were really fascinating!

  • parade 遊行　marching band 遊行樂隊

- 因為今天是國慶日，所以我掛起了國旗。

  Because of National Day, I hung up the national flag today.

  • hang up 掛起來　　　國旗

- 最近很少人在國慶日掛國旗了。

  There are few people nowadays hanging up national flags on National Day.

- 爸爸教我要怎麼把國旗掛起來。

  My dad taught me how to hang my national flag up.

- 每年的 4 月 5 日是清明節。

  Every April 5 is Qingming Festival.

  清明節

- 清明節時我們全家回老家掃墓。

  All of our family members went back to our hometown to sweep our ancestors' tombs on Qingming Festival.

  • sweep 清掃、打掃

- 我們在今年的清明節連假會回老家。

  We are going to go back our hometown during this Qingming Festival holidays.

- 當我們要去掃墓的時候，我們要事先準備一些用來祭拜祖先的鮮花和水果。

  When we are going to sweep our ancestors tombs, we need to prepare some flowers and fruits beforehand to worship our ancestors.

- 媽媽在清明節的時候做了一些潤餅捲。

  My mom made some steamed spring rolls on Qingming Festival. — 潤餅捲

- 我喜歡在潤餅捲裡面加上很多花生糖粉。

  I like to put a lot of powdered peanuts with sugar into a steamed spring roll.

- 今天是端午節。

  Today is Dragon Boat Festival.

- 端午節是農曆的 5 月 5 日。

  Dragon Boat Festival is on May 5 in lunar calendar.

- 因為今天是端午節，所以我和媽媽一起去廟裡拜拜。

  Because today is Dragon Boat Festival, my mom and I went to a temple to worship.

- 我們準備了一些粽子和水果來祭拜神靈。

  — 粽子

  We prepared some rice dumplings and fruits to worship gods and spirits.

  • spirit 精神、靈魂

- 我最喜歡吃裡面有蛋黃的粽子。

  The rice dumpling with yolk into it is my favorite.

  • yolk 蛋黃

- 媽媽包了很好吃的粽子。

  My mom made delicious rice dumplings.

- 教師節是在每年的 9 月 28 日。

  Teacher's Day is on September 28.

- 學校辦了教師節的慶祝活動。

  My school held a celebration for Teacher's Day.
  教師節

- 我們班一起做了卡片給老師。

  Students in our class made a card for my teacher.

- 老師對我們很好，所以我覺得我們應該要送一張感謝卡給她。

  My teacher is nice to us, so I think we should give her a thank-you card.
  感謝卡

- 老師收到感謝卡後很開心。

  My teacher was happy to get a thank-you card.

- 行憲紀念日在每年的 12 月 25 日。

  Every December 25 is our national Constitution Day.

  • constitution 憲法

- 行憲紀念日是為了紀念我們國家的憲法正式實行。

  紀念
  Constitution Day is in honor of the official enforcement of our national constitutional system.

  • enforcement 實行

- 因為行憲紀念日和聖誕節是同一天，很多人都不記得它了。

  Because Constitution Day and Christmas are on the same date, few people still remember our Constitution Day.

- 以前行憲紀念日有放假，但現在沒有放假了。

  Constitution Day used to be a holiday, but it's not now.

- 我希望所有的節日都能夠放假。

  I wish all the festivals could be holidays.

- 如果有更多假日，我就能夠更常出去和朋友一起玩了！

  If there are much more holidays, I can go out and play with my friends more often!

各種節日

Valentine's Day

Friday, February 14, Freezing

Today is Valentine's Day. In Taiwan, Valentine's Day is a day when girls give chocolates to the boys they like. Lisa passed out chocolates to all of her classmates. Adam received valentines from two girls. Oh, I envy him!

情人節　2月14日星期五，超級冷

今天是情人節。在台灣，情人節是女生送巧克力給她們喜歡的男生的日子。Lisa 分送了全班同學巧克力。Adam 收到兩個女生送的情人節禮物。喔，我好羨慕他！

· pass out 分送

情人節 ★ Valentine's Day

- 今天是情人節。

  Today is Valentine's Day.

- 在台灣，情人節是女生送巧克力給她們喜歡的男生的日子。

  In Taiwan, Valentine's Day is a day when girls give chocolates to the boys they like.

- 我和媽媽在家一起做了巧克力。

  I made chocolates at home with my mom.

- 我買了巧克力，並且把它和一張可愛的小卡一起包得漂漂亮亮的。

  I bought chocolates and wrapped them beautifully together with a cute little card.
  • wrap 包裝

- 我給了爸爸和弟弟巧克力。

  I gave chocolates to my father and younger brother.

- 因為是情人節，我分送了巧克力給我的同學們。

  I gave out chocolates to my classmates since it was Valentine's Day.
  分送

- Amy 給了全班同學巧克力。

  Amy gave chocolates to the entire class.

- 我有幾個朋友送了巧克力給她們喜歡的男生。

  Some of my friends gave chocolates to the boys that they like.

- Alice 送了巧克力給 Adam。

  Alice gave chocolates to Adam.

- 今天我收到了很多巧克力。我真受歡迎！

  Today, I received a lot of chocolates. I'm so popular!

- 今天我收到了 Amy 送的巧克力，我覺得很開心。

  Today, I received chocolates from Amy. I feel so good.

- 有個我不怎麼喜歡的男生一直來跟我要巧克力。

  A boy that I don't really like kept asking me for chocolates.
  • keep+Ving 一直～

白色情人節 ★ White Day

- 今天是白色情人節。

  Today is White Day.

- 白色情人節是男生送他們喜歡的女生糖果的日子。

  White Day is a day when boys give candy to the girls they like.

- 聽說白色情人節是由日本一間甜點公司所發明的。

  It is said that White Day was made up by a confectionery company in Japan.
  發明
  • confectionery 糕點糖果

- 我給了媽媽糖果。

  I gave candy to my mom.

- 今天我在學校收到了一些男生送的很多糖果。

  Today, I received a lot of candy from some boys at school.

- 我很開心可以收到這麼多糖果。

  I was so happy to get lots of candy.

- 我很開心,因為我原本沒有預期會收到糖果。

  I felt happy because I wasn't expecting candy presents.

- 我收到一個我不太喜歡的男生送的糖果。

  I got candy from a boy that I don't really like.

- 我很難過,因為我沒有收到任何糖果。

  I am so upset because I didn't get any sweets.
  • sweets 甜食、糖果

- 我很羨慕那些有收到糖果的朋友。

  I envied my friends who got sweets.

- 我桌子的抽屜裡有好幾盒糖果。

  There were candy packs inside my desk drawer.
  • packs 包、盒　drawer 抽屜

- 我很好奇是誰放的。

  I wonder who put them there.

- 送別人糖果的時候我既害羞又緊張。

  I was shy and nervous when giving candy.

- 我沒有想要送糖果的對象。

  There's no one that I want to give candy to.

- 爸爸送了媽媽和我糖果籃。

  My father gave candy baskets to my mother and me.

  • basket 籃

- 果然我爸爸是最棒的！

  No wonder my dad is the best!

兒童節 ★ Children's Day

- 今天是 4 月 4 號兒童節！

  Today is April 4, Children's Day!

- 因為是兒童節，我和家人一起去了遊樂園。

  遊樂園

  I went to an amusement park with my family because it was Children's Day.

- 因為是兒童節，所以我去了主題樂園。

  I went to a theme park because it was Children's Day.

- 爸爸買了一台腳踏車給我當兒童節禮物。

  My dad bought me a bicycle as a Children's Day present.

- 爺爺給了我一些零用錢當兒童節禮物。

  Grandpa gave me some pocket money as a Children's Day gift.

- 我收到了書和衣服當兒童節禮物。

  I received books and clothes as Children's Day presents.

- 兒童樂園有兒童節活動。

  There was a Children's Day event at the Children's Amusement Park.

- 有很多有趣的活動。

  There were a lot of fun events.

- 因為兒童節而有送免費的氣球和糖果。

  Free balloons and candy were given out 給 for Children's Day.

- 我很開心我拿到了很多禮物。

  I am happy that I got a lot of presents.

- 我參加了臉部彩繪和手環製作的活動。

  I participated in the face-painting and bracelet-making activities.

  • participate 參與　bracelet 手環

- 因為是兒童節，我們家一起到家庭餐廳吃飯。

  Because it was Children's Day, my family ate out at a family restaurant.

  • eat out 外食

- 其實我想吃義大利麵，可是弟弟堅持要吃牛肉麵，所以我們去了中式餐廳。

  Actually, I wanted to eat spaghetti, but my younger brother insisted on eating beef noodles. So we went to a Chinese restaurant. 堅持～

- 我真希望每天都是兒童節。

  I wish everyday were Children's Day.

母親節／父親節 ★ Mother's Day / Father's Day

- 今天是 5 月的第二個星期日，母親節。

  Today is the second Sunday of May, Mother's Day.

- 我在學校做了康乃馨胸花，並且將它們別在媽媽的胸前。

  I made carnation corsages at school and put them on my mother's chest.

  • corsage 胸花（別在衣服上的花飾）　chest 胸膛

- 我給了媽媽康乃馨胸花和卡片當作禮物。

  I gave carnation corsages along with a card to my mother as presents.

- 我和妹妹一起唱了爸媽最喜歡的歌。

  I sang my parents' favorite song to my parents together with my younger sister.

- 我在卡片上寫著，我不會再和妹妹吵架，也會聽爸爸的話。

  I wrote on the card that I won't fight with my younger sister anymore and will obey my father.
  • obey 遵守

- 媽媽說她被我的卡片感動了。

  Mom told me that she was moved by my card.

- 從現在開始我會當一個更好的兒子／女兒。

  I will be a better son/daughter from now on.

- 爸爸對他的父母親很孝順。

  My dad is such a good son to his parents.

- 我想要像爸爸一樣孝順。

  I want to be a good son like my dad.

萬聖節 ★ Halloween

- 今天是萬聖節，所以我們英文課的時候舉辦了萬聖節派對。

  Today was Halloween, so we had a Halloween party at my English class.

- 在從國外流傳進來的眾多節日之中，萬聖節最好玩了。

  Among the holidays coming from other countries, Halloween is most fun.

- 今天是學校的萬聖節扮裝派對。

  Today is school's costume party for Halloween.

- 我戴了女巫帽到學校。

  I went to school wearing a witch's hat.

- 我打扮成吸血鬼德古拉。

  I dressed up as Dracula.
  裝扮

- 我扮成白雪公主。

  I dressed up as Snow White.

- Eric 扮成蜘蛛人來了。

  Eric came as Spiderman.

- 男生的服裝看起來很可怕。

    The boys' costumes looked scary.

- 因為男生們都戴著面具，我分不出誰是誰。

    Because the boys were wearing masks, I couldn't tell who was who.

- 因為是萬聖節，學校發糖果給我們。

    My school gave out candy to us because it was Halloween.

- 外籍老師裝扮成女巫發糖果。

    My native teacher dressed up as a witch and gave out candy.

- 我們應該要說「不給糖就搗蛋」來拿糖果。

    We are supposed to say, "Trick or treat," to get candy.

    • trick or treat 不給糖就搗蛋（萬聖節時，孩子會挨家挨戶拜訪，當他們要糖果時所說的話）

- 我和弟弟一起去玩「不給糖就搗蛋」。

    I went trick or treating with my younger brother.

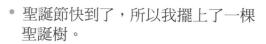 聖誕節 ★ Christmas

- 聖誕節快到了，所以我擺上了一棵聖誕樹。

    Christmas is coming soon, so I put up a Christmas tree.
    裝設、設置

- 我和弟弟一起裝飾聖誕樹。

    I decorated the Christmas tree with my younger brother.

    • decorate 裝飾

- 燈泡一閃一閃的真是漂亮。

    The twinkling lights of the bulbs are so beautiful.

    • twinkling 閃閃發光的　bulb 燈泡

- 擺上聖誕樹讓我有了聖誕節的感覺。

    Putting up the Christmas tree gave me a Christmas feeling.

- 我和妹妹一起開心地唱著聖誕歌。

I joyfully sang Christmas carols with my younger sister.

• joyfully 開心地

- 我最喜歡的聖誕歌是《耶誕鈴聲》。

My favorite Christmas carol is *Jingle Bells*.

- 我在英文課學了一些聖誕歌曲。

At my English class, I learned some carols.

- 我們今天在學校有一個聖誕派對。

Today, we had a Christmas party at my school.

- 我在學校做了一張聖誕卡。

I made a Christmas card at school.

- 當媽媽稱讚我的卡片看起來很漂亮的時候，我覺得很開心。

I felt good when my mom said that my card looked good.

- 我做了聖誕卡送給爺爺奶奶。

I made a Christmas card and gave it to my grandparents.

- 終於，聖誕節來了！

Finally, Christmas is here!

- 聖誕節是為了慶祝耶穌誕生。

Christmas celebrates Jesus's birth.

• celebrate 慶祝、紀念　birth 誕生

- 因為是平安夜，所以我們外出用餐。

It was Christmas Eve, so we ate out.

- 平安夜的時候我們買了蛋糕慶祝聖誕節。

We bought a cake and celebrated Christmas on Christmas Eve.

- 因為是平安夜，所以街上有很多人。

There were so many people on the streets since it was Christmas Eve.

- 我在平安夜到教堂參加耶誕彌撒。

On Christmas Eve, I went to church for the Christmas mass.

• mass 彌撒

- 我邀了朋友參加聖誕禮拜。

  I invited my friends to the Christmas service.

  • service 禮拜

- 聖誕節的時候，教會有耶穌誕生劇的表演。

  （聖誕節的時候孩子們表演的）耶穌誕生劇

  A (nativity play) was performed at my church on Christmas.

  • perform 表演

- 我希望今年聖誕節可以下很多雪。

  I hope it snows a lot on Christmas this year.

- 我希望今年會是白色聖誕節。

  I hope that we will have a White Christmas.

- 很遺憾地，聖誕節沒有下雪。

  Sadly, it didn't snow on Christmas.

聖誕禮物／聖誕老人 ★ Christmas Presents / Santa Claus

- 爸媽買了最新的手機給我當聖誕禮物。

  My parents bought me the latest (mobile phone) as a Christmas present.

  • latest 最新的　手機

- 弟弟收到機器人，而我則是收到滑板車當聖誕禮物。

  As a Christmas present, my younger brother got a robot, and I got a kickboard.

- 媽媽說不可以要貴的禮物。

  My mom told me not to ask for an expensive gift.

- 我在睡覺前把襪子掛在聖誕樹上。

  I hung the stockings on the Christmas tree before going to bed.

- 當我起床的時候，我知道聖誕老人有來看過我。

  When I woke up, I knew that Santa had visited me.

- 聖誕老人給了我幾本書。

  Santa Claus gave me some books.

- 也許聖誕老人不知道我想要什麼。　　　Maybe Santa doesn't know what I want.

- 我向他要了遊戲機。　　　I asked him for a game machine.

- 聖誕老人怎麼會知道我想要什麼？　　　How did Santa know what I wanted?

- 我家沒有煙囪，聖誕老人要怎麼進來？
  My house doesn't have a chimney. How can Santa come in?
  • chimney 煙囪

- 媽媽告訴我，因為我整年都很乖，所以聖誕老人給我禮物。
  My mom told me Santa gave me a gift because I had been good throughout the year.
  • throughout ～期間、總是

- 我覺得聖誕老人就是爸爸。　　　I think that Santa is my dad.

- 有一些朋友說聖誕老人是真的存在，可是其他人說不是。
  Some of my friends say that Santa is real while others say he isn't.

- 他們說聖誕老人是爸媽假扮的，禮物也是爸媽給的。
  They say that it is our parents who pretend to be Santa and give presents to us.
  —— 假裝～

- 弟弟還是相信有聖誕老人。
  My younger brother still believes in Santa.
  —— 相信～

Chapter 19

家族活動

Happy Birthday, Eric! Tuesday, November 11, Sunny

We had a birthday party for my little brother Eric. Several kids from his nursery school were invited. When I saw Eric receiving lots of gifts, I envied him. I wish my birthday would come soon. Anyway, happy birthday, my lovely cute bro!

Eric，生日快樂！　　11 月 11 日星期二，晴天

我們幫弟弟 Eric 辦了一個生日派對。他的幾個幼稚園同學也受邀參加。當我看到 Eric 收到很多禮物時，我好羨慕他。我希望我的生日可以快點來。不管怎樣，生日快樂，我可愛的弟弟！

· **nursery school** 幼稚園　　**envy** 羨慕　　**anyway** 不管怎樣　　**bro** brother 的縮寫

我的生日 ★My Birthday

- 我的生日是 4 月 8 號。

  My birthday is April 8.

- 星期三是我的生日。

  Wednesday is my birthday. /
  My birthday is coming up on Wednesday.

  （活動或是時間點）接近

- 今天是我期待已久的生日。

  Today is my birthday, which I have been badly waiting for.

  • badly 非常、很

- 因為今天是我的生日，所以我和朋友們一起開了一場生日派對。

  Since today is my birthday, I had a birthday party with my friends.

- 跆拳道班為這個月生日的人舉辦了生日派對。

  We had a birthday party at my taekwondo school for people whose birthdays are in this month.

- 我和朋友們一起在 VIPS 開了一場生日派對。

  I had a birthday party at VIPS with my friends.

- 我和朋友們在家裡辦了場生日派對。

  I had a birthday party at home with my friends.

- 我邀請了 Alice、Adam 和 Eric 來參加我的派對。

  I invited Alice, Adam, and Eric to my party.

- 我邀請了全班同學。

  I invited the entire class.

  • entire 整個的

- 我做了邀請卡給我的朋友們。

  I made invitations and gave them to my friends.

  • invitation 邀請卡

- 媽媽幫我們訂了披薩和炸雞。

  Mom ordered pizza and fried chicken for us.

- 媽媽做了炸雞和炸薯條給我們。

  My mother cooked fried chicken and French fries for us.

- Alice 送了我一本書，Adam 給了我一個陀螺當禮物。

  Alice gave me a book, and Adam gave me a top for presents.

- 因為 Sam 生病沒辦法來參加派對，我覺得很難過。

  I was sad that Sam couldn't make it to the party because he was sick.　到～、去～

- 今年我只和家人一起舉行了生日派對。

  This year, I had a birthday party with only my family.

- 爸爸帶了我最喜歡的冰淇淋蛋糕回家。

  My dad brought my favorite ice cream cake home.

- 爸爸買了一雙球鞋給我當禮物。

  My dad bought me sneakers as a present.

  • sneakers 運動鞋

- 奶奶給了我一些零用錢當生日禮物。

  Grandma gave me some pocket money for my birthday.

- 我很難過我的生日剛好在假期之中。

  I am so sad my birthday is during vacation.

- 我從朋友那裡收到很多禮物。

  I received plenty of presents from my friends.　很多

父母的生日 ★ Parents' Birthdays

- 我們去外面吃了晚餐，因為今天是媽媽的生日。

  We went out for dinner since it was my mother's birthday today.

- 因為今天是爸爸的生日，媽媽煮了一些很好吃的菜。

  Since it is my dad's birthday, my mom cooked some delicious food.

- 媽媽今年就 40 歲了。

My mom is turning 40 this year.

• turn （年紀）成為

- 我準備了一張生日卡片給媽媽。

I prepared a birthday card for my mother.

- 爸爸為媽媽買了蛋糕。

My dad bought a cake for my mom.

- 我用存起來的零用錢買了個鑰匙圈
給爸爸。

With my saved-up allowance, I bought a
key chain for my dad.
（存起來的）
（鑰匙圈）

• allowance 零用錢

- 我做了愛的兌換券當作爸爸的生日
禮物。

I made love coupons for my dad's birthday
present.

- 我和弟弟一起唱了一首歌。

Together with my younger brother, we
sang a song.

- 爸爸很謝謝我們。

My dad was grateful to us.

• grateful 感激的

- 媽媽收到我們的禮物很開心。

My mom was so happy to receive our
presents.

- 爸爸說我們就是最棒的禮物。

My dad said that we were the biggest gifts.

- 我們在回家以後吃了蛋糕。

After coming back home, we ate cake.

- 爸爸買了一些花和一條項鍊當作媽
媽的生日禮物。

My dad brought some flowers and a
necklace for mother's birthday present.

- 今天是媽媽的生日，不過家裡沒有
人記得這件事。

Today was my mother's birthday, but
everyone in my family had forgotten about
it.

- 我們感到很抱歉。

We felt really sorry.

- 我明年一定會送她生日禮物。

I will make sure to give her a birthday
present next year.
（確信、一定）

祖父母的生日 ★ Grandparents' Birthdays

- 因為爺爺生日，所以我們去了爺爺家。

  It was my grandfather's birthday, so we went to his house.

- 因為奶奶生日，所以我們全家人都聚在一起。

  Since it was my grandmother's birthday, all of my family members (were gathered) together.

  （因為活動）
  聚集

- 爺爺今年要 70 歲了。

  My grandfather is turning 70 this year.

- 奶奶用農曆來算她的生日日期，所以每年都不一樣。

  Grandma counts her birthday by using the (lunar calendar), so it changes each year.

  農曆

- 爺爺的生日其實是下週三，但是我們今天提前開了生日派對。

  Grandpa's birthday is actually next Wednesday, but we had an early birthday party today.

- 因為奶奶生日，我們出去吃了很棒的中華料理。

  We ate out at a nice Chinese restaurant because it was my grandmother's birthday.

- 我寫了一張生日卡片給奶奶。

  I wrote a birthday card for my grandmother.

- 奶奶在看我送的生日卡片時看起來好開心。

  Grandma looked so pleased when she was reading my birthday card.

  • pleased 愉悅的

- 我沒有給爺爺禮物，而是幫他按摩。

  I gave my grandfather a massage, instead of giving him a present.

  • massage 按摩

- 我很大聲地唱《生日快樂歌》。

  I sang *Happy Birthday* really loudly.

- 我拉小提琴祝他生日快樂。

I played the violin to congratulate him on his birthday.
- congratulate 恭喜

- 奶奶很喜歡我送的禮物。

My grandmother really liked my present.

- 媽媽準備了奶奶最愛的蛋糕。

My mom prepared Grandma's favorite cake.

- 為了慶祝爺爺的 70 歲生日，我們全家到濟州島旅行。

To celebrate Grandpa's 70th birthday, all of my family members went to Jeju Island for a trip.

- 我們送奶奶的 70 歲生日禮物是到中國旅行。

For my grandmother's 70th birthday, we sent her on a trip to China for a present.

兄弟姊妹的生日 ★ Siblings' Birthdays

- 今天是姊姊的生日。

Today is my older sister's birthday.

- 我們一家人的生日都在秋天。

All of my family members' birthdays are in autumn.

- 哥哥的生日在九月，我的在十月。

My older brother's birthday is in September, and mine is in October.

- 姊姊和我的生日只差五天。

My older sister's birthday and my birthday are only 5 days apart.
- apart 距離

- 媽媽和弟弟的生日只差一天，所以我們幫他們兩個一起辦生日派對。

My mother's birthday and my younger brother's birthday are only a day apart, so we had a birthday party for both of them.

- 姊姊和她的朋友們在餐廳開生日派對。
  My older sister had a birthday party at a restaurant with her friends.

- 我買了一台玩具車給弟弟當生日禮物。
  I bought a toy car for my younger brother's birthday present.

- 弟弟很喜歡我送的禮物。
  My younger brother really liked my present.

- 姊姊好像不太喜歡我買給她的生日禮物。
  My sister did not seem to like the present that I bought for her.

- 媽媽買了手機給哥哥當生日禮物。
  My mother bought my older brother a (cell phone) for his birthday.
  手機

- 我很羨慕哥哥。我也想要一隻手機。
  I really envy my brother. I want to have a cell phone, too.

- 看到妹妹收到很多朋友送的禮物，我真的很羨慕她。
  Seeing my younger sister receiving a lot of presents from her friends, I really envied her.

- 我希望我的生日可以快點到。
  I hope my birthday comes soon.

婚禮 ★ Wedding

- 今天是阿姨的婚禮。
  Today was my aunt's wedding.

- 我很開心可以有一個姨丈。
  I am so happy to get a new uncle.

- 我因為阿姨要結婚了而有一點難過。
  I am (kind of) sad about my aunt getting married. 一點

- 阿姨穿婚紗看起來好漂亮。
  My aunt looked so pretty in her wedding dress.

- 我也想要像她一樣穿漂亮的婚紗。

  I want to wear a pretty wedding dress like her.

- 媽媽穿了漂亮的洋裝。

  Mom wore a pretty dress.

- 姨丈穿了帥氣的燕尾服，看起來就像電影明星。

  My uncle looked like a movie star in his gorgeous tuxedo.

  • gorgeous 帥氣的　tuxedo 燕尾服

- 很多親戚都來了。

  A lot of relatives came.

- 爺爺奶奶也從很遠的地方來參加婚禮。

  My grandparents also came to the wedding from far away.

- 我因為要參加表哥的婚禮而去了台中。

  Because of my cousin's wedding, I went to Taichung.

- 因為週末塞車，我們在婚禮上遲到了 10 分鐘。

  We were ten minutes late to the wedding because of the weekend traffic.

- 當我到達婚禮現場，儀式已經結束了。

  When I arrived at the wedding, the ceremony was over.

- 外婆在阿姨的婚禮上哭了。

  Grandma cried at my aunt's wedding.

- 阿姨在婚禮上哭得好傷心，讓我也跟著哭了。

  My aunt was crying so much during her wedding that it made me cry, too.

- 婚禮在戶外舉行，幸好天氣非常好。

  The wedding was held outside. Thankfully, the weather was very nice.

  • thankfully 幸好、幸虧

- 證婚人的致詞太冗長了，讓整個儀式變得有點無聊。

  The officiator's speech was rather long, making the ceremony a bit boring.

  • officiator 證婚人

- 姨丈的朋友在婚禮上唱了祝賀歌曲。

  My uncle's friends sang a congratulatory song at the wedding.

  • congratulatory 祝賀的

- 婚禮在教堂舉行，所以非常莊嚴。

The wedding was held at a church, so it was very solemn.

• solemn 莊嚴的

- 婚禮在教堂舉行，所以有很多祈禱文。

The wedding was held at a church, and there were a lot of prayers.

• prayer 禱告

- 在結婚儀式結束以後拍了照片。

After the wedding ceremony, there was a photo shoot.
　　　　　└ 拍照

- 婚禮會場的自助餐真的很好吃。

The buffet at the wedding hall was really delicious.

- 在婚宴上，新娘和新郎穿得很漂亮地向賓客敬酒。

At the wedding reception, the bride and groom dressed up beautifully and toasted to the guests.

• reception 宴會　bride 新娘　groom 新郎

- 姨丈說他們蜜月要去泰國。

My uncle said they are going to Thailand for their honeymoon.

• honeymoon 蜜月

- 阿姨的禮車用花朵裝飾。

My aunt's wedding car was decorated with flowers.

葬禮／悼念儀式 ★ Funerals / Memorial Ceremonies

- 爺爺昨天過世了。

My grandfather passed away yesterday.
　　　　　　　　└ 過世

- 奶奶今天因為癌症過世了。

My grandmother passed away due to cancer today.
　　　　　　　　　　└ 由於～

• cancer 癌症

- 我很難過爺爺就這樣過世了。

  I am so sad that Grandpa just passed away.

- 我和其他人一樣穿了黑色。

  I dressed up in black just like everyone else.
  穿著

- 很多人都前來葬禮。

  A lot of people came to the funeral.
  • funeral 葬禮

- 爺爺在火化後被葬在公墓裡。

  Grandpa was cremated and then buried at a memorial park.
  • cremate 火化   公墓

- 爸爸哭得很慘，讓我也跟著哭了。

  Dad cried a lot, and it made me cry, too.

- 今天是奶奶的祭日，所以我們去了叔叔家。

  Today was the memorial service day for my grandma, so we went to my uncle's house.
  悼念儀式

- 悼念儀式應該要在半夜舉行。

  The memorial service is supposed to be held at midnight.
  應該要～

- 爺爺生前特別疼愛我，因為我是他的第一個孫子。

  Grandpa especially adored me when he was alive because I was his first grandchild.
  • adore 疼愛   grandchild 孫子

- 我真的很想念過世的奶奶。

  I really miss my grandmother who passed away.

搬家 ★ Moving Day

- 我們今天搬家。

  We moved today.

- 我很開心我終於有自己的房間了。

  I am so happy that I am finally getting my own room.

- 我們必須要搬家，因為妹妹需要有自己的房間。

  We had to move because my younger sister needed her own room.

- 我很開心新家比舊家還要大。

  I am glad the new house is bigger than the old one.

- 搬到大一點的房子後，我們有一個看起來像操場一樣大的客廳。

  Moving into a bigger house, we have a living room that looks like a schoolyard.

- 我不喜歡這間房子，因為它太老舊了。

  I don't like this house because it is too worn out.
  老舊的

- 這間房子比舊家還小，所以感覺上有點空氣不流通。

  The house is smaller than the old one, so it feels stuffy.
  • stuffy 空氣不流通的

- 新家離學校很近，這非常棒。／我很開心新家離學校很近。

  The new house is near my school, which is very good. / I am happy that the new house is near my school.

- 因為新的社區離公園很近，所以我很喜歡。

  I like this new neighborhood because it is close to a park.
  • neighborhood 社區

- 因為我們搬家了，所以我轉學到新學校。

  Because we moved, I transferred to a new school.

- 我很難過我必須要離開朋友們和可愛的小鎮。

  I was so sad that I had to leave my friends and the lovely town behind.
  • leave A behind 留下 A 離開

- 我新搬進的小鎮離舊的並不是很遠。

  The new town that I moved to is not so far away from my old town.

- 我們以前住在公寓裡，不過現在搬到別墅了。

  We used to live in an apartment, but we moved into a private house now.

- 我很開心我可以盡情奔跑了。

  I am so happy that I can run around as much as I want.

- 因為我們還沒整理完東西，所以我們訂了披薩當晚餐。

  Because we haven't finished sorting our stuff, we ordered pizza for dinner.

  • sort 分類、整理　stuff 物品

- 我很擔心能不能交到新朋友。／我很懷疑我能不能輕鬆交到新朋友。

  I am worried about making new friends. / I wonder if I can make new friends easily.

  • make friends 交朋友　好奇～

- 我真的不想搬家。

  I really didn't want to move.

- 我希望我可以住在這裡很久都不用搬家。

  I hope I can live here for a long time without moving.

家族旅行

At the Zoo

Saturday, May 18, Sunny

Today, I went to the zoo with my family. We saw elephants, giraffes, zebras, snakes, and birds. There was an anteater that I had never seen before. It looked really bizarre. The most fun was that we fed the deer. I would like to go there again.

在動物園裡　5月18日星期六，晴天

今天我和家人一起去了動物園。我們看到了大象、長頸鹿、斑馬、蛇和小鳥。我還看到了以前從來沒有看過的食蟻獸，牠真的長得很奇特。最有趣的事情是我們餵了鹿。我還想再去一次動物園。

·anteater 食蟻獸　bizarre 奇異的、奇特的　feed (feed-fed-fed) 餵食　would like to 想要

- 吃過晚餐以後，我們全家一起到公園散步。

  After eating dinner, everyone in my family went out for a walk in the park.

  外出散步

- 星期天我和家人一起去公園野餐。

  On Sunday, I went on a picnic in the park with my family.　去野餐

- 我們在公園草地上鋪了墊子，吃了午餐便當。

  We spread a mat on the grass and ate a packed lunch in the park.

  • spread 展開　mat 草蓆　午餐便當

- 爸爸和我在公園裡溜直排輪。

  My father and I went inline skating in the park.

- 媽媽和我在公園散步了三圈。

  My mom and I walked around the park three times.

- 很多人都來公園運動。

  A lot of people went to the park to exercise.

  • exercise 運動

- 因為天氣很溫暖，所以在公園裡有很多人。

  Because of the warm weather, there were a lot of people in the park.

- 我們在晚上可以看到很多人沿著河邊散步。

  In the evening, we can see many people walking along the river.

- 弟弟溜滑板車，而我騎腳踏車。

  My younger brother rode a kickboard, and I rode my bicycle.

- 媽媽和我騎腳踏車到淡水河岸。

  My mom and I went up to the Tamsui River bank by riding our bikes.

- 美麗的花朵在公園裡盛開。

  Beautiful flowers are blooming in the park.

  • bloom （花）盛開

- 我在公園裡看到一隻漂亮的小狗狗。
  I saw a pretty puppy in the park.

- 公園裡有噴水池，所以我玩了水。
  There was a floor fountain in the park, so I played in the water.
  • fountain 噴泉

- 我用公園裡的運動器材來運動。
  I worked out by using the sports equipment in the park.
  運動
  運動器材

- 住在公園附近真好。／
  在我家附近有公園真好。
  It is really nice to live near the park. /
  It is so good having a park near my house.

遊戲場 ★ Playgrounds

- 因為天氣很好，我和妹妹一起在遊戲場玩。
  Because the weather was fine, I played with my younger sister on the playground.

- 我和同學在遊戲場玩。
  I played with my classmates on the playground.

- 我在遊戲場玩溜滑梯。
  I went down the slide on the playground.
  玩溜滑梯

- 我在遊戲場玩沙。
  I played with the sand on the playground.

- 弟弟從鞦韆上摔下來，所以他哭了。
  My younger brother fell off the swing, so he cried.
  從～摔下

- 今天我在遊戲場和朋友們一起玩棒球。
  Today, I played baseball on the playground with my friends.

- 遊戲場裡沒有很多小孩。
  There were not many kids on the playground. / Not many kids were seen on the playground.

購物 ★ Shopping

- 我星期六去了市場。

  I went to the market on Saturday.

- 週末我們全家一起去了市場採買。

  All of my family went to the market for groceries on the weekend.

  • groceries 食品雜貨

- 我很喜歡去逛市場。

  I really like to look around the market.

- 弟弟坐在一台汽車形的推車上。

  My younger brother rode in a car-shaped cart.

  • car-shaped 汽車形的

- 媽媽負責採買,我和爸爸則去了試吃區。

  My mother did the grocery shopping while my dad and I went to the free food sample corners.

  買菜、採買

- 因為我們吃了太多免費試吃,肚子都飽了。

  Because we ate too many free food samples, we were full.

- 我拜託媽媽買一個玩具陀螺給我。

  I begged my mother to buy a toy top.

  • beg 哀求、請求

- 爸爸買了我想要的玩具給我。

  My dad bought me the toy that I wanted.

- 採買完了以後,我們在美食街吃午餐。

  After doing the grocery shopping, we ate lunch at the food court.

- 我和媽媽一起到百貨公司買了一些衣服。

  I went to the department store with my mom to buy some clothes. 百貨公司

- 我沒找到想買的球鞋，所以我就回家了。

  I could not find any sneakers that I liked, so I just came home.

  • sneakers 運動鞋

- 媽媽買了一個新的背包給我。

  My mom bought me a new backpack.

遊樂園／職業體驗館 ★ Amusement Parks / Children's Job Experience Centers

- 我和家人一起去了遊樂園。

  I went to an amusement park with my family.

  遊樂園

- 因為那天是學校的校慶，所以我和朋友們一起去了遊樂園。

  It was my school's foundation day, so I went to an amusement park with my friends.

  • foundation 建立

- 因為是星期六，所以遊樂園裡擠滿了人。

  Because it was Saturday, there were so many people at the amusement park. / Because it was Saturday, the amusement park was crowded with many people.

  擠滿了～

- 熱門的遊樂設施大排長龍。

  The popular rides were packed with long lines of people.

  擠滿

  • ride 遊樂設施

- 只為了搭一項遊樂設施，我就必須排 40 分鐘的隊。

  In order to go on just one ride, I had to wait in line for 40 minutes.

- 因為人實在太多了，所以我只搭了四樣遊樂設施。

  Because there were too many people, I took only 4 rides.

- 因為是平日，所以人並不多。

It was a weekday, so there weren't a lot of people. / There were only a few people because it was a weekday.

- 因為人不多，所以遊樂設施我愛搭幾次就搭幾次。

Because there weren't a lot of people, I enjoyed the rides as many times as I wanted.

- 我最喜歡海盜船了。

The pirate ship was my favorite. / I liked the pirate ship the most.

- 因為現在我長大了，摩天輪實在太無聊了。

Now that I am older, the ferris wheel was just too boring.

- 妹妹不搭雲霄飛車，因為她說太恐怖了。

My younger sister didn't ride on the rollercoaster because she said that it was too scary.

- 我去了鬼屋，它非常可怕。

I went into the haunted house, and it was really scary.

• haunted 鬧鬼的

- 雖然海盜船很可怕，不過還是很好玩。

Although the pirate ship was scary, it was still fun.

- 因為遊樂園晚上也有營業，所以我可以在那裡玩到很晚。

Because the amusement park opened at night, I could play there till late at night.

- 在兒童職業體驗館裡，我體驗了很多種職業。

At Children's Job Experience Center, I got to experience many types of jobs.

• experience 體驗　type 種類

- 我到了兒童職業體驗館去體驗許多不同種類的職業。

I went to Children's Job Experience Center and experienced many different occupations.

• occupation 職業

動物園／植物園 ★ Zoos / Botanical Gardens

- 今天我們一家人去了動物園。

  Today, my family went to the zoo.

- 在動物園裡，我看到了獅子、大象、長頸鹿和許多其他的動物。

  I saw lions, elephants, giraffes, and many other animals at the zoo.

- 我到動物園去餵了鹿。

  I went to the zoo and fed the deer.

  • feed (feed-fed-fed) 餵食

- 北極熊看起來很哀傷。

  The polar bear looked very sad.

- 獅子在睡覺。

  The lion was sleeping.

- 那裡有很多有趣的動物。

  There were a lot of interesting animals.

- 在植物園裡，我看到很多漂亮的花朵。

  At the botanical garden, I saw plenty of beautiful flowers.

  植物園　很多

- 有一些植物非常大又很漂亮。

  Some plants were very big and really wonderful.

- 在我今天看到的植物裡面，捕蠅草是最有趣的一種。

  Among the plants that I saw today, the Venus flytrap was the most interesting one.

  捕蠅草

- 我去了樹園，看見很多漂亮的植物。

  I went to the arboretum and saw lots of beautiful plants.

  • arboretum 樹園

電影院 ★ Movie Theaters

- 週末我們全家一起去看了電影。

  Everyone in my family went to see a movie on the weekend.

- 我和媽媽一起在電影院看了《蜘蛛人》。

  I saw *Spiderman* with my mom at the movie theater.
  電影院

- 我爸媽很喜歡電影。

  My parents love movies.

- 我喜歡動作片。

  I like action movies.

- 我們家一個月至少會去看一次電影。

  My family goes to the movie theater at least once a month.
  至少

- 爸爸已經買好《蝙蝠俠》的票，所以我們就去看了。

  My dad had already bought tickets for *Batman*, so we went to see it.

- 因為妹妹說她討厭看恐怖片，所以我們看了別部片子。

  Because my younger sister said that she hated horror movies, we watched a different one.
  恐怖片

- 我看了最近最熱門的電影。

  I watched the movie that is most popular these days.

- 那部電影很有趣。

  The movie was so much fun.

- 那部電影太幼稚了。

  The movie was too childish.
  • childish 幼稚的

- 結局太令人失望了。

  The ending was too disappointing.
  • disappointing 令人失望的

- 那部電影非常感人。

  The movie was very moving/touching.
  • moving/touching 感人的

- 那部電影好悲傷，讓我流了很多眼淚。

  The movie was so sad that I cried a lot.

- 看電影的時候，我吃了爆米花也喝了汽水。

  While watching the movie, I ate popcorn and drank soda.

- 我背後有人在講話，所以我沒辦法專心看電影。

  Someone was talking behind me, so I couldn't concentrate on the movie.

  • concentrate 專心

- 當我們到電影院看電影的時候，應該要把手機關機。

  When we watch a movie at the theater, we should turn off our cell phones.

  關掉（電源）

- 我的手機在電影院突然響了，讓我覺得很尷尬。

  My cell phone suddenly rang at the movie theater, so I was really embarrassed.

- 這部電影給了我很多可以思考的地方。

  The movie gave me a lot to think about.

- 這部電影聽說已經吸引了超過千萬人次的觀眾。

  The movie was said to have drawn more than ten million viewers.

  • draw 吸引　viewer 觀眾

- 我想要像電影裡的人物那樣生活。

  I want to live like the character in the movie.

  • character 登場人物

- 這個演員真的太棒了。

  The actor was really incredible.

  • incredible （因為太好、太厲害而）無法置信的

博物館／展覽／音樂會 ★ Museums / Exhibitions / Concerts

- 我們去了故宮博物院。

  We went to the National Palace Museum.

- 參觀博物館是我的假期作業，所以我去了故宮博物院。

  Visiting a museum was my vacation homework, so I went to the National Palace Museum.

- 我去了兒童博物館，然後體驗了很多東西。

  I went to the Children's Museum and experienced a lot of things.

- 我在故宮看到了一件很厲害的藝術品。

  I saw a piece of wonderful artcraft at the National Palace Museum.

- 我想要看看我們的祖先是怎麼生活的。

  I would like to see how our ancestors had lived.

  • ancestor 祖先

- 在博物館的體驗中心裡，我試著打了鼓。我很喜歡打鼓，因為很刺激。

  In the museum's experience center, I tried the drum set. I liked it because it was very exciting.

- 逛完博物館以後，我買了一個紀念品。

  After looking around the museum, I bought a souvenir.

  • souvenir 紀念品

- 今天媽媽和我一起去了台北市立美術館。

  My mother and I went to the Taipei Fine Art Museum today.

- 今天我去看了夏卡爾的展覽。

  Today, I went to see a Chagall exhibition.

  • exhibition 展覽

- 那裡人很多，因為現在正在放假。

  There were so many people because it was the vacation season.

- 因為那裡人太多，所以我必須排隊。

  Because there were too many people, I had to wait in line.

  排隊

- 我跟著導覽員聽他／她的解說。

  I was following a docent and listened to his/her explanation.

  • docent （博物館等）導覽員　explanation 解說

- 能夠親眼看到名作真是太感動了。

  Seeing the masterpieces in real was unbelievably impressive.

  • masterpiece 傑作　unbelievably 不可置信地
    impressive 印象深刻的、感人的

- 我真的不知道為什麼這一幅畫會是名畫。

  I really don't know why this painting is a masterpiece.

- 我今天去參加了新年音樂會。

  I went to a new year's concert today.

- 今天是給兒童聽的音樂會，所以有很多首曲子我都聽過。

  It was a concert for children, so there were a lot of musical pieces that I knew.
  歌曲

- 我很開心可以在音樂會上聽到這麼好聽的曲子。

  I was so happy that I got to listen to such beautiful songs at the concert.

- 音樂會有點無聊。

  The concert was a bit boring.

- 我不太喜歡古典音樂。

  I don't really like classical music.
  古典音樂

暑假 ★ Summer Vacation

- 我們家在夏天去了濟州島度假。

  My family went to Jeju Island for our summer holiday.

- 今年的暑假我們去了澎湖。

  As for this year's summer vacation, we went to Penghu.

- 我們去釜山玩了三天，度過了一段美好的時光。

  We went to Busan for three days and had a fun time.

- 暑假的時候，阿姨全家和我們一起去了海邊。

  My aunt's family went along with us to beach on summer vacation.

- 我們暑假時沒辦法去旅行度假。

  We could not go on a vacation trip during our summer break.
  暑假

- 高速公路很塞。

  The expressway had heavy traffic.

  • expressway 高速公路

- 當我把雙腳伸進山谷裡的小溪裡時，我覺得又涼又清爽。

When I put my feet into the creek in the valley, it felt so cold and refreshing.
  - creek 小溪　valley 山谷　refreshing 清爽的、爽快的

- 整個假期的天氣都很好。

The weather was so nice during the entire vacation.

- 我很難過，因為整個假期都在下雨。

I was very sad that it rained during the entire vacation.

- 媽媽幫我塗了防曬油。

My mom put sunscreen on me.
  - sunscreen 防曬油

- 我和爸爸去釣了魚。

I went fishing with my dad.

- 爸爸幫我在釣鉤上放了一些蚯蚓。

My dad put the earthworms in the hooks for me.
  - earthworm 蚯蚓　hook 釣鉤

- 我釣到三隻魚！

I caught three fish!

- 我沒有釣到魚，所以我很不開心。

I didn't catch any fish, so I was really upset.

- 媽媽用我們釣到的魚給我們煮了魚湯。

With the fish that we caught, my mom cooked us some fish soup.

- 因為爸爸很忙，所以我們暑假不能去旅行。

Because my dad was so busy, we couldn't go on a summer trip.

- 我們去了一個叫做「Paradise」的渡假村。

We stayed at a resort called "Paradise."
  - resort 渡假村

- 那個地方很棒，因為渡假村的正前方就是海灘。

It was really nice because there was a beach right in front of the resort.

- 和家人一起去旅行真的很棒。

It is really nice to travel with my family.

游泳池／海灘 ★ Swimming Pools／Beaches

- 補習班放假了，所以我去了游泳池。

  I had a cram school break, so I went to the swimming pool.

- 游泳池擠滿了人潮。

  The swimming pool was crowded with people.

- 我玩了滑水道。

  I went down the waterslide.

- 衝浪是在海灘最有趣的活動了。

  Surfing was the most fun activity at the beach.

- 玩了水之後我覺得好餓。

  I was so hungry after playing in the water.

- 午餐之後我休息了一下子，然後又跑去玩水。

  I took a short rest after lunch and then went into water to play again.

  • take a rest 休息

- 我在海邊盡情的游泳。

  I swam as much as I wanted at the beach.

- 游泳的時候發現我的腳踩不到地，讓我嚇了一跳。

  I was shocked while swimming because I found my feet could not touch the bottom.

- 我在岸邊游泳。

  I swam near the shore.

  • shore 岸邊

- 海水好冷。

  The ocean water was so cold.

- 我和弟弟一起玩沙玩得很開心。

  I had such a fun time playing in the sand with my younger brother.

- 我和弟弟一起在海灘上堆了沙堡。

  I made a sandcastle with my younger brother at the beach.

- 我在泥灘上挖出了很多蛤蠣。

  At the mud flat, I dug out a lot of clams.

  • clam 蛤蠣   泥灘   挖出

- 在海灘，我和哥哥抓了一隻小魚和一些蛤蠣。 | At the beach, my brother and I caught a small fish and some clams.

登山 ★ Hiking / Climbing

- 我今天去了附近的陽明山。 | I went to Mt. Yangming, a nearby mountain, today.

- 山不高，所以我可以很輕鬆地爬。 | The mountain isn't so high, so I could climb up it easily. /
It was easy for me to climb up because the mountain is not that high.

- 雖然山不太好爬，不過到山頂的感覺真好。 | Although it was difficult to climb up, it felt so good at the top.

- 我覺得爬山可以讓我的身體和心靈變得神清氣爽。 | I feel like hiking refreshed my body and mind.
  • refresh 使神清氣爽

- 當我下山的時候，我的雙腳在顫抖。 | When I was going down the mountain, my legs were shaking.

- 我在山上看到了一隻松鼠。 | I saw a squirrel on the mountain.

- 山上到處充滿綠意。 | The mountain was green everywhere.

- 秋色覆蓋了整座山。 | The fall colors covered the mountain sides.

- 山上的花朵盛開得很漂亮。 | Flowers were blooming so beautifully on the mountain.

- 我吃了小黃瓜當點心。 | I ate cucumbers for a snack.

- 當我從山頂往下看，所有的房子和建築物看起來就像模型玩具似的。 | When I looked down from the mountain top, all of the houses and buildings looked like miniature toys.
  模型玩具

「登山」的幾種說法

- 很好爬的山會說 **hiking**，爬高度比較高的山則會用 **mountain climbing**。
- **hiking** 的意思是沿著登山步道走的那種爬山。
- **(mountain) climing** 指的是爬險峻的山、需要登上岩壁的登山。
- **trekking** 指的是攜帶裝備齊全的登山。
- **backpacking** 是指包含露營行程的登山。

- 妹妹說她的腿很痛，所以我們爬到一半就折返下山了。

My younger sister said that her leg hurt, so we turned around in the middle of climbing and came down.

- 爬完山以後，我們吃了海鮮煎餅。

After finishing hiking, we ate seafood pancake.

- 從現在開始，我會更常去山上。

From now on, I will go to the mountain more often.

 露營 ★ Camping

- 星期六我去了陽明山露營。

I went to Mt. Yangming to go camping on Saturday.

- 我們家常常去露營。

My family goes camping a lot.

- 我們在帳篷裡睡覺。

We slept in a tent.

- 和爸爸一起搭帳篷很好玩。 | (Setting up) the tent with my dad was really fun. 搭、設置

- 我在帳篷裡睡覺，還被蚊子叮了好幾個包。 | I slept in a tent and got a lot of (mosquito bites). 蚊子叮咬

- 雖然是一樣的泡麵，可是在露營地的吃起來美味多了。 | Although they are the same old instant noodles, the one that I eat at the campsite taste so much better.
  - campsite 露營地

- 我們在面對大海的地方搭了帳篷。 | We set up a tent in front of the ocean.

- 我在帳篷裡睡覺，可是晚上變冷了。 | I slept in a tent, and it got colder at night.
  - get＋比較級 變得～

- 我希望我們可以更常去露營。 | I wish we could go camping more often.

滑雪／滑雪板 ★ Skiing / Snowboarding

- 這個冬天我第一次去滑雪。 | For the first time this winter, I went skiing.

- 我和跆拳道班的同學一起去滑雪。 | I went skiing together with my taekwondo school friends.

- 我不太會滑雪。 | I am not really good at skiing.

- 爸爸教我要怎麼滑雪。 | My dad taught me how to ski.

- 我上了一堂滑雪課。 | I took a skiing lesson.

- 我練習要怎麼站起來練習了好多次。 | I practiced getting up many times.

- 練習了幾次以後，我已經可以站得很好了。 | After practicing several times, I was able to stand up well.

- 教練說我的姿勢很棒。

  The coach told me that I had good posture.
  - posture 姿勢

- 我滑雪的時候摔了好幾次，所以我的屁股好痛。

  I fell down a lot while skiing, so my hips hurt.　摔倒

- 教練叫我在停下來的時候要讓雙腿呈現 A 字形，可是這並沒有那麼簡單。

  The coach told me to make my legs into an A shape when pausing, but it was not that easy.
  - pause 停止

- 我滑了初學者的滑雪道。

  I skied down the beginner's course.

- 我第一次挑戰了中級的滑雪道。

  I tried the intermediate course for the first time.
  - intermediate 中級的

- 這其實沒有我想像中的那麼恐怖。

  It was not as scary as I had imagined.

- 光是搭纜車就夠好玩了。

  Just taking the ski lift was fun enough.

- 當我試著在脫掉滑雪靴後走路，那感覺很詭異。

  When I tried to walk after taking off my ski boots, it felt weird.
  - weird 奇怪的、詭異的

- 滑雪非常好玩，讓我甚至沒有注意到時光飛逝。

  Skiing was so fun that I did not even realize how much time had passed. /
  I did not even know that time had passed that quickly while I was having fun skiing.

- 滑雪板比滑雪還要有趣多了。

  Snowboarding is much more fun than skiing.

- 我第一次學怎麼玩滑雪板。

  I learned how to snowboard for the first time.

- 滑雪板沒有我想像中的那麼困難。

  Snowboarding was not as difficult as I had thought.

- 我明年想要學怎麼玩滑雪板。

  I want to learn how to snowboard next year.

雪橇 ★ Sledding

- 今天我和家人一起去了雪橇樂園。

  I went to a sledding park with my family today.

- 我在雪橇樂園玩了一整天。

  I played all day long at the sledding park.

- 雖然中級的雪道路線有點可怕，可是還是很有趣。

  Although the intermediate course was a little scary, it was still fun.

- 媽媽抱著弟弟一起滑雪橇。

  Mom rode on the sled while holding my little brother in her arms.

- 因為太好玩了，讓我在滑雪橇的時候完全感覺不到寒冷。

  It is so fun that I don't feel cold at all when riding on a sled.

- 在雪橇樂園我也體驗了釣魚。

  I also went fishing at the sledding park.

- 你在那裡可以馬上把魚炸來吃。

  You could have the fish fried instantly there.

  • instantly 立刻、及時

- 那些炸魚好好吃。

  The fried fish was so delicious.

到國外旅行 ★ Overseas Trips

- 我們家族旅行去了泰國四天。

  We went to Thailand on a family trip for 4 days.

- 這是我第一次出國。

  It was my first time to go abroad.

- 這是我人生中第一次搭飛機。

  For the first time in my life, I got to ride on an airplane.

- 我覺得既開心又興奮，因為這是我第一次出國旅行。

  I was so excited and thrilled because it was my first trip overseas.

  • thrilled 非常興奮的　overseas 海外地

- 我們趕著要去搭飛機。

  We hurried to catch the airplane.

- 搭飛機到塞班島要四個小時。

  It took 4 hours to fly to Saipan by airplane.

- 長時間坐在飛機裡非常無聊。

  It was so boring to sit on the airplane for such a long time.

- 我很害怕，因為我不知道入境審查時會問什麼問題。

  I was terrified because I did not know what they would ask me at the immigration counter.

  • terrified 害怕的　immigration 移民、入境

- 我們住在君悅酒店。

  We stayed at the Hotel Hyatt.

- 第一天的下午，我們在飯店的泳池度過了美好的時光。

  I had such a fun time at the hotel's pool in the afternoon of our first day there.

- 第二天我們去了市內觀光。

  On the second day, we went on a city tour.

- 導遊很親切。

  The guide was really kind.

- 我在購物中心買了紀念品給朋友們。

  I bought souvenirs for my friends at a shopping mall.

  • souvenir 紀念品、禮物

- 海岸線的景色真是難以言喻的美。

  The scenery of the coastline was indescribably beautiful.

  • scenery 景色、風景　indescribably 無法言喻地

- 因為行程很緊湊，我們花了好幾個小時在搭巴士。

  Because of our tight schedule, we spent many hours riding on buses.

  • tight （時間上）緊湊的

- 去過國外以後，我發現我應該要更努力學英文。

  外國

  Having visited a foreign country, I realized that I should study English harder.

Part 6

情緒、個性、興趣與煩惱

情緒

It Wasn't Me!

Thursday, September 3, Rainy

I got scolded by my teacher because of Eric. He was the one that was making noise in class, but the teacher thought I was doing it. I swear I never talked aloud. That was so unfair, and I felt furious. I will never hang out with Eric again. Never!

不是我啦！　　9月3日星期四，雨天

我因為 Eric 而被老師罵。他就是那個在上課時吵鬧的人，但老師認為是我在吵鬧。我發誓我從來沒有大聲講話。那真是太不公平了，讓我覺得很生氣。我不會再和 Eric 出去玩了，絕對不會！

· **get scolded** 被罵　**make noise** 製造噪音、吵鬧　**unfair** 不公平的　**furious** 狂怒的
hang out 去某處閒晃、玩耍

喜悅／高興 ★ Gladness / Joy

- 今天真是幸福愉快的一天。

  Today was a really happy day. /
  It was such a blessed day today.
  • blessed 被祝福的、幸福的　如此的、非常的

- 我覺得自己好像在做夢一樣。

  I felt as if I were dreaming.
  好像〜、彷彿〜

- 我開心到可以飛上天了。

  I am so glad that I could fly in the sky.

- 我高興到跳了起來。

  I was jumping for joy.
  由於高興

- 我既開心又興奮。

  I was happy and excited.

- 我不敢相信這不是一場夢！

  I can't believe that this isn't a dream!

- 我開心到不敢置信！

  I was so happy that I couldn't believe it!

- 我捏了自己一下來確認自己不是在做夢。

  I pinched myself to check that I wasn't dreaming.
  • pinch 捏、掐

- 我高興得跳上跳下的。

  I was jumping up and down for joy.

- 我高興到哭了。

  I was so happy that I cried.

- 我高興到說不出話來。

  I was speechless because I was very happy.
  / I was so happy that I could not say anything.
  • speechless 無法言語的
    so＋形容詞＋that… 如此〜以至於〜

- 我很高興聽到這個消息。

  I was glad to hear the news.

- 我開心到無法相信這是真的！

  I was so happy that I could not believe it was true!

- 我很高興能在數學競賽裡得獎。

  I was happy to win a prize in the math competition.

  • competition 比賽、競賽

- 我無法相信自己得到了第一名！感覺像做夢一樣！

  I can't believe that I won first place! It feels like a dream!

  第一名

- 我高興到合不攏嘴。

  I was so glad that I was grinning from ear to ear.

  張開嘴巴咧嘴而笑

- 當我聽到這個消息時，我大聲歡呼！

  When I heard the news, I cheered loudly!

  • cheer 歡呼、喝采　loudly 大聲地

- 我忍不住一直笑。

  I couldn't stop laughing.

快樂 ★ Happiness

- 我今天過了很開心的一天。

  I had a really fun day today.

- 我很高興收到了意想不到的禮物。

  I was happy to receive an unexpected gift.

  • unexpected 意想不到的

- 老師的稱讚讓我覺得很開心。

  The compliment from my teacher made my day.

  • compliment 稱讚　make one's day 使某人感到開心

- 和朋友一起玩很有趣。

  It was fun to hang out with my friends.

  和～一起玩耍

- 太好玩了，讓我都沒發現到時間的流逝。

  It was so fun that I didn't know time had passed.

- 當我在做好玩的事時，時間過得飛快。

  When I am doing something fun, time just flies.

- 早上的一些稱讚，讓我一整天都覺得很開心。 Some compliments in the morning make me feel happy for the entire day.

- 我不自覺地哼起歌來。 I was humming to myself without knowing it. / I didn't realize I was humming to myself.
  　　　　　　　　　　　自己哼起歌來

- 當我在彈鋼琴時，我覺得很愉快。 When I play the piano, I feel good.

- 當我心情好的時候，我和朋友們相處得更好。 When I am in a good mood, I get along with my friends better. 心情好

- 當我心情好的時候，我對我的兄弟姊妹們會比較友善。 When I am in a good mood, I am friendlier to my siblings.
  • sibling 兄弟姊妹

- 當我覺得快樂時，所有人看起來都很快樂。 When I feel good, everyone I see looks happy.

生氣 ★ Anger

- 我很生氣。 I am so angry.

- 我氣到幾乎無法忍受了。 I am so angry that I can hardly stand it.
  • hardly 幾乎不～　 stand 忍受、忍耐

- 我真的受夠了。 I am so fed up.
  • be fed up 對～感到厭煩
  　　　　　　　十分生氣、發火

- 我真的氣炸了。 I am boiling mad.

- 我無法冷靜下來。 I can't cool down.
  　　　　　　　　冷靜下來

- Adam 沒有遵守他的諾言，這使我感到非常生氣。

  Adam did not keep his promise, and that made me angry.
  　　　　　　　　　　　　　　遵守諾言

- 我對於因為朋友而惹上麻煩，感到十分生氣。

  I am angry for getting into trouble because of my friend.
  　　　　　　　　　　　受罪，給～找麻煩

- 我弟弟把我的回家功課給毀了，所以我覺得非常生氣。

  My younger brother ruined my homework, so I am very upset.

  • ruin 破壞、搞砸

- Amy 很容易生氣。

  Amy easily gets angry.

- Adam 幾乎從來不發脾氣。

  Adam hardly ever gets angry.

- 是哥哥先對我發火的。

  My brother got angry at me first.
  　　　　　　　　　　　因不重要的事
- 姊姊為了不重要的事而生氣。

  My sister got upset over nothing.

- 這件事也讓我覺得生氣，因此我狠狠地罵了她。

  It made me angry, too, so I lashed out at her.
  　　　　　　　　　　猛烈抨擊、斥責

- 我知道對著姊姊大罵是不對的，但是她先開始的。

  I know that it's wrong to lash out at my older sister, but she started it.

- 我的老師因為班上太吵而生氣。

  My teacher got angry because our class was too noisy.

  • noisy 吵鬧的

- 我媽媽因為我沒有在考試上得到好成績而生氣。

  My mother was angry with me for not getting a good score on the exam.

- 我媽媽生氣時真的很可怕。

  My mother is really scary when she is angry.

- 我媽媽很常生氣。

  My mother gets angry often.

- 我媽媽每天都對我發脾氣。

  My mother gets angry at me every day.

- 我爸爸不常生氣，但他生氣的時候真的很可怕。

  My father doesn't really get angry, but when he does, he is really scary.

- 我媽媽今天心情不好，所以我安靜地寫我的作業。

  My mother was in a bad mood today, so I did my homework quietly. 心情不好

- 雖然我非常生氣，但我盡我所能的保持冷靜。

  I felt furious, but I tried my best to remain calm.

  • furious 狂怒的　remain 保持～　calm 沉著冷靜的

- 我太生氣了，所以向妹妹大吼大叫。

  I was so furious that I screamed at my younger sister. 向～大吼大叫

- 我因為生我弟弟的氣而打了他。

  I hit my younger brother because I was angry at him.

- 即使我當時很生氣，我也應該要保持耐心的。

  I should have been more patient 即使～ even though I was angry.

  • patient 有耐心的、能容忍的

不耐煩 ★ Feeling Irritated

- 我最近沒來由地感到煩躁。／我最近沒來由地感到心煩。

  These days, I feel irritated for no particular reason. / I haven't been myself for no reason lately.

  • irritated 感到不耐煩／煩躁的　particular 特別的
    not oneself 感到心煩

- 所有的事情都讓我煩躁不耐。

  Everything bothers and irritates me.

  • bother 煩擾、打擾　irritate 使～心煩

- 我姊姊很挑剔。

My older sister is fussy.
- fussy 挑剔的、難以取悅的

- 我哥哥最近時常無故對我大呼小叫的。

My older brother has been (roaring at) me a lot for no reason lately. 向～大聲吼叫
- lately 最近

- 我早上的心情通常不太好。

I tend to be in a bad mood in the morning.

- 我因為在早上發脾氣而被媽媽罵。

I got into trouble with my mother for (throwing a fit) in the morning. 發脾氣、使性子

- 一旦你覺得煩躁，那任何事情都會讓你覺得生氣。

Once you feel annoyed, everything seems annoying.
- annoyed 煩躁、生氣的
  annoying 使人感到生氣的、煩躁的

- 當我聽到別人的抱怨時，這些抱怨會讓我感到煩躁。

When I heard a complaint from someone, it irritated me.
- complaint 不滿、抱怨

- Amy 很容易就會覺得不耐煩，所以和她在一起時，我也會覺得不耐煩。

Amy is easily irritated, so when I am with her, I get irritated as well.

- 每當我媽媽對我嘮叨時，我就感到十分煩躁。

Whenever my mom nags me, I feel so annoyed.
- nag 嘮叨

- 因為我太煩躁了，所以我對媽媽發了脾氣。

Since I was so annoyed, I threw a fit at my mom.

- 我知道我做錯了，但當我的錯誤被直接指出時，我還是覺得很惱火。

I knew that I was wrong, but when my mistake was (pointed out) directly, I got so annoyed. 指出

- 因為我妹妹不斷地煩我，所以我感到很心煩。

My younger sister kept bothering me, so I was upset.

- 我試著不那麼挑剔，但是效果並不是很好。

  I tried not to be fussy, but it didn't work well.

  • work 有效果

- 我很後悔對媽媽發脾氣。

  I regret throwing a fit at my mother. / I was sorry that I had thrown a fit at my mother.

- 從今以後我會盡力別這麼挑剔的。

  I will try my best not to be fussy from now on.

難過／沮喪 ★ Sadness / Depression

- 今天是很難過的一天。

  Today was a really sad day.

- 因為某些原因，我今天覺得心情沮喪。

  Today, I felt depressed for some reason.

  • depressed 心情沮喪的

- 今天是令人沮喪的一天。

  Today was a depressing day.

  • depressing 令人沮喪的

- 今天我和朋友吵架了，所以我一整天都覺得很沮喪。

  Today, I had a fight with my friends, so I felt depressed for the entire day.

- 我因為考試沒考好而感到沮喪。

  I am depressed because I didn't do well on my test.

- 我因為被老師罵而感到十分難過。

  I was so sad because I got into trouble with my teacher.

- 我弄丟了我的手機，所以我感到既難過又苦惱。

  I lost my cell phone, so I was sad and distressed.

  • distressed 苦惱的、難受的

- 我因為 Amy 搬走了而感到非常難過。

  I am so sad because Amy moved away.

  搬家、轉學

- 我的狗死了，所以我覺得十分心痛。

  My dog died, so I was heartbroken.
  - heartbroken 心痛的

- 這部電影太令人難過了，讓我哭了出來。

  The movie was so sad that I burst into tears.
  - burst into tears (burst-burst-burst) 哭了出來

- 我哭得太厲害，讓我的雙眼都腫起來了。

  I cried so much that my eyes swelled up.

  — 腫眼

- 我盡力忍住淚水。

  I tried my best to hold back the tears.

  — 忍住、抑制住

- 當我聽到這個消息時，我感到十分難過。

  When I heard the news, I was sad.

- 我因為媽媽不理解我，而感到很受傷。

  I was hurt because my mother didn't understand me.
  - hurt 覺得受傷、心裡不是滋味

- 我因為奶奶好像比較偏愛弟弟而覺得受傷。

  I was hurt because my grandma seemed to favor my younger brother over me.
  - favor 偏愛

- 我因為沒被邀請參加生日派對而覺得非常受傷。

  I was hurt so much because I didn't get invited to the birthday party.

- 我只要一想到要被媽媽罵了就覺得很沮喪。

  I was depressed just by thinking about getting scolded by my mother. / Thinking my mom was going to scold me, I felt depressed.
  - scold 罵

- 我試著去安慰十分悲痛的媽媽。

  I tried to comfort my mother, who was deeply grieving.
  - comfort 安慰   grieving 感到悲痛的

- 我媽媽安慰了我。

  My mom consoled me.
  - console 安慰、安撫

擔心 ★ Worry

- 我很擔心明天的報告。

  I am worried about tomorrow's presentation.
  • presentation 報告、發表

- 我很擔心明天的章節小考,因為我沒看什麼書。

  I (am concerned about) tomorrow's chapter test because I didn't study much. ⟨擔心～⟩
  • chapter test 章節小考

- 考試快到了,我現在開始感到有點擔心了。

  I am starting to get a little worried now that the exam is coming up.

- 我考試考得很糟,所以我很擔心。

  I did badly on the test, so I was very worried.

- 我擔心我的成績。

  I was worried about my grades.

- 我擔心會犯錯。

  I was worried about making mistakes.

- 我擔心會被媽媽罵。

  I was worried about getting into trouble with my mother.

- 我因為太過擔心而睡不著。

  I couldn't sleep because I was too worried.

- 我媽媽告訴我別太擔心。

  My mother told me not to worry.

- 我擔心會被和惡霸分到同一班。

  I am afraid that I will (be assigned) to the same class as the bully. ⟨被指派到～、被分配到～⟩
  • bully 惡霸、霸凌

- 我很擔心我的弟弟。

  I was worried about my younger brother.

- 我擔心我的朋友們會對我生氣。

  I was worried that my friends might be mad at me.
  • be mad at 對～生氣

我擔心我明天是否能表演得好。	I was worried whether I would be able to do well on the performance tomorrow. • performance 表演
我整天都在擔心他們是否已經發現我說了謊。	All day long, I was worried about if they had found out that I had lied.
我本來對這個考試感到很緊張,但是這個考試比我預想的簡單。	I was nervous about the test, but it was easier than I had thought. • nervous 緊張的
總之擔心也無法解決任何事。	Worrying doesn't solve anything anyway.
我媽媽憂心忡忡。	My mother worries a lot.
我擔心那裡會沒有我認識的人。	I was afraid that there would be no one I knew there.
擔心這種事情是無濟於事的。	It was useless to worry about such things. • useless 無用的、無濟於事的
我擔心的事情進行得很順利。	The thing that I was worried about went well.
我昨天非常的擔心,但當我實際面對它時,發現根本沒什麼。	I was worried so much yesterday, but when I actually faced it, it was nothing. • face 面對、面臨

害怕 ★ Scared

我很容易感到害怕。	I get scared easily.
我無法一個人睡覺,因為我會覺得害怕。	I can't sleep alone because I feel scared.
我晚上害怕自己單獨待在家裡。	I was scared to stay at home alone at night.

- 當媽媽外出辦事，而留我一個人在家時，我會覺得害怕。

  I felt scared when my mother went on some errands and left me at home alone.
  - go on an errand 辦事情

- 我去了鬼屋，那真的很恐怖。

  I went to the haunted house, and it was really terrifying.
  - haunted 鬧鬼的　terrifying 恐怖的

- 弟弟因為害怕而哭了。

  My younger brother cried because he felt scared.

- 我坐了雲霄飛車，而且害怕得要命。

  I rode on the rollercoaster, and I was scared to death.　極度、（程度）至死

- 看牙醫是我最害怕的事情。

  Going to the dentist is the thing that I fear the most.
  - fear 害怕、畏懼

- 我和朋友們一起看了一部很恐怖的電影。

  I watched a movie together with my friends, and it was very scary.

- 我無法停止的想著這部電影裡的恐怖場景。

  I can't stop thinking about the horrible scenes in the movie.
  - horrible 可怕的、令人毛骨悚然的

- 看了恐怖片以後，我晚上做了個惡夢。

  After seeing the horror movie, I had a nightmare at night.
  - horror 恐怖

- 我從朋友那裡聽到了一個恐怖的故事，而我無法停止的一直想著它。

  I heard a horror story from my friend, and I couldn't stop thinking about it.

- 我做了一個惡夢。

  I had a nightmare.

- 因為做了惡夢，我醒了。

  Because of my nightmare, I woke up.

- 我因為太害怕而開始流汗。

  I was so scared that I started to sweat.
  - sweat 流汗

- 我因為害怕而顫抖。

  I was shivering from fear.

  • shiver 顫抖

- 我起了雞皮疙瘩。

  I got goose bumps.　— 起雞皮疙瘩

- 那令人心驚膽顫。

  It was bloodcurdling.

  • bloodcurdling 令人心驚膽顫的

- 在我回家的路上，因為我覺得非常害怕，所以我非常努力地跑。

  On my way home, I was very scared, so I ran really hard.

- 我感到令人毛骨悚然的恐懼。

  I felt hair-raising horror.　— 毛骨悚然的

- 我很害怕，因為我在一個黑暗的地方。

  I was scared because I was in a dark place.

- 我很怕大隻的狗。

  I am afraid of big dogs.

- 我妹妹很怕打針。

  My younger sister is afraid of getting shots.　— 打針

- 因為我聽到一個奇怪的聲音，所以我覺得害怕。／奇怪的聲音讓我覺得害怕。

  I was scared because I heard a strange sound. / A strange sound made me frightened.

  • frightened 害怕的、受驚嚇的

- 我開著燈睡覺，因為我很怕黑。

  I sleep with the light on because I'm afraid of the dark.

後悔／可惜 ★ Regret

- 我後悔沒有早一點開始做我的回家功課。

  I regret not doing my homework earlier.

  • regret 後悔　earlier 早一點

- 我後悔浪費自己的時間。

  I regretted wasting my time.

- 在考完試以後，我後悔沒有念書。

  After taking the test, I regretted not studying for it.

- 我後悔我一直在玩。

  I regret playing all the time.

- 我對打了妹妹感到抱歉。

  I was sorry that I had hit my younger sister.

- 我後悔嘲笑了我的朋友。

  I regret teasing my friend.

  • tease 取笑、嘲弄

- 我當時應該要更有耐心。

  I should have been more patient.

  • should have + 過去分詞 當時應該～

- 我當時應該要更小心。

  I should have been more careful.

- 在玩樂之前，我應該要先做完我的回家功課。

  I should have done my homework before playing.

- 我當時不應該看電視的。

  I should not have watched TV.

- 我當時應該要聽媽媽的話的。

  I should have listened to my mother.

- 我不知道為什麼我沒聽媽媽的話。

  I don't know why I didn't listen to my mother.

- 我當時不應該聽媽媽的話的。

  I should not have listened to my mother.

- 我當時不應該隨著我的朋友起舞的，現在我惹上麻煩了。／我因為跟著朋友做了蠢事而惹上了麻煩。

  I shouldn't have followed my friend. Now I am in trouble. / I am in trouble because I did a stupid thing by following my friend.

- 失去這個重要的機會讓我感到十分難過。

  I am really sad about losing this important opportunity.

  • opportunity 機會

- 我對結果感到有點難過，但我沒有任何遺憾，因為我已盡了全力。

  I am a bit sad about the result, but I don't have any regrets because I did my best.

- 我答錯了四題，所以我考試考不及格了。

  I got four wrong answers, so I failed the test.

- 覆水難收。（為打翻的牛奶哭泣也沒有用。）

  It's no use crying over spilt milk.
  - spill (spill-spilt-spilt) 打翻、溢出

- 嘗試過後後悔，比起後悔什麼都沒做來得好。

  It's better to regret after trying something than regretting doing nothing.

- 我會盡我的全力，讓我在未來不會有任何遺憾。

  I will try my best so that I don't have any regrets in the future.

- 我明天會開始運動。

  I will exercise starting tomorrow.

- 從明天開始我不會再吃太多。

  Starting tomorrow, I will never eat too much.

- 下次說話前我會再多思考一下。

  I will think one more time before I speak the next time.

驚訝 ★ Feeling Surprised

- 當我聽到這個消息，我真的感到很驚訝。

  When I heard the news, I was really surprised.

- 那個消息真的很讓人震驚。

  That news was really shocking.

- 我無法相信自己得了第一名！

  I couldn't believe that I had won first place!

  得到第一名

- 在聽到這個消息之後，我的心臟真的跳得很快。

  My heart was beating really fast after hearing the news.

- 我驚訝到無法言語了。

  I was so surprised that I became speechless.

- 我一動也不動地站著，因為我實在太過驚訝了。

  I stood still because I was too dumbfounded. ――一動也不動地站著

  • dumbfounded （受到驚嚇）目瞪口呆

- 你真的讓我大吃一驚。

  You could have knocked me down with a feather.

  • knock A down with a feather 使 A 大吃一驚

- 那樣的事情怎麼會發生？

  How could something like that happen?

尷尬／困惑／害羞 ★ Feeling Embarrassed / Confused / Shy

- 當著同班同學的面被罵，讓我感到很尷尬。

  I was embarrassed to be scolded in front of my classmates. ――被罵

  • embarrassed （人感到）窘迫的、尷尬的

- 我在賽跑時跌倒，這讓我覺得真的很丟臉。

  I fell down while racing, and I felt so embarrassed.

  • ashamed 丟臉的

- 在跌倒之後，其實我覺得比起疼痛，我更覺得丟臉。

  After falling down, I thought it was actually more embarrassing than painful.

- 我的褲襪破了個洞，這讓我覺得很丟臉。

  It was embarrassing because I got a hole in my stocking. / I was embarrassed to have a hole in my tights.

  • tights 褲襪

- 我忘了帶我的回家功課，所以我得要在教室後面罰站。我覺得自己很丟臉。

  I forgot to bring my homework, so I had to stand in the back of the classroom. I was ashamed of myself.

- 我因為覺得尷尬而臉紅了。

  I was blushing because I was embarrassed.

  • blush 臉變紅

- 我尷尬到想直接消失。

  I was so embarrassed that I wanted to disappear.
  - disappear 消失

- 儘管這是我知道的事情，但我無法說出任何話，因為我覺得太尷尬了。

  Although it was something I knew, I couldn't say anything because I was too embarrassed.

- 當我的名字突然被叫到時，我不知道該怎麼辦。

  When my name was suddenly called, I didn't know what to do.

- 因為我感到不知所措，所以我說出的話完全不合理。

  I was at a loss, so my words didn't make any sense.　茫然不知所措的
  - make sense 合理、行得通

- 我實在太混亂了，以致於我忘了所有我之前記下來的東西。

  I was so confused that I forgot everything I had memorized.
  - memorize 背熟、記住

- Amy 真是個害羞的女孩。

  Amy is such a shy girl.

- 我想參與課堂討論，但我太害羞了，所以沒辦法這樣做。

  I want to participate in the class discussion, but I am too shy to do so.

- 老師突然問了我一個問題，結果我結巴的回答不出來。

  My teacher suddenly asked me a question, and I stammered instead of answering.
  - stammer 口吃、講話結巴的

- 教室裡的所有人都在看我，讓我的臉紅了起來。

  Everyone in the class was looking at me, so it made me blush.

- 我很緊張，但我很冷靜地回答。

  I was so nervous, but I answered calmly.
  - calmly 沉著冷靜地

個性

My Friend Eric

Wednesday, April 20, Sunny

Eric is the kindest of my friends. A mother brought some snacks for the class, but there was not enough for everyone. Eric said he would not have anything. He always thinks of others first. Everyone likes to hang out with him. I will try to be kind to others like Eric.

我的朋友 Eric　　4 月 20 日星期三，晴天

Eric 是我的朋友當中最體貼親切的。有同學的媽媽帶了點心給全班吃，但是點心不夠分給班上的每個人，Eric 就說他不要吃。他總是先想到別人。大家都喜歡和他一起玩。我會試著像 Eric 一樣的體貼親切地對待別人。

· snack 點心　enough 足夠的

個性急躁 ★ Short-Tempered Personalities

- 我的個性有點急躁。

  I am kind of short-tempered.
  • short/quick-tempered 急性子的、脾氣暴躁的

- 我們家的人都是急性子。

  Everyone in my family is quick-tempered.

- 我就像我爸一樣個性急躁。

  Just like my dad, I am quick-tempered.

- 我爸爸的個性暴躁。

  My dad is hot-tempered. 性情暴躁、易怒的

- 我爸爸是個積極能幹的人。

  My dad is a real go-getter. 能幹、積極的人

- 當我決定要做些什麼，我就會努力去做。

  When I decide on something, I just go for it. 積極嘗試、努力爭取

- 我哥哥的個性太過急躁，以至於他很容易就會生氣。

  My older brother is so quick-tempered that he gets angry easily.

- 我總是想趕快做好所有的事。

  I want to do everything fast. /
  I want to get everything done fast.

- 因為我做事總是急急忙忙的，所以我很常會犯很多錯誤。

  Since I am always in a hurry, I tend to make many mistakes. 匆忙地、急切地

- 我做每件事都做得很快，但總是做得不夠徹底。

  I do everything fast but not thoroughly.
  • thoroughly 徹底地

- 我的個性比較急，所以當我看到別人的動作不夠迅速時，我就會覺得很不耐煩。

  I am quick-tempered, so I get frustrated when I see someone who is not fast enough.
  • frustrated 覺得沮喪、不快的

- 當我看到朋友做事不夠迅速的時候，我就想乾脆替他們做。

  When I see friends who do not act fast enough, I just want to do things for them.

- 為什麼我的個性這麼急躁呢？　　　　Why am I so short-tempered?

- 我應該要更有耐心的，但我做不到。　I should be more patient, but I can't.
  - patient 有耐心的

個性隨和 ★ Easygoing Personalities

- 我是個隨和的人。
  I am an easygoing person.
  - easygoing 隨和的、悠哉的

- 我往往用緩慢的步調來做每一件事。
  I tend to do everything at a slow pace.
  用緩慢的步調

- 我動作和講話都很慢。
  I act slowly and talk slowly.

- 烏龜是我的綽號。
  Turtle is my nickname.

- 我弟弟就是一個這麼隨和的人。
  My younger brother is such an easygoing person.

- 我妹妹就像我媽媽一樣非常隨和。
  My younger sister is very easygoing just like my mother.

- 我弟弟做事的步調很慢。
  My younger brother acts at a slow pace.

- 我不喜歡急急忙忙的。
  I don't like hurrying.

- 我總是我們班上最後一個去拿午餐的人。
  I am always the last one to get lunch in my class.

- 雖然我的步調常常比較慢，但我的思考速度可不慢。
  Although I tend to be slow, my thoughts do not run at a slow pace.
  - thought 思考

- 爸爸說媽媽的慢步調讓他覺得很不耐煩。
  My father says my mom's slow pace frustrates him.

- 我覺得隨和的人事實上有比較好的個性。

  I think easygoing people actually have nicer personalities.

  • personality 個性

- 我想要用更快的速度做事，但即使我努力了也還是做不到。

  I want to act at a faster speed, but I can't even though I try.

  即使～

- 我因為那些動作比較快的小孩總是能拿到好東西而感到不高興。

  I am upset because it's always the faster kids who get the good things.

個性善良 ★ Nice / Kind Personalities

- Eric 人很好。

  Eric is very nice.

- Eric 有很好的個性。

  Eric has such a nice personality.

- Eric 是我班上個性最好的學生。

  Eric is the nicest student in my class.

- Eric 是我朋友中最親切善良的。

  Eric is the kindest of my friends.

- Eric 十分親切善良。

  Eric is very kind.

- Eric 對別人相當體貼。

  Eric is very considerate of others.

  • considerate 體貼的

- Eric 十分顧及他人的需求。／Eric 總是先為他人設想。

  Eric takes good care of others' needs. / Eric always thinks of others first.

- Eric 不太會生氣。

  Eric hardly gets angry.

- Eric 總是笑容滿面。

  Eric always smiles.

- Eric 很有禮貌。

  Eric is polite.

- Eric 很尊敬年長者。／Eric 對年長者很有禮貌。

  Eric respects the elderly. / Eric is polite to the elderly.

  • respect 尊敬　　　　年長者

個性差勁 ★ Bad/Mean Personalities

- Adam 的個性很差勁。

  Adam has a bad personality.

- Adam 有著強硬的個性。

  Adam has such a strong personality.

- Adam 很卑鄙。

  Adam is very mean.

- Adam 有點自私。

  Adam is kind of selfish.

  • selfish 自私的

- Adam 很自我中心。

  Adam is egotistic.

  • egotistic 自我中心的

- Adam 老是想要為所欲為。／
  Adam 老是想要使喚我們。

  Adam always wants to get his way. /
  Adam always wants to boss us around.

  • get one's way 為所欲為　boss around 使喚、頤指氣使

- Adam 很容易生氣。

  Adam gets angry easily.

- Adam 非常調皮搗蛋。／
  Adam 很愛玩鬧。

  Adam is very mischievous. /
  Adam is very playful.

  • mischievous 調皮搗蛋的　playful 愛玩鬧的

- Adam 很高傲自負。／
  Adam 很喜歡炫耀。

  Adam is arrogant. /
  Adam likes to show off.

  • arrogant 高傲自負的　　　炫耀

- Adam 總是在別人背後說壞話。

  Adam is always talking behind people's backs.

  • talk behind one's back 在別人背後說壞話

- Adam 說他的朋友們的壞話。

  Adam speaks badly of his friends.

  說～壞話

個性開朗活潑 ★ Cheerful / Lively Personalities

- 我的個性很開朗。

  I have a cheerful personality.
  • cheerful 開朗的、愉悅的

- 我是個快樂的人。

  I am a jolly person.
  • jolly 愉快的、高興的

- 我是個外向的人。

  I am an outgoing person.
  • outgoing 外向的

- 我的個性可用「開朗」來形容。

  Bright is the word for my personality.

- 多虧我的開朗個性，我有許多的朋友。

  幸虧～、多虧～
  (Thanks to) my cheerful personality, there are a lot of friends.

- 我的綽號是「快樂病毒」。

  Happy Virus is my nickname.

- Amy 很活潑且精力旺盛。

  Amy is lively and energetic.
  • lively 活潑的　energetic 精力旺盛的

- Amy 非常開朗。

  Amy is very cheerful.

- Amy 笑口常開。

  Amy laughs a lot.

- Amy 對每件事都抱持著積極的態度。

  Amy has a positive attitude about everything.
  • positive 積極的　attitude 態度

- Alice 非常友善。／
  Alice 是個很善於交際的人。

  Alice is very friendly. /
  Alice is a very sociable person.
  • sociable 善於交際的

- Alice 很外向，所以她很容易就能交到朋友。

  Alice is very outgoing, so she makes friends easily.

- Alice 就是一個這麼健談的人。 | Alice is such a talkative person.
  • talkative 健談的

- 弟弟總是這麼活潑。 | My younger brother is always so lively.

- 妹妹總是充滿活力。 | My younger sister is always full of energy.

- 當我看到快樂的弟弟，我也會覺得快樂。 | When I see my jolly brother, I get happy, too.

個性幽默 ★ Humorous Personalities

- 我的幽默感絕佳。 | I have a pretty good sense of humor.
  幽默感

- 我很擅長逗笑別人。 | I am good at making people laugh.
  擅長

- 我的夢想是當一個喜劇演員。 | My dream is to be a comedian.

- 朋友跟我說我應該去當喜劇演員。 | My friends tell me that I should be a comedian.

- 爸爸的幽默感十足。 | My dad is full of humor.

- 爸爸總是捉弄我們。 | My dad always plays tricks on us.
  捉弄

- 爸爸總是在開玩笑。 | My dad makes jokes all the time.
  開玩笑　　總是

- 爸爸讓同樣的老笑話聽起來更好笑。 | My dad makes the same old joke sound funnier.

- 弟弟很會做鬼臉。 | My younger brother makes excellent funny faces.

- 媽媽總是會因為我的笑話而大笑。 | My mother laughs at my jokes all the time.

我們班上有很多有趣的學生。	There are so many funny students in my class.
Jason 真的很有趣。	Jason is really funny.
Jason 是我們班上的開心果。	Jason is the class clown. • clown 小丑、詼諧的人
Jason 是班上最有趣的學生。	Jason is the funniest student in my class.
Jason 擅長表現得像個喜劇演員一樣。	Jason is good at acting like a comedian.
我羨慕 Jason 說有趣的笑話的天分。	I envy Jason's talent at telling funny jokes. • talent 天分
我喜歡有趣的朋友。	I like my friends who are funny.
我今天在才藝表演上模仿了一個喜劇演員。	I did an impression of a comedian at the talent show today. （對名人）的模仿
我的朋友們覺得那非常有趣。	My friends found it very funny.
老師跟我說我是班上的開心果。	My teacher told me that I am the class clown.
看到朋友們大笑也會讓我感到心情愉快。	Seeing my friends laugh made me feel good, too.

個性沉著冷靜／注重細節
★ Calm Personalities / Meticulous Personalities

我是個文靜的人。	I am a quiet person.
我個性挺冷靜的。	I am kind of calm.

- 我個性有點膽小。

  I am kind of timid.
  - timid 膽怯、膽小的

- 我很容易害羞。

  I get shy easily.

- 我是個內向的人。

  I am an introvert.
  - introvert 內向的人

- 每當我必須在班上發表意見時，我都會覺得很緊張。

  Whenever I have to speak in class, I feel so nervous.

- Jason 的話不多。

  Jason doesn't really talk a lot.

- Jason 不怎麼愛講話。

  Jason rarely talks. /
  Jason talks little.
  - rarely 幾乎不～

- 雖然 Jason 不怎麼愛講話，但當他開口說話時，他說的非常條理分明。

  Although Jason hardly speaks, when he does, he is very articulate.
  - articulate 說話清楚且條理分明

- Jason 是個思慮非常周到的人。

  Jason is a very considerate person.
  - considerate 思慮周到的

- 我是個注重細節的人。

  I am a meticulous person.
  - meticulous 注重細節的

- 我對所有事情都十分小心。／
  我對所有事情都非常注意。

  I am cautious about everything. /
  I pay close attention on everything.
  - cautious 十分小心的   pay attention 關注、注意

- 我試著在說話前三思。

  I try to think twice before I speak.

- 我在午休時喜歡看書，勝過於出去玩。

  I prefer reading books to playing outside during lunch break.

- 我喜歡待在家裡勝過於出去玩。

  I like staying at home more than playing outside.

- 我想改變我膽小的個性。 I want to change my timid personality.

- 我想變成外向的人。我想要和各種 I want to be an outgoing person. I want to
  類型的人好好相處。 get along with all types of people.
  • type 種類　　　　　和～和睦相處

- 我是個文靜的人。我和我妹妹正好 I am a quiet person. I'm the exact opposite
  相反。 of my younger sister.
  • opposite 相反的

- 雖然 Amy 很文靜，而我精力旺盛， Although Amy is quiet and I am
  但我們相處得極為融洽。 energetic, we get along perfectly well.

個性誠懇 ★ Earnest Personalities

- 我認為我是個誠懇的人。 I think I am an earnest person.
  • earnest 誠懇的

- 我認為我是個負責任的人。 I think I am a responsible person.

- 我自己把該做的事完成。 I do what I have to do by myself.
  （沒有別人的協助）自己做

- 我朋友 Amy 是個模範生。 My friend Amy is a model student.
  模範生

- Amy 是個真誠的人。 Amy is a sincere person.
  • sincere 真誠、真摯的

- 坐我旁邊的同學很和藹可親且誠 My seatmate is very kind and earnest, so
  懇，所以大家都叫他模範生。 everyone calls him a model student.

- 我覺得 Eric 是我們班上最認真的學 I think Eric is the hardest working
  生。 student in my class.

- 我幾乎沒有從我媽媽那裡聽到任何 I have hardly heard any nagging from my
  的嘮叨。 mother.
  • nag 嘮叨

- 我回到家就先去完成我的回家功課。

  I finish my homework first when I come home.

- 當我做完回家功課後，我覺得放心了。

  I feel relieved when I am done with my homework.

  做完〜

  • relieved 覺得放心的

- 我上學幾乎不會遲到。

  I am hardly late for school.

- 我的朋友們都說我是一個努力認真的人。

  My friends all call me a hard worker.

- 如果我繼續這樣做，恐怕我會被說成是不負責任的人。

  If I keep doing this, I am afraid I might be called irresponsible.

  • irresponsible 不負責任的

- 我想成為一個親切又誠懇的人。

  I want to be a kind and earnest person.

我的優點 ★ My Strengths

- 我的優點是什麼？

  What is my strength?

- 我覺得我的優點就是能夠對朋友讓步。

  I think my strength is that I am able to give up things for my friends.

- 我最大的優點就是能和我所有的朋友和睦相處。

  My strongest point is that I get along with all of my friends.

- 我擅長演奏樂器。而在所有樂器之中，我的鋼琴彈得非常好。

  I am good at playing instruments. Among them, I play the piano very well.

  • instrument 樂器

- 我的字非常工整，我在寫字比賽上有得獎。

  My handwriting is very neat. I won an award at the handwriting competition.

  • handwriting 書寫、筆跡

- 我很擅長跑步，所以我在體育課時很受歡迎。

  I am good at running, so I am very popular during P.E.

- 我朋友很羨慕我，因為我的英文發音很棒。

  My friends envy me because my English pronunciation is good.

  • pronunciation 發音

- 我很會管理我的錢，每當我拿到零用錢，我就會把一部分存下來。

  I manage my money well. Whenever I get my allowance, I put some of it in my savings.

  • manage 處理、管理　allowance 零用錢　savings 存錢

- 我往往完整規劃每件事情，並盡我最大的努力依照計畫進行。

  I tend to plan everything thoroughly and try my best to stand by it.
  遵守～

  • thoroughly 徹底地

- 當我做完我的功課，我總會幫助我的朋友。

  When I am done with my work, I always help my friends.

- 我上課時很專注。

  I concentrate really well during class.

  • concentrate 專注、集中

- 我早上不需要媽媽幫忙就能自己起床。

  I can wake up by myself in the morning without my mother's help.

- 我喜愛看書。我是圖書館的常客，所以圖書館館員對我很好。

  I love reading. I am a regular visitor at the library, so the librarian treats me really well.
  常客

  • librarian 圖書館館員

- 我很擅長課堂參與，我總是信心滿滿地提供我的意見。

  I am good at participating in class. I always give my opinion with confidence.
  有信心地

- 我很擅長畫畫，我在校內寫生比賽上得了一個獎。

  I am good at drawing. I won an award at the school's nature drawing competition.

- 我很擅長寫作，我曾經是我們學校參加寫作比賽的代表。

I am good at writing. I was once my school's representative at a writing competition.

• once（過去）曾經、一度　representative 代表

- 我總是先和別人打招呼，所以我總是得到來自鄰居的稱讚。

I always say hello to others first, so I always get compliments from my neighbors.

• compliment 稱讚

- 我總是仔細傾聽朋友們的心聲。

I always (listen closely) to my friends.
　　　　　┗ 仔細傾聽

- 我很注重細節，所以我的朋友們常會問我要帶什麼去學校。

I am meticulous, so my friends often ask me what to bring to school.

- 我是個天生的領導者，所以很多我的朋友們想和我在同一組。

I am a born leader, so a lot of my friends want to be in the same group with me.

• born 天生的

- 我總是打扮得很好看，因為我很有時尚感。

I always dress up nicely because I have a good (sense of fashion).
　　　　　　　　┗ 時尚感

- 我很有運動細胞，所以我的同學們都想要和我在同一隊。

I am athletic, so my classmates want to be in the same team with me.

• athletic 擅長運動的

- 我很擅長讀書，所以我的成績總是很好。

I am good at studying, so my grades are always high.

- 我的同學們常會帶著問題來找我，因為我很擅長解釋事情。

My classmates often come to me with questions because I am good at explaining things.

- 我擅長除了讀書之外的所有事。

I am good at everything except studying.

• except 除了～以外

我的缺點 ★ My Weaknesses

- 我的缺點就是缺乏恆心。

  My weakness is that I am not persistent.
  - persistent 堅持不懈的

- 我的缺點就是我很急躁。

  My weakness is that I am short-tempered.

- 我的缺點就是情緒化。

  My weakness is my moodiness.
  - moodiness 情緒化、喜怒無常

- 我的缺點就是容易被周邊的言語所影響。

  My weakness is that I get carried away easily with my surroundings.　被別人所影響
  - surrounding 周邊情況

- 我的缺點就是我無法拒絕別人。

  My weakness is that I cannot say no to others.

- 我很容易感到不開心。

  I get upset easily.

- 我常會記恨，當我感到不開心的時候，我就會維持那個狀態很久。

  懷抱恨意、記恨
  I tend to hold grudges. When I am upset, I stay that way for a long time.

- 我既不會唱歌也不會跳舞。／
  我唱歌和跳舞都很糟。

  I can neither sing nor dance. /
  I am a terrible singer and dancer.

- 我有點敏感，所以我朋友的話常會使我感到受傷。

  I am kind of sensitive, so my friends' words often hurt me.
  - sensitive 神經過敏的、易受傷害的

- 我有拖延的習慣。

  I have a habit of delaying things.
  - delay 耽擱、拖延

- 我覺得我睡太多了，對我來說要在早上起床很難。

  I think I sleep too much. It's so difficult for me to wake up in the morning.

- 我是個笨手笨腳的人。

  I am a clumsy person.
  - clumsy 愚笨的、手腳不靈活的

- 我常會掉東西。

  I lose things easily.

- 我缺乏自信。

  I lack self-confidence. (自信)

- 我缺乏專注力。／
  我很難專心。

  I lack concentration. /
  I have trouble paying attention.

  • concentration 專注（力）

- 我很優柔寡斷且顧慮太多。

  I am indecisive and think about things too much.

  • indecisive 優柔寡斷的

- 我不認為我有什麼特別的缺點。

  I don't think I have any particular flaws.

  • particular 特別的　flaw 缺點

- 我唯一的缺點就是我沒有缺點，哈哈哈！

  My only flaw is that I don't have any flaws at all. Ha-ha-ha!

- 如果我有缺點的話，我認為我必須接受它，並且專注在發展我的優點上。

  I think I need to accept my weakness if I have one and focus on developing my strengths. (集中於～、專注於～)

- 我雖然很清楚我的缺點，但是很難去改過來。

  I am well aware of my weakness, but it's hard to fix it. (很清楚知道～)

  • fix 修正

嗜好和興趣

My Dream Job: Diplomat Wednesday, October 20, Windy

My dream is to be a brilliant diplomat like Mr. Kimoon Ban, the UN Secretary-General. I read a book about him once. Since then, I have been interested in being a diplomat. I heard academic excellence is very important to be a diplomat. I will study harder to achieve my goal.

我夢想中的工作:外交官　　10月20日星期三,強風

我的夢想是成為一位像聯合國祕書長潘基文先生一樣傑出的外交官。我曾經看過一本關於他的書。在那之後,我就對成為一位外交官產生了興趣。我聽說在課業上的優異表現對成為一位外交官來說很重要,我會更努力念書以達成我的目標。

·**brilliant** 傑出的　**diplomat** 外交官　**Secretary-General** 祕書長
　academic excellence 課業上的優異表現　**achieve** 達成、實現

嗜好 ★ Hobbies

- 我的嗜好是閱讀。   My hobby is reading.

- 我的嗜好是聽音樂。   My hobby is listening to music.

- 我的嗜好是看電影。   My hobby is watching movies.

- 可以說我的嗜好就只是閒坐著。   I could say my hobby is just sitting around. 〔閒坐、無所事事〕

- 我爸爸的嗜好是打高爾夫球。   My father's hobby is playing golf.

- 我媽媽的嗜好是編織。   My mother's hobby is knitting.
  - knit 編織、針織

- 在我有空的時候，我會健身。   During my free time, I work out. / 〔健身、運動〕
  I work out when I find the time.

- 當我在運動的時候，我可以紓解我的壓力。   When I exercise, I can relieve my stress.
  - relieve 紓解

- 我通常用聽音樂來紓解我的壓力。   I usually relieve my stress by listening to music.

- 我真的很喜歡畫畫。   I really enjoy drawing.

- 我沒有什麼特別的嗜好。   I don't have a particular hobby.

特長、天分 ★ Talents

- 我很擅長畫畫。   I am good at drawing.

- 我對語言有天分。   I am talented at languages.
  - talented 有天分、才能

- 我有藝術天分。　　　　　　　　　I have a talent at art.

- 我擅長做手工藝。　　　　　　　　I am good at making crafts.
  - craft 手工藝品

- 我妹妹的手很巧。　　　　　　　　My younger sister is handy.
  - handy 手巧的

- 我是我們班上足球踢得最好的人。　I am the best soccer player in my class.

- 我滿擅長運動的。　　　　　　　　I am quite athletic.

- 我是個全能型的運動員。　　　　　I am an all-around athlete.
  　　　　　　　　　　　　　　　　全能的、多才多藝的
  - athlete 運動選手、擅長運動的人

- 我對運動很有天分。　　　　　　　I am talented at sports.

- 我不擅長運動。　　　　　　　　　I am not good at sports.

- 我沒有運動細胞。　　　　　　　　I am not athletic.

- 我對音樂很有天分。　　　　　　　I have a good ear for music.

- 我的小提琴老師告訴我說我對小提　My violin teacher told me that I am
  琴很有天分。　　　　　　　　　　talented at the violin. 對～有天賦、才能

- 雖然我喜歡芭蕾，但我不認為我在　I like ballet, but I don't think I'm
  芭蕾上有天分。　　　　　　　　　talented for ballet.

未來夢想、目標 ★ Dreams / Future Goals

- 我的夢想是成為一名廚師。　　　　My dream is to be a chef.

- 我想成為時尚設計師。　　　　　　I want to be a fashion designer.

- 當我長大後，我想成為一位足球選手。

  When I grow up, I want to be a soccer player.

- 我在一年級的時候，我的夢想是成為一位喜劇演員。

  When I was in the 1st grade, my dream was to be a comedian.

- 我的夢想是成為像愛因斯坦一樣的科學家。

  My dream is to be a scientist like Einstein.

- 我想成為像麥可・喬丹一樣的籃球員。

  I want to be a basketball player like Michael Jordan.

- 我想成為像麥可・菲爾普斯一樣棒的游泳選手。

  I want to be a fantastic swimmer like Michael Phelps.

- 我的夢想是成為一位像潘基文一樣傑出的外交官。

  My dream is to be a brilliant diplomat just like Kimoon Ban.

  • diplomat 外交官

  （因尊敬而想效仿的）榜樣

- 潘基文是我的榜樣。

  Kimoon Ban is my role model.

- 我想成為跆拳道教練，並教授世界各地的孩子跆拳道。

  I want to be a taekwondo instructor and teach taekwondo to children all over the world.

  • instructor 教練、指導者

- 我想和我爸爸一樣成為獸醫。

  I want to be a vet like my father.

  • vet 獸醫

- 我熱愛棒球，所以我想成為一名棒球選手。

  I love baseball, so I want to be a baseball player.

- 雖然我喜歡芭蕾，但長大後我想當一名律師。

  Although I like ballet, I want to be a lawyer when I grow up.

- 自從我在二年級看了音樂劇《Wicked》以後，我就夢想成為音樂劇演員。

  Ever since I watched the musical *Wicked* in the 2nd grade, I've dreamed of becoming a musical actor.

- 我的夢想是成為外交官，因此我必須會說流利的英語來實現這個夢想。

  My dream is to be a diplomat, and I have to be fluent in English to make it come true.
  • fluent 流利的　實現

- 為了要達成我的夢想，我必須要很會讀書。

  In order to achieve my dream, I have to be good at studying.
  • achieve 達到、實現

- 我想成為電影導演，所以我看了很多電影。

  I want to become a movie director, so I watch a lot of movies.　電影導演

- 我仍然不知道長大後想要做什麼。

  I still don't know what I want to be when I grow up.

- 我對未來有著太多的夢想，所以我不知道該選擇哪一個好。

  I have too many dreams for my future, so I don't know which one to pick.

- 我仍然還沒決定我的夢想是什麼。

  I still haven't made up my mind about my dream.　決定、下定決心

- 我認為當科學家很酷，當老師也很棒。

  I think being a scientist is cool, and being a teacher is also wonderful.
  • cool 酷的、很棒的

- 有一天，我想成為足球員，但隔天我又想成為外交官。

  One day, I want to be a soccer player, but then the next day, I want to be a diplomat.

- 我也真的很想找到我的夢想。

  I really want to find my dream, too.

- 決定要追求哪個夢想是很困難的。

  It is difficult to decide which dream to pursue.
  • pursue 追求

- 我認為我必須盡可能的多體驗不同事物。

  I think I have to experience as many things as possible.

- 爸爸告訴我，當我全心投入手邊的工作時，那我就可以找到正確的方向。

  My dad told me that when I am devoted to the task at hand, then I should find the right path.

  全心投入～

  在手邊的

  • task 工作、任務　path 路徑、方向

- 在未來會有更多的工作被創造出來。

  In the future, more jobs will be created.

- 未來的工作會和現在盛行的工作不同。

  Future jobs will be different from the jobs that are popular now.

- 我的夢想是當足球選手，但是我爸媽想要我當醫生。

  My dream is to be a soccer player, but my parents want me to be a doctor.

- 我媽媽建議我當設計師，因為她認為我有藝術天分。

  My mom suggests I become a designer because she thinks I am talented at art.

- 我的夢想是在演藝圈工作，但是我媽媽極其反對。

  My dream is to work in the entertainment area, but my mother is extremely opposed to that.

  • entertainment area 演藝圈　extremely 極其、非常地
    be opposed to 反對～

- 我只想成為像我媽媽那樣的人。

  I just want to be someone like my mother.

我的決心 ★ My Decisions

- 我決定要更加用功讀書。

  I have decided to study harder.

- 從今以後，我會當個好兒子／女兒。

  From now on, I will be a good son/daughter.

- 我對老師承諾說我從明天開始上學不會再遲到。

  I promised my teacher that I will not be late for school starting tomorrow.

- 我弟弟和我達成了停戰協議。

  My younger brother and I made an agreement to stop fighting.

  • agreement 協議、協定

- 我決定早上要早點起床，不要睡過頭。

  I have decided to wake up early in the morning instead of oversleeping.

- 我每個月會至少讀十本書。

  I will read at least 10 books every month.

  至少

- 我一定會在接下來的考試中得到前五名的成績。

  For the upcoming exam, I will make sure to get one of the top five scores.

  • upcoming 即將來臨的

- 我一定會在這次期中考的所有科目上都拿到滿分。

  I will make sure to get a perfect score in every subject this midterm.

- 我會盡全力來一直堅持我的決心。

  I will try my best to stick to my resolution for a long time.

  堅持～

  • resolution 決心、決定

- 距離許下我的新年新希望已經一年了，但是我大部分都沒有達成。

  It has already been a year since I came up with my new year's resolutions, but I've failed to keep most of them.

- 我決定要更努力地念數學，但我還是沒做到。

  I decided to study math harder, but I don't do well.

- 我和媽媽達成協議要在早上早起，但是實踐起來真的非常困難。

  I made an agreement with my mother to wake up early in the morning, but it's so difficult to put it into practice.

  • put... into practice 實行～、實踐～

- 每當我碰到麻煩的時候，我會提醒自己要記得自己的決心，但是我老是忘記這件事。

  Every time I get into trouble, I remind myself about my decision, but I keep forgetting it.

  • remind 使～想起

- 我會證明我是言出必行的男生／女生。

  I will show that I am a boy / girl of my word.

- 我無論如何都會保持每天至少運動一小時。

  Exercising at least an hour every day, I will do it no matter what.

  無論如何

- 我的字典裡沒有不可能。　　The word impossible is not in my dictionary.

- 遵守計畫比訂出計畫來得重要。　　It is more important to follow the plan than to come up with one.
  想出～

電腦／遊戲 ★ Computers / Games

- 在我家，電腦是放在客廳裡的。　　At my house, the computer is in the living room.

- 在我家，每個家庭成員都有排定使用電腦的時間。　　In my family, each member has a scheduled time to use the computer.
  • scheduled 計畫好的

- 老師要我們用 PowerPoint 來做我們的回家功課。　　My teacher told us to use PowerPoint for our homework.

- 我找到一些網路資料來做我的回家功課。／我利用一些網路資料來做我的回家功課。　　I found some Internet resources for my homework. / I did my homework by using some online resources.
  • resource 資源、資料

- 我做了一些網路搜尋，然後上傳了一些資料到我們的班網上。　　I did some Internet research and then uploaded the resources on the class's webpage.
  • research 調查、搜尋

- 我有三張和電腦相關的證照。　　I have three certificates related to computers.
  和～有關的
  • certificate 證照

- 我擅長使用 PowerPoint。　　I am good at using PowerPoint.

- 我一分鐘可以打兩百個英文字母。

  I can type about 200 English letters in a minute.

- 我應該要練習英打。

  I should practice typing in English.

- 我朋友 Amy 有經營她自己的部落格。

  My friend Amy runs her own blog.

- 我無法想像沒有電腦的世界。

  I can't imagine a world without computers.

- 我家的電腦壞了。

  The computer in my house is broken.

  • broken 故障

- 我只能在週末玩電腦遊戲。

  I can play computer games only on weekends. / I am supposed to play computer games only on weekends.

- 我因為可以在週末玩電腦而感到很開心。／我很喜歡週末，因為我可以玩電腦！

  I am so excited because I can play with my computer on weekends. / How I love weekends because I am allowed to use the computer!

- 我被媽媽抓到在玩電腦遊戲，所以我麻煩大了。

  I got caught 〔被抓住〕 playing a computer game, so I got in big trouble with my mother.

- 我媽媽深信所有的遊戲都是不好的。

  My mother believes that all games are bad.

- 事實上有一些遊戲是需要用很多腦力思考的。

  There are actually some games that require a lot of thinking.

- 當我在玩遊戲的時候，我幾乎不會注意到時間的流逝。

  When I play games, I hardly notice time passing by.

- 最近我無法不一直想著遊戲。

  These days, I can't stop thinking about games.

- 我覺得我可能有線上遊戲成癮。

  I think I might have an online game addiction.

  • addiction 成癮、中毒

- 我應該克制我自己別玩太多電腦遊戲。

I should refrain from playing computer games too much. 克制～、避免～

手機 ★ Cell Phones

- 我還沒有手機。

I don't have a cell phone yet. 手機

- 生活沒有手機很不方便。

It is so hard to live without a cell phone. / It is really inconvenient to live without a cell phone.

• inconvenient 不方便的

- 爸爸說等我升上四年級後，他會給我一支手機。

My father told me that he would get me a cell phone when I become a fourth grader.

- 我還要再等一年才能有手機。

I still have to wait for one more year for a cell phone.

- 在我的朋友之中，沒有人是沒有手機的。

Among my friends, there is no one who doesn't have a cell phone.

- 我爸爸買了支手機給我當生日禮物。

My father bought me a mobile phone for a birthday present. 手機

- 我終於得到自己的手機了！

I finally got my own cell phone!

- 我們不被允許帶手機到學校。

We are not allowed to bring cell phones to school.

- 當我踏進教室時，我應該要把手機放進包包裡。

When I step into my classroom, I should put my cell phone into my bag.

- 老師因為我的手機在上課的時候響了而罵我。

  My teacher scolded me because my cell phone rang during class time.

- 我忘記把手機調成震動模式。

  I forgot to put my cell phone on vibration mode.

  • vibration 震動

- 我的手機壞了，因為我摔到它了。

  My cell phone is broken because I dropped it.

- 我的手機掉了。

  I lost my cell phone.

- 我到底有可能會把它放在哪裡呢？我到處都找不到它！

  Where could I have possibly placed it? I can't find it anywhere!

  • possibly 可能、也許　place 放置

- 我因為被媽媽抓到我在玩手機遊戲而被罵。

  I was scolded by mother because she caught me playing a game on my cell phone.

- 我爸媽注意到我下載了一個遊戲到手機裡了。

  My parents noticed that I had downloaded a game on my cell phone.

- 我爸媽因為我不聽他們的話而沒收了我的手機。

  My parents confiscated my phone because I hadn't obeyed them.

  • confiscate 沒收　obey 聽從、遵守

- 我覺得我對手機上癮了。

  I think I have a cell phone addiction.

- 因為當時是考試期間，所以我暫時把手機交給媽媽保管。

  I temporarily gave my phone to my mom because it was my exam period.

  • temporarily 暫時

- 我已經決定在考試期間不用手機了。

  I have decided not to use my phone during my exam period.

- 我的手機很快就沒電了。

  My cell phone's battery dies fast.

- 我無法打電話給媽媽，因為我的手機沒電了。

  I couldn't call my mom because my cell phone's battery went dead.

- 我把手機放在家裡了。

  I left my phone at home.

- 我一整天都焦慮不安，因為我的手機不在身上。

  I was anxious all day because I didn't have my phone with me.

  • anxious 焦慮不安的

- 最近幾乎每個人都用智慧型手機。

  These days, almost everyone uses a smartphone.

- 我也想把我的手機換成最新型的。

  I also want to exchange my phone for the newest model.

- Adam 的手機真的很酷。

  Adam's cell phone is really cool.

- 媽媽告訴我說如果我考試考得好，她就會買一支智慧型手機給我。

  Mom told me that she would buy me a smartphone if I do well on the test.

- 爸爸告訴我再過一陣子他就會把我的手機換成智慧型的。

  Dad told me that he would exchange my phone for a smartphone a little later.

簡訊／數據資料／電信資費 ★ Texting / Data / Phone Plans

- 我和朋友時常用簡訊溝通。

  My friends and I usually communicate by texting.

  • communicate 溝通　text 簡訊

- Adam 經常傳簡訊。

  Adam often sends text messages.

- 我用簡訊詢問我朋友關於回家功課的事。

  I asked my friend about our homework through a text.

- 我傳簡訊給朋友，但是她還沒有回我。

  I texted my friend, but she has not replied.

  • reply 回覆

- 我傳了一封簡訊給爸爸，簡訊裡寫著：「我愛你。」。

  I sent a text to my dad that said, "I love you."

- 我收到很多垃圾訊息。

  I get a lot of spam messages.

- 我已經用光所有的免費簡訊了。

  I have already used all of my free texts.

  • free 免費的

- 媽媽因為我的手機費太高而罵我。

  My mom scolded me because my cell phone bill was too high.

  • bill 帳單

- 我只能用很少的手機數據服務。

  I am allowed to use a very limited data service with my phone.

  • limited 有限的

- 我應該要更小心別傳太多簡訊。

  I should be more careful not to send too many text messages.

- 比起一般的簡訊，我比較喜歡用 Line。

  I prefer Line texts to regular texts.

- 當我在用 Line 聊天時，我沒有注意到時間的流逝。

  I did not notice time passing by while I was chatting on Line.

電視 ★TV

- 我喜歡看電視。

  I like watching TV.

- 我是個電視動漫迷。

  I am a TV animation maniac.

  • maniac ～的迷、～的狂熱者

- 我家沒有電視。

  There is no TV in my house.

- 我只能在週末看電視。

  I can watch TV only on weekends.

- 我在家會留時間看電視。

  I set aside time for TV at home.

  留出、騰出

- 我已經決定一天只看一小時的電視。

  I have decided to watch TV only one hour a day.

- 我們家用電腦看電視。

  My family watches TV through a computer.

- 媽媽總是在電視上看肥皂劇。

  My mother always watches soap operas on TV.
  肥皂劇

- 我爸媽因為我看太多電視而罵我。

  My parents scold me for watching TV too much.

- 爸爸看電視只看新聞。

  My father watches TV only for the news.

- 爸爸只在週末時看電視。

  My father watches TV only on weekends.

- 我最喜歡的電視頻道是 Discovery。

  My favorite TV channel is Discovery Channel.

- 哥哥喜歡看紀錄片。

  My older brother enjoys watching documentaries.

- 我一定要看完所有的綜藝節目，不然我會發瘋。

  I have to watch all the variety shows on TV, or else I'll go crazy.
  綜藝節目

- 我的朋友們常常討論最近流行的電視劇。

  My friends often talk about popular dramas on TV these days.

- 我很少看電視，所以我真的沒辦法參與他們的對話。

  I hardly watch TV, so I can't really participate in the conversation.
  • participate 參與

- 為了和朋友聊天，我必須去看流行的電視劇。

  I have to watch the popular dramas in order to talk with my friends.

- 如果我可以選擇看好的節目，那麼看電視也可以是非常有好處的。

  If I can choose good programs to watch, then watching TV can be quite beneficial.
  • beneficial 有好處的

- 我在奶奶家愛看多久電視就看多久。

  At my grandmother's house, I watched TV as long as I wanted.

- 我喜歡奶奶家有各式各樣頻道的電視。

  I love that Grandma's TV has a variety of channels.
  多樣的

- 我們只有幾個頻道而已，像是公共電視網。

  We only have a few channels, such as the public TV networks.

- 媽媽把電視叫作笨蛋箱。

  My mother calls TV the idiot box.

- 媽媽從不讓我看電視，除非我是在看英文的 DVD。

  My mom never lets me watch TV unless I am watching an English DVD.

  • let A ＋原形動詞 讓 A～

- 我喜歡和朋友們到外面玩，勝過待在家裡看電視。

  I like playing outside with my friends more than watching TV at home.

- 媽媽因為我看太多電視而罵我。

  My mother scolded me for watching TV too much.

- 每當我在看電視，時間就過得飛快。

  Whenever I am watching TV, time flies.

- 從今以後，我會不要看太多的電視。

  From now on, I will watch TV for the right amount of time.

  • amount 量

- 我會減少看電視的時間。

  減少

  I will cut down my TV-watching hours.

- 現在我不看電視了，所以我有更多的時間可以看書。

  Now that I don't watch TV, I have more time to read books.

零用錢 ★ Allowances

- 我每週領一次零用錢。

  I get my allowance on a weekly basis.
  以週為單位

- 我每個禮拜一領零用錢。

  I get my allowance every Monday.

- 我朋友一個月領一次零用錢。

  My friend gets her allowance once a month.

- 我的零用錢是一個禮拜三百元。

  My allowance is 300 NT dollars a week.

- 我聽說 Eric 一個禮拜的零用錢是一千元。

  I heard Eric receives 1000 NT dollars for his weekly allowance.

- 我好羨慕 Eric 能領到這麼多零用錢！

  I envy the big amount of money Eric gets!

- 我好羨慕那些能領到很多零用錢的朋友。

  I envy my friends who receive large allowances.

- 在我的朋友之中，我領到的零用錢最少。

  Among my friends, I get the lowest allowance.

- 領到零用錢的時候，我會存一百元起來。

  When I get my allowance, I save 100 NT dollars.

- 我的銀行帳戶裡有三萬元。

  I have 30,000 NT dollars in my bank account.

  銀行帳戶

- 我沒有零用錢。

  I don't get an allowance.

- 我只在需要時才會開口要錢。

  I just ask for money when I need it.

- 今天我花了一整個星期的零用錢去買了一些垃圾食物當作點心。

  Today, I spent all of my weekly allowance buying some junk food for snacks.

  （營養價值低的）垃圾食物

- 距離我領到零用錢才過了兩天，但我已經全花光了。

  It has been only two days since I received my allowance, but everything is already gone.

- 因為我沒有整理房間，媽媽扣了我的零用錢。

  Because I didn't clean up my room, my mother cut my allowance.

• 我對我的支出做了徹底的記錄。	I keep a thorough record of my spending. • keep a record of 記錄～ thorough 徹底的 spending 支出
• 我必須記錄我的支出，但是這真的很煩人。	I have to keep track of my spending, but it's too annoying. 記錄～
• 因為我長大了，所以媽媽增加了我的零用錢。	Because I got older, my mother increased my allowance. • increase 增加
• 我希望媽媽能增加我的零用錢。／我希望我的零用錢能增加。	I hope my mother will increase my allowance. / I hope I get a raise in my allowance. 獲得提高
• 我存下了我的零用錢，買了個禮物給媽媽。	I saved my allowance and bought a gift for my mother.
• 我會存下我的零用錢來買遊戲機。	I will save my allowance and buy the game player.
• 我的目標是存到十萬元。	My goal is to save up to 100,000 NT dollars. 到～
• 爺爺給了我一些零用錢去買點好吃的東西。	My grandfather gave me some pocket money to buy some goodies. • goodies 好吃的東西
• 爸爸多給了我一些零用錢，因為我考試考得好。	My father gave me some extra spending money for doing well on my exam.
• 我幫忙做家事，然後得到了一些零用錢做為獎勵。	I helped with the chores and received some money for a reward. • chore 雜事、家事
• 我保證會聰明地使用我的零用錢。	I will make sure that I use my allowance wisely.

電影 ★ Movies

- 我超喜歡電影的！

  I love movies!

- 我們家的人常一起去電影院。

  My family often goes to the movie theater together.

  電影院

- 我們家的人一個月去一次電影院。

  My family visits the movie theater once a month.

- 爸爸其實不是很喜歡去電影院。

  My father is not really a fan of going to the movie theater.

- 爸爸通常在家看電影。

  My dad usually watches movies at home.

- 我喜歡動作片。

  I love action movies.

- 我最喜歡的演員是傑森史塔森。

  My favorite actor is Jason Statham.

- 媽媽是裘德洛的超級大粉絲。

  My mother is a huge fan of Jude Law.

- 在所有的好萊塢演員當中，我最喜歡的是安海瑟薇。

  Of all the Hollywood actors, Anne Hathaway is my favorite.

- 她／他是個很棒的演員。

  She/He is such a great actress/actor.
  • actress 女演員

- 我最喜歡的電影是《哈利波特》。

  My favorite movie is *Harry Potter*.

- 《哈利波特》系列我已經看過三次以上了。

  I have watched the *Harry Potter* series more than three times.

- 那其實是小說《哈利波特》的電影版。

  It is actually a movie version of the novel *Harry Potter*.
  • novel 小說

- 我透過有線電影頻道看《暮光之城》。

  I watched *Twilight* on a cable movie channel.

- 我透過下載的方式在家看電影。

  I watched a movie at home by downloading it.

- 非法下載電影是不對的。

  It is wrong to illegally download movies.

  • illegally 非法地

- 我週末和朋友看了場電影。

  I watched a movie with my friends on the weekend.

- 和朋友們一起看電影，比自己單獨看有趣多了。

  It is much more fun to watch movies with my friends than to watch them alone.

- 有部電影我真的很想看，但是它被列為滿十八歲以上才能看的電影，所以我沒辦法看。

  There was a movie that I really wanted to see, but it was rated 18 and over, so I couldn't watch it. 被列為某等級

- 我去看電影，而且買了汽水和爆米花。

  I went to see a movie, and I bought soda and popcorn.

  • soda 汽水

- 這部電影應該看 3D 版的。

  This movie should be watched in 3D.

電影評論 ★ Movie Critics

- 這部電影真的很有趣。

  This movie was really fun.

- 這部電影真的很感人。

  The movie was really touching.

  • touching 感人的

- 這部電影實際上比我預期的更好。

  The movie was actually better than I had expected.

- 看這部電影時我哭得很慘。

  I was crying a lot while watching the movie.

- 這部電影不錯，但是有些部分有點暴力。

  The movie was good, but some parts were a bit violent.
  - violent 暴力的　有點

- 我因為主角死了而感到十分難過。

  I was so sad because the main character died.
  - 主角

- 這部電影其實不好看，我想是我對它的期待太高了。

  The movie was actually not good. I guess I was expecting too much.

- 男主角的演技太過生硬了。

  The lead actor was too stiff in his role.
  - stiff 生硬不自然的　男主角

- 這個劇情太容易預測了。

  The plot was too predictable.
  - plot 劇情　predictable 可預測到的

- 結局太過單調乏味了。

  The ending was too dull.
  - dull 單調乏味的、無趣的

- 結局看起來很荒謬。

  The ending seemed ridiculous.
  - ridiculous 荒謬的、可笑的

名人 ★ Celebrities

- 我的朋友們對名人很有興趣。

  My friends are so into celebrities.
  - be into 對～極有興趣、熱衷於～　celebrity 藝人、名人

- 我對名人不是這麼的有興趣。

  I am not really interested in celebrities.

- Alice 知道很多關於名人的事。

  Alice knows a lot about celebrities.

- Alice 講的全都是有關名人的話題。

  All Alice talks about is celebrities.

- 我喜歡偶像。

  I like idols.

- 我是 EXO 的粉絲。 — I am a fan of EXO.

- 我最喜歡的名人是劉在錫。 — My favorite celebrity is Jaeseok Yoo.

- 我今天去遊樂園玩，而且看到了一個藝人。 — I went to the amusement park today and saw a celebrity.

- 這是我第一次親眼看到藝人。 — It was my first time to see a celebrity in person.
  in person — 親自、本人

- 他本人比電視上帥多了。 — He was much more handsome in real life than on TV.

- 親眼看到藝人真的很令人驚訝。 — It was so surprising to see a celebrity in person.

- 藝人們都太瘦了。 — Celebrities are too thin.

- 我希望自己擁有像藝人們一樣的小臉。 — I wish I had a small face like those of celebrities.

- 我也想成為藝人。 — I want to be a celebrity, too.

- 我覺得藝人們很快樂，因為他們很受歡迎，而且又賺很多錢。 — I think celebrities are happy because they are popular and make a lot of money.
  • popular 受歡迎的、大眾的

- 我很羨慕藝人們，因為我不覺得他們需要讀書。 — I envy celebrities because I don't think they have to study.

音樂／流行歌曲 ★ Music / Pop

- 我喜歡古典樂勝過於流行樂。 — I prefer classical music to pop music.

• 我喜歡舞曲。	I like dance music.
• 我喜歡抒情歌。	I like ballads.
• 我喜歡愉快的音樂。	I like exciting/fun music.
• 只要是 BigBang 的歌都是我的最愛。	Any songs by BigBang are my favorites.
• 我想去看演唱會。	I want to go to a concert.
• 那位歌手有如此棒的嗓音。	That singer has such a nice voice.
• 那位歌手真的很會唱歌。	That singer is really good at singing.
• 那位歌手很會跳舞。	That singer is a great dancer.
• 我常用手機聽音樂。	I often listen to music with my cell phone.
• 我常在 YouTube 上看音樂錄影帶。	I often watch music videos on YouTube.
• 我也希望我很會唱歌。	I wish I could sing well, too.

運動 ★ Sports

• 我喜歡戶外運動。	I like exercising outdoor. / I love outdoor sports. • outdoor 戶外的
• 體育課是我最喜歡的課。	P.E. is my favorite class. • P.E. (= physical exercise) 體育課
• 我是一個青少年足球俱樂部的成員，而且我一個禮拜踢一次球。	屬於～ I belong to a youth soccer club, and I play soccer once a week.
• 我有跆拳道黑帶二段。	I have a second-degree black belt in taekwondo.

- 我從一年級就開始學跆拳道了。

  I've been learning taekwondo since I was in the 1st grade.

- 我喜歡任何和球類有關的運動。

  I like any sports involving balls.

  • involving 與～有關的

- 下課之後，我在回家之前會和朋友們在學校運動場上踢足球。

  When school is over, I play soccer with my friends on the schoolyard before I go home.

- 我是我們鎮上棒球隊的投手。

  I am the pitcher on my town's baseball team.

  • pitcher 投手

- 從假期開始時，我就開始在鎮上的游泳池學游泳。

  Since vacation, I've started to learn to swim in my town's swimming pool.

- 我參加了市政府辦的比賽，而且在自由式上得到了一個獎。

  I participated in the competition held by the city and received an award for freestyle swimming.

  • competition 競賽

- 我們學校針對課後活動提供各式各樣的運動項目。

  My school has a variety of sports for after-school activities.

- 最近我正在學花式溜冰。

  These days, I am learning figure skating.

- 在我的跆拳道課裡，我也在學習跳跳繩。

  In my taekwondo class, I am also learning to jump rope.

  跳繩

- 鎮上的健身俱樂部有一堂隨音樂跳繩的課程，所以我在放假期間去上了這門課。

  The fitness club in my town has a class for jumping rope with music, so I took the class during vacation.

- 我學校有辦跳繩的認證，所以我正在練習。

  There is a certificate for jumping rope at my school, so I am practicing it.

  • certificate 證照

- 在冬天的時候，我喜歡去滑雪和玩滑雪板。

  When it's winter, I enjoy skiing and snowboarding.

- 我們這隊和另一隊比賽，結果我們這隊以二比一輸了比賽。

  My team competed against another team, and we lost two to one.

  • compete 競爭、對抗

- 我的家人有時會在我家附近的公園慢跑。

  My family jogs at the park near my house from time to time.

  有時

- 我家每一個人都有運動天分。

  Everyone in my family was born with a talent for sports.

  • talent 才能、天分

- 爸爸打高爾夫，而媽媽上瑜珈課。

  My father goes golfing, and my mother attends a yoga class.

  • attends 上（某課程）

- 弟弟正在學游泳。

  My younger brother is learning to swim.

- 爸爸在我們鎮上的健身中心運動。

  My father works out at our town's fitness center.

  運動
  健身中心

- 我討厭挪動我的身體，所以我不知道要怎麼去做運動。

  I hate moving my body, so I don't know how to play any sports.

- 我的醫生告訴我規律的運動會幫助我變得健康。

  My doctor told me that regular exercise would help me to be healthy.

  • regular 規律的

- 我對運動很不拿手，所以我討厭體育課。

  I am terrible at sports, so I hate P.E. class.

  對～不擅長

- 終於，我今天成功地溜了直排輪。

  Finally, I succeeded at inline skating today.

外表和煩惱

I Am Not Fatty!

Tuesday, April 15, Sunny

Recently, I gained a lot of weight. My clothes are too tight for me. My dad makes fun of me and calls me Fatty. I know he is just joking, but sometimes I get really angry. I guess I should start on a diet!

我不胖！　　4月15日星期二，晴天

最近我的體重增加了很多，我的衣服對我來說太緊了。爸爸取笑我，而且叫我胖子。我知道他只是在開玩笑，但有時候我真的覺得很生氣。我想我應該要開始節食了！

·**gain weight** 體重增加　**tight** 緊的　**make fun of** 取笑～、嘲笑～　**fatty** 肥胖的人　**diet** 節食

身高 ★ Height

- 我的身高是一百三十公分。

  My height is 130 cm. /
  I am 130 cm tall.
  • height 身高

- 我有一點矮／高。

  I am a bit short/tall.
  有點

- 我是我們班上最高的。

  I am the tallest (one) in my class.

- 我在我們班上是中等身高。

  I am average height in my class.
  • average 一般的、普通的、中等的

- 以我的年齡來說我的身高很一般。

  I am average height for my age.

- 最近我長高很多。

  Recently, I have grown a lot.

- 我很擔心我的身高，因為我很矮。

  I am worried about my height because
  I am short.

- 我擔心我可能會長得不夠高。

  I am worried I might not grow tall enough.

體重／身材 ★ Weight / Size

- 我的體重是三十二公斤。

  I weigh 32 kg.
  • weigh 重～、體重是～

- 我的體重超過四十公斤一點點。

  I am a bit over 40 kg.
  有點、以某個程度上來說

- 我有點過重。

  I am kind of overweight.
  • overweight 體重過重

- 我體重過輕。

  I am underweight.
  • underweight 體重過輕

- 就算我吃東西，體重也不會增加。

  Even if I eat, I don't gain any weight.
  - gain weight 體重增加

- 我量體重的時候，發現我的體重增加了。

  I found I had gained weight when I weighed myself.
  - weigh oneself 測量體重

- 我最近體重增加了一點。

  Recently, I have gained some weight.

- 我沒有一件衣服是合身的，因為我的體重增加了。

  None of my clothes fit me because I have gained weight.
  - fit 合於（外觀、大小）

- 因為我的體重增加了，所以我的衣服對我來說太緊了。

  Because I have gained weight, my clothes are too tight for me.
  - tight 緊的

- 我必須減肥。

  I have to lose weight.
  └─ 減肥

- 我的腿太粗了。

  My legs are too thick.

- 我的腰太粗了。

  My waist is too big.

- 我的肚子很大。

  I have a big stomach.

- 我想要變瘦。

  I want to be thin/skinny.

- 我弟弟不斷地取笑我，並說我胖嘟嘟的。

  My brother keeps teasing me and calling me chubby.
  - tease 取笑　chubby 胖嘟嘟的

節食 ★ Diets

- 我必須要節食了。

  I have to go on a diet.
  └─ 節食、控制飲食

- 從今天開始我不吃晚餐了。 Starting today, I won't eat dinner.

- 我今天才剛開始節食。 I just started a diet today.

- 為了減肥，我已經開始節食了。 To lose weight, I have started a diet.

- 我已經開始進行單一食物節食法了。 I have started a one-food diet.

- 我沒吃晚餐。 I didn't eat dinner.

- 因為我跳過晚餐，所以覺得很餓。 Since I skipped dinner, I am starving.

  • skip 省略　starving 飢餓的

- 因為我跳過了幾餐沒吃，所以我覺得沒力氣／精神。 Because I have been skipping meals, I don't have any strength/energy.

  • strength 力氣

- 因為我現在減少了每天吃的餐數，所以我很容易生氣。 Now that I am skipping meals, I get annoyed so easily.

  • annoyed 生氣的、惱怒的

- 我吃了一些蒸地瓜來代替晚餐。 Instead of having dinner, I ate some steamed sweet potatoes.

  • steamed 蒸的

- 我應該停止在正餐之間吃零食。 I should stop snacking between meals.
  在正餐之間吃零食

- 為了減肥，我決定晚餐要吃少一點。 To lose weight, I have decided to eat less for dinner.

- 為了減肥，我決定要停止吃披薩和炸雞。 To lose weight, I have decided to stop eating pizza and fried chicken.

- 我必須要節食，但爸爸不斷要我多吃一點。 I have to go on a diet, but my dad keeps telling me to eat more.

- 爸爸跟我說我現在看起來很不錯。 My dad says that I look good for who I am right now.

- 我為了減肥而跳繩。

  To lose weight, I jumped rope.

- 為了減肥，在吃過晚餐後我繞著公園跑了五圈。

  To lose weight, I ran around the park 5 times after eating dinner.

- 我因為搖了很多呼拉圈，肚子上的肥肉都消失了。

  Since I used a hula hoop a lot, all of the fat around my stomach has disappeared.

  • fat 脂肪、肥肉　disappear 消失

- 過度的節食對你的健康不好。

  Excessive dieting is not good for your health.

  • excessive 過度的

- 我一個星期就減了三公斤。

  In just a week, I have lost 3 kg.

- 在我開始節食後，大家都說我看起來更漂亮了。

  After I went on a diet, people tell me that I look prettier.

- 我復胖了。

  I regained the weight that I had lost.

  • regain 再次得到

- 從明天開始，我會再次開始節食。

  Starting tomorrow, I will go on a diet again.

- 我從明天開始會努力運動。

  Starting tomorrow, I will work out hard. / I will exercise hard starting tomorrow.

外表的煩惱 ★ Worries about Appearances

- 我沒有那麼漂亮／醜陋。

  I am not that pretty/ugly.

- 我其實覺得自己滿漂亮的。

  I actually think that I am kind of pretty.

- 我的臉太大了（和我的身體大小比起來）。

  My face is too big (for the size of my body).

- 我的大餅臉是我的煩惱。／
  我不喜歡我有一顆大頭。

  煩惱、焦慮

  My big face is my hang up. /
  I don't like how I have a big head.

- 我的眼睛很小。

  My eyes are small. /
  I have small eyes.

- 我希望可以像別人一樣擁有大眼睛。

  I wish I had bigger eyes like others.

- 我希望可以像別人一樣擁有雙眼皮。

  I wish I had double eyelids like others.
  　　　　　　　　雙眼皮

- 我想去割雙眼皮。

  I want to have plastic surgery to create double eyelids.
  　　　　　　　整形手術

- 我的鼻子太扁／大了。

  My nose is too flat/big.
  • flat 扁平的

- 我的嘴唇太厚／薄了。

  My lips are too thick/thin.

- 我的嘴唇太突出了。

  My lips are too protruding.
  • protrude 突出

- 我不喜歡我的暴牙。

  I don't like my buckteeth.
  • buckteeth 暴牙

- 我有方形的下巴。

  I have a square jaw.

- 我有突出的下巴。

  I have a lantern jaw.
  　　　　　突出的長下巴

- 我的皮膚太黑了。

  My skin is too dark.

- 我臉上有太多痣了。

  I have too many moles on my face.
  • mole 痣

- 我身上的毛很多。

  I am hairy.

- 我的頭髮很乾燥，而且毫無生氣。

  My hair is so dry and lifeless.
  • lifeless 無生氣的、死的

- 我太胖了。

  I am too fat/big.

- 我瘦到別人都叫我「排骨」。

  I am so skinny that others call me "ribs."
  - skinny 瘦到皮包骨的、極瘦的

- 我希望我可以再高一點、皮膚再白一點。

  I hope I can be a bit taller and have a lighter skin.
  - light （顏色）淺色的

- 我的朋友們取笑我胖。

  My friends make fun of me by calling me fat.

- 爸爸說我是世界上最漂亮的女孩。

  Dad says that I am the prettiest girl in the world.

- 我覺得只有爸爸會覺得我漂亮。

  I think I am pretty only in my dad's eyes.

- 我妹妹很漂亮，但是我很醜。

  My younger sister is pretty, but I am ugly.

- 我和妹妹看起來怎麼會差這麼多？

  How come my sister and I look so different?

髮型 ★ Hairstyles

- 我留長髮／短髮。

  I have long/short hair.

- 我留短髮。

  I have bobbed hair.
  - 短髮

- 我的頭髮很捲。

  My hair is curly.

- 我希望我有又長又直的頭髮。

  I wish I had long, straight hair.

- 我想把頭髮留長一點。

  I want to grow my hair longer.

- 長髮不適合我。

  Long hair doesn't suit me.
  - suit 適合

- 中等長度的髮型最適合我。 | Medium-length hair suits me the best.

  中等長度的

- 我在美容院剪了頭髮，但是我不喜歡。 | I got a haircut at a salon, but I don't like it.

  • (beauty) salon 美容院　剪頭髮

- 我剪了頭髮，但這髮型真的不適合我。 | I got a haircut, but it really doesn't suit me.

- 我只要求髮型設計師幫我稍微修一下，但是她剪得太短了。 | I asked the hairstylist just to trim it, but she cut it too short.

  • trim 修剪

- 我今天把頭髮燙直了。 | Today, I got my hair straightened.

  • straighten 把～弄直

- 我想把頭髮燙得像我朋友一樣。 | I want to get a perm just like my friend.

  燙頭髮

- 我想染髮，但我媽媽不讓我染。 | I want to have my hair dyed, but my mom won't let me.

  • dye 染髮

- 我把瀏海放下來了。 | I put down my bangs.

  • bang 瀏海

  既然、因為～

- 因為我現在把瀏海放了下來，所有人都說我看起來很可愛。 | Now that I have put down my bangs, everyone says that I look cute.

- 在剪完頭髮以後，我的瀏海太短了。 | After my haircut, my bangs were too short.

- Amy 的頭髮很漂亮。 | Amy has really nice hair.

- Amy 的頭髮總是很柔順。 | Amy's hair is always silky.

  • silky 像絲綢一般柔順的

- Amy 總是把她的頭髮綁得很漂亮。 | Amy always ties her hair in a pretty way.

  • tie 綁

- 我的頭髮很沒有光澤。

My hair is so dull.
• dull 無光澤的

- 我喜歡長髮，但媽媽叫我去剪短。

I like long hair, but mother tells me to cut it.

- 我因為自己連喜歡的髮型都無法選擇，而覺得生氣。

I am angry because I can't even choose my favorite hairstyle.

受歡迎 ★ Popularity

- 我很受朋友們的歡迎。

I am popular with my friends.

- 我不是很受朋友們的歡迎。

I am not really popular with my friends.

- Sam 是我們班上最受歡迎的學生。

Sam is the most popular student in my class.

- 有很多女孩喜歡 Sam。

There are a lot of girls who adore Sam.
• adore 喜歡、愛慕

- Amy 非常的可愛，因此她很受男孩子們的歡迎。

Amy is so cute that she is very popular with the boys.

- 我因為受歡迎而被選為這學期的班長。

被選中

I (was elected) this semester's class president because I am popular.
• semester 學期

- 我在一、二年級的時候不怎麼受歡迎。

I was not so popular when I was in the 1st and 2nd grades.

- 我真希望我也能受到朋友們的歡迎。

I wish I were popular with my friends, too.

單戀／約會 ★ One-Sided Love／Dating

- 我迷戀一個女孩。

  I have a crush on a girl. 迷戀、喜歡某人（通常是對不熟的異性產生單方面的迷戀）

- 我已經喜歡她兩年了。

  I have had a crush on her for 2 years.

- 我因為她人很善良而喜歡她。

  I like her because she is nice.

- 她既聰明又受歡迎。

  She is smart and popular.

- 我應該告訴她我喜歡她嗎？

  Should I tell her that I like her?

- 如果她拒絕我的告白怎麼辦？

  What if she says no to me after I talk to her? 拒絕

- 我在情人節那天送了他巧克力。

  I gave him chocolates on Valentine's Day.

- 我向喜歡的對象告白了，但是她拒絕了我。

  I told my crush that I liked her, but she turned me down.

  • crush 喜歡的對象　turn down 拒絕

- 我不知道我喜歡的對象有喜歡的人了！

  I had no idea that my crush liked someone else!

- 單戀很痛苦。

  One-sided love is so painful.

  • painful 痛苦的　單戀

- Eric 喜歡我嗎？

  Does Eric have a crush on me?

- Eric 告訴我他喜歡我。

  Eric told me that he liked me.

- 不知怎麼地，這變成了三角關係。

  Somehow, it became a love triangle. 三角關係

- 我有男朋友了。

  I have a boyfriend.

- 我和 Adam 正在交往中。

  I am going out with Adam. 和～交往、約會

- 我和男朋友分手了。

  和～分手

  I broke up with my boyfriend.

- 從今以後，我會只專注在課業上。

  From now on, I will just focus on studying.

  專注於～

青春期 ★ Adolescence

- 我最近很容易沒來由地感到煩躁。

  For no reason, I get annoyed easily these days.

  無緣無故、沒來由

- 我最近就是不想講話。

  I just don't want to talk these days.

- 我的心情一直在好與壞之間擺盪。

  My mood swings from good to bad all the time.

  • mood 心情　swing 搖擺、擺盪

- 我想我正在經歷青春期。

  I think I am going through puberty.

  • puberty 青春期

- 我哥哥正在經歷青春期。

  My older brother is going through puberty.

- 我姐姐總是在生氣。

  My older sister always gets upset.

- 我的額頭上開始長青春痘了。

  I am starting to get pimples on my forehead.

  • pimple 青春痘

- 我在鼻子下方開始長鬍鬚了。

  I am starting to get a mustache under my nose.

  • mustache 鬍鬚

- 我覺得很怪，因為我的聲音開始在改變了。

  I feel strange because my voice has started changing.

- 最近我和媽媽相處的不太好。

  These days, my mom and I do not get along.

- 我媽媽總是叫我去讀書。

  My mom always tells me to study.

- 我媽媽總是對我嘮叨。

  My mom always nags me.

  • nag 嘮叨

- 我和我爸媽無法理解彼此。

  My parents and I can't understand each other.

- 我媽媽因為我向她回嘴而罵我。

  My mother scolded me for talking back to her.

  向～回嘴

- 我不知道自己為何活著。

  I don't know why I live.

- 我不知道自己是誰。

  I don't know who I am.

課業煩惱 ★ Worries about Academics

- 我真的很討厭念書。

  I really hate studying.

- 我想去外面玩，但是我有很多回家功課。

  I want to play outside, but I have a lot of homework.

- 學校出太多回家功課了。

  My school gives out too much homework.

- 我每天都在晚上十一點後才做完回家功課上床睡覺。

  Every day, I do my homework and go to bed after 11 p.m.

- 我這次的考試考糟了。

  I messed up on this exam. /
  I screwed up on the test.

  • mess up / screw up 把～弄糟

- 我真的很想得到更好的成績。 I really want to get better grades.
  • grade 成績

- 我羨慕那些拿到好成績的人。 I envy those who get good grades.

- 學無止境。 There is never an end to studying.

- 我羨慕那些再也不用念書的大人 I envy adults who don't have to study
  們。 anymore.

謊言 ★ Lies

- 我對朋友說了謊。 I told a lie to my friend.

- 我對媽媽說謊說我已經做完回家功 I lied to my mother by telling her I had
  課了。 finished doing my homework.

- 我向媽媽說謊，然後去了網咖。 I lied to my mother and went to the
  Internet café.
  網咖

- 我向老師說謊說我因為身體不舒服 I lied to my teacher by saying that I
  而不能寫回家功課。 couldn't do my homework because I was
  sick.

- 雖然我考得很糟，但我跟媽媽撒謊 弄糟、搞砸
  說我考得很好。 Although I messed up on my exam,
  I lied to my mother and said that I had
  done well.

- Amy 常說謊。 Amy often lies.

- 我們班上有個說謊慣犯。 There is a habitual liar in my class.
  • habitual 習慣的

- 我不經意地就說了謊。

  I lied without even realizing it.

  • realize 意識到、了解

- 我向媽媽說謊，並在被她發現後被狠狠地教訓了一頓。

  I lied to my mother and got into huge trouble after she found out about it.

  • find out (find-found-found) 發現、查明

- 媽媽總能看穿我的謊言。

  My mother always sees through my lies.

  看穿、識破

- 我認為謊言總是會被揭穿的。

  I think it is true that lies always come out.

  （指真相）周知、透露

- 如果你說了一個謊，就會讓你必須再說其他的謊。

  Once you tell a lie, it leads to another lie.

  導致

- 只要我一說謊，我就會變得非常緊張不安。

  Whenever I lie, I become so nervous.

- 我向媽媽坦承我曾向她說謊。

  I confessed to my mother that I had lied to her.

  • confess 坦白、承認

- 爸爸常跟媽媽說她很苗條的善意的謊言。

  善意的謊言

  My father often tells my mother a white lie by telling her that she is slim.

  • slim 身材苗條的

- 說善意的謊言是可以的嗎？

  Is telling white lies okay?

- 爸爸從不遵守他的承諾。我無法信任他。

  Dad never keeps his word. I cannot trust him.

  • keep one's word 遵守承諾 trust 信任

- 說謊會成習慣的。

  Lying becomes a habit.

- 從今以後我不會再說謊。

  From now on, I will never lie.

Part

7

飲食與健康

Chapter

25

飲食

I Hate Curry!

Wednesday, December 5, Sunny

Mom cooked curry and rice for dinner. My older sister likes it, but I don't, because it smells weird. Mom said I should eat various foods to grow taller. I know being a picky eater is not good, but I wonder if it is bad not to love curry.

我討厭咖哩！　12 月 5 日星期三，晴天

媽媽晚餐煮了咖哩飯。我姊姊喜歡，但我不喜歡，因為那聞起來味道怪怪的。我媽媽說為了長得更高，我應該要吃各式各樣的食物。我知道當個挑食的人不好，但我想知道不喜歡咖哩是否也是不好的呢？

·**weird** 奇怪的　**picky eater** 挑食的人（**picky**：挑剔的）　**wonder if** 想知道是否～

最喜歡的食物 ★ Favorite Foods

- 漢堡是我最喜歡的食物。

  Hamburger is my favorite food.

- 在整個世界上我最喜歡牛肉麵。

  I like beef noodles the most in the whole world.

- 我是個只喜歡台灣食物、真正土生土長的台灣人。

  I am a true native Taiwanese who only likes Taiwanese food.

  • native 土生土長的

- 我喜歡中式和日式料理。

  I like Chinese and Japanese food.

- 在各種義大利麵裡，培根蛋麵是我最喜歡的。

  Among pastas, carbonara is my favorite.

- 在所有水果裡，西瓜是我最喜歡的。

  Among fruits, watermelon is my favorite.

- 我喜歡吃魚，特別是白帶魚。

  I like eating fish, especially cutlassfish.

  • cutlassfish 白帶魚

- 我很能吃辣。

  I can eat spicy food well.

  • spicy 辣的

- 沒有肉的話，我就吃不下飯。

  When there's no meat, I can't eat a meal.

  • meal 餐食、一餐

- 我喜歡吃肉。

  I love meat.

- 只要在餐桌上有一盤有肉的菜餚，那一切就很美好了。

  只要～
  As long as there's a meat dish on the table, everything is fine.

- 我喜歡海鮮勝過於肉類。

  I prefer seafood to meat.

- 我們家的人喜歡吃湯麵。

  My family loves noodle soup.

- 夏天最適合吃涼麵了。

  Cold noodles are the best in summer.

- 巧克力餅乾是最棒的餅乾。

  Chocolate cookies are the best cookies.

- 當你沒有食慾的時候，泡麵是最棒的食物。

  When you lose your appetite, instant noodles are the best.
  - appetite 胃口、食慾

- 比起正餐，我更喜歡吃零食。

  I like snacks more than eating proper meals.
  - proper 正確的、適當的

- 我喜歡麵包勝過於白飯。

  I like bread more than rice.

- 我喜歡新鮮的水果。

  I love fresh fruit.

- 我的生活無法沒有水果。

  I can't live/do without fruit.
  — 沒有～也行

- 我喜歡甜食。

  I love sweets.

- 我吃完飯後總是想吃點甜的東西。／我在吃完飯後相當渴望吃甜食。

  I always want to eat something sweet after a meal. / I have a craving for sweets after a meal.
  — 熱切渴望～

- 我妹妹只吃零食。

  My younger sister only eats snacks.

- 媽媽晚餐煮了炙烤肋排。那真的很好吃。

  Mother cooked us grilled ribs for dinner. It was so delicious.

- 炙烤肋排是如此的美味，以致於我吃掉了兩碗飯。

  Grilled ribs was so delicious that I ate two bowls of rice.
  - bowl 碗

我最不喜歡的食物 ★ My Least Favorite Foods

- 蘑菇是我最不喜歡的食物。

  Mushrooms are my least favorite food.

- 我討厭蘑菇的口感。

  I hate the texture of mushrooms.

  • texture 質感、結構

- 我無法吃辣的東西。

  I can't eat anything spicy.

- 我不喜歡辣的或鹹的食物。

  I don't like spicy or salty food.

- 我不喜歡泡菜，因為它很辣而且很臭。

  I don't like kimchi because it's spicy and smelly.

- 我不喜歡漢堡或披薩。

  I don't like hamburgers or pizzas.

- 我很少吃蔬菜。

  I rarely eat vegetables.

  • rarely 很少、難得

- 我討厭魚肉，因為它很臭。

  I hate fish because it stinks.

  • stink 散發惡臭

- 每當我聞到魚的味道，我都覺得想吐。

  Whenever I smell fish, I feel like puking.

  • puke 嘔吐

- 我無法吃生魚片。

  I can't eat sashimi.

- 我對蛤蜊過敏。

  I am allergic to clams.

  • clam 蛤蜊　　對～過敏

- 每當我吃了蛤蜊以後，我就會起疹子。

  Whenever I eat clams, I get a rash.

  • rash 疹子

- 我討厭白醬義大利麵，因為它太油膩了。

  I hate spaghetti with cream sauce because it is too greasy.

  • greasy 油膩的

- 炸薯條冷掉以後就不好吃了。

When fries get cold, they do not taste good.
- fries 炸薯條

- 我不喜歡水果，因為水果很酸。

I don't like fruits because they are sour.
- sour 酸的

- 我無法忍受胡蘿蔔。／我不能吃胡蘿蔔，我討厭它們。

I can't stand carrots. /
I can't eat carrots. I hate them.

- 粥難吃死了。

Porridge tastes horrible.
- porridge 粥　horrible 極討厭的、糟透的

- 我討厭有很多湯的食物。

I hate dishes with a lot of soup.

- 我討厭吃麵食。

I hate noodle dishes.

- 我很少吃螃蟹，因為要從蟹殼挖出肉來太費工了。

I rarely eat crabs because it's too much work to get the flesh from the shell.
- crab 蟹　flesh 肉　shell（堅硬的）殼

- 我奶奶無法吃酸的食物。

My grandmother can't eat sour food.

挑食 ★ Picky Eating

- 我不喜歡五穀雜糧飯。

I don't like rice with mixed grains. /
Rice with mixed grains is not my favorite.
- grain 穀物

- 我喜歡白米飯。

I like plain rice.
- plain 單純的、不參雜的

- 我不喜歡混合豆類的飯。

I hate beans mixed with rice.

- 我在吃的時候會把豆子從飯中挑出來。

  When I eat, I pick the beans out of the rice.

  • pick out 挑選出

- 我因為把豆子挑出來而被媽媽罵。

  I got scolded by mom for picking out the beans.

- 當菜裡有蔥時，我會把它們挑掉。

  When there are (green onions) inside dishes, I pick them out.
  青蔥

- 我妹妹從來不吃甜瓜。她不知道那有多好吃真是她的損失。

  My younger sister never eats melons. It's such a loss that she doesn't know how good it is.

  • melon 甜瓜、香瓜　loss 損失

- 我又吃一顆煎蛋當一餐了。

  I had a fried egg for a meal again.

- 餐桌上只有泡菜而已。

  Kimchi was the only dish on the table.

- 餐桌上只有蔬菜而已。我又不是吃草的綿羊！

  There were only vegetables on the table. I am not a grass-eating sheep!

- 沒有可以吃的東西！

  There was nothing to eat!

- 我喜歡像火腿和香腸之類的食物。

  I love foods like ham and sausage.

- 沒有配菜可以吃，所以我只吃了白飯而已。

  There were no (side dishes) to eat, so I just ate rice.
  配菜

- 我媽媽只煮了豆芽菜和豆腐而已。

  My mom only cooked (bean sprouts) and tofu.
  豆芽

  • tofu 豆腐

- 我對每天在家裡吃一樣的食物感到厭煩。

  I am so sick of eating the same food at home every day.

  • be sick of 對～感到厭煩

- 今天的晚餐是我最討厭的咖哩。

  Today's dinner was curry, which I hate the most.

- 我覺得我自己是個十分挑食的人。

  I think I am a very picky eater.
  • picky 挑剔的

- 我媽媽告訴我不要成為一個挑食的人。

  My mom told me not to be a picky eater.

- 我媽媽告訴我要把盤子裡的所有東西都吃掉。

  My mom told me to eat everything on my plate.

- 為了長得更高，我不應該挑食。

  I shouldn't be picky in order to grow taller.

- 我討厭吃蔬菜。

  I hate eating vegetables.

- 我弟弟因為幾乎不吃蔬菜而便祕。

  My younger brother is constipated because he hardly eats vegetables.
  • constipated 有便祕的

- 我最小的弟弟太瘦了，因為他是個非常挑食的人。

  My youngest brother is too skinny because he is such a picky eater.

- 我哥哥什麼都吃，所以很少生病。

  My older brother eats everything, so he hardly gets sick.

- 奶奶說吃對食物會讓我健康。

  Grandma says that eating right will make me healthy.

- 從現在開始，我一定會吃健康的餐點。

  From now on, I will make sure I eat healthy meals.

- 當我在學校吃午餐時，我必須吃我不想吃的東西。

  When I have lunch at school, I have to eat things that I don't want to.

- 如果我在我的餐盤裡留下任何食物，我們這一組的所有人就會受到處罰。

  If I leave any food on my plate, everyone in my group gets a penalty.
  • penalty 處罰、行為造成的不利結果

烹飪 ★ Cooking

• 我洗了米後煮了飯。 | I washed rice and then cooked it.
• grain 穀物、穀粒

• 我煎了一顆蛋。 | I fried an egg.

• 我煮了一包泡麵。 | I cooked a pack of instant noodles.

• 我烤了條魚。 | I broiled fish.
• broil 燒烤

• 我煎了培根。 | I fried bacons.

• 我煎了一些鬆餅。 | I fried some pancakes.

• 我炸了一些蝦子。 | I fried some shrimp.

• 我煮了海帶湯。 | I boiled seaweed soup.

• 我蒸了些玉米。 | I steamed some corn.

• 我炒了一些青菜。 | I stir-fried some vegetables.
• stir-fry 炒

• 我煮了些餃子。 | I boiled some dumplings.
• dumplings 餃子

• 這些馬鈴薯已經煮得差不多可以吃了。 | The potatoes are cooked enough to eat.

• 蒸蛋蒸得夠軟嫩，所以很好吃。 | The steamed eggs are cooked soft enough to taste great.

• 馬鈴薯燒焦了。 | The potatoes are burned.

• 蛋還沒煮熟。 | The egg is not yet boiled.
• boiled 煮熟的

- 麵煮過頭了。

  The noodles are overcooked.
  • overcooked 煮過頭的

- 泡麵煮過頭了。

  The instant noodles are overcooked.

- 魚煎得太老了。

  The fried fish is too hard.

- 栗子被烘烤得香噴噴的。

  The chestnuts are deliciously baked.

廚藝 ★ Cooking Skills

- 我媽媽很會做菜。

  My mother is very good at cooking.

- 我媽媽真的很會做菜。

  My mother cooks really well.

- 我媽媽做的餅乾真的很好吃。

  My mom's cookies are really delicious.

- 我最喜歡媽媽做的食物，那是世上最棒的。

  I like food my mom makes the most. It is the best in the world.

- 我媽媽常做我喜歡的食物。

  My mother often cooks food that I like.

- 我媽媽做的食物比餐廳做的要好吃多了。

  The food my mom makes is much more delicious than the food at restaurants.

- 我媽媽很會做牛肉麵。

  My mother can cook beef noodles really well.

- 牛肉麵是我媽媽的拿手好菜。

  Beef noodles are my mom's specialty.
  • specialty 專門、專業

- 我媽媽做的紅燒魚是最棒的。

  My mother's braised fish is the best.
  • braise 用小火燉煮

- 我媽媽做的紅燒魚比餐廳做的好吃多了。

  My mother's braised fish is much more delicious than that served at restaurants.

- 我覺得這樣說很抱歉，不過我媽媽的廚藝很糟。

  I am so sorry to say this, but my mother's cooking is horrible.

- 因為我媽媽不會做菜，所以所有她煮的食物都不好吃。

  Because my mother has no ability to cook, everything she cooks is not good.

- 我媽媽除了做菜之外其他都很在行。

  My mom is good at everything except for cooking.

  除了～

- 我爸爸也是一位優秀的廚師。

  My dad is also a good cook.

- 我爸爸比我媽媽會做菜。

  My dad cooks better than my mom.

味道／飲食愛好 ★Tastes

- 這湯太鹹了。

  The soup was too salty.

- 這菠菜沒什麼味道。

  The spinach was too tasteless.

  • tasteless 沒味道的

- 這盤炒豬肉太辣了。

  The stir-fried pork was too spicy.

- 這份炒年糕太辣了，它辣到幾乎要燒傷我的嘴了。

  The stir-fried rice cake was too spicy. It almost burned my mouth.

- 這蛋糕太甜了，以致於我無法把它全部吃完。

  The cake was so sweet that I couldn't finish the whole thing. / The cake was so sweet that I left it unfinished.

  • unfinished 未完成的、未結束的

- 這西瓜一點也不甜。

  The watermelon was not sweet at all.

- 這些橘子太酸了。 The tangerines were too sour.

- 我家所有人都吃得又鹹又辣。 Everyone in my family eats salty and spicy food.

- 我們家的食物都有點甜。 All the food in my house is kind of sweet.

- 我們家所有人的飲食愛好都不同。 All of my family members have different tastes in food.
  - taste 味道、飲食愛好

- 我爸爸和哥哥喜歡吃肉，而媽媽和我則喜歡吃蔬菜。 My father and brother love meat while my mom and I love vegetables.

- 我的胃口很小。 I have a small appetite.
  - appetite 胃口

- 我不喜歡同樣的菜吃兩次。 I don't like eating the same dish more than once.

- 如果桌上沒有肉的話我爸爸就不吃了。 My father doesn't eat if there's no meat dish on the table.

吃零食和外食

No More Snacks!

Sunday, March 20, Sunny

My dad likes snacks. After each meal, he always eats a snack. He said he has two stomachs, one for meals and the other for snacks. I also eat snacks whenever he eats them, so I am gaining weight. I should cut down on cookies from tomorrow.

別再吃零食了！　　3月20日星期日，晴天

我爸爸喜歡吃零食。在吃完飯後，他總會吃個零食。他說他有兩個胃，一個裝正餐，另一個裝零食。每當他在吃零食時我也會跟著吃，所以我的體重增加了。我應該從明天起少吃些餅乾。

· snack 零食、點心　stomach 胃　meal 一餐　cut down on 削減～

零食／甜食 ★ Snacks / Sweets

- 我喜歡甜食。

  I love sweets.

- 我喜歡像糖果、巧克力、冰淇淋等甜食。

  I love sweets like candy, chocolates, and ice cream.

- 我弟弟沉迷於吃零食。

  My younger brother indulges in snacks.

  沉迷於～

- 我弟弟把我買回來的所有零食都吃掉了。

  My younger brother ate up all of the snacks that I bought.

- 我爸爸喜歡吃零食。

  My father loves snacks.

- 在爸爸下班回家的路上，他常會買好吃的東西給我們。

  On his way home from work, my dad often buys goodies for us.

  • goodies 好吃的東西

- 我爸爸從不在正餐之間吃零食。

  在正餐之間吃零食

  My father never eats between meals.

- 我在吃飯前吃了零食，所以我沒什麼胃口吃飯。

  I ate a snack before eating a meal, so I lost my appetite.

- 我的體重增加了。我應該克制自己不要吃太多的零食。

  抑制～、忍住～

  I am gaining weight. I should refrain from eating too many snacks.

- 我會停止吃零食。

  I will cut out eating snacks.

  停止

- 我爸爸常吃消夜。

  My father often eats late-night snacks.

  消夜

- 我們家常叫炸雞外送。

  My family often orders fried chicken for delivery.

  • delivery 運送

- 我把我大部分的零用錢都花在買零食上。

I spend most of my allowance on buying snacks.

- 糖果餅乾等零食有很多種類，但可以用 snacks 來表示全部的種類。

- 補習班結束以後，我和我朋友們一起到餐館買了些點心。

After finishing at my cram school, I went to a cafeteria with my friends and bought some snacks.

- cafeteria 小吃店、自助餐館

- 今天 Amy 請我吃了一些巧克力糖。

Today, Amy treated me to some chocolates.

- treat A to B 招待 A 吃 B

- 因為我吃太多甜食了，我有些牙齒已經蛀掉了。

Because I ate too many sweets, some of my teeth are decayed.

- decayed 蛀蝕的

- 我媽媽幾乎不買餅乾給我，因為她說那些東西對我的健康不好。

My mother hardly buys me cookies because she says that they're not good for my health.

- 我媽媽說加工食品含有很多有害的食品添加物。

My mother says that there are a lot of harmful food additives in processed foods.
食品添加物　　　加工食品

- 有些零食含有太多的糖。

Some snacks contain too much sugar.

- contain 含有

- 我在吃了太多的洋芋片後就沒有胃口了，所以我最後就沒吃飯了。

After eating too many chips, I lose my appetite, so I end up skipping a meal.

- end up Ving 結果成為～

- 不管我吃了多少次的洋芋片，我從來不會覺得膩。／
不管我吃了多少，我從來不會厭倦吃零食。

No matter how many times I eat chips, I never get tired of them. /
I never get sick of eating snacks no matter how many I eat them.

- get tired/sick of 對～感到厭惡

- 我們在學校辦了一場同樂會。

At school, we had a snack party.

點心 ★ Snacks

- 我媽媽給了我一些西瓜當點心。 My mother gave me some watermelon for a snack.

- 我媽媽給我帶了一些餅乾當點心。 My mom packed me some cookies for a snack.

- 我媽媽常做點心給我。 My mother often makes snack for me.

- 我帶了一些洋芋片當作在補習班的點心。 I packed some chips for snacks at my cram school.

- 我帶了一些柳橙當我在校外教學時的點心。 I packed some oranges for snacks for my field trip.

- 我們老師跟我們說不要帶洋芋片和餅乾當點心。 My teacher told us not to pack chips and cookies for snacks.

- 我忘了帶我的點心。 I forgot to bring my snack.

- Amy 分享了一些她的櫻桃番茄給我。 Amy shared her (cherry tomatoes) with me.
  — 櫻桃番茄

- 我沒有吃任何點心，所以我在補習班真的餓扁了。 I didn't eat any snacks, so I was really hungry at the cram school.

- 我吃了一些地瓜當點心，所以我仍然覺得肚子飽飽的。 I ate some sweet potatoes for a snack, so I am still full.

飲料—水 ★ Drinks – Water

- 我幾乎不怎麼喝水。 I hardly drink water.

- 我常常會喝很多水。 I tend to drink a lot of water.

- 我喜歡麥茶。

  I love barley tea.
  麥茶

- 在家裡，我們煮麥茶當水喝。

  At home, we boil barley tea for drinking water.

  • boil 煮

- 在家裡，我們買礦泉水來喝。

  礦泉水
  At home, we buy mineral water to drink.

- 在家裡，我們喝從淨水器出來的水。

  At home, we drink from the water purifier.
  淨水器

- 我喜歡喝冷水。

  I love drinking cold water.

- 我喜歡喝溫水勝過於冷水。

  I prefer tepid water to cold water.

  • tepid 微溫的

- 我聽說喝非常冰的水對你的健康不好。

  I heard that drinking very cold water is not good for your health.

- 每天喝兩公升的水對你的健康很好。

  Drinking 2 liters of water a day is good for your health.

- 我早上做的第一件事，就是在起床後馬上喝一杯水。

  First thing in the morning, I drink a cup of water as soon as I get out of bed.
  一～就～

- 我們必須把水煮沸後再飲用。

  We must boil water before drinking it.

- 在上完體育課後我渴死了。

  I was so thirsty after P.E. class.

- 從明天起，我會帶水到學校去。

  Starting tomorrow, I will bring water to school.

- 因為我喝了很多水，所以我必須要頻繁地去廁所。

  Since I drank a lot of water, I had to go to the bathroom frequently.

  • frequently 頻繁地

- 我上床睡覺前喝太多水了，所以我半夜醒來去上廁所。

  I drank water too much before going to bed, so I woke up in the middle of the night to go to the bathroom.

飲料—牛奶 ★ Drinks – Milk

- 我喜歡牛奶，所以我一天至少喝三至四杯。
  I love milk, so I drink at least 3 to 4 glasses a day.

- 我們有訂牛奶宅配。
  We have milk delivered.

- 我家的人都喜歡牛奶。
  Everyone in my family loves milk.

- 麵包和牛奶非常配。
  Bread goes perfectly with milk.
  和～完美地搭配

- 我一天喝一公升的牛奶來長得更高。
  I drink 1 liter of milk a day to grow taller.

- 我們學校提供我們牛奶。
  Our school provides milk to us.
  • provide 提供

- 我無法喝純鮮奶。
  I can't drink white milk.

- 當我喝純鮮奶的時候，我會胃痛。
  When I drink white milk, I get a stomachache.

- 我不喜歡牛奶，因為我每次喝牛奶都會拉肚子。
  I don't like milk because I get a diarrhea whenever I drink it.
  • diarrhea 腹瀉

- 我無法喝純鮮奶。取而代之的，我會喝草莓或香蕉口味的牛奶。
  I can't drink white milk. Instead, I drink strawberry- or banana-flavored milk.
  • flavored 有～味道的

- 我不喝牛奶，而是喝豆漿。
  Instead of milk, I drink soymilk.
  • soymilk 豆漿

飲料—汽水 ★ Drinks - Soft Drinks

- 我喜歡可樂和雪碧。／我喜歡可樂和叫做蘋果西打的汽水。

  I love cola and Sprite. / I love cola and a soft drink called Apple Sidra.

- 我不是很喜歡汽水。

  I don't really like soft drinks.
  無酒精飲料、汽水

- 當我吃炸雞或漢堡時，我會喝可樂。

  When I eat fried chicken or hamburgers, I drink cola.

- 我喜歡汽水，但我媽媽從不允許我喝任何汽水。

  I love soft drinks, but my mother never allows me to drink any.

- 在夏天喝碳酸飲料太讚了。

  Drinking carbonated soft drinks in the summer is fantastic.
  碳酸飲料

- 我喜歡可樂勝過於蘋果西打。

  I prefer cola to Apple Sidra.

- 如果你喝太多的汽水，你的體重很有能會增加。

  If you drink too many soft drinks, you are likely to gain weight.

  • be likely to 有～的可能；易於～

- 我喜歡可樂那種刺刺的口感。

  I love the tingly taste of cola.

  • tingly 有刺痛感的、引起刺痛的

- 這可樂沒氣了。

  The cola lost its fizz.

  • fizz （飲料裡的）氣泡

- 可樂不冰就不好喝了。

  When cola is warm, it tastes bad.

- 當我喝可樂的時候，我總會打嗝。

  When I drink cola, I always burp.

  • burp 打嗝

- 我喜歡喝運動飲料勝過於汽水。

  I like sport drinks more than soft drinks.
  運動飲料

- 我聽說汽水和運動飲料都含有很多糖。

  I heard that both <u>soft</u> drinks and sport drinks contain tons of sugar.

  有很多的～

- 我幾乎不喝汽水。

  I hardly drink soft drinks.

- 在所有的飲料當中，我認為檸檬水是最好的。

  Of all drinks, I think lemonade is the best.

- 我買了一瓶柳橙汁當作校外教學的飲料。

  As a drink for my field trip, I bought a bottle of orange juice.

- 在所有果汁當中，我最喜歡葡萄汁。

  Of all juices, I love grape juice the most.

- 我聽說喝太多果汁很有可能造成會蛀牙。

  I heard that drinking juice too much is likely to cause tooth decay.

  • decay 蛀蝕、腐爛

冰淇淋／冰沙／刨冰 ★ Ice Cream / Smoothie / Shaved ice

- 我最喜歡的冰淇淋口味是香草。

  My favorite flavor of ice cream is vanilla.

  • flavor 口味

- 因為天氣炎熱，所以我吃了兩支雪糕／甜筒。

  Because of the hot weather, I ate two ice cream bars/cones.

- 因為天氣潮溼悶熱的關係，冰淇淋很快就融化了。

  Because of the steamy weather, the ice cream melted so fast.

  • steamy 潮濕悶熱的　melt 融化

- 當我在操場玩的時候，Alice 的媽媽買了冰淇淋給我。

  When I was playing on the playground, Alice's mom bought me an ice cream.

- 吃完飯後，我吃了冰淇淋當飯後甜點。

  After eating my meal, I ate ice cream for dessert.

- 我喜歡我們鎮上的中式餐廳，因為它提供冰淇淋做為飯後甜點。

  I like the Chinese restaurant in my town because it serves ice cream for dessert.

  • serve 供應

- 放學後，我朋友和我各自買了一杯冰沙。

  After school, my friend and I each bought a smoothie.

- 我買了一杯哈密瓜口味的冰沙。

  I bought a melon-flavored smoothie.

- 我媽媽買了一些刨冰。

  My mom bought some shaved ice.

- 這是我今年第一次吃刨冰。

  It was my first time to eat shaved ice this year.

- 我喜歡吃在紅豆刨冰裡面的麻糬。

  I love the rice cakes inside the red bean shaved ice.

- 在夏天吃刨冰是最棒的。

  The shaved ice is the best for summer.

外食 ★ Eating Out

- 我們家常在外面吃。

  My family often eats out.

- 我們家常在週末時去外面餐廳吃飯。

  My family often eats out on weekends.

- 我們家的人通常去日式餐廳吃飯。

  My family usually goes to Japanese restaurants.

- 為了慶祝我哥哥比賽得獎，我們全家人一起到外面吃飯。

  To celebrate my older brother's award in the competition, my family ate out.

  • celebrate 慶祝

- 因為今天是媽媽的生日，所以我們到外面吃飯。

  It was my mom's birthday today, so we ate out.

- 我爸爸在一家家庭餐廳訂了位子。

  My dad made a reservation at a family restaurant. 訂位

- 每當我們要在外面吃飯，我弟弟總是想去吃中式餐廳。

  Whenever we eat out, my younger brother always wants to go to a Chinese restaurant.

- 我們去了一間中式餐廳，並吃了牛肉麵和滷肉飯。

  We went to a Chinese restaurant and ate beef noodles and braised pork rice.

- 我對去吃中式餐廳已經感到很厭煩了。

  I am so sick of going to Chinese restaurants.

  • be sick of 對～感到厭煩

- 我真的很想吃義大利麵。

  I really wanted to eat pasta.

- 我們家幾乎不會外食。

  My family hardly eats out.

- 我爸爸不怎麼喜歡餐廳的食物，所以我們從未在外面吃飯。

  My father doesn't really like food at restaurants, so we have never eaten out.

- 我喜歡在家吃飯勝過於在外面吃飯。

  I like eating at home more than eating out.

- 我央求到外面吃飯，但是媽媽說飯已經煮好了。

  I begged to eat out, but my mother said that our meal was ready.

  • beg 央求

- 我媽媽討厭在外面吃飯，因為她認為那是浪費錢。

  My mother hates eating out because she believes that it's a waste of money.

- 因為是爺爺的生日，所以我們就在一間自助式餐廳舉辦家庭聚會。

It was my grandfather's birthday, so we had a (family gathering) at a buffet restaurant. —— 家庭聚會

- 我們今天去的餐廳有很好的氣氛，而且提供非常美味的食物。

The restaurant that we went to today had a good atmosphere and served really delicious food.

• atmosphere 氣氛

- 我想再去那裡一次。

I want to go there again.

健康和感冒

Get Well Soon, Sam!

Monday, June 29, Warm

Today, Sam missed school because he has a cold. I felt bored without him all day long. The flu is spreading these days, so lots of other kids have also caught colds. I should wash my hands often to avoid catching a cold. I hope Sam gets well soon.

早日康復，Sam!   6 月 29 日星期一，天氣溫暖

今天 Sam 沒來上學，因為他感冒了。少了他我整天都覺得好無聊。這個流感最近正在大流行，所以有很多其他的小朋友也感冒了。我應該要經常洗手來避免感冒。我希望 Sam 能早日康復。

·miss 遺漏 bored 感到無聊的 all day long 一整天 flu 流感 spread 傳播、普及
 catch a cold 得到感冒 avoid 避免 get well （從生病狀態中）好轉

健康狀態 ★ Health Conditions

- 我是個相當健康的人。

  I am a pretty healthy person.
  • pretty 相當、頗、很

- 我很健康。

  I am really healthy.

- 我身體很強壯。

  I am physically strong.
  • physically 身體上

- 我的體力不太好。

  I don't have a lot of physical strength.
  體力

- 我天生就比較虛弱。／
  我常常覺得很虛弱。

  I was born weak. /
  I often feel weak.

- 我的身體很虛弱。／
  我沒有什麼精神。

  I am physically weak. /
  I have low energy.

- 我最近很容易感到疲憊。

  I easily get tired these days.

- 最近我有時會覺得昏昏欲睡。

  These days, I feel sleepy
  every now and then.
  有時

- 我覺得我好像變虛弱了。

  I feel like I am getting weak.

- 我應該要讓我的身體更強壯。

  I should strengthen my body.
  • strengthen 加強、使強壯

感冒／流感 ★ Colds / The Flu

- 我感冒了。

  I caught a cold.

- 我覺得我身體有點不舒服。

  I am feeling under the weather.

  └─ 身體有點不舒服

- 我想我是被弟弟傳染的。

  I think I got a cold from my younger brother.

- 我因為穿輕薄的衣服而感冒。

  I caught a cold by wearing light clothes. / I wore light clothes, so I caught a cold.

  • light 輕薄的

- 我因為太常吹冷氣而感冒。

  I caught a cold from using the air conditioner too much.

- 我因為睡覺沒蓋被子而感冒。

  I caught a cold because I slept without tucking myself in.

  • tuck in 幫～蓋好被子

- 最近我們學校有很多學生感冒。

  These days, lots of students at my school are catching colds.

- 我聽說這個流感最近正在流行。

  I heard that the flu is spreading these days.

  • spread 傳播、普及

- 在季節交替時我總會感冒。

  I always catch a cold when the seasons change.

- 我不能去學校，因為我感冒了。

  I couldn't go to school because I had caught a cold.

- Alice 因為感冒已經兩天沒來上學了。

  Alice has been absent for two days because of her cold.

  • absent 缺席

- 我看完醫生後才去上學。

  I went to school after visiting the doctor.

- 我克服了感冒而且覺得好多了。

  I got over my cold and felt better.

  └─ 克服、恢復

- 我媽媽說她因為我很容易感冒而覺得擔心。

My mom says she worries because I easily catch colds.

- 天氣溫暖時很難得會感冒。

It is very rare to catch a cold when it is warm.

• rare 稀有的、罕見的

- 為了避免感冒，我們必須勤洗手。

To avoid catching a cold, we need to wash our hands often.

- 我因為感冒而沒有什麼胃口。

I've lost my appetite because of my cold.

• appetite 胃口、食慾

- 我這次的感冒真的很嚴重。

This time, my cold is really bad.

- 我的感冒一點都沒有比較好。

My cold is not getting any better.

- 充足的休息是克服感冒的最佳良藥。

Getting enough rest is the best medicine to get over a cold.

• medicine 藥

- 今年冬天我沒有感冒過。一次也沒有！

I didn't suffer from a cold this winter. Not even once!
受～之苦

- 我討厭得到流感，但我喜歡不用去補習班。

I hate having the flu, but I love not going to my cram school.

- 我因為感冒而沒去補習班，所以現在我有一大堆的功課要做。

I missed my cram school because of my cold, so now I have tons of homework to do.
有很多的～

• miss 遺漏

- 當我起床時，我的感冒不可思議地消失了。

When I woke up, my cold had magically disappeared.

• magically 不可思議地、魔法般地

- 我因為發燒而有點昏昏欲睡。

  I am a bit drowsy because of a fever.
  - drowsy 昏昏欲睡的、懶散的　fever 發燒

- 我發高燒而且在發抖。

  I had a high fever, and I was shivering.
  - shiver 打顫、發抖

- 我整個晚上都在發燒。

  I suffered from a fever throughout the night.
  - throughout 從頭至尾

- 當我量體溫的時候，它顯示是三十七度。

  When I took my temperature, it was 37 degrees.
  - take one's temperature 量體溫

- 我發燒超過四十度，所以我服用了退燒藥。

  I had a fever over 40 degrees, so I took a fever reducer.
  退燒藥

- 我發燒好幾天都還沒有降下來。

  My fever has not come down for days.

- 我白天的時候還好，但晚上又發燒了。

  I was fine during the day, but at night I had a fever again.

- 我在學校發燒了，所以我去了保健室。

  I had a fever at school, so I went to the nurse's office.
  保健室

- 我弟弟發了嚴重的高燒，所以他住院了。

  My younger brother had a very high fever, so he has been hospitalized.
  - be hospitalized 住院治療

- 我發燒了，而且全身痠痛。

  I have a fever, and my entire body is aching.
  - ache 持續性地疼痛

- 我還是有點發燒。

  I still have a slight fever.
  - slight 輕微的

- 我吃了藥丸後就退燒了。

  I took a pill, and my fever came down.

- 我在流鼻水。

  I have a runny nose.
  - runny 流鼻涕的

- 我擤太多次鼻子了，導致我的鼻子又紅又腫。

  I blew my nose so much that it is all red and swollen.
  - blow one's nose 擤鼻子 swollen 腫起的

- 因為我一直擤我的鼻子，所以我覺得頭很痛。

  Because I kept blowing my nose, my head hurts.

- 我的鼻子塞住了，所以我感覺要窒息了。

  塞滿

  My nose is (stuffed up), so I feel suffocated.
  - suffocated 窒息的

- 我的鼻子過敏。

  I have a nasal allergy.
  - nasal 鼻的

- 因為季節正在轉換，我的鼻子過敏變得更糟了。

  Because the season was changing, my nasal allergy got worse.

- 我的喉嚨裡都是痰。

  My throat is full of phlegm.
  - phlegm 痰

- 我的喉嚨痛。

  My throat hurts. /
  I've got a sore throat.
  - sore 疼痛發炎的

- 當我去醫院的時候，醫生說我的喉嚨很腫。

  When I went to the hospital, the doctor said that my throat was swollen a lot.

- 我因為腫脹的喉嚨而發不出聲音。

  I lost my voice because of my swollen throat.

- 我一直在咳嗽。

  I can't stop coughing.
  - cough 咳嗽

- 我的咳嗽一直沒好。

  My cough is not going away.
  ——消失

- 我咳嗽咳得很厲害。

  My cough is very severe.
  • severe 嚴重的

- 我咳嗽咳了整個晚上。

  I was coughing all night.

- 我覺得很難過，因為我在上課的時候一直咳嗽。

  I felt terrible because I kept coughing during class.

- 我聽說桔梗根對治療咳嗽很有效。

  I heard that balloon flower root is good for coughs.
  ——桔梗根

- 我媽媽煮了梨子給我，並說那對治療咳嗽很有效。

  Mom served me boiled pears and said that they were good for coughs.
  • boiled 煮熟的

感冒藥／醫院 ★ Cold Medicine / Hospitals

- 我忘了吃感冒藥。

  I forgot to take my cold medicine.

- 我覺得這藥的藥效很強。

  I think the medicine is really strong.

- 這個感冒藥吃起來真的很苦。

  The medicine for my cold tasted really bitter.
  • bitter 味道苦的

- 我應該要在三餐飯後的三十分鐘吃藥。

  應該～、認為必須～
  I am supposed to take the medicine 3 times a day 30 minutes after meals.
  • meal 一餐

- 我因為發燒而去看了醫生。

  I went to see a doctor because of my fever.

- 醫院人很多。我想原因是因為現在正在換季。

  The hospital was very crowded. I guess the reason is that the seasons are changing.

- 醫生說我感冒了。

  The doctor told me that I had caught a cold.

- 醫生說我的喉嚨腫起來了。

  The doctor told me that my throat was swollen.

- 醫生吩咐我暫時待在家裡。

  The doctor told me to stay at home (for a while).
  ┗━ 暫時、一會兒

- 他吩咐我要吃一些藥並好好休息。

  He told me to take some medicine and to get some good rest.

- 我的感冒還沒好，所以我去給耳鼻喉科醫生看病，而不是小兒科醫生。

  My cold is not going away, so I went to an ENT(ear, nose, and throat) specialist instead of the pediatrician.
  • ENT 耳鼻喉科　specialist 專家　pediatrician 小兒科醫生

- 醫生說我有中耳炎。

  The doctor told me that I had an inflammation in my middle ear.
  • inflammation 發炎

- 醫生開了抗生素。

  The doctor prescribed antibiotics.
  • prescribe 開立處方籤　antibiotic 抗生素

- 我媽媽囑咐我別忘了吃藥。

  Mom told me not to forget to take the medicine.

- 我因為吃了一些感冒藥，而覺得想睡和疲倦。

  I felt sleepy and tired because I took some cold medicine.

- 我吃了一些感冒藥，而感冒藥讓我一整天都昏昏欲睡。

  I took some cold medicine, and it made me feel drowsy all day.
  • drowsy 昏昏欲睡的、懶散的

- 我媽媽很討厭吃藥。

  My mother hates taking medicines.

- 我的感冒嚴重到必須要打針。

  My cold was so severe that I had to get a shot.

  • severe 嚴重的　shot 注射

預防接種 ★ Vaccinations

- 我今天注射了流感疫苗。

  I got a flu shot today.

  • shot 注射

- 我去了醫院做 B 型肝炎的預防接種。

  I went to the hospital and got a vaccination for hepatitis B.

  • vaccination 預防接種　hepatitis B B 型肝炎

- 打針真的很可怕。

  Getting a shot is really scary.

- 只是看到了注射器，我就不禁發抖。

  Just by looking at the syringe, I couldn't stop trembling.

  • syringe 注射器　tremble 發抖

- 打針不像我之前所想的那麼痛。

  Getting a shot didn't hurt as much as I had thought.

- 打針一點也不痛，我真不敢相信。

  Getting a shot didn't hurt at all. I couldn't believe it.

- 那只是有一點刺痛。

  It just stung a little.

  • sting (sting-stung-stung) 刺痛

- 我弟弟像瘋了似地大哭。

  My younger brother cried like crazy.

- 在打完針以後，我得到了一些糖果做為獎勵。

  After getting a shot, I got some candy as a reward.

  • reward 獎賞、獎勵

- 我媽媽病了。

  My mother is sick.

- 我爸爸因為腸子發炎而住院。

  My father is hospitalized due to the inflamed intestine.

  住院

  腸子發炎

- 我媽媽住院了，所以我必須要自己吃飯。

  My mother was in the hospital, so I had to eat my meals on my own.

  自己

- 我妹妹突然發高燒了，所以我們帶她到急診室。

  My younger sister suddenly had a high fever, so we took her to the emergency room.

  急診室

- 我妹妹因為肺炎住院。

  My younger sister is hospitalized because of pneumonia.

  • pneumonia 肺炎

- 我爺爺生病了，所以他住院接受治療。

  My grandfather got sick, so he was hospitalized.

- 我奶奶因為椎間盤突出而做了手術。

  My grandmother had surgery for a slipped disk.

  • surgery 手術   椎間盤突出

- 我希望爺爺能早日康復。

  I hope my grandfather gets well soon.

  康復

- 我奶奶覺得好多了，所以她就出院了。

  My grandmother got better, so she left the hospital.

- 我希望我的祖父母都能長壽健康。

  I hope my grandparents live long and healthy lives.

Chapter

28

疾病和症狀

Food Poisoning

Friday, July 3, Sunny

After lunch at school, my stomach began hurting. The pain grew worse and worse, so I left school early. As soon as I got home, I threw up everything I had eaten. I went to see a doctor, and he said I had food poisoning. I hope to feel better soon.

食物中毒　　7月3日星期五，晴天

在學校吃完午餐以後，我的肚子就開始痛。因為漸漸地越來越痛，所以我提早回家。當我一回到家，我就把我之前吃的所有東西給吐了出來。我去看了醫生，醫生說我食物中毒了。我希望能趕快好起來。

· food poisoning 食物中毒　　pain 疼痛　　grow 漸漸變得～　　throw up 吐

肚子痛 ★ Stomachaches

- 我的肚子痛。

  I have a stomachache.

  • stomachache 肚子痛

- 我突然感到肚子痛。

  I got a stomachache all of a sudden.

  突然

- 我無法忍受肚子的疼痛。

  I couldn't stand the pain in my stomach.

  • stand 忍受

- 我的肚子痛到讓我快要哭了。

  My stomachache was so bad that I felt like crying.

- 從早上開始，我的肚子就一直微微地痛。

  Since morning, my stomach has been hurting slightly.

  • slightly 輕微地

- 我覺得腸胃不舒服。

  I have an upset stomach.

  腸胃不適

- 我把我吃的所有東西都吐掉了。

  I threw up everything I ate.

  吐

- 我整天都在拉肚子。

  I had diarrhea all day.

  • diarrhea 腹瀉

- 我因為肚子痛而提早離開學校。

  Because of my stomachache, I left school early.

- 我沒有任何力氣，因為我把所有東西都吐出來了。

  I don't have any strength because I threw up everything.

- 也許我吃了太多冰冷的食物。

  Maybe I had too much cold food.

- 也許我吃到一些壞掉的食物。

  Maybe I ate some spoiled food.

  • spoiled 壞掉的

- 我想我必定是吃到了不好的東西。

I think I must have eaten something bad.

• must have+過去分詞 一定是做了～

- 我在街上吃了一些臭豆腐，而且我覺得那個食物是壞掉的。

I ate some stinky tofu on the street, and I think that food was spoiled.

- 醫生跟我說我食物中毒了。

The doctor told me that I had food poisoning. 食物中毒

- 醫生吩咐我要常喝溫開水。

The doctor told me to drink warm water often.

- 因為腸炎，我嘔吐和腹瀉了一整天。

Because of enteritis, I threw up and had diarrhea all day.

• enteritis 腸炎

- 我媽媽煮了些粥給我。

My mother made me some porridge.

• porridge 粥

- 那感覺就像我死過了一次。

It feels like I came back from death.

- 我因為討厭的肚子痛而不能吃任何東西！我不敢相信！

I can't eat anything because of my stupid stomachache! I can't believe this!

- 我的家人在我遭受腹痛之苦時在我面前吃炸雞。

遭受～之苦

My family ate fried chicken in front of me while I was suffering from a stomachache.

- 當我肚子痛好了以後，我就要去吃炸雞。

When my stomachache goes away, I am going to eat fried chicken. 消失

- 在我睡了一整晚以後，我的肚子不可思議地不痛了。

My stomachache magically went away after I slept all night.

• magically 不可思議地、如魔法般地

蛀牙 ★ Cavities

- 我的牙齒開始痛了。

  My tooth started hurting.

- 我的牙齒痛了好幾天了。／
  我好幾天前就開始牙痛了。

  My teeth have hurt for a few days. /
  My toothache started a few days ago.

- 我想我蛀牙了。／
  牙齒好像蛀掉了。

  I think my tooth is decayed. /
  The tooth seems to be decayed.

  • decayed 腐爛、蛀蝕

- 我真的很害怕去看牙醫。

  I am really afraid of
  going to see the dentist.

  • dentist 牙醫師   看牙醫

- 今天我去看牙醫並治療了蛀牙。

  Today, I went to the dentist and had a
  cavity treated.

  • cavity 蛀牙   treat 治療

- 我的牙齒中有三顆蛀掉了。

  Three of my teeth are decayed.

- 醫生把蛀掉的部分去除，並填補上
  黃金。

  The doctor removed the decayed part and
  then filled it with gold.

  • remove 去除

- 多虧有麻醉，這不會太痛。

  Thanks to anesthesia, it didn't hurt much.

  • anesthesia 麻醉

- 但是機器發出的聲音使我感到毛骨
  悚然。

  But the sound from the machine gave me
  the chills.

  • chill 毛骨悚然

- 當麻醉消退以後，我的牙齒就開始
  痛了。

  When the anesthesia wore off, my tooth
  started to ache.

  • wear off (wear-wore-worn) 慢慢消失

- 因為我已經治好了我的蛀牙，所以現在就能舒舒服服地吃東西了。

Now that I got my cavity treated, it is comfortable to eat food.

- 在治好我的蛀牙以後，我覺得舒服了很多。

I feel so much better after getting my cavity treated.

- 我到目前為止還沒有任何蛀牙。

I don't have a single cavity so far.

- 我每天都很努力刷牙，但我發現我有一顆蛀牙。

I brush my teeth very hard every day, but I found I had a cavity.

- 牙醫師吩咐我要用牙線。

The dentist told me to use floss.

• floss 牙線

- 從今天起，我一定會好好刷牙。

Starting today, I will make sure I brush my teeth well.

- 我會更仔細地刷牙。

I will brush my teeth more carefully.

- 從今以後我不會再忘記刷牙。

I will never forget to brush my teeth from now on.

拔牙 ★ Pulling Teeth

- 我的門牙在晃動。／
  我有一顆在晃動的門牙。

My front tooth is wobbling. /
I have a wiggly front tooth.

• wobble 擺動、不穩定　wiggly 擺動的

- 我有一顆牙齒從幾天前就開始晃動了。

One of my teeth has been wobbling for several days. / One of my teeth started shaking a few days ago.

- 我可以感覺到我的牙齒在晃動。

I could feel my tooth hanging loose.

鬆動、晃動

- 我去看了牙醫，並把我晃動的牙齒拔掉。

  I went to the dentist and got my loose teeth pulled out.

  拔掉

- 儘管我的牙齒被拔了也一點都不會痛。

  It didn't hurt at all even though my tooth was pulled.

- 聽說我正在長恆牙。

  I heard that my permanent teeth are coming in.

  恆牙

- 我鬆動的牙齒自行脫落了。

  My loose tooth fell out by itself.

  脫落　自行、自動地

- 我自己拔掉了那顆鬆動的牙齒。

  I pulled out the loose tooth by myself.

- 我抓住我的牙齒並搖了一下，然後它就掉了。

  I held the tooth and shook it a little, and then it just fell out.

- 我有個朋友的牙齒在他在學校吃午餐時掉了。

  I have a friend whose tooth fell out while he was eating lunch at school.

- 因為我掉了一顆牙齒，所以我吃東西的時候很不舒服。

  Since I am missing a tooth, it is quite uncomfortable to eat.

- 我爸爸說我沒了門牙看起來更可愛了。

  Dad says I look cuter without my front tooth.

- 我打算把這顆牙齒交給牙仙子。

  I am going to give this tooth to the tooth fairy.

  牙仙子〈來自「把脫落的牙齒放在枕頭底下，牙仙子就會拿零用錢來交換那個落齒」的童話故事〉

- 我在游泳池那邊被傳染眼疾了。／
  我在游泳池玩之後得到了結膜炎。

  I got an eye infection from the swimming pool. / I got pink eye after I played in the swimming pool. 結膜炎
  - infection 感染

- 我聽說眼疾正在傳染。

  I heard that eye infections are spreading.
  - spread 傳播、普及

- 我的眼睛流了很多眼淚。

  My eyes watered a lot.

- 我的眼睛充血了。

  My eyes are bloodshot.
  - bloodshot 充血的、有血絲的

- 我的眼睛裡有眼屎。

  I have sleep in my eyes.
  - sleep 眼屎

- 我點了眼藥水到眼睛裡。

  I put eye drops into my eyes.
  - eye drops 眼藥水

- 眼疾需要一段時間痊癒。／
  據說眼疾沒有辦法很快治好。

  An eye infection takes some time to heal. / It is said that an eye infection cannot be cured quickly.
  - heal 治癒

- 我被我弟弟傳染了眼疾。

  I got an eye infection from my brother.

- 我的眼疾已經被完全治療好了。

  My eye infection is completely cured.
  - completely 完全地　cure 治療

- 我已經戴眼罩戴了一個禮拜了。

  I have been wearing an eye patch for a week. 眼罩

- 醫生吩咐我不要去學校，因為眼疾是會傳染的。

  The doctor told me not to go to school because eye infections are contagious.

  • contagious 具傳染性的

- 我因為眼疾而一個禮拜沒去學校了。

  I missed school for a week because of my eye infection.

視力 ★ Eyesight

- 我的視力不好。

  My eyesight / vision is bad.

  • eyesight/vision 視力

- 我的視力很好。

  My eyesight is good.

- 我兩眼的視力都是0.5。

  My eyes are 0.5 on both sides.

- 我的視力比起去年變差了。

  My eyesight got worse than it was last year.

- 我無法清楚地看見黑板上的字。

  I can't see the words on the board clearly.

- 我去看了眼科並檢查了我的視力。

  I went to see an eye doctor and had my 〔眼科醫生〕 eyesight examined. / I went to an ophthalmic clinic and took an eyesight 〔眼科〕 test.

  • examine 檢查

- 醫生跟我說我需要戴眼鏡，因為我的視力變差了。

  The doctor told me that I should wear glasses because my eyesight got worse.

- 我去了眼鏡行配眼鏡。

  I went to an optical store to get glasses. 〔眼鏡行〕

- 我配了一副白框的眼鏡。

  I got white-framed glasses.

  • -framed ～框的

- 我還不習慣自己戴眼鏡的樣子。

I am not used to seeing myself with glasses.

• be used to +Ving 習慣於～

- 戴眼鏡很不舒服。

Wearing glasses is uncomfortable.

• uncomfortable 不舒服的

- 現在我戴了眼鏡，所以我能看得很清楚。

I can see clearly now that I am wearing glasses.

- 在我班上有很多人戴眼鏡。

There are many students in my class who wear eyeglasses.

- 我聽說小孩子不要戴隱形眼鏡比較好。／據說隱形眼鏡對孩子不好。

I heard that contact lenses are not recommended for children. /
It is said that contact lenses are not so good for children.

• recommend 推薦

- 我會更加小心讓我的視力不會再變差。

I will be more careful so that my eyesight doesn't get any worse.

- 我不會再玩一大堆電腦遊戲了。

I will not play a lot of computer games.

- 我不應該看這麼多電視。

I should not watch a lot of TV.

便祕 ★ Constipation

- 我便祕了。

I am constipated.

• constipated 有便祕的

- 我受嚴重的便祕之苦。

I am suffering from serious constipation.

• constipation 便祕

- 即使我在馬桶上坐了很久，我也大不出來。

  Even if I sit on the toilet for a long time, I can't poop.

  • poop 排便

- 我的肚子在痛，但依然大不出來。

  My tummy hurt, but poop still did not come out.

  • tummy 肚子

- 今天早上又來了，我坐在馬桶上三十分鐘，但什麼也沒大出來。

  Again this morning, I sat on the toilet for 30 minutes, but nothing came out.

- 因為我有便祕，所以我臉上長了青春痘。

  Because I'm constipated, I have pimples on my face.

  • pimple 青春痘、面皰

- 已經過了三天了，但我仍然沒有排便。

  It has been three days already, and still I haven't pooped.

- 我吃進肚子的東西完全排不出來，這真是要命。

  What I eat doesn't come out at all, so it's killing me.

- 因為我便祕了，所以我開始喝優酪乳。

  Because I'm constipated, I have started to drink yogurt.

- 我這幾天吃了很多蔬菜，而這讓我不再便祕了。

  I ate a lot of vegetables for the past few days, and that made my constipation go away.

- 從今以後我一定會吃很多蔬菜。

  I will make sure I eat a lot of vegetables from now on. 一定～

- 我會停止當一個挑食的人，並吃所有種類的食物。

  I will stop being a picky eater and will eat all kinds of food.

青春痘 ★ Pimples

- 我臉上有青春痘。

  I have pimples on my face.
  - pimple 青春痘、面皰

- 我的額頭上有一顆青春痘。

  I have a pimple on my forehead.

- 在我臉頰上有紅紅的東西，而且非常腫。

  There is something red on my cheek, and it's all swollen.
  - swollen 腫脹的

- 我媽媽看了看它，就說那是痘痘。

  Mom looked at it and said it was acne.
  - acne 面皰

- 我發現我的青春痘變嚴重了。

  I found my acne getting worse.

- 我用手擠了一顆青春痘。

  I squeezed a pimple with my hands.
  - squeeze 擠出

- 我臉上有一顆煩人的青春痘。

  I have a pimple on my face, and it is bothering me.

- 我的朋友們因為我臉上長了青春痘而嘲笑我。

  My friends made fun of me for having pimples on my face. 嘲笑～

- Eric 的青春痘很嚴重。

  Eric acne is pretty serious.
  - serious 嚴重的

- 我同班同學裡有很多人的臉上有青春痘。

  A lot of my classmates have pimples on their faces.

- 我因為臉上的青春痘而去看醫生。

  I went to the hospital because of the pimples on my face.

- 醫生開了一些軟膏給我擦。

  The doctor prescribed some ointment for me.
  - prescribe 開處方籤　ointment 軟膏

- 在我塗了軟膏以後，青春痘就消失了。

  After I applied the ointment, the pimples disappeared.
  - apply 塗抹

- 儘管我塗了軟膏，這些青春痘還是在那裡。／這個軟膏對我的青春痘沒有什麼用。

  Even though I put on the ointment, the pimples are still there. / The ointment did not work really well on my acne.
  - work 有效、管用

- 我想知道這些青春痘什麼時候會消失。

  I wonder when these pimples will go away.

- 我聽說當某人開始長青春痘，那就是進入青春期的徵兆。我想知道那是否是真的。

  I heard that when someone gets pimples, it is a sign of puberty. I wonder if that is true.
  - puberty 青春期

- 我覺得我的聲音在開始長青春痘以後就聽起來怪怪的。

  I think my voice has started to sound weird since I have gotten pimples.

生理期 ★ Menstruation

- 我剛開始了第一次的生理期。

  I just started my first period.
  - period 生理期

- 我開始有生理期了。

  My period started.

- 我還沒有生理期。

  I still haven't had a period.

- Amy 已經開始有生理期了。

  Amy already started her period.

- 我希望我的生理期別太快開始。

  I hope I don't start my period any sooner.

- 媽媽恭喜我，並對我說我要變成大人了。

  Mom congratulated me and said that I am becoming an adult.
  - congratulate 祝賀　adult 大人

- 每當我生理期來的時候，我就不想去上學。

  Whenever I have my period, I don't want to go to school.

- 我的生理痛很嚴重。

  I have bad cramps.

  • cramps 生理痛

- 因為生理痛，我必須要躺在保健室裡。

  Because of my cramps, I had to lie down in the nurse's office.

- 我的生理痛嚴重到我必須吃藥。

  My cramps were so severe that I had to take some medicine.

- 我的衛生棉用完了。

  I am out of pads.

  • pad 衛生棉

- 為什麼只有女人有生理期？

  Why do only women have periods?

受傷 ★ Injuries

- 我跑步時跌倒了。

  I fell down while running.
  跌倒

- 我在操場跌倒了，而且我的膝蓋都擦破皮了。

  I fell down on the playground, and my knees are all scraped.

  • scraped 擦傷、刮破

- 我的膝蓋在流血。

  My knee was bleeding.

  • bleed 流血

- 我被紙割傷了。

  I got a paper cut.

- 我塗了一些軟膏，並在流血的地方用繃帶包紮。

  I applied some ointment and put a bandage on the bleeding.

  • bandage 繃帶　bleeding 流血的

- 我的傷口結痂了。

A scab formed over my wound.

• scab 傷口的痂　wound 傷口

- 我的頭撞到床，並在我的額頭造成了一個傷口。

I bumped my head on the bed, and got a cut on my forehead.

- 我去醫院縫了三針。

I went to the hospital and got three stitches.

• stitch 縫合

- 我的額頭留下了一個疤痕。

It left a scar on my forehead.

• scar 疤痕

- 我因為和朋友們一起玩時跌倒而手臂骨折。

I broke my arm because I fell while fooling around with my friends.
　　　　　　　　　遊玩

- 我在騎自行車時跌倒了，所以我的腿骨折了。

I fell down while riding my bicycle, so I broke my leg.

- 我因為手臂骨折而必須打石膏。

I broke my arm, so I had to wear a cast.

• cast 石膏

- 我必須打石膏一個月。

I have to wear a cast for a month.

Part

8

我的家和家鄉

Chapter 29

住家和房屋

A Wish for My Own Bedroom
Thursday, September 23, Sunny

We only have two bedrooms in my house. I share a bedroom with my big brother. He tells me to go out of the room. He argues that it is his room. So I usually study in the living room. I wish I had my own bedroom.

我希望有自己的臥室　　9月23日星期四，晴天

我們家只有兩間臥室。我和我大哥共用一間臥室。他叫我離開房間，他主張那是他的房間。因此我通常在客廳讀書。我希望能擁有自己的臥室。

·**share** 共用、分享　**argue** 主張、爭辯

住家 ★ Homes

- 我住在台北市大安區。

  I live in Daan, Taipei City.

- 我的住址是台北市大安區仁愛路 211號。

  My address is 211, Renai Road, Daan District, Taipei City.

  • address 住址

- 我住在一個新市鎮。

  I live in a new town.

- 我最近因為爸爸工作的關係搬家搬到花蓮。

  I recently moved to Hualien due to my father's job.
  因為～

  • recently 最近

- 我家住在鄉下。

  My home is in the countryside.

  • countryside 鄉村

- 我居住的地方是個人口不到一萬人的農村。

  The place I live in is a rural town which has a population of fewer than ten thousand people.

  • rural 農村的　population 人口

- 從我們家開車到市區要四十分鐘。

  It takes us 40 minutes to drive to the downtown area from my house. /
  From my house, it is a 40-minute drive to reach the downtown area.

  • reach 到達～　市區、市中心

- 我家是在離花蓮市市區有一段小距離的郊區。

  My house is in a suburb a little away from the downtown of Hualien City.

  • suburb 郊區

- 我住在一個坐船要花一小時才能抵達的島上。

  I live on an island which takes an hour to reach by ship.

  • reach 抵達～

公寓 ★ Apartments

- 我住在公寓裡。

  I live in an apartment.
  - apartment 公寓（在英國被稱為 flat）

- 我的地址是 Happy 公寓第 10 棟樓的 1208 號。

  My address is unit number 1208 in building 10 of Happy Apartment.

- 我住的公寓有十五層樓。

  There are 15 stories in my apartment.
  - story 樓層

- 我家在五樓。

  My house is on the 5th floor.

- 我住在大林公寓。

  I live at Daelim Apartment.

- 我的公寓是一棟一樓有店面的住商混合大樓。

  My apartment is a multipurpose building with stores on the ground floor.
  　　　　　　　　　　　　　　一樓
  - multipurpose 多用途的

- 我很多的同班同學跟我住在同一棟大樓裡。

  Many of my classmates live in the same building where I live.

- 在我的公寓裡有很多遊戲場。

  There are many playgrounds in my apartment.

- 我喜歡我的公寓附近有條小路。

  I like that there is a trail near my apartment.
  - trail 小路、小徑

- 在我們公寓社區的購物中心裡有很多間補習班。

  There are many cram schools in the shopping center at my apartment complex.
  - complex 綜合設施

- 我的公寓大樓的隔音很差。

  Noise travels so well through the floors of my apartment building.
  - travel 移動

- 我公寓的牆壁幾乎不能隔音。

My apartment building's walls are hardly soundproof.

• soundproof 隔音的

別墅 ★ Private Residences

- 我住在別墅裡。

I live in a private residence.
別墅

- 我住在別墅區裡。

I live in a condominium private residence.

• 如同社區一樣聚集了同種類的住宅，例如公寓大樓或是別墅，再分戶出售產權的住宅形式，在英文裡稱為 condominium。

過去經常

- 我以前一直是住在公寓大樓裡，但是我在一年前搬來了這棟房子。

I used to live in a tall apartment building, but I moved to this house a year ago.

- 因為我家是別墅，所以我可以隨心所欲地盡情奔跑。

Because my house is a private residence, I can run as much as I want to.

- 我們家裡有個庭院。

We have a yard at my house.

- 在我家後院的樹上結了柿子。

There are persimmons on the tree in the backyard of my house.

• persimmon 柿子　backyard 後院

櫻花樹

- 我家花園裡的櫻花樹開了很多櫻花。

The cherry blossom tree in the garden of my house has many blossoms.

• blossom 花

- 我媽媽在她的果菜園裡種蔬菜。

My mother grows vegetables in her kitchen garden.

〈我種僅供自家食用的〉果菜園

房屋構造 ★ House Structures

- 我們家有兩個房間。

  There are two rooms in my house.

- 我們家有三個房間和兩個浴室。

  There are three rooms and two bathrooms in my house.

- 我們家只有一間房間。

  There is only one room in my house.

- 我和哥哥共用一個房間。

  I share a room with my older brother.

- 我和奶奶共用一個房間，而且她不斷要我去關燈和早點上床睡覺。

  I share a room with my grandmother, and she keeps telling me to turn off the light and to go to bed early.

- 我希望我擁有自己的房間。

  I wish I had my own room.

- Adam 住在一個有閣樓的兩層樓的房子裡。

  Adam lives in a two-story house with an attic.

  　　　　　　　　　　　兩樓的、雙層的

- 我們家客廳裡沒有電視。

  There is no TV in our living room.

- 我們家客廳裡擺滿了書籍。

  My living room is filled with books.

- 我們把客廳當成書房，並在裡面擺滿了書架。

  We use the living room as a study room and have filled it with bookshelves.

  • bookshelf 書架、書櫃

- 在我們家的陽台上有很多的花盆。

  很多～

  There are plenty of flowerpots on the balcony of my house.

  • flowerpot 花盆　balcony 陽台

- 我可以從我家的陽台看到海。

  I can see the ocean from the balcony/veranda of my house.

- 我家是面向南方的，所以採光非常好。

  My house faces south, so it receives a lot of sunlight.

我的家鄉

Kenting: My Hometown Wednesday, August 28, Scorching

I live in Kenting in Pingtung. It is famous for its beautiful beach.
In the summer, many tourists from all over the country come to
enjoy the beach. Recently, lots of foreigners have been visiting
here. I am proud to live in Kenting.

我的家鄉：墾丁　　8月28日星期三，酷熱的天氣
我住在屏東的墾丁。墾丁以她美麗的海灘聞名。在夏天時會有來自全國各地的觀光客前來享受這個海灘。
最近也有很多外國觀光客造訪這裡。我很驕傲能住在墾丁。
·be famous for 以～聞名　tourist 觀光客　foreigner 外國人　proud 驕傲的

介紹我住的城鎮 ★ Introducing My Town

- 我住的城鎮以蘋果聞名。

  The town that I live in is famous for apples.

- 松子是我住的城鎮的特產。

  松子
  Pine nuts are a specialty of my town.
  • specialty 特產

- 我住的城鎮是一個有很多海灘和旅遊勝地的知名度假景點。

  My town is a famous vacation spot with a lot of beaches and resorts.
  度假景點

- 因為我住的城鎮就在沿海地區，所以我可以吃到很多新鮮的魚。

  Because my town is on the coast, I can eat a lot of fresh fish.
  • coast 海岸

- 我住的城鎮附近有一座山。

  There is a mountain near my town.

- 我住的城鎮空氣很新鮮。

  My town has fresh air. /
  The air is very fresh in my town.

- 我住的城鎮周邊有很多公園。

  There are many parks around my town.

- 我住的城鎮的人口相當少。

  The population of my town is pretty small.
  • population 人口

- 我的朋友們和我每天都在我們鎮上的小山丘上玩耍。

  My friends and I hang out on a hill in our town every day.
  一起～玩耍

- 我住的城鎮每年都會舉辦蝴蝶節。

  There is a butterfly festival in our town every year.

- 在我們鎮上，農夫市集每隔五天開市一次。

  In my town, the farmers' market opens once every 5 days.
  位於～

- 我住的城鎮位在一個小山丘上，所以有很多上坡路。

  My town is located on a hill, so there are many uphill roads.
  上坡路

餐廳 ★ Restaurants

- 我們鎮上有很多好吃的餐廳。

  There are so many delicious restaurants in my town.

- 我們鎮上沒有很多好吃的餐廳。

  There are not many good restaurants in my town.

- 在市區的義大利麵餐廳真的很有名。

  The pasta restaurant downtown is really famous.

- 人們總是會在那家餐廳前排隊等候。

  People are always waiting in line in front of that restaurant.

- 我們鎮上的烘焙坊有很好吃的奶油泡芙。

  My town's bakery has perfect creampuffs.
  • creampuff 奶油泡芙

- 我們鎮上剛開了一家新的披薩店。

  A new pizza restaurant just opened up in my town.

- 我們家的人經常會去燒肉店吃飯。

  My family usually goes to a barbecue restaurant.

文具店 ★ Stationery Stores

- 在我家附近沒有文具店很不方便。

  It is very inconvenient not having a (stationery store) near my house.
  • inconvenient 不便的   文具店

- 在我學校前面有一家文具店。

  There is a stationery store in front of my school.

- 我去文具店買了明天美勞課要用的一些材料。

  I went to the stationery store to buy some materials for tomorrow's art class.
  • material 材料

- 我去文具店買了一份禮物給我朋友。

  I went to the stationery store and bought a present for my friend.

- 我媽媽在文具店買了一個玩具給我，因為我完成了好寶寶獎賞貼紙的收集。

  Mom bought me a toy at the stationery store because I completed my collection of reward stickers.

  • complete 完成、結束

- 我們鎮上的文具店裡有很多有用的學校用品。

  The stationery store in my town has so many useful (school supplies).

  學校用品

- 我們鎮上的文具店老闆為人非常和善。

  The owner of my town's stationery store is really kind.

圖書館／書店 ★Libraries / Bookstores

- 市立圖書館在我家附近。／
  在我家附近有一間市立圖書館。

  The city library is near my house. /
  There is a city library in my neighborhood.

- 我家附近有幾間圖書館。

  There are a few libraries around my house.

- 圖書館離我家真的很遠。

  The library is really (far from) my house.

  離～很遠

- 開車去圖書館要花二十分鐘。

  It takes us 20 minutes to drive to the library.

- 在我們鎮上的圖書館，你一次可以借三本書。

  You can borrow 3 books at once from the library in my town.

  • borrow 借

- 我們家有四個人，所以我們總共可以借十二本書。

  There are 4 people in my family, so we can borrow a total of 12 books.

- 因為是考試期間，所以圖書館裡有很多人。

  There were so many people in the library because it was an (exam period).
  └─ 考試期間

- 我家常會在週末時去圖書館。

  My family often visits the library on weekends.

- 我如果要去書店的話就必須去市區。

  I have to go downtown if I want to go to the bookstore.

- 我和爸爸在週末一起去了書店。

  On the weekend, I went to the bookstore with my father.

- 我去書店買了本參考書。

  I went to the bookstore and bought a (reference book).
  └─ 參考書

- 我通常透過網路書店買書。

  I usually buy books through an online bookstore.

超級市場／傳統市場 ★ Supermarkets / Traditional Markets

- 我去超級市場買了一些零食。

  I went to a supermarket and bought some goodies.
  • 糖果餅乾有很多種類，所以表達吃零食的意涵時，利用 goodies 或 snacks 來表達是比較恰當的。

- 我家附近的超級市場有宅配的服務。

  The supermarket in my neighborhood offers a (delivery service).
  └─ 外送、宅配服務

- 超級市場的西瓜正在促銷。

  Watermelons are (on sale) at the supermarket.
  └─ 促銷

- 我們鎮上的超級市場開到晚上十點。

  The supermarkets in my town stay open until 10 p.m.

- 我家前面的雜貨店關了，所以我就到便利商店買要去校外教學的一些零食。

  The grocery store in front of my house was closed, so I bought some snacks for my field trip at the convenience store.

  便利商店

- 我們家的人會在週末去超級市場採買日常雜貨。

  My family goes grocery shopping at the supermarket on weekends. 採買日常雜貨

- 我爸爸和我在雜貨店裡四處走動來吃店裡所有的試吃品，所以我真的覺得很飽。

  My father and I went around to taste all of the samples in the grocery store, so I was really full.

  • taste 嚐味道

- 我喜歡大型的超級市場，因為它們有試吃攤位。

  I love big supermarkets because they have sample food stands.

  • stand 攤位

- 我們鎮上有個傳統市場。

  There is a traditional market in my town.

  • traditional 傳統的

- 傳統市場裡有很多有趣的東西可以看。

  There are so many interesting things to see at the traditional market.

- 我和奶奶一起到傳統市場並買了一些涼鞋。

  I went to the traditional market with my grandmother and bought some sandals.

 學校 ★ Schools

- 從我家裡到學校有走路二十分鐘的距離。

  My school is twenty minutes' walking distance from my home.

  • distance 距離

- 搭公車去學校要花十分鐘。

  It takes ten minutes to get to school by bus.

- 我上的小學就在我家對面。

  The elementary school that I am attending is right in front of my house.

- 有一間國中就正對著我住的公寓大樓。

  There is a middle school directly facing my apartment building.

  • directly 直接、馬上

- 因為我的學校很遠,所以我必須搭校車上下學。

  Because my school is far away, I have to take the school bus.

- 我上的學校就在路邊。

  The school that I go to is located on the roadside.

- 我的學校在山丘的頂端。

  My school is on top of a hill.

- 我姊姊上的高中附近有一間警察局。

  There is a police station around the high school that my sister goes to.

- 為了上學,我姊姊必須要搭捷運搭四站。

  My older sister has to take the MRT and go 4 stops in order to go to school.

  • stop 站

- 有一間小學和一間國中彼此相鄰。

  An elementary school and a middle school are right beside one another.

- 我弟弟上的幼兒園就在公寓社區裡。

  The kindergarten that my younger brother attends is inside the apartment complex.

- 我住在島上,而且我每天都要搭船去上學。

  I live on an island, and I ride on a ship to go to school every day.

BOOK 2

Book Report Expression

英文讀書心得
寫作寶典

Intro

英文讀書心得
核心句型20句

20 Useful Patterns for

Your Book Reports

在這裡整理出根據不同情況用英文撰寫讀書心得時有用的必備句型。這些句型可以用來表達從整體的故事大綱到具體的說明及感想。

因為讀書心得是將書本的內容精簡摘要並自由發揮地寫出感想的作文，使用這些句型雖然沒辦法把人們各式各樣的想法全都表達出來，但如果我們現在對英文寫作還不是很熟悉的話，這些句型對我們在英文寫作時會有很大的幫助。

注意事項

● 在傳達書的內容時，雖然句子的時態用現在式或過去式都可以，但通篇所有句子的時態應該要一致。

● 在句型中能省略 that 的情況雖然不少，但在撰寫時最好能用完整的句型書寫。

read 的動詞三態變化雖然都是不變的 read-read-read，但是請注意它們的發音有所不同，依序為 [rid]-[rɛd]- [rɛd]。在這個句型是使用過去式的[rɛd]。要表達「是由～寫的」的意涵時，可用簡單的「by + 作者名字」來表達就可以了。

- 我讀了羅爾德・達爾的《神奇魔指》。

  I read Roald Dahl's *The Magic Finger*.

- 我讀了一本有關海倫・凱勒的書。

  I read a book about Helen Keller.

- 我今天讀了露薏絲・勞瑞的《記憶傳承人》。

  Today, **I read** *The Giver* by Lois Lowry.

📝 更進一步！ 這樣表達也可以

- 這本書的書名是《巧克力冒險工廠》。

  The title of the book is *Charlie and the Chocolate Factory.*

- 我今天讀的書是安德魯・克萊門斯寫的《我們叫它粉靈豆》。

  The book I read today was *Frindle* by Andrew Clements.

Pattern

02

這本書的作者是～

The author of the story is ~

★介紹作者

「作家、作者」可用 author 或 writer 來表達。也可以用動詞 write（書寫）來表達出是哪位作者的意涵。

- 這個故事的作者是瑪莉・波・奧斯本。

  The author of the story is Mary Pope Osborne.

- 《愚蠢的莎莉》的作者是奧黛莉・伍德。

  The author of *Silly Sally* **is** Audrey Wood.

- 這個故事的作者是喬伊・考莉。

  The writer of the story is Joy Cowley.

更進一步！ 這樣表達也可以

- 《神奇魔指》是由羅爾德・達爾所撰寫的。

  The Magic Finger **was written by** Roald Dahl.

- 瑪莉・波・奧斯本寫了這個故事。

  Mary Pope Osborne **wrote** the story.

Pattern
03

這個故事的插畫家是～　　　　　　　　　★介紹插畫家
The illustrator of the story is ~

「插畫家」的英文是 illustrator，要注意字尾是用 or 結尾的。或者可用 be illustrated by~（由～畫插圖的、由～畫的），也就是利用「由～畫了～」這樣的句型來說明也可以。

- 這個故事的插畫家是昆汀・布萊克。

  The illustrator of the story is Quentin Blake.

- 《好餓的毛毛蟲》的插畫家是艾瑞克・卡爾。

  The illustrator of *The Very Hungry Caterpillar* **is** Eric Carle.

- 這個故事的插畫家是唐・伍德。

  The illustrator of the story is Don Wood.

- 《月亮晚安》是由克雷門‧赫德畫插圖的。
  Good Night Moon **was illustrated by** Clement Hurd.

- 那是由湯米‧狄波拉所撰寫及插畫的。
  It **was written and illustrated by** Tomie dePaola.

Pattern 04　這個故事是關於～
This is a story about ~
★ 用一個句子來說明內容大綱

這是用來介紹書的內容是在講「誰」和「什麼」時可以用得上的句型。這個用來表達「誰 / 什麼」的名詞的後面，很多時候會出現由 who / that 所引導的關係代名詞子句。

- 這是一個有關希臘和羅馬眾神的故事。
  This is a story about the Greek and Roman gods.

- 這是一個關於讓我們大笑的學校的故事。
  This is a story about a school **that** makes us laugh.

- 這是一個關於我們已親眼目睹的氣候變遷的故事。
  This is a story about climate changes **that** we have witnessed.

更進一步！　這樣表達也可以

- 《我們叫它粉靈豆》是一個關於一個很會創造新名字的男孩的故事。
  Frindle **is a story about** a boy **who** is good at making new names.

- 這告訴我們如何規劃我們的人生。
  This tells us about how to plan our lives.

我因為～而讀了這本書   ★ 說明看這本書的原因

I read this book because ~

把看這本書的原因或動機放在 because 的後面來表達就可以了。

- 因為我的很多朋友們都在讀這本書，所以我也讀了這本書。

  I read this book because many of my friends read it.

- 我看這本書是因為它得到了紐伯瑞獎。

  I read this book because it received the Newbery Medal.

- 我因為老師的推薦而讀了這本書。

  I read this book because my teacher recommended it.

✎ **更進一步！** 這樣表達也可以

- 我想看這本書是因為它的書名看起來很有趣。

  I wanted to read this book because the title looked interesting.

- 我選擇這本書是因為它的插圖很好笑。

  I chose this book because the pictures were funny.

這是本～的書   ★ 說明書的類型

This is a(an) ~

想要說明「小說」、「詩集」、「科幻類」等書籍類型（genre）時可以使用這個句型，而在說明「圖畫書」、「分章節的書」、「紙本書籍」等不同形態的書籍時也可以使用這個句型。

- 這是本圖畫書。

  This is a picture book.

- 這是本神祕小說。

  This is a mystery novel.

- 這本書不是虛構的小說。

  This is a nonfiction book.

  📝 更進一步！ 這樣表達也可以

- 《神奇樹屋》是一本分章節的書籍。

  Magic Tree House **is a** chapter book.

- 夏洛克‧福爾摩斯的作品類型是偵探小說。

  The genre of *Sherlock Holmes* **is** detective.

Pattern **07** 這個故事的背景是設定在～ ★ 介紹故事背景

The setting of the story is ~

setting 指的是（戲劇或小說等）的背景，也就是「故事發生的時間和地點」。順帶一提，「在～年代」的表達方式就如 in the 1930s（在 1930 年代），也就是在該年代數字後加上 s 來表達，因此「2000 年代」就是 in the 2000s。

- 這故事的背景是設定在 1930 年代。

  The setting of the story is in the 1930s.

- 這故事的背景是設定在海上的一艘船上。

  The setting of the story is on a ship at sea.

- 這本書的背景是設定在第二次世界大戰爆發時。

  The book's setting is when World War II broke out.

- 這個故事發生在賓州蛙溪鎮的樹林裡。
  The story takes place in the woods of Frog Creek, Pennsylvania.

- 《芭蕾小精靈安吉莉娜》是被設定在一個叫做切達起司碎片的小鎮裡。
  Angelina Ballerina **is set in** a small village called Chipping Cheddar.

Pattern 08 這故事的主角是～　　　　★介紹故事的主角
The main character of the story is ~

通常因為故事中的登場人物有很多，所以在介紹登場人物時，要用複數形 characters 來表達。其中，「主角」是用 main character 來表達，如果主角有兩位以上的話，就用 main characters 來表達就可以了。

- 這個故事的主角是安吉莉娜。
  The main character of this story is Angelina.

- 這本書的主角是一隻青蛙和一隻蟾蜍。
  The main characters of this book are a frog and a toad.

- 這個故事的主角是貝貝熊。
  The main characters of this story are the Berenstain Bears.

更進一步！ 這樣表達也可以

- 這本書的主角是一個叫做艾洛思的六歲女孩。
  This book's main character is a six-year-old girl named Eloise.

- 《洞》的主角是史丹利・葉納慈四世。
  The main character of *Holes* **is** Stanley Yelnats IV.

Pattern
09
配角是～   ★介紹故事的配角
The supporting character is ~

協助主角展開故事的人，也就是書中的「配角」，在英文裡是用 supporting character(s) 來表達的。

● 配角是 D.W. 亞瑟的妹妹。
The supporting character is D.W., Arthur's little sister.

● 配角是安妮，一隻兇猛的狗狗的主人。
The supporting character is Annie, the owner of a fierce dog.

● 故事的配角是尼克和斯圖亞特，他們是馬文最好的朋友們。
The supporting characters are Nick and Stuart, Marvin's best friends.

更進一步！ 這樣表達也可以

● 也有像零和 X 光等其他的角色。
There are also other characters like Zero and X-ray.

● 其他重要的角色有山姆及賽雷娜。
Other important characters are Sam and Serena.

Pattern
10
～是一個～的男孩   ★介紹登場人物的特徵
~ is a boy who...

介紹登場人物時在 a person / a boy / a girl 等名詞的後面，連接由 who 引導的關係代名詞子句來給予說明。這樣就可以呈現出更具體且有生動感的句子。

- 主角是一個總是在惹麻煩的男孩。

  The main character **is a boy who** always makes trouble.

- 卡勒娜是一個被困在一個小島上很多年的年輕女孩。

  Karana **is a young girl who** was stranded on an island for years.

- 喬治是一隻喜歡學習一切事物的好奇的猴子。

  George **is a curious monkey who** likes to learn everything.

✏️ 更進一步！ 這樣表達也可以

- 主角馬文長得不像他其他的家人。

  Marvin, the main character, doesn't look like the rest of his family.

- 配角巴斯特是亞瑟最好的朋友。

  Buster, a supporting character, is Arthur's best friend.

| Pattern **11** | 在一開始～（故事以～為開端）
In the beginning, ~ | ★ 說明故事的序幕 |

這是在開始介紹故事劇情時很有用的表達句型。當要將故事做摘要時要整理好各個劇情情節（plot），此時利用英文當中的六何法（5W1H）：who, when, where, what, how, why（人物、時間、地點、事件、經過、原因）會比較容易整理。

- 故事以燒鼠老師要求亞瑟他們班寫下一個有趣的故事為開端。

  In the beginning, Mr. Ratburn told Arthur's class to write an interesting story.

- 在一開始，安吉莉娜騎著她的舊腳踏車幫忙跑腿。

  In the beginning, Angelina went on an errand by riding her old bike.

- 在一開始，整個家族參與了太多的活動了。

In the beginning, the whole family was involved in too many activities.

🖊️ **更進一步！** 這樣表達也可以

- 故事以太忙碌而記不得事情的媽媽為開端。

The story begins with Mama, who is too busy to remember things.

- 故事以一位解說鎮裡謎團的口述者為開端。

The story begins with a narrator explaining the mystery of the town.

Pattern
12

在故事的中間，～
In the middle, ~

★ 說明故事中半部的劇情

這個句型對於說明故事的中半部進展很有用，動詞的時態用現在式或過去式都可以。但是在這邊使用的時態，要和敘述故事的序幕（In the beginning,～）時所用的時態一致。

- 在故事的中間，亞瑟想寫一個好故事，但他不知道要怎麼寫。所以他在和身邊的其他人討論後，試著寫了一遍又一遍。

In the middle, Arthur wanted to write a good story, but he did not know how. So he tried to write again and again after talking to people around him.

- 在故事的中間，安吉莉娜在和她的朋友艾莉絲比賽的時候弄壞了她的腳踏車。為了買台新的腳踏車，她試著靠幫忙她的鄰居來賺點錢。

In the middle, Angelina broke her bike while racing her friend Alice. To buy a new bike, she tried to earn some money by helping her neighbors.

- 在故事的中間，熊媽媽緊張又焦慮的哭了，她發現自己實在壓力太大了。所以熊熊們決定先選擇優先要做的事。

In the middle, Mama Bear got stressed out and cried. She found she was feeling too much pressure. So the bears decided to choose what to do first.

Pattern 13 最後，～　　　　　　　　　　★ 說明故事的結局
In the end, ~

這個句型用來說明故事在解決了衝突和矛盾等情節後如何收尾。「In the end, ~」後方句子的時態，要和說明故事的開頭以及中段劇情時所使用的時態一致。

- 最後，燒鼠老師給他第二次機會來寫一個真正的好故事。

In the end, Mr. Ratburn gave him a second chance to write a truly good story.

- 最後，安吉莉娜的祖父母買了一台漂亮的腳踏車給她當生日禮物。

In the end, Angelina's grandparents bought a beautiful bike for her birthday present.

- 最後，貝貝熊們回到了他們平常的生活。

In the end, the Berenstain Bears went back to their normal lives.

更進一步！ 這樣表達也可以

- 故事的結局是主角回到了他家。

The story ends when the main character went back to his family.

- 故事以孩子們散著步並想起汪達做為結束。

The story ends with the children taking a walk and thinking of Wanda.

Pattern 14

起初，～ / 然後，～ / 接下來，～ / 之後，～ / 最後，～　　★ 總結全文

At first, ~ / Then, ~ / Next, ~ / Later, ~ / Finally, ~

這些都是在把故事全文按照時間順序來敘述時可以用得到的副詞片語。除了起初（At first, ~）和最後（Finally, ~）會固定出現在讀書心得的開頭和結尾之外，其餘的副詞可以視文章的長度和內容需要，省略或反覆使用來自由撰寫。此時，在這些副詞的後面加上逗號，接著開始寫我們想表達的內容。在撰寫的時候也可以利用 First, Second, Third… Last 等順序來寫。

● 燒鼠老師吩咐亞瑟他們班寫一個有趣的故事。

　Mr. Ratburn told Arthur's class to write an interesting story.

● 起初，亞瑟想要寫一個好故事，但他不知道要怎麼寫。

　At first, Arthur wanted to write a good story, but he did not know how.

● 接下來，他和很多人討論寫作的事情。

　Next, he talked about writing with many people.

● 然後，他聽從了他們的意見，一遍又一遍地重寫他的故事。

　Then, he followed their ideas and rewrote his story again and again.

● 之後，他的故事最後變得很奇怪，因此燒鼠老師給了他第二次的機會。

　Later, his story turned out weird, so Mr. Ratburn gave him a second chance.

● 最後，亞瑟自己想到了一個非常棒的故事。

　Finally, Arthur came up with a very good story on his own.

問題是～

★ 說明故事中的衝突與矛盾

The problem is (that) ~

一個故事有不有趣很大一部分取決於主角經歷了什麼「問題（problem）」，還有主角解決問題的過程。這些問題也可叫做「衝突（conflict）」。

- 問題是膠水太黏了，以致於椅子黏在了小孩身上。

The problem is that the glue is so strong that the chairs get stuck to the kids.

- 問題是那個壞公主總是欺負其他的公主。

The problem is the mean princess always bullied the other princesses.

- 問題是主角意外地捲入一個不幸的事件當中。

The problem was that the main character accidentally got involved in an unfortunate event.

更進一步！ 這樣表達也可以

- 故事的衝突從艾薇和她姊姊的關係不好時開始。

The conflict starts when Ivy and her sister are not on good terms.

- 故事的衝突從主角被無根據地指控偷東西開始。

The conflict started when the main character was falsely accused of stealing.

問題在～時被解決　　　　　　　　　　　　　　★ 說明解決問題的方法

The problem is solved when ~

在敘述問題以後，想說明這個問題的解決過程時可以使用這個句型。用 be resolved（解決、消除）來代替 be solved（解決）也可以。

● 問題在索菲向她的朋友道歉時被解決了。

The problem is solved when Soffie apologizes to her friend.

● 問題在奈特從照片中找到一個重要的線索時被解決了。

The problem is solved when Nate finds an important clue from the picture.

● 問題在他終於成功地達到他的目標時被解決了。

The problem was resolved when he eventually succeeded in reaching his goal.

✎ 更進一步！　這樣表達也可以

● 他們藉由帶一些禮物給貝爾先生，解決了他們的問題。

They solved their problem by bringing some presents to Mr. Bell.

● 他們藉由聽從他們媽媽的勸告，解決了他們的問題。

They solved their problem by following their mom's advice.

在這個故事裡，我最喜歡的部分是～ ★介紹最喜歡的部分

My favorite part of the story is when ~

利用這個句型，可以寫出書中內容令人印象最深刻的部分。比起單純回憶並寫出書中有趣的部分，透過重新思考並整理出自己的想法，來選擇自己最喜歡的部分，是在撰寫一篇讀書心得時最重要的部分。

- 在這個故事裡，我最喜歡的是龍載公主們一程的部分。

  My favorite part of the story is when the dragon gave a ride to the princesses.

- 在這個故事裡，我最喜歡的是當皮諾丘說謊時，他的鼻子會變長的部分。

  My favorite part is when Pinocchio's nose grows long as he tells lies.

- 在這個故事裡，我最喜歡的是當愛麗絲喝了藥水後，身體就會變小的部分。

  My favorite part is when Alice got smaller after drinking some liquid.

✏ 更進一步！ 這樣表達也可以

- 哈利在天空中飛得高高的去參加比賽，是我在這個故事裡最喜歡的地方。

  I liked the story best when Harry flew high in the sky to play the game.

- 哈利對抗佛地魔和食死人的時候是最有趣的部分。

  The most interesting part was when Harry fought against Voldemort and his Death Eaters.

Pattern 18 　從這個故事裡，我學到了～　★ 整理出從書中學到的東西
From the story, I learned that ~

透過這個句型，可以把從書中整理出的、能學習到的東西表達出來。在寫的時候，可以寫誰都可以想得到的一般道理和感想，也可以寫具有創意和個人風格的感想。

- 從這個故事裡，我學到了我們應該要一直遵守規定。

  From the story, I learned that we should follow the rules all the time.

- 從這個故事裡，我學到了只要不放棄，你的夢想就會實現。

  From the story, I learned that your dream will come true if you don't give up.

- 從這個故事裡，我學到在人生中有時有機會冒險是幸運的。

  From the story, I learned that you are lucky to have an adventure sometime in your life.

更進一步！ 這樣表達也可以

- 這個故事的教訓就是貪婪的人最終會受到懲罰。

  The lesson of the story is that a greedy man gets punished in the end.

- 我所學到的就是在我們的人生中友情的重要性。

  What I learned is the importance of friendship in our lives.

Pattern 19 我喜歡這個故事因為～　　　★ 說明喜歡這本書的理由

I like the story because ~

在寫讀書心得時如果只寫「這本書好有趣呀！」，那內容就太單調乏味了。因此就算只是一些簡單的理由，訓練自己利用這個句型清楚具體的寫下喜歡這本書的理由，這是讀書心得中很重要的部分，可以讓內容更豐富。

● 我喜歡這個故事，因為有很多有趣的角色。

I like the story because there are many fun characters.

● 我喜歡這個故事，因為它的插圖很漂亮。

I liked the story because the pictures were very beautiful.

● 我喜歡這個故事，因為主角和我所想的和想做的都一模一樣。

I like this story because the main character thinks and acts just like I do.

✏️ **更進一步！** 這樣表達也可以

● 那個非常勇敢的主角讓我喜歡這個故事。

The very brave main character **made me like the story**.

● 有趣的劇情設定使我想繼續看下去。

The interesting setting **made me want to keep reading**.

Pattern 20

我想把這本書推薦給～　　　　　　　　　　　★ 推薦書籍

I want to recommend this book to ~

recommend A to B 是「把 A 推薦給 B」的意思。推薦書籍給別人時加上 because（因為）等詞來說明推薦的理由會更好。

● 我想把這本書推薦給我的朋友們，因為它教了我們很多事情。

I want to recommend this book to my friends **because** it teaches us many things.

● 我想把這本書推薦給一直都很喜歡看有關皇室家族故事的賽蘭。

I want to recommend this to Seran, who always likes to read about royal families.

● 我想把這本書推薦給敏熙，讓她知道如何當一個好妹妹。

I want to recommend this to Minhee to let her know how to be a good sister.

✏️ 更進一步！ 這樣表達也可以

● 我弟弟應該要讀這本書，因為他喜歡冒險故事。

My brother **should read this book because** he likes adventure stories.

● 想要大笑的人一定要讀這本書。

A person who wants to laugh a lot **must read this book**.

Part

1

介紹書籍

書的簡介

A Great Fan of Robert Munsch

I read *Something Good* by Robert Munsch to my little sister. I love all of his books because the illustrations are full of humor. His books are fun just when looking at the illustrations. I also like his writing because it is easy to read. He is good at describing how the characters feel. I am also amazed by the author's brilliant imagination. My sister is not good at English, but she liked the story. I think a great writer makes even little children enjoy the story.

羅伯特‧曼斯基的超級粉絲

我讀了羅伯特‧曼斯基的《有些好事》給我妹妹聽。我喜歡他的所有作品,因為插圖都充滿幽默。光是看他書中的插圖就很有趣了。我也很喜歡他的文字,因為讀起來很容易。他擅長描寫角色們的內心感受。我也對於這位作者卓越的想像力感到驚訝。我妹妹的英文不太好,但是她喜歡這個故事。我覺得一個很棒的作家就是連小孩子都會喜愛他的故事。

·illustration 插圖　be good at 擅長～　describe 描寫、敘述　character 角色、登場人物
　be amazed by 驚訝於～　brilliant 傑出的　imagination 想像力

書名 ★ Book Titles

- 我讀的這本書的書名是《夏綠蒂的網》。

  The title of the book that I read is *Charlotte's Web.*

- 我今天要介紹的書是《法蘭妮》。它是我最喜歡的系列故事。

  The book that I'll be introducing today is *Franny.* It is my favorite story series.

  • introduce 介紹

- 今天我看了一本叫做《吃書的狐狸》的書。

  Today, I read a book called *The Fox Who Ate Books.*

- 我今天讀了羅爾德・達爾的《神奇魔指》。

  Today, I read Roald Dahl's *The Magic Finger.*

- 為了今天學校的回家功課，我讀了《神奇樹屋》。

  For today's school homework, I read *The Magic Tree House.*

- 我今天在圖書館讀了《老鼠記者》的第二十集。

  At the library today, I read the 20th volume of *Geronimo Stilton.*

  • volume （系列叢書的）一冊

- 這是我最喜歡的《老鼠記者》系列的最新一集。

  This is the newest volume of my favorite book series, *Geronimo Stilton.*

  • newest 最新的

- 我從圖書館借了《內褲超人》的最後一集來看。

  I borrowed the final volume of *Captain Underpants* from the library and read it.

  • borrow 借

- 我在學校的圖書館借了《A 到 Z 的謎團》系列，這個系列讀起來十分有趣。

  I borrowed the *A to Z Mysteries* series from the school library, and it was so much fun to read.

書的簡介 ★ Brief Introduction

- 今天我看了一本有關海倫・凱勒的書。

  Today, I read a book about Helen Keller.

- 今天我看了一本討論霸凌的書。

  Today, I read a book discussing bullying.
  - discuss 討論、論述　bullying 霸凌

- 《大偵探奈特》是一個關於小男孩當偵探的故事。

  Nate the Great is a story about a young boy working as a detective.
  - detective 偵探

- 《夏綠蒂的網》是一本關於小豬和蜘蛛之間的友誼的書。

  Charlotte's Web is a book about a friendship between a baby pig and a spider.

- 《老鼠記者》是關於一隻名叫謝利連摩的老鼠的冒險故事。

  Geronimo Stilton is about the adventures of a mouse named Geronimo.
  - adventure 冒險

- 《青蛙和蟾蜍》系列是關於青蛙和蟾蜍這兩個好朋友之間的日常生活。

  The *Frog and Toad* series is about the daily lives of two best friends, Frog and Toad. 日常生活

- 《神奇樹屋》是一本關於一對兄妹跨越時空的冒險故事。

  The Magic Tree House is about an adventure of siblings across time and space.
  - sibling 兄弟姊妹　across 橫越、穿過

- 《我觀察》系列是一系列讓讀者在書頁之間尋找隱藏圖片的書。

  The *I SPY* series is a book series in which the readers find the hidden pictures on pages.
  - hidden 隱藏的

- 《好奇猴喬治》系列是根據主角，一隻名叫喬治的猴子的各種有趣經驗的故事所組成的。

  The *Curious George* series is made up of a variety of stories based on the interesting experiences of the main character George, a monkey. 主角
  - based on 根據~

- 《調皮的亨利》是關於最愛調皮搗蛋的男孩亨利的故事。

Horrid Henry is about Henry, the most mischievous boy of all.

　• mischievous 調皮的、淘氣的

- 這本書呈現出被霸凌的主角的學校生活。

This book shows the school life of the main character who is being bullied.

　• bully 霸凌

- 在這個故事裡，主角得到他的家人的所有關愛，然而在他的弟弟／妹妹出現後所歷經的一些轉變。

In the story, the main character gets all of the attention from his family and goes through some changes with the arrival of a younger sibling.

　• attention 注意、關照　arrival 登場、出現

- 這本書是關於一個有幻想中的朋友的主角。

This book is about the main character who has an imaginary friend.

　• imaginary 想像中的、幻想的

- 《邪惡壞女巫》是根據西方國家的壞女巫故事《綠野仙蹤》所改編而成的衍生故事。

Wicked is a spin-off story about the Wicked Witch of the West from *The Wizard of Oz*.

　　　　　　副產品、附帶的產品

- 《三隻小豬的真實故事》是以大野狼的觀點來改寫的《三隻小豬》的故事。

The True Story of the Three Little Pigs is the story *The Three Little Pigs* told from the wolf's perspective.

　• perspective 觀點

- 這本書是《青蛙王子》的續集，並描寫了青蛙王子和公主之間永遠幸福快樂的生活。

This book is a sequence of the *Frog Prince* and tells about the happily ever after of the frog prince and the princess.

　• sequence 續集

- 這本書提到一隻名叫喬治的好奇猴子所經歷的各種事件。

This book deals with various events that a curious monkey named George goes through.

　　　　　　處理、論述到

　• event 重要的事件　　經歷

- 在這本書裡，一位有名的編輯帶領讀者們體驗在世界各地生動的冒險和旅程。

  In this book, a famous editor leads readers on vivid adventures and trips around the world.
  - vivid 生動的

- 這本書是一本讓讀者和三位年輕偵探一起解決謎團的偵探故事。

  This book is a detective story in which readers solve mysteries together with three young detectives.

- 這本書是關於一位名叫傑克的祕密特務，以及他為了祕密任務在全世界展開的令人興奮的冒險故事。

  This book is about a secret agent, Jack, and his thrilling adventures on secret missions all over the world.
  - thrilling 令人興奮的、令人毛骨悚然的

- 這是一本強調實踐的重要性的品格教育書。

  This is a character education book (品格教育) emphasizing the importance of taking action.
  - emphasize 強調　　實行、實踐

- 這是一本有關青少年校園生活的詼諧故事。

  This book is a comical story of teenagers' school life.
  - teenager 青少年

書的類型 ★ Genre

- 這是一本人物傳記。

  This book is a biography.

- 這是一本小說。

  This book is a novel.

- 這是一本歷史小說。

  This book is a historical novel.

- 這是一本偵探小說。

  This book is a detective novel.

- 這是一本神祕小說。

  This book is a mystery novel.

- 這是一本漫畫。

  This book is a comic book.

- 這是一本詩集。

  This book is a poetry book.

- 這是一部科幻小說。

  This book is a work of science fiction.

- 這是一本奇幻小說。

  This book is a fantasy novel.

- 這是一本言情小說。

  This book is a romance novel.

- 這本小說來自美國。

  This novel is from the USA.

- 這本書來自日本。

  This book is from Japan.

- 這是一本自傳。

  This book is an autobiography.

- 這是一本自我成長的書。

  This book is a self-help book.

- 這本書是根據一個真實故事所撰寫的。

  This book is based on a real story.

- 這是一本童話故事書。

  This book is a fairy tale.

- 這本書裡有關於科學的文章。

  This book has essays on science in it.

- 這是一本具教育意義的書。

  This is an informative book.

  • informative 具教育意義的、有益的

- 這是一本經典的小說。

  This book is a classic novel.

- 這本書改編自一本古典小說。

  This book is an adaptation of a classic novel.

  • adaptation 改編

- 這是一本武俠小說。

  This book is a martial arts novel.
  武術

- 這本書適合給零至三歲的小孩閱讀。

  This book is for children from 0 to 3 years old.

- 這本書是給正在學走路的年齡的小孩閱讀的。

  This book is for toddlers.

  • toddler 學習走路的小孩〈一般來說是指零至三歲的小孩〉

- 這本書是給小學生閱讀的。

  This book is for elementary school students.

- 這本書是給國中以上的讀者閱讀的。

  This book is for readers older than middle school students.

- 這本小說是關於一個家族的故事。

  This novel is about a family.

- 這本書是關於第三世界國家孩童的報告。

  This book is a report about children from the Third World countries.

  第三世界的國家們

- 這本書是跟占星術有關的非文學書。

  This is a nonfiction book about horoscopes.

  • horoscope 占星術

關於書名 ★ About Book Titles

- 根據書名，我猜想這本書也許會很有趣。

  Based on the book title, I imagined the book might be interesting.

- 我喜歡《沒有媽媽嘮叨的一天》這個書名。

  I love the title *A Day without Mom's Nagging.*

- 在看到這個書名之後，我真的很想看這本書。／這個書名讓我想看這本書。

  After seeing the title, I really wanted to read it. / The title made me want to read the book.

- 我看的這本書的書名是《我不想站在黑板前面》。這個書名和這個故事真是絕配。

  The book that I read is titled *I Don't Want to Stand in Front of the Blackboard.* It is perfect for the story.

- 我是因為書名很有趣而選擇這本書的，但是故事實際上沒有這麼好。

  I chose the book based on the interesting title, but the story was actually not so good.

  • actually 實際地

- 書名和故事情節都非常有趣。

  Both the book title and the plot were really interesting.

  • plot 情節

- 作者是如何想出這樣的書名的？

  How did the author come up with such a title?

  — 想出～

- 我很好奇作者為什麼會取《時間的皺紋》這個書名。

  I wonder why the author created the title *A Wrinkle in Time*.

  • wonder 好奇

- 當我在讀這本書的時候，我很好奇為什麼作者會給它取這樣的書名。

  While I was reading the book, I was wondering why the author gave it such a title.

- 我因為它的書名而選了這本書，但是實際的故事情節和我原先想像的有所不同。

  I chose the book based on the title, but the actual plot was different from what I had imagined.

- 如果是我的話，我不會取這樣的書名。

  If it were me, I wouldn't have put such a title.

- 當我看到書名的時候，這本書似乎是一個艱深難懂的故事。然而，它實際上既好玩又有趣。

  When I looked at the title, the book seemed like a difficult story. However, it was actually fun and interesting.

介紹作者 ★ Introduction of Authors

- 這本書的作者是艾瑞克・卡爾。

  The author of this book is Eric Carle.

- 這本書是由艾瑞克・卡爾所寫的。

  This book was written by Eric Carle.

  — 由～所寫

- 我聽說這個作者是凱迪克獎的得獎者。／我聽說這個作者獲頒凱迪克獎。

  I heard that this author is a winner of the Caldecott Medal. / I heard this author was awarded a Caldecott Medal.

  — 得獎

- 這本書是由羅爾德‧達爾所寫，並由昆丁‧布雷克繪製插圖。／這本書的作者是羅爾德‧達爾，插畫家是昆丁‧布雷克。

  This book was written by Roald Dahl and illustrated by Quentin Blake. / The author of this book is Roald Dahl, and the illustrator is Quentin Blake.

  • illustrate 繪製插圖　illustrator 插畫家

- 安東尼‧布朗是寫《朱家故事》的人。

  Anthony Browne is the person who wrote *Piggybook*.

- 安東尼‧布朗是一位以《威利》系列聞名的作家。

  Anthony Browne is an author who is famous for the *Willy* series.

- 羅爾德‧達爾以他的作品《巧克力冒險工廠》聞名。

  Roald Dahl is known for his work *Charlie and the Chocolate Factory*.

- 據說羅爾德‧達爾得了兩次愛倫坡獎。

  It is said that Roald Dahl was awarded the Edger Allen Poe Prize two times.

- 我已經看過了羅爾德‧達爾大部分的書。

  I've read most of Roald Dahl's books.

- 所有由安東尼‧布朗所寫的書都很有趣。

  All of the books written by Anthony Brown are so much fun.

- 這本書的作者是位作家兼插畫家。

  The author of this book is both a writer and illustrator.

- 我聽說這本書的作者不只寫了這個故事，還幫這本書畫了插圖。

  I heard that the author not only wrote the story but also drew the pictures for this book.

- 露薏絲‧勞瑞是一位得過紐伯瑞獎的作家。

  Lois Lowry is an author who has received a Newbery Medal.

- 露薏絲‧勞瑞以她的作品《記憶傳承人》得到紐伯瑞獎。

  Lois Lowry won a Newbery Medal for her book *The Giver*.

- 我看了這個作者所有的書。因為它們保證會既好玩又有趣。

  I read all of the books by this author. They are guaranteed to be fun and interesting.

  ── 保證

- 我聽說這位作者以前是位老師，但她後來轉為撰寫兒童故事。

  以前是～

  I heard that this author used to be a teacher, but she came to write children's stories.

- 這位作者說他是根據自身經驗來寫這本書。

  The author said that he wrote this book based on his own experiences.

- 書中有很大一部分是跟作者出生和長大的地方有關。

  A lot of the parts in the book are about the place where the author was born and grew up.

- 當我長大以後，我想成為像他一樣的作家。

  When I grow up, I want to be an author like him.

最喜歡的作家 ★ Favorite Authors

- 安東尼・布朗是我最喜歡的作家。

  Anthony Browne is my favorite author.

- 我喜愛這位作家，所以我看過他大部分的作品。

  I love this author, so I've read most of his works.

- 羅伯特・曼斯基的書光是看插圖就很有趣。

  Robert Munsch's books are fun just by looking at the illustrations.

- 所有羅伯特・曼斯基執筆的故事都很感人。

  All of Robert Munsch's stories are very touching.

  • touching 感人的

- 這位作家擅長描寫主角的情緒。

  This author is good at describing the main character's emotions. /
  The author is good at describing how the main character feels.

  • describe 描寫　emotion 情緒

- 這位作家的插圖充滿幽默，且他的文字很容易閱讀。

  This author's illustrations are full of humor, and his writing is easy to read.

- 我喜歡這個作家的書，因為他的插圖很好笑。

  I like this author's book because the illustrations are funny.

- 我喜歡能寫出有趣故事的作家。

  I love authors who can write fun stories.

- 我驚訝於這位作家卓越的想像力。

  I am amazed at the author's brilliant imagination.

  • amazed 吃驚的

- 這位作家能透過幽默傳遞寓意。

  This author can deliver a message through humor.

  • deliver 傳遞　message 啟示、寓意

- 我喜歡這位作家，因為他總是能想出獨特的故事。

  I like this author because he always comes up with a unique story.
  想出

- 這位作家的故事總是非常有趣且令人興奮。

  This author's stories are always very interesting and exciting.

- 我喜歡能讓我在讀完他們的作品後，對他們感到欽佩的作家們。

  I like authors who make me admire them after reading their work.

  • admire 欽佩、欣賞

- 我喜歡這位作家，因為她能捕捉到其他人無法看到的觀點。

  I like this author because she catches aspects that others fail to see.

  • aspect 觀點

- 每當我讀這位作家的故事時，我的內心就充滿了溫暖。

  Whenever I read this author's stories, my heart is filled with warmth.

  • warmth 溫暖

- 這位作家成功地透過簡單的句子傳達了他的寓意。

  This author successfully delivers his message through simple sentences.

  • successfully 成功地

插圖 ★ Illustrations

- 我發現這本書的插圖特別有趣。

  I find the book's illustrations to be especially fun.

  • especially 特別地

- 這本書的插圖很漂亮。

  This book's illustrations are so pretty.

- 這本書的插圖有點陰森 / 可怕。

  The illustrations in this book are somewhat gruesome/scary.

  • somewhat 有點　gruesome 陰森的、令人毛骨悚然的

- 這位插畫家的插圖很獨特。

  This illustrator's pictures are very unique.

  • unique 獨特的

- 我光看插圖就可以知道這是關於什麼的書。

  I can tell what the book is about just by looking at the illustrations.

  • tell 區別、了解

- 我因為書中滑稽的人物插圖而喜歡上這本書。

  I like this book because of the comical illustrations of the characters.

  • comical 滑稽的、詼諧的

- 我很難理解這本書的插圖。

  It was difficult for me to understand the illustrations in the book.

- 這本書幾乎沒有插圖，所以我一開始真的不想看它。

  This book has few illustrations, so I really didn't want to read it at first.

  一開始

  • few 幾乎沒有

書的資訊 ★ Book Information

- 這本書有一百頁。

  This book has 100 pages.

- 這本書超過兩百頁！

  This book is over 200 pages long!

- 我很快就讀完了這本書，因為它的內容不長。

  I finished reading the book quickly because it was not long.

- 我可以快速地看完這本書，因為它的每一頁裡有很多的插圖和少許文字。

  I could read this book quickly because there were many illustrations and a few words on each page.

- 雖然這本書很厚，但我可以很快看完，因為故事很有趣。

  Although the book was thick, I could finish it quickly because the story was interesting.

- 我很不想看這本書，因為它太厚了。

  I didn't want to read the book because it was too thick.

- 這本書的內容太長了，所以我甚至在看之前就感到無聊了。／我不想看這本書，因為它的內容很長。

  The text of the book is too long, so I felt bored even before reading it. / I did not feel like reading the book because of its lengthy text. 想做～
  - lengthy 冗長的

- 我希望書中字母的大小可以再大一點。

  I wished that the size of letters on the book were a bit bigger.
  - letter 字母、文字

- 這是一本平裝本。

  This book is a paperback.
  - paperback 平裝本、紙面裝訂的書

- 這是一本精裝本。

This book is a hardcover.

• hardcover 精裝本、硬皮材質裝訂的書

- 這是一本立體書而且非常有趣。

This book is a pop-up book, and it was really interesting.

- 這本書是由藍燈書屋出版的。

This book was published by Random House.

• publish 出版

- 這本書來自藍燈書屋。

This book is from Random House.

- 學者出版社是美國有名的出版社之一。

Scholastics is one of the famous publishing companies in the USA.

出版社

- 學者出版社是一家出版了很多兒童文學的出版社。

Scholastics is a publishing company producing plenty of children's literature.

• produce 出版、生產　literature 文學

選書動機

You Can Count on the Newbery

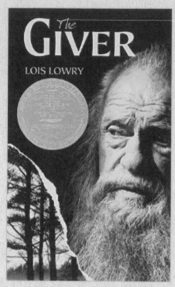

I finished reading *The Giver* by Lois Lowry.
I chose this book because it won the
Newbery Medal in 1994. It is said that more
than 10 million copies have been sold. I
think all of the books with Newbery Medals
are flawless. *The Giver* provides us with fun as well as important
messages. Many of my friends read the book in Chinese and are
talking about it. I did not tell them I was reading it in English. I
can't believe I finished a Newbery Medal-winning book in English!

紐伯瑞獎值得你信賴

我讀完了由露薏絲・勞瑞所寫的《記憶傳承人》。我選這本書,是因為它在一九九四年獲得了紐伯瑞獎。據說它已經賣出了一千萬本以上。我認為所有獲得紐伯瑞獎的書都是完美無缺的。《記憶傳承人》不只帶給我們樂趣,同時也帶給我們一些重要的啟示。我的許多朋友們都讀了這本書的中文版並討論著它。我沒有告訴他們我是讀英文版的。我無法相信我用英文讀完了一本獲得紐伯瑞獎的書!

· count on 相信～　choose (choose-chose-chosen) 選擇　copy 書的本、冊　flawless 完美的
　provide A with B 把 B 提供給 A

其他人的推薦 ★ Recommendations from Others

- 我選擇這本書的原因是我朋友 Amy 說這本書很有趣。

  The reason why I chose the book is that my friend Amy said it was fun.

- 這本書是由 Amy 推薦給我的。

  This book was recommended to me by Amy.

  • recommend 推薦

- Amy 借了這本書給我,並說這本書很有趣。

  Amy lent this book to me and said it was fun.

  • lend (lend-lent-lent) 借給

- 我去看了這本書,因為我的朋友們說這本書很有趣。

  I came to read this book because my friends said it was fun.

- 我看這本書的原因是我姊姊推薦我去看它。

  The reason why I am reading this book is that my older sister recommended it.

- 我姊姊之前就看過這本書,而且告訴我這本書很有趣。

  My older sister had read this book before and told me that it was fun.

- 這本書是我姊姊的,而且它看起來很有趣。因此我選擇看它。

  This book belongs to my older sister, and it looked fun. So I chose to read it.

  屬於～

- 我所有的朋友們都已經看過這本書了。

  All of my friends have read this book.

- 這是在我們學校的圖書館裡最受歡迎的書。

  This is the most popular book in my school library.

- 我讀這本書是因為 Adam 把它送給我當生日禮物。

  I read this book because Adam gave it to me as a birthday present.

- 這本書是我爸爸給我的禮物。

  This book is my father's present to me. / This book is a present from my father.

- 我爸爸買了這本書給我，並說這本書對我有益。

  My father bought me this book and said it would be good for me.

- 我的老師跟我說我應該要讀這本書。

  My teacher told me that I should read this book.

- 多虧有老師的推薦，我才會看了這本書。

  I read this book thanks to my teacher's recommendation. 多虧～

  • recommendation 推薦

- 我媽媽從圖書館借了這本書給我。

  My mother borrowed this book from the library for me.

- 我因為媽媽買了這本書而看了它。

  I read this book because my mother bought it.

個人喜好 ★ Personal Preferences

- 我選擇看這本書，是因為它是由我最喜歡的作家埃爾文‧布魯克斯‧懷特所寫的。

  I chose and read this book because it was written by my favorite author, E.B. White.

- 我選擇這本書是因為它的封面看起來很有趣。

  I selected this book because the cover looked interesting.

  • select 選擇、挑選

- 我選擇這本書是因為它的書名很有趣。

  I chose this book because the title was interesting.

- 我選擇這本書是因為它是一本偵探小說。

  I chose this book because it is a detective novel.

  • detective 偵探

- 我選擇這本書的理由是它有漂亮的插圖。

  The reason I chose this book was that it had pretty illustrations.

  • illustration 插圖

- 我對這本書感興趣，是因為它的主題是關於我最喜歡的恐龍。

  I got interested in this book because it is about my favorite topic, dinosaurs.

- 我因為它顯眼的封面而去看了這本書。

  I came to read this book because of its outstanding cover.

  • outstanding 顯眼的、傑出的

- 我從圖書館借了這本書，因為它的書名很酷。

  I chose this book from the library because of the cool title.

- 當我看到書名的時候，它看起來似乎很有趣。這就是為什麼我會開始看這本書。

  When I looked at the title, it seemed really interesting. That's why I came to read it.

- 在看了書名以後，我對書的內容感到十分好奇，因此我決定讀這本書。

  I was so curious about what the book was about after looking at the title, so I decided to read it.

- 我看了這本書，因為它的插圖很有趣。

  I read the book because the illustrations were fun.

- 我最喜歡的系列剛出了新的一集，所以我馬上把它買了下來。

  A new volume in my favorite series just came out, so I bought it (right away).

  └─ 馬上、立刻

推薦好書／得獎作品 ★ Recommended Books / Award Books

- 我看這本書的原因，是因為它被放在二年級推薦閱讀書單裡。

  I read this book because it was on the recommended (reading list) for grade 2.

  └─ 閱讀書單

- 這本書被推薦給小學生。

  This book is recommended for elementary school students.

- 這本是二年級學生的必讀書籍之一。

  This book is one of the (must-read books) for 2nd graders.

  └─ 必讀書籍

- 這本書在圖書館的推薦閱讀書單上。

  This book is from the library's recommended reading list.

- 我選這本書是因為它得到了凱迪克獎。

  I chose this book because it received the Caldecott Award.

- 得到凱迪克獎的書籍都充滿了漂亮的插圖。

  Books which received a Caldecott Award are filled with beautiful illustrations.

- 當我選書的時候，我傾向會先尋找得過獎的書籍。

  When I choose books, I tend to look for books that have received awards first.

- 這本是獲得紐伯瑞獎的書。

  This book is a winner of the Newbery Medal.

- 這是由獲得紐伯瑞獎的作者所寫的最新作品。

  This is the newest book by a Newbery Medal-winning author.

- 所有獲得紐伯瑞獎的書都是完美無缺的。

  All of the books that have received Newbery Medals are flawless.

  • flawless 無缺點的、完美的

- 我不敢相信自己用英文讀了一本得到紐伯瑞獎的書！

  I can't believe I am reading a Newbery Medal-winning book in English!

- 這本書被收錄在三年級的教科書裡。

  This book is included in third grade textbooks.

  • include 包含　textbook 教科書

- 這是最近的暢銷書。

  This is a (bestselling book) these days.
  　　　　　暢銷書

其他 ★ Others

- 我讀這本書是因為它是我的回家功課。

  I read the book because it was my homework.

- 因為我的回家功課是要研究螞蟻，所以我看了這本書。

  I read the book because my homework was to research ants.

  • research 研究、調查

- 我的回家功課是要讀這本書並寫一篇讀書心得。

  My homework is to read this book and to write a (book report).
  讀書心得

- 我讀這本書是因為它是我英文補習班的回家功課。

  I read the book because it was my English cram school's homework.

- 老師跟我說她要根據這本書來給我們辦一場閱讀測驗競賽。

  My teacher told me that she is going to give us a reading (quiz bowl) based on this book.
  測驗競賽

- 這本書是根據一部電視劇來寫的。

  This book is based on a TV drama.

- 看這本書前，我先看了它的電影。

  I watched the movie before I read the book.

- 這本書有被翻拍成電影。因為我喜歡這部電影，所以我也想看這本書。

  This book was made into a movie. Because I liked the movie, I wanted to read the book, too.

- 這本書是電影《飢餓遊戲》的原著，所以我真的很想看它。

  （電影等的）原著
  This book is the (original story) of the movie *The Hunger Games*, so I really wanted to read it.

- 我先看了這本書的中文版，然後我決定要讀英文版的。

  I read this book in Chinese first, and I decided to read the (English version).
  英文版

- 我能夠看英文版的，是因為在先看過中文版以後，我已經知道故事情節了。

  I could read the English version because I knew the plot already after reading the Chinese version earlier.

- 我聽說這本書得到很有名的獎，而且真的很有趣。

  I heard that this book received a famous prize, and it was really fun.

- 我喜歡所有和歷史有關的書，而這本書對我而言也真的很有趣。

  I like all books about history, and this was also really fun for me.

- 我在學校學到了亞瑟王，而我想藉由看這本書知道更多關於這位國王的事情。

  I learned about King Arthur at school, and I wanted to know more about the king by reading this book.

Part **2**

介紹登場人物和故事情節

登場人物和故事情節

A Summary of Earthquake in the Early Morning

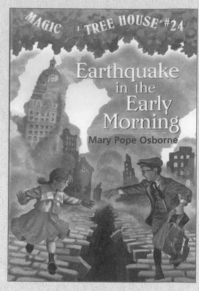

I read *Magic Tree House: Earthquake in the Early Morning* by Mary Pope Osborne. First, Jack and Annie went to San Francisco to find some special writings for Morgan's library. When they arrived, it was 1906. A big earthquake happened, so they had trouble finding the writings. Then, they helped a poor family by giving them their boots and received a writing in return. Finally, they got all of the necessary writings and went back to the tree house. They were glad to complete their adventure successfully.

《清晨的地震》摘要

我讀了由瑪麗・波・奧斯本所寫的《神奇樹屋》系列裡的《清晨的地震》這集。起初，傑克和安妮為了找一些特別的文件給摩根圖書館，而去了舊金山。他們到達的那年是 1906 年。當時發生了一個很大的地震，因此他們在找文件時遇到了困難。之後，他們送出了他們的靴子來幫助一個窮困的家庭，並收到一份文件做為回報。最後，他們得到了所有必要的文件並回到了樹屋。他們很高興可以成功地完成他們的冒險。

・have trouble + Ving 做～時遭遇困難　in return 做為回報、做為交換　necessary 必要的
complete 完成

介紹主角 ★ Main Characters

- 這個故事的主角是亨利。

  The (main character) of this story is Henry.
  　　　　主角

- 這本書的主角是一隻青蛙和一隻蟾蜍。

  A frog and a toad are the main characters of this book.

  • toad 蟾蜍

- 一對叫做麥斯和露比的姊弟是這本書的主角。

  A brother and a sister named Max and Ruby are the main characters of this book.

- 一個叫做貝貝熊的熊家族是這個故事的主角。

  A bear family called the Berenstain Bears are the main characters of this story.

- 這本書的主角是一個叫做艾洛思的六歲女孩。

  This book's main character is a six-year-old girl named Eloise.

- 這本書的主角亞瑟是三年級的學生。

  This book's main character, Arthur, is in third grade.

- 這個故事的主角亨利是一個總是製造麻煩的男孩。

  Henry, the main character of the story, is a boy who always (makes troubles).
  　　　　　　　　　　　　　　製造麻煩

- 《巫婆與黑貓》裡的溫妮是一個有趣而不可怕的女巫。

  Winnie, from *Winnie the Witch*, is a witch who is funny (rather than) scary.
  　　　　　　　　　　　而不是～

- 這本書的主角朱妮 B 是一個就像我一樣的孩子。

  This book's main character, Junie B, is a child just like me.

- 這本書的主角是一隻叫做小熊的熊寶寶。

  This book's main character is a baby bear called Little Bear.

- 亞瑟有很多好朋友。

  Arthur has a lot of good friends.

- 艾洛思總是能想出既古怪又有創造力的點子。

  Eloise always comes up with weird and creative ideas.

  • weird 古怪的

- 奈特把困難的案件解決得很好，因為他很聰明。

Nate solves difficult cases very well because he is really smart.
- case 事件、案子

- 隨著詹姆士長大，他經歷了許多困難。

As James grows up, he (goes through) lots of difficulties.
經歷

- 不管情況有多困難，詹姆士從不放棄。／不論遇到什麼樣的困難，詹姆士從不感到沮喪挫折。

James never gives up no matter how difficult the situation is. / James never gets frustrated whatever difficulties may come.
- frustrated 感到沮喪的、感到挫折的

- 這本書的主角是個就像我一樣膽小的孩子。

This book's main character is a timid child just like me.
- timid 膽小的

- 這本書的主角非常勇敢。

This book's main character is very brave.

- 這本書的主角和我有許多相似之處。

This book's main character and I have a lot (in common).
共同的

- 這個主角和我妹妹很相似，因為她們都很古怪。

和～相似
This main character (is similar to) my younger sister in that both of them are weird.

介紹反派角色 ★Villains

- 詹姆士的兩個阿姨都心地很壞且殘酷。

Both of James's aunts are mean and cruel.
- cruel 殘酷的

- 詹姆士有兩個心腸不好的阿姨。

James has two mean aunts.

- 主角的姊姊們對主角非常不好。

The older sisters are so mean to the main character.

- 史高治是一個貪婪的老人。

  Scrooge is a greedy old man.
  - greedy 貪婪的

- 白雪公主的後母對白雪公主非常不好。

  Snow White's stepmother was really mean to Snow White.
  - stepmother 後母、繼母

- 在《瑪蒂達》裡，有一位叫做川契布爾的邪惡校長。

  In *Matilda*, there is an evil principal called Ms. Trunchbull.
  - evil 惡毒的、邪惡的

- 川契布爾校長用非常可怕的方式來對待學生。

  Principal Trunchbull treats the children in a really horrible way.
  - horrible 可怕的、極為可憎的

- 亞瑟的老師是燒鼠先生，他以喜歡出無止盡的回家功課而惡名昭彰。

  Mr. Ratburn, Arthur's teacher, is notorious for giving out endless homework.
  - notorious 惡名昭彰的

- 加法爾是一個折磨阿拉丁的邪惡巫師。

  Jafar is the evil wizard who torments Aladdin.
  - wizard 巫師、魔法師　torment 使～痛苦、折磨

- 這個邪惡的巫師總是為阿拉丁帶來麻煩。

  This evil wizard always causes trouble for Aladdin.

- 我不認為大野狼有這麼壞。

  I don't think that the wolf was bad after all.

- 如果我們觀察得仔細一點，即使是反派角色也有好的一面。

  If we look closely, even the villains have good sides. 好的一面
  - villain 反派角色

- 當我們仔細地觀察一個做了某些壞事的人，在他們的行為背後總是有他們的原因的。

  When we look closely at a person who does something bad, there are always reasons behind his/her actions.

- 在羅爾德・達爾的故事裡，大人們總是反派角色。／在羅爾德・達爾的書裡總是有壞心的大人。

  In Roald Dahl's stories, it is always the adults that are the villains. / There are always mean adults in Roald Dahl's books.

- 在這個故事裡沒有壞人。

  There are no bad people in this story.

介紹其他配角 ★ Supporting Characters

- 克勞德很傲慢。／
  克勞德很愛炫耀。

  Claude is so arrogant. /
  Claude likes to show off.
  炫耀
  • arrogant 傲慢的

- 查爾斯是一個非常害羞的男孩。

  Charles is a very shy boy.

- 葛莉絲是一個不怎麼討人喜歡的模範生。

  Grace is a model student who is not likable.
  模範生
  • likable 可愛的、討人喜歡的

- 佛瑞茲是一個喜歡科學的奇妙男孩。

  Fritz is a whimsical boy who likes science.
  • whimsical 奇妙的、奇怪的

- 詹金斯老師很了解孩子們。

  Mrs. Jenkins understands children really well.

- 巴斯特是亞瑟最好的朋友。

  Buster is Arthur's best friend.

- 奈特總是和泥泥一起遊玩。

  Nate always travels together with Sludge.

- 麥斯不是一個壞男孩，但他總是讓露比不高興。

  Max is not a bad boy, but he always makes Ruby feel upset.

- 藍仙子是一個幫助皮諾丘的仙女。

  The Blue Fairy is a fairy who helps Pinocchio.

- 查理的祖父母很慈祥和藹。

  Charley has kind grandparents.

- 小熊的媽媽非常的溫柔且和藹可親。

  Little Bear's mother is very gentle and kind.

- 有很多不同的朋友出現在亞瑟的故事裡。

  A lot of different friends appear in Arthur's story.
  - appear 出現

- 叫做《卡由》的這本書是關於卡由和他的家人的故事。

  The book titled *Caillou* is a story about Caillou and his family.

- 這本書是關於哈利波特和朋友們的冒險故事。

  This book is about the adventures of Harry Potter and his friends.

- 在這個故事裡，我們看到有個人會在主角遇到一些困難時幫助他。

  In this story, we see a person who helps the main character when he has some difficulties.
  - difficulty 困難

- 奈特藉著泥泥的幫助來解決案子。

  Nate solves the case with the help of Sludge.
  - case 案子

故事背景─時間及地點 ★ Setting – Time and Place

- 這本書是以中世紀的歐洲為背景。

  This book is set in medieval Europe. / The setting of the book is medieval Europe.
  - set 設定背景　medieval 中世紀的　setting 背景

- 這本書的背景是設定在古希臘。

  This book's setting is ancient Greece.
  - ancient 古代的

- 這本書的背景是在第二次世界大戰。

  This book's setting is the Second World War. / The setting of the story is World War II.

- 這本書是根據一個發生在德國 1940 年代的真實事件。

  This book is based on a true event that took place in Germany during the 1940s.

  根據～ / 發生

- 這本書是背景設定在韓戰時期的小說。

  This book is a novel which is set during the Korean War.

- 這個故事帶著我們回到 1930 年代。／這個故事可以回溯到 1930 年代。

  This story takes us back to the 1930s. / The story dates back to the 1930s.

  回溯到～

- 這個故事的背景是設定在一個波蘭的農村。

  A rural village in Poland is the setting of this story.

- 這本書寫的是有關於未來世界的科幻小說。

  This book is a work of science fiction written about the future world.

  科幻小說

- 主角回到了過去的時光。

  The main characters travel back in time.

- 這個故事的背景是現在，但主角為了他們的冒險而回到了過去。

  The story is set in the present day, but the main characters travel back in time for their adventures.

- 這是一個關於主角回到了久遠的過去和前往未來的故事。

  It is a story about the main characters traveling far back into the past and ahead into the future.

- 每個章節都是根據一個歷史事件。

  Each episode is based on a historical event.

  • historical 和歷史有關的、歷史的

- 這本書是關於一個住在小村莊的動物家庭。

  This book is about one animal family living in a small village.

- 這本書是關於在一個夏日裡發生的事情。

  This book is about what happened one summer day.

- 這個故事的背景是在一所美國的小學。

  This book's setting is an elementary school in the United States of America.

- 這是一個關於進入人類的身體裡，並看看身體裡發生什麼事情的故事。

  It is a story about going inside the human body and what happens there.

- 這個故事以孫子去探望住在附近村子的奶奶為開端。

  The story starts with a grandson visiting his grandmother in a neighboring village.

  • neighboring 鄰近的、附近的

故事摘要 ★ Summaries

- 這是這本書的摘要。

  Here is a summary of this book.

  • summary 大意、總結

- 整個故事是這樣的。

  The entire story happens like this.

  • entire 整體的、全體的

- 主角偶然地碰到了一連串的事件，並面臨了一些問題。

  （偶然地）碰到

  The main character runs into a series of events and faces problems.

  一連串的

- 這本書的通篇故事是在講當主角回到過去時所發生的事情。

  This book's overall story is what happens to the main character as he goes back in time.

  • overall 全盤的、全體的

- 衝突從主角被錯誤地指控偷了一些運動鞋開始。

  The conflict starts when the main character is falsely accused of stealing some sneakers.

  • conflict 衝突　falsely 錯誤地　be accused of 被指控～

- 問題就是主角意外地被捲入了一件不幸的事件當中。

  The problem was that the main character accidently gets involved in an unfortunate event.

  與某事件有關、涉入某事件

- 主角雖然在一開始進行的很困難，但問題在主角最後成功時被解決了。

  The problem is solved when the main character eventually succeeds though he struggles at first.
  - struggle 奮鬥、艱難的進行

- 在這個過程中，主角和一個叫做零的小孩變成了朋友。

  During the process, the main character becomes friends with a child named Zero.
  - process 過程

- 這個故事的結局是主角平安地回到了家。

  The story ends with the main character safely returning home.

時間軸／其他事件 ★Timeline / Events

- 起初，他們去了法國巴黎。

  First, they went to Paris, France.

- 接著，他們到了埃及的蘇伊士。

  Next, they went to Suez, Egypt.

- 然後，他們在印度救了酋長的妻子。

  Then, they saved the chief's wife in India.

- 接著，他們去了美國並遭到印地安人襲擊。他們勉強地逃了出來。

  Next, they went to America and were attacked by Indians. They barely escaped.
  - attack 攻擊 barely 勉強、僅僅 escape 逃脫

- 在那之後，他們回到了英國。

  After that, they returned to Britain.

- 最後，他們在時間用盡的三秒前回到了協議好的地點。

  Finally, they were able to go back to the agreed place 3 seconds before time ran out.
  - agreed 議定好的、協議好的   全部用盡

- 一開始，男孩因為無聊，就撒謊說狼來了。

  First, the boy lied that there was a wolf because he was bored.

- 接著，他又再次撒謊說狼來了。

  Then, he lied again that there was a wolf.

- 隔天他又重複地開了相同的玩笑。 He repeated the same joke the next day.

- 然後，隔天真的有狼出現了！ Then, the next day, there was a real wolf!

- 最後，沒人前去幫忙，所以全部的羊都被吃掉了。 Finally, no one came to help, so all of the sheep were killed.

故事架構 ★ Story Structures

- 這本書是一本有名的經典作品的詼諧版仿作。

  This book is a parody of a famous classical piece.

  • parody 詼諧版的模仿作品　classical 經典的

- 雖然它是根據一個經典作品改編，但它的時間背景設定是現在。

  Although it is based on a classic, its time setting is present.

  • classic 古典（作品）　present 現今

- 他以幽默的方式把這個民間故事重新創作。

  It recreated the (folk tale) by telling it in a humorous way. 民間故事

  • recreate 重新創作

- 這個故事以回到過去的時光來展開。

  The story unfolds/begins by going back in time.

  • unfold 展開、呈現

- 這個故事顯示出這兩個事件是如何進行的，以及它們是如何被連繫起來的。

  The story shows how the two events progress and how they are related.

  • related 有連繫的、相關的

- 這個故事是以主角述說自己的經驗的形式來撰寫的。

  The story is written in the form of the main character telling his experiences.

- 在故事的中間有用插圖描繪出主角的內心世界。

  In the middle of the text, there are illustrations portraying the main character's (inner side). 內心

  • portray 描繪、描寫

- 這本書獨特的地方在於讀者可以同時享受到看童話故事和看漫畫的樂趣。

  This book is unique in that readers can enjoy the pleasure of a fairy tale and a comic book.

- 這本書是一個關於在一個禮拜內所發生的事情的故事。

  This book is a story about what happened during one week.

- 這本書藉由發生在我們日常生活的故事，把艱深的科學事實用較為簡單的方式來說明。

  By using stories from our everyday lives, this book explains difficult science facts in easier ways.

- 每個人都經歷過的極為平凡的事件，被變成了一個有趣的故事。

  Very ordinary events that everyone has experienced are turned into a fun story.
  - ordinary 平凡的、平常的　　變成～

- 有一天，主角一直想像的一些事情真的成真了。

  One day, something that the main character has been imagining happens for real.
  　真的

- 過去的祕密是如何被揭穿的這個部分非常的吸引人。

  How the secrets from the past are revealed is really fascinating.
  - reveal 揭穿、洩露　fascinating 迷人的、吸引人的

我的想法

Bad Parents in *Charlie and the Chocolate Factory*

Let's think about the parents of the naughty children in *Charlie and the Chocolate Factory* by Roald Dahl. They all love their kids very much. I can see it when they worry when something happens to their kids. But giving unconditional love without discipline is not love. In the end, they cannot protect the bad children from danger because the children are out of control. In my opinion, Roald Dahl is saying that those parents don't know how to be good parents. Neglecting children without love is not right, but giving too much love is also foolish.

《巧克力冒險工廠》裡的壞父母

讓我們來想想由羅爾德·達爾寫的《巧克力冒險工廠》裡調皮小孩的父母。他們都很愛他們的孩子。當他們在擔心他們的孩子發生了什麼事情的時候，我可以看出他們對孩子的愛。但是缺乏原則的給予無條件的愛並不是愛。最終，他們無法保護壞孩子們遠離危險，因為這些孩子已經不受控制了。依我的見解，羅爾德·達爾是要說這些父母不知道該如何當好父母。毫無關愛地忽視孩子固然是不對的，但給予過多的關愛也是很愚蠢的。

· **naughty** 頑皮的、淘氣的　**unconditional** 無條件的　**discipline** 原則、紀律　**out of control** 失去控制
　neglect 忽略

表達想法—支持的理由 ★ Opinions – Supporting Reasons

- 我認為小紅帽做錯了，因為她走了一條她不應該走的路。

  I think Little Red Riding Hood was wrong because she took a path that she was not supposed to.
  - path 小路、小徑　be supposed to 應該～

- 我認為蚱蜢沒有做任何不對的事。

  I think the grasshopper didn't do anything wrong.

- 第一，蚱蜢一點都不懶惰。它一直在唱歌，而這也是它能做得最好的事。

  First, the grasshopper wasn't being lazy at all. He sang all the time, which was what he could do best.

- 第二，每個人對於快樂都有不同的標準。

  Second, everyone has a different standard of happiness.
  - standard 標準

- 第三，說耕種很重要，而演奏音樂沒有用是不對的。

  Third, saying that farming is important while playing music is useless is wrong.
  - useless 無用的、無益的

- 因此，蚱蜢其實只是個藝術家，而不是一個懶骨頭。

  Therefore, the grasshopper wasn't actually a lazybones but was just an artist.
  - lazybones 懶骨頭

表達想法—表達反對 ★ Opinions – Expressing Opposition

- 我覺得主角太優柔寡斷了。

  I think the main character is too indecisive.
  - indecisive 優柔寡斷的

- 這本書的主角太善良了，讓我覺得鬱悶。／在我看到太過善良的主角時，我覺得很鬱悶。

  The book's main character is too nice, which frustrates me. / I am upset when I see the main character who is being too nice.

- 我無法理解主角的行為。／我不知道主角為什麼要這麼做。

  I don't understand the main character's actions. / I don't understand why the main character acts like that.

- 我不喜歡主角的表現。

  I don't like how the main character acts.

- 我認為這本書的主角很善良，但他並不聰明。

  I think the book's main character is nice but not wise.

- 我不認為沈清做了正確的決定。

  I don't think that Shim Chung made the right decision.

- 我認為沈清當時應該要留在她父親的身邊。

  I believe that Shim Chung should have stayed with her father.

- 我覺得留下她失明的父親獨自一人是不對的。

  I think it was wrong to leave her blind father alone.

  • blind 眼瞎的

- 她當時就應該要想到當她父親發現時，他會有多難過。

  She should have thought about how sad her father would be when he found out.

- 當她父親最終能張開眼睛看東西時，他會快樂嗎？

  Will her father be happy when he can finally open his eyes?

- 要當個好女兒，並不意謂著無論如何都要犧牲自己。

  Being a good daughter does not mean one has to sacrifice herself no matter what.

  • sacrifice 犧牲

- 對於沈清的行為是否是好女兒的表現，我感到困惑。

  I am puzzled to call Shim Chung's action being a good daughter.

  • puzzled 困惑的、茫然的

- 說她和某人結婚不是因為她愛對方，而是因為對方是國王，這是胡說八道。

  It is nonsense that she marries someone not because she loves him but because he is a king.
  - nonsense 胡說八道

- 只為視障者辦一場派對也是不公平的。

  It is also unfair to (throw a party) only for blind people.

  → 辦一場派對

最喜歡的部分 ★ Favorite Parts

- 最讓人印象深刻的是皮諾丘變成一個真正的人類的部分。

  The most impressive part is when Pinocchio becomes an actual (human being). 人類
  - impressive 令人印象深刻的

- 最難忘的就是媽媽親吻賈斯特的手當作禮物的部分。

  The most memorable part is when Mother gives a kissing hand to Chester as a gift.
  - memorable 難忘的

- 我最喜歡的就是紙袋公主離開王子的那一幕。

  The scene that I liked the most is when the Paper Bag Princess leaves the prince.

- 我很喜歡這本書的結局。

  I really love the ending of this book.

- 結束的那一幕是這個故事的大翻轉。

  The ending scene was a real twist to the story.
  - twist 轉折、扭轉

- 老師被大猩猩抓住的那一幕真的是個意外轉折。

  The scene where the teacher was captured by the gorilla was a real twist.
  - capture 捕獲、俘虜

- 當我看到兒子給了媽媽一個擁抱的部分時，我流下了眼淚。

  Tears came to my eyes when I was reading the part where the son (gave a hug) to his mother.

  → 給予一個擁抱

- 《彩虹魚》的結尾真的很感人。 The ending of *Rainbow Fish* is really moving/touching.

- 我發現小青蛙最後睡著的結局十分有趣。 I found the ending so funny when Froggy finally falls asleep.

- 《花盼》的最後一部分告訴了我們很多教訓。 The last part of *Hope for the Flowers* teaches a lot of lessons.
  - lesson 教訓

- 《雪人》的結局有點讓人難過。 The ending of *The Snow Man* is a bit sad.

 ## 難忘的引言 ★ Memorable Quotes

- 我記得最清楚的就是：「最重要的東西是眼睛看不到的」這句引言。 The quote that I remember the most is "What is essential is invisible to the eye."
  - quote 引言　essential 最必要的、極為重要的
    invisible 看不到的

- 「最重要的東西是眼睛看不到的」這句引言是這本書中最令人印象深刻的想法。 The quote "What's essential is invisible to the eye" was the most impressive idea from the book.
  - impressive 令人印象深刻的

- 「最重要的東西是眼睛看不到的」，這句引言是本書中最令人難忘的一句話。 The quote "What's essential is invisible to the eye" is the most memorable saying from the book.
  - memorable 難忘的

- 在這本書中有句引言：「最重要的東西是眼睛看不到的」，這句話真的打動了我的心。 In this book there is a quote saying, "What's essential is invisible to the eye." It really touched my heart.
  - touch 感動人心

- 「我無法回到昨日了，因為我已是一個不同的人」，這句引言是由愛麗絲說的，而我覺得她說的真的非常棒。

  "I can't go back to yesterday because I was a different person then." This is a quote said by Alice, and I think it is really wonderful.

- 讀完這本書以後，最令人難忘的引言就是愛麗絲所說的：「我無法回到昨日了，因為我已是一個不同的人。」

  After reading this book, the most memorable quote was when Alice said, "I can't go back to yesterday because I was a different person then."

- 我寫下下面的書中引言，因為我太喜愛這句話了。

  I wrote down the following quote from the book because I love it so much.

  • write down 寫下～

- 看到「真愛就是比起自己優先想到某人」這句話後，我開始反省過去的許多事，並對自己曾經做過的事情感到後悔。

  After looking at the expression "True love is putting someone else before yourself," I came to reflect on many things from the past and regretted what I had done.

  • expression 表達　reflect 反省　regret 後悔

- 每當你遭受困難的時候，想想這句引言：「不到最後就不是結束」，這將給你很多幫助。

  Whenever you are going through a hard time, think about the quote "It is not over until it is over." It will help you a lot.

- 我想跟朋友分享「不到最後就不是結束」這句引言，因為如果我們能努力奮鬥到最後，所有事情最後都會變得不一樣。

  I want to share the quote "It is not over until it is over." with my friends because if we try hard till the very end, everything can turn out differently.

  • the very end 最後　turn out 最終變為～

如果我是～的話—假設 ★ Rewriting the Story

- 如果我是這本書的主角,我會如何反應呢?

  If I were the main character of the book, how would I have reacted?
  - react 反應

- 如果當時我和主角在同一個情境裡的話,我會如何反應呢?

  How would I have reacted if I had been in the same situation as the main character?

- 如果我當時在這樣的環境裡長大,我會有怎樣的行為舉止呢?

  How would I have behaved if I had been brought up in this kind of environment?
  - behave 表現、舉動　　養育、扶養

- 假如我是這本書的主角,我當時就會去救老師。

  Supposing I were the main character of this book, I would have saved the teacher.
  - suppose 假設、假定

- 如果我生在唐朝,我會過著怎樣的生活呢?

  If I had been born during the Tang Dynasty, what kind of life would I have lived?

- 如果當時我碰到了像瑪蒂達的父母一樣的雙親,那我一定會很悲慘。

  If I had met parents like Matilda's, I would have been so miserable.
  - miserable 悲慘的

- 如果有像麥斯這樣的弟弟,我想會很有趣。

  I think it will be really fun to have a younger brother like Max.

- 如果我是哈利波特,我會有勇氣站出來對抗佛地魔嗎?

  If I were Harry Potter, would I have the courage to stand up against Voldemort?
  - courage 勇氣　　站出來對抗

- 如果海倫‧凱勒沒有遇到像蘇利文這樣棒的老師,那她會發生什麼事呢?

  What would have happened to Helen Keller if she had not met a great teacher like Sullivan?

- 我希望我能像瑪蒂達一樣施展魔法。

  I wish I could work magic like Matilda.
  施展魔法、操縱魔法

- 如果我是作者，我才不會讓小美人魚死掉。絕對不會！

  If I were the author, I would not have let the Little Mermaid die. Never!

- 如果我能在現實生活裡遇到這本書的主角，我想要稱讚他的勇氣。

  If I were to meet the main character in this book for real, I want to praise him for his courage.

  • praise 稱讚

- 如果我是作者的話，我就不會讓故事這樣子結束。

  If I were the author, I would not have ended the story that way.

寫信給書中的人物 ★ Letters to the Characters

- 親愛的皮諾丘：
  我想知道當你成為一個真正的人類時，你的感受是什麼？

  Dear Pinocchio,
  I want to know how you felt when you became an actual human being.
  人類

- 對我而言，為了考試而念書真的很辛苦。如果你是我你會怎麼做？

  To me, studying for exams is really hard. What would you do if you were me?
  惹出麻煩

- 當你惹出麻煩時，我完全不會討厭你，因為我能理解你。

  When you were causing trouble, I didn't hate you at all because I could understand you.

- 但是你不去學校上學還是不對的。

  But it is still wrong for you not to go to school.

- 然而，你能透過你的勇氣來克服所有困難還是很棒的。

  However, it is still great of you to overcome all of your difficulties through your courage.

  • overcome 克服

- 我想要有像你一樣的朋友。

  I want to have a friend like you.

- 葉芽，我真欽佩你能逃離雞舍。

  Leafie, I really admire you for escaping from the henhouse.

  • admire 欽佩、欣賞　escape 逃離、逃脫　henhouse 雞舍

- 我很欽佩你能幫助你的朋友。

  I admire you a lot for helping your friend.

- 我覺得你到最後都沒有失去勇氣真的很偉大。

  I really think you are great for not losing your courage till the end.
  到最後

- 蘇利文老師，我從這本書裡學到了很多。

  Miss Sullivan, I learned a lot by reading this book.

- 蘇利文老師，我想要有像妳一樣的老師。

  Miss Sullivan, I want to have a teacher like you.

- 非常感謝妳幫助海倫‧凱勒。

  Thank you very much for helping Helen Keller.

- 就像您一樣，我會成為一個能幫助別人的人。

  Like you, I will be a person who can help others.

- 當事情變得棘手的時候，我會一直抱怨並想馬上放棄。

  When things get difficult, I become whiney and want to give up right away.
  馬上、立刻

  • whiney 愛抱怨的

- 在想到海倫‧凱勒以後，我覺得自己很慚愧。

  I felt so ashamed of myself after thinking about Helen Keller.
  因～而感到慚愧、羞恥

Part

3

寫結論

整體的感受

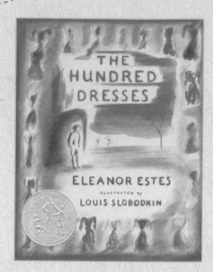

The Hundred Dresses: A Sad But Beautiful Story

I read *The Hundred Dresses* by Eleanor Estes. I cried while reading the book. In the story the kids made fun of Wanda because she wore the same blue dress every day. I was heartbroken when Wanda kept saying she had one hundred dresses at home. The truth was she drew one hundred dresses. I also felt bad for Maddie who did not speak up for Wanda. She thought teasing Wanda was wrong, but she was not brave enough. After Wanda left the town, the kids found Wanda was a talented artist. They felt guilty. Later, they were glad Wanda wrote a nice letter to the class. It is a beautiful story that teaches us the importance of respect for others.

《一百件洋裝》：一個悲傷但美麗的故事

我讀了由艾蓮諾・艾斯提斯所寫的《一百件洋裝》。在讀這本書時我哭了。在書中孩子們嘲笑汪妲，因為她每天都穿一樣的藍色洋裝。當我看到汪妲不斷地說她在家裡有一百件洋裝時，我的心就好痛。事實上是她畫了一百件的洋裝。瑪蒂不敢站出來幫汪妲出聲也讓我覺得難過。她覺得嘲笑汪妲是不對的，但她不夠勇敢。在汪妲離開這個城鎮以後，孩子們發現汪妲是個天才藝術家。他們覺得有罪惡感。之後，他們很高興汪妲寫了一封友善的信給班上。這是一個教導我們尊重別人的重要性的美麗故事。

・make fun of 嘲笑～　heartbroken 心痛的、悲傷的　speak up for 幫～出聲　respect 尊重

- 這本書有趣到讓我幾乎沒注意到時光流逝。

  The book was so fun that I hardly noticed time passing by.
  • hardly 幾乎不　notice 注意到

- 這本書很有趣，以致於我很快就讀完了。

  It was so fun that I finished the book very fast.

- 這本書有趣到甚至讓我跳過吃飯繼續看下去。

  The book was so fun that I even skipped my meals and kept reading.
  • skip 省略、漏掉　meal 一餐　keep -ing 持續做～

- 這本書有趣到讓我把它一口氣給讀完了。

  The book was so fun that I finished it in one sitting.
  一口氣地

- 這本書有趣到讓我想再看一遍。

  The book was so fun that I want to read it again.

- 這個故事太有趣，讓我愛上它了。

  The story was so interesting that I fell in love with it.

- 這本書的插圖十分有趣。

  The book's illustrations are so funny.

- 我一口氣讀完了一本書。

  I read one book in a single sitting.

- 因為我太好奇結局了，以致於我無法把它放下。

  I was so curious about the ending that I could not let go of the book.
  鬆手、放過

- 我覺得我只看了一半，但其實我已經看完了。

  I thought I had read about half, but I had already finished it.

- 那感覺就好像是故事太短了。

  It almost felt as if the story was too short.

- 我真的不想闔上這本書的最後一頁。

  I really didn't want to close the last page of the book.

- 我通常看書看得很慢，但這本書我真的很快就讀完了。它就是那麼地有趣。

  I am usually a slow reader, but I finished this book really quickly. It was that much fun.

- 我對這麼美麗的故事感到驚豔。

  I am amazed at such a beautiful story.

- 因為這個故事進行得很快，所以沒有覺得無聊的空檔。

  The story moved so quickly that there was no time to be bored.

- 一個又接著另一個的事件發生，讓我甚至無法眨眼。

  One event was immediately followed by another so I could not even blink my eyes.
  • immediately 即刻　blink 眨眼睛

- 這是我到目前為止看過最有趣的書。

  So far, this is the most fun book that I've ever read.

- 書受歡迎總是有原因的。

  There are always reasons for a book's popularity.
  • popularity 受歡迎

- 我聽說這本書很受歡迎，而我也能看出其中原因。它就如同我聽說的有趣。

  I heard that the book was pretty popular, and I can see why. It was fun like I had heard.

- 難怪！這是羅爾德・達爾寫的。

  No wonder! It is Roald Dahl.
  難怪、不足為奇

- 我十分確定這位作家是個天才。

  I am pretty sure that this author is a genius.

- 儘管這位作家是個大人，但他怎麼會這麼了解小孩的情感呢？

  How does the author know so much about children's emotions even though he is an adult?

很好笑 ★ It was so funny.

- 主角很古怪且有趣。

  The main character was weird and funny.
  • weird 古怪的

- 主角的行為真的很愚蠢。

  The main character's actions were really silly.

- 主角所有的行為都很荒謬。

  All of the main character's actions are so absurd.
  • absurd 荒謬的、不合理的

- 那實際上幾乎不太可能會發生，但這個故事還是很有趣。

  It is highly unlikely to happen for real, but the story is really funny.
  • unlikely 不太可能發生的

- 當我在看這本書時，我突然大笑了出來。

  I burst into laughter when I was reading the book. 突然（哭泣、大笑）
  • cannot help+Ving 忍不住～

- 在看的時候我笑得太厲害，讓我覺得好像快窒息了。

  I was laughing so hard while reading that I felt like I was suffocating.
  • suffocate 窒息

- 我差點笑到要流眼淚了！

  I laughed so hard that I almost cried!

- 這是我第一次看書的時候笑到哭。

  It was my first time to cry while laughing when reading a book.

- 故事裡古怪的轉折讓我笑得很厲害。

  The weird twist in the story made me laugh so hard.
  • twist 轉折

- 我感覺就好像看了部喜劇電影。

  I felt as if I had watched a comedy movie.

- 我已經有一段時間沒有笑得那麼厲害了。

  I haven't laughed that hard for a while.

- 在大笑之後，我覺得精神恢復了。

  After laughing so hard, I felt so refreshed.

  • refreshed 恢復精神的

- 這是我到目前為止看過最好笑的書。

  It is by far the funniest book that I've ever read. 到目前為止

- 這本書的作者很有幽默感。

  This book's author has a very good sense of humor. 幽默感

- 這本書既好笑又很感人。

  This book is funny and moving at the same time.

  • moving 動人的

很無趣 ★ It was so boring.

- 情節太老套了而顯得無趣。／因為這故事的情節太容易預測而顯得無趣。

  The plot was so common that it was boring. / The plot was so predictable that it was boring.

  • common 常見的　predictable 可預測的

- 這本書無趣到讓我在看的時候睡著了。

  The book was so boring that I fell asleep while reading it.

- 這本書不是我喜歡的類型。

  This book is not my style.

- 我不自覺地一直打哈欠。／我發現我在看的時候打了哈欠。

  I kept yawning unintentionally. / I found myself yawning while reading it.

  • yawn 打哈欠　unintentionally 非故意地

- 書裡幾乎沒有對話，並且充滿敘述。

  There are hardly any dialogues, and it is full of descriptions.

  • dialogue 對話　description 敘述

- 甚至連一個有趣的部份都沒有。／我在這個故事裡找不到任何有趣的地方。

  There is not even one part that is interesting. / I can't find anything interesting in the story.

- 故事情節無趣到光是要讀完這本書都很吃力。

  The plot was so boring that it was really hard just to finish the book.

- 我根據一篇推薦而選了這本書，但它不是我原先所預期的那樣。

  I selected the book based on a recommendation, but it was not what I had expected.

  • select 選擇　recommendation 推薦

- 因為這本書非常有名，所以我原本期待很高，但它卻十分無趣。

  Since the book was so famous, I had expected a lot, but it was so boring.

- 每個人都說它有趣，但我發現它不如我原先所想的那般有趣。

  Everyone said it was fun, but I found it was not as much fun as I had thought.

- 我因為之前先看過了電影所以看了這本書，但是它不如我原先所預期的有趣。

  I read the book because I've seen the movie before, but it was not as fun as I had expected.

- 故事情節太簡單了。

  The plot is too simple.

- 我因為看到精美的封面而選了這本書，但實際的故事內容太幼稚了。

  I chose the book by looking at the artistic cover, but the actual story was too childish.

  • childish 幼稚的

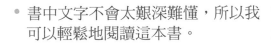

易／難以閱讀 ★ It was easy/difficult to read.

- 書中文字不會太艱深難懂，所以我可以輕鬆地閱讀這本書。

  The words were not so difficult, so I could read the book easily.

- 書中的句子又短又簡單，因此這本書讀起來很容易。

The sentences are short and simple, so the book is easy to read. /
The book is easy to read because the sentences are short and simple.

- 這本書看起來很難，因為它是 AR 3 等級的書，但它比我之前所想的還要容易閱讀。

The book seemed difficult since it was an AR 3 book, but it was more readable than I had thought.

• AR 3 是「適合美國小學三年級學生閱讀」的意思
  readable 易讀的

- 當我上次閱讀這本書的時候，我還無法理解書中的內容。但是這次我理解了大部分的內容。

When last time I read the book, I could not understand it. But this time, I understood most of it.

- 當我還小的時候，我覺得這本書讀起來太過困難，但現在對我而言就顯得簡單了。

I felt this book was too difficult to read when I was younger, but it is easy for me now.

- 我因為這本書很厚而覺得不安，但它其實是很好閱讀的。

I was nervous because the book was thick, but it was actually easy to read.

- 雖然這本書很厚，但它是用很淺白的英文寫的，這讓它讀起來很好理解。

Although the book was thick, it was written in plain English, which made it easy to understand.

• plain 普通的、單純的

- 書中的文章沒有那麼長，因此我可以十分快速地翻閱。

The text was not that long, so I could (flip through) the pages pretty quickly.
快速瀏覽、翻閱

- 因為這本書是用小的字體書寫，所以看起來不好讀，但是它比我原先想的要簡單。

Written in small font, the book looked difficult, but it was easier than I had thought.

• font 字體

- 雖然它是一本具教育性的書，但我能輕易地理解它，因為它談的是我已經知道的事情。

Although it was an informative book, I could understand it easily because it talked about something I already knew.

• informative 具教育性的

- 這內容太過艱深難懂。

The content/story was too difficult.

• content 內容

- 當我打開這本書的瞬間，我的頭就開始痛了。

The moment that I opened the book, my head started to ache.

• ache 疼痛

- 有太多我不知道的單字。

There were too many words that I did not know.

- 因為大部分的單字是我不知道的，因此這本書讀起來很困難。

Since I did not know most of the words, it was too difficult to read.

- 我不知怎麼搞地看了這本書，但我完全不知道它是在寫些什麼。

I somehow read the book, but I had no idea what it was about.

勉強完成、設法做到

- 我勉強地看完了這本書，但我不覺得我充分地理解它了。

I managed to finish the book, but I don't believe I fully understood it.

• fully 充分地

- 因為這本書的故事情節太過艱深難懂，而讓它顯得無趣。

The book's plot was so difficult that it was boring.

- 這故事情節太過難懂而且無趣。

The plot was too difficult to understand and was boring.

- 在這本書中沒有插圖，有的只是滿滿的文字。

There are no illustrations in this book, but it is just full of words.

- 我不認為這本書適合我的程度。

I don't think this book is good for my level.

- 我對於自己能讀完這麼艱深難懂的書而感到驕傲。

I was so proud of myself for finishing such a difficult book.

- 這本書光是讀一次是不可能讀懂的。我之後會再找一天再看一次。

This book is impossible to understand just by reading it once. I will read it again someday.

- 我常搞不清誰是誰,因為在這個故事裡有太多人了。

I often got mixed up trying to figure out the characters because there were too many people in the story.

搞混、搞不清
理解、明白

- 因為這本書是一本古典小說,所以它的用字很艱深,而且句子都很長。

Because the book is a classic novel, its words are difficult, and the sentences are long.

- 我對科學的專有名詞不熟悉,因此這本書對我來說很難。

I wasn't used to the scientific terms, so it was difficult for me. /
The book was difficult because I was not familiar with the scientific terms.

習慣於～

• scientific 科學的　term 專有名詞
　be familiar with 對～熟悉

- 醫學用語對我來說太陌生了。

The medical terms were too foreign to me. / The medical terms sounded very unusual to me.

• foreign 異質的、陌生的

- 我無法理解故事情節,也許是因為我沒有任何的背景知識。

I could not understand the plot maybe because I didn't have any background knowledge.

背景知識

- 因為我看不懂,所以我把這本書讀了又讀。然後我知道它的意思了。

I read it over and over because I couldn't understand it. Then, I got what it meant.

反覆地

- 我會先讀這本書的中文版,接著再讀一次英文版的。

I will read the book in the Chinese version first, and then the English version later again.

悲傷／感人 ★ It was sad/touching.

- 在看完這本書以後，我幾乎要哭了。

  I almost cried after finishing the book.

- 我在看這本書時潸然淚下。

  Tears rolled down my face while I was reading the book.　眼淚流下來

- 這是我第一次看書看到哭。

  It was my first time to cry while reading a book.

- 在看這本書的時候，我就忍不住一直哭。

  I couldn't stop crying while reading the book.

- 主角最後的話讓我哭了。

  The main character's last words made me cry.

- 這是我看過最悲傷的書。

  This is the saddest book that I've ever read.

- 在看完這本書以後，我領悟到自己是個幸福的孩子。

  I realized that I am a happy child after reading this book.

  • realize 領悟、了解

- 當我看到主角和她妹妹分開的場面時，我的心好痛。

  I was heartbroken while reading the part when the main character and her younger sister parted ways.　分開

- 我覺得藍鬍子很可憐。

  I felt bad for Bluebeard.

- 在痛快地大哭一場以後，我居然覺得精神恢復了。

  After crying my heart out, I actually felt refreshed.

  • cry one's heart out 大哭　refreshed 感到恢復精神的

- 在看了一個悲傷的故事之後，我的心情也低落了下來。

  After reading a sad story, my spirits went down, too.

  • spirit 精神、心情

- 我就是不喜歡悲傷的故事，也許是因為我還年輕。

  I just don't like sad stories maybe because I am still young.

- 這本書很感人。

  This book is so moving/touching.

- 這本書告訴了我一個很好的教訓。

  This book teaches a good lesson.

- 透過這本書，我學到了我們應該要珍惜我們的歷史。

  Through this book, I've learned that we should cherish our history.

  • cherish 珍惜

- 這個結局真的很感人。

  The ending is really touching.

- 雖然它是悲劇，但很美麗。

  Although it is a tragedy, it is beautiful.

  • tragedy 悲劇

- 這棵樹的愛情十分動人。

  The love of the tree is so moving.

很恐怖／殘忍 ★ It was scary/cruel.

- 我覺得這本書有點暴力。

  I think the book is a bit violent.

- 這本書的結局真的很可怕。

  The book's ending is really scary.

- 這本書的插圖真的的很恐怖。

  The book's illustrations are really terrifying.

  • terrifying 極為恐怖的、駭人聽聞的

- 關於這個結局，我越是想著它，就越覺得害怕。

  About the ending, the more I think about it, the more scared I get.

  • the＋比較級, the＋比較級 越～越～

- 我不知道這是個恐怖故事，而且它太令人毛骨悚然了。

  I did not know it was a horror story, and it was too gruesome.

  • horror 恐怖　gruesome 令人毛骨悚然的

- 我不知道這本書會這麼恐怖！ / I had no idea that the book would be this scary!

- 當我闔上這本書的那瞬間，我覺得很害怕。 / The moment I closed the book, I felt scary.

- 我依然記得書中可怕的場景。 / I can still remember the scary scenes from this book.

- 看完這本書以後，我很害怕自己一個人去廁所。 / After reading the book, I am scared to go to the bathroom alone.

- 這本書所講的戰爭故事太過恐怖，而且讓人覺得害怕。 / The war story that the book told was too horrific and scary.
  - horrific 恐怖的

- 因為這本書實際上是個真實的故事，所以似乎更可怕。 / It seems scarier since the book is actually a true story.

- 我的朋友們說他們一點都不害怕，但是我是真的很害怕。 / My friends said they were not scared at all, but I was really scared.

- 我不打算去看後面兩集了，因為這本書太可怕了。 / I am not going to read the next two volumes because this is too scary.

- 在看完這本書以後，我覺得好像有鬼會在什麼地方出現一樣。 / After reading the book, I felt as if a ghost might appear somewhere.

- 我會有一陣子不看恐怖故事了。 / I will not read horror stories for a while.

- 我覺得我今天沒有辦法自己一個人睡覺。 / I don't think I can't sleep alone tonight.

- 我當時不應該看它的。 / I shouldn't have read it.
  - should not have＋過去分詞 當時不該～

結論和推薦

Book Recommendation: *Frindle*

I would like to recommend *Frindle* by Andrew Clements because it is very funny. I've read this book three times, and I hope others will read it, too. If you want to laugh a lot, then you should read this. It is even more fun than any comic books. You will be amazed to see how a boy named Nick comes up with brilliant ideas. You will love the ending when Nick becomes rich and gives Mrs. Granger a gold frindle, actually a pen. My favorite part is when Nick turns the classroom into a beach resort. How much I wish I also could do that! That is why I love *Frindle* and I wish all of my classmates read it.

推薦好書：《我們叫它粉靈豆》

我想推薦由安德魯‧克萊門斯所寫的《我們叫它粉靈豆》，因為它很好笑。我已經看這本書看了三遍了，而且我希望其他人也看這本書。如果你想捧腹大笑，那麼你一定要看這本書。它甚至比任何的漫畫都還有趣。你會對於一個名叫尼克的小男孩所想出的聰明點子感到訝異。你會喜歡它的結局，也就是當尼克變得有錢，並給葛蘭潔老師其實是一支筆的黃金粉靈豆。我最喜歡的部分是尼克把教室變成一個海邊假勝地。我多麼希望我也能那樣做！這就是我為何喜歡《我們叫它粉靈豆》的原因，而且我希望我們班上的所有同學都能看它。

· recommendation 推薦　Frindle 音譯為粉靈豆，書中為筆的代稱　amazed 感到驚訝的 named 名為～　turn A into B 把 A 變成 B

我學到的東西 ★ Things I Learned

- 我認為這個故事的主題是全球暖化的嚴重影響。

  I think the theme of the story is the serious effects of (global warming).
  - theme 主題　　　　　　全球暖化

- 看了這本書後，我了解到家庭的重要性。

  After reading this book, I realized the importance of family.
  - importance 重要性

- 這本書給了我一個機會去思考自由的重要性。

  This book gave me an opportunity to think about the importance of freedom.
  - opportunity 機會　freedom 自由

- 這本書讓我領悟到戰爭的殘酷。

  This book taught me about the cruelty of war.
  - cruelty 殘忍、殘酷

- 我得知這世上有很多正在幫助別人的人。

  I learned that there are many people in the world who are helping others.

- 書的主題就是我們應該要感激那些以犧牲自己的性命為代價，保衛我們國家的偉人。　　以～為代價

  The theme is we should appreciate the great people who defended our country (at the cost of) their lives.
  - appreciate 感激、感謝　defend 防禦、保衛

- 我再次領悟到我們今日能存活下來，都是因為有偉大的人為了我們國家犧牲了自己的緣故。

  再次
  I realized (yet again) that we can exist today because of the great men who sacrificed themselves for our nation.
  - sacrifice 犧牲

- 我決定盡我最大的努力來節省能源。

  I've decided to do my best to save energy.

- 我想效法主角的挑戰精神。

  學習、效法
  I want to (take after) the main character's (spirit of challenge).
  挑戰精神

- 我得知了在這世界上有很多孩童正在飽受飢餓之苦。

  I've learned that there are many children in the world who are suffering from starvation.
  - starvation 飢餓

- 我已經為不斷煩我爸媽買一隻新手機給我而感到後悔。

  I've come to regret pestering my parents for a new cell phone.
  - pester 不斷煩擾、糾纏

- 我因為當事情變得棘手時就容易惱怒的自己感到羞愧。

  為～感到羞愧的

  I feel ashamed of myself for being easily irritated when things get difficult.

- 壞人總會受到懲罰的。所以我們要當善良的人。

  Bad people always get punished. So we have to be good.

  受到懲罰

- 從今以後，我會當個好兒子／女兒。

  From now on, I will be a good son/ daughter.

- 從今以後，我會和我的兄弟姊妹好好相處。

  From now on, I will get along with my siblings.

- 當我的朋友處境艱難時，我會幫助他／她。

  When my friend is having a hard time, I will help him/her.

  處境艱難

- 就像表現得很勇敢的主角，我也會勇敢。

  Just like the main character who acted bravely, I will be courageous.
  - courageous 勇敢的

- 我會像故事裡的人一樣，設定一個目標，並盡我最大的努力去實現它。

  設立目標

  I will set a goal and do my best to achieve it just like the person in the story.
  - achieve 實現、達成

期待下一集 ★ Anticipation for the Next Volume

- 我期待這個系列的下一本書。

  I am looking forward to the next book in the series.

  期待～

- 我希望下一本書快點出！

  I hope the next volume comes out soon!

- 因為我現在已經看了這本書，所以我等不及的想要新的一集出版。

  而今～、因為～

  Now that I have read the book, I can't wait for the next volume to come out.

- 這個故事是由五本書組成的。我已經每本書都想看了。

  This story is made up of 5 books. I want to read everything already. 由～所組成

- 我對結局感到很驚訝，但我發現還有下一集。

  I was surprised at the ending, but I found out that there was a next volume.

- 我對接下來會發生什麼事感到十分好奇。

  I am so curious as to what will happen next. 關於～

- 我想知道主角會發生什麼事情。

  I wonder what will happen to the main character.

- 我希望主角在下一集裡能變得快樂。

  In the next book, I hope the main character becomes happy.

- 我對犯人的真實身分感到十分好奇。

  I am so curious about the true identity of the criminal.

  • identity 身分　criminal 犯人

- 作者，請您趕緊出這系列的下一集吧！

  Writer, please hurry with the next book in the series!

推薦本書 ★ Books Recommendations

- 我真的很想推薦這本書做為必讀好書。

  I really want to recommend this book as a must-read. 必讀好書

- 如果還有人沒看過這本書，我會推薦這本書給那個人。

  If there is anyone who hasn't read this book, I recommend it to that person.

- 你在讀這本書的時候，你會發現這本書越讀越有趣。所以我強力推薦它。

  You will find the book gets more fun as you read it, so I strongly recommend it.

- 我已經看這本書看了三遍了，而我希望其他人也會看這本書。

  I've read this book three times, and I hope others will read it, too.

- 它甚至比任何的漫畫都還要有趣。

  It is even more fun than any comic books.

- 我相信這本書甚至連不覺得看書有趣的人都會覺得有趣。

  I believe it is fun even for people who don't usually find reading fun.

- 這本書適合各種年齡層的人閱讀。

  This book is good for anyone regardless of age.

  不論～

- 雖然這本書是寫給兒童的，但我覺得它對大人而言也是本好書。

  Although the book is for children, I think it is a good book for adults as well.

  也、同樣地

- 我希望我的父母也能看這本書。

  I wish my parents would read this book, too.

- 這是對於喜歡偵探故事的孩子來說必看的一本書。

  This book is a must-read for children who like detective stories.

- 如果你夢想當一名科學家，那麼你應該要看這本書。

  If you are dreaming of becoming a scientist, then you should read this book.

- 如果你喜歡科學，那麼這本書會對你有幫助。

  If you like science, then this book will be good for you.

- 如果你喜歡好笑且古怪的故事，那這本書正適合你。

  If you like funny and strange stories, this is the book for you.

- 如果你覺得歷史很困難，那麼這本書會給你很多幫助。

  If you find history difficult, then this book will help you a lot.

- 我想把這本書推薦給目前和朋友之間的關係發生問題的人。

  I want to recommend this book to those who are having troubles with their friends.

- 我想把這本書強力推薦給目前正在努力尋找夢想的人。

  I strongly recommend this book to those who are struggling to find their dreams.

  • struggle 奮鬥、掙扎

- 我想推薦這本書給像我一樣非常害羞的人。

  I want to recommend this book to people who are extremely shy, just like me.

  • extremely 極度地、非常

- 如果你想要看感人的故事，那麼我會推薦這本書給你。

  If you want a touching story, then I recommend this book to you.

- 如果你想知道兄弟間的手足之情是什麼，那麼你應該要讀這本書。

  If you want to know what brotherhood is, then you should read this book.

  • brotherhood 兄弟關係、手足情誼

附錄

- **10 種組織圖**
  (Graphic Organizer)
- **我的讀書宣言**
  (My Reading Contract)

About the Book

Tip 寫下書名、作者姓名、插畫家姓名等資訊，並對書的內容作簡略說明。

Title〈書名〉：

Date〈日期〉：

I like it!	It's okay!	I don't like it!
😄	🙂	😞

● Draw the cover of the story.
  畫出這本書的封面

The title of the book is

The author is

I   reading this book.

(enjoyed / didn't enjoy)

我的筆記

About People

Tip 分析登場人物的外表、個性、行為、思想、成就等，讓人一眼就可以了解各角色之間的關係。

Title〈書名〉：_____

Date〈日期〉：_____

I like it!	It's okay!	I don't like it!
😄	🙂	😣

● Who do you like most? Draw your favorite character.
  你最喜歡的角色是誰？畫出你最喜歡的角色。

● Write about your favorite character.
  寫出你最喜歡的角色。

My favorite character is _____

He/She _____

He/She _____

我的筆記

I Guess...

Tip 試著對書中內容展開的形式做預測，再與實際的故事做比較。

Title〈書名〉：_____

Date〈日期〉：_____

I like it!	It's okay!	I don't like it!
😄	☺	😣

● Before reading, draw and write what might happen.
  After reading, draw and write what really happened.
  在開始看之前，先寫下和畫下你想像中的故事；在看過之後，把真正的故事寫下和畫下來。

Before reading

I think _____

After reading

我的筆記

I Found...

Tip 在故事的結構裡透過重要的衝突矛盾和解決問題的方法來幫助理解內容。

Title〈書名〉：

Date〈日期〉：

I like it!	It's okay!	I don't like it!
😄	🙂	😣

● Draw and write about the problem and its solution.

把故事裡發生的問題和解決方法畫下及寫下來。

Problem

Solution

我的筆記

The Story Goes...

Tip 順著時間軸列出故事裡出現的重要事件來理解各事件之間的關係。

Title〈書名〉：

Date〈日期〉：

I like it!	It's okay!	I don't like it!
😄	🙂	😣

● Write the important events in order.
按照先後順序把書裡的重要事件寫下來。

First

Second

Third

Last

我的筆記

Story Map

Tip Story Map 是能一眼了解故事構成的必需要素，如文章的背景、登場人物之間的關係、解決方式等，如此就能輕易整理出文章的重點。

Title〈書名〉：

Author〈作者〉：

Illustrator〈插畫家〉：

Date〈日期〉：

I like it!	It's okay!	I don't like it!
😄	🙂	😣

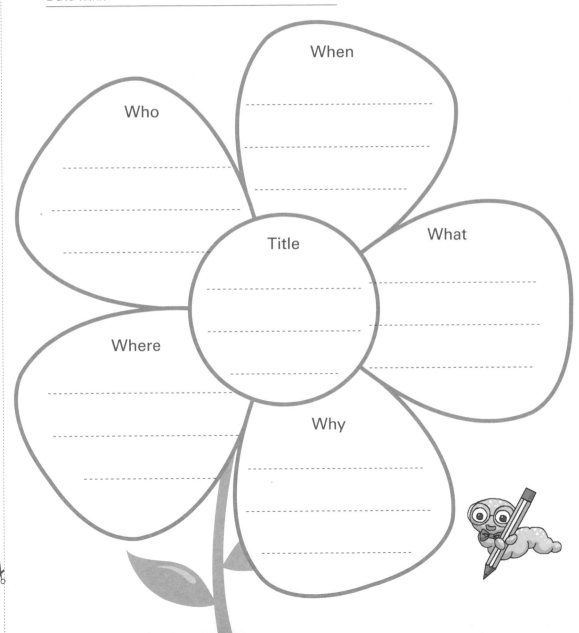

When

Who

Title

What

Where

Why

我的筆記

Summary Chart

Tip Summary Chart 是用來把故事的內容整理出開頭、中段、結論，可以概略地表達出書的內容給其他人。

Title〈書名〉：

Author〈作者〉：

Illustrator〈插畫家〉：

Date〈日期〉：

I like it!	It's okay!	I don't like it!
😄	🙂	😖

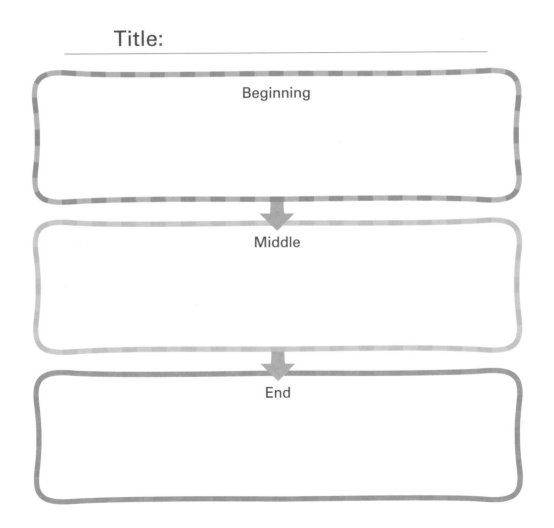

Title:

Beginning

Middle

End

我的筆記

Compare & Contrast

Tip Compare & Contrast 是在觀察文章的概念、主題、人物以後，分析自己和人物的共通點和差異性來幫助掌握文章的內容。

Title〈書名〉：

Author〈作者〉：

Illustrator〈插畫家〉：

Date〈日期〉：

I like it!	It's okay!	I don't like it!
😄	☺	😣

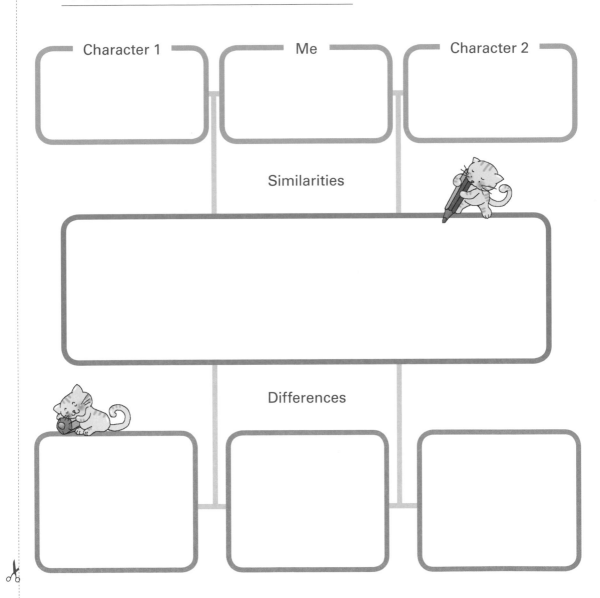

Character 1

Me

Character 2

Similarities

Differences

我的筆記

Problem & Solution

Tip 掌握在故事裡的重要衝突矛盾和解決問題的方法，透過這樣的過程就能輕易了解文章的結構。

Title〈書名〉：

Author〈作者〉：

Illustrator〈插畫家〉：

Date〈日期〉：

I like it!	It's okay!	I don't like it!
😄	🙂	😣

What was the problem?

Why did it happen?

Who made the problem?

How was the problem solved?

我的筆記

KWL

Tip KWL 是 Know, Want to know, Learned 的縮寫，透過自己所擁有的背景知識來了解非小說的書籍。

Title〈書名〉：

Author〈作者〉：

Illustrator〈插畫家〉：

Date〈日期〉：

I like it!	It's okay!	I don't like it!
😄	🙂	😣

Before Reading	After Previewing	After Reading
K	**W**	**L**
What do I already know?	What do I want to know?	What did I learn?
1.	1.	1.
2.	2.	2.
3.	3.	3.
4.	4.	4.
5.	5.	5.

我的筆記

My Reading Contract
我的讀書宣言

Date _____

I, _____ agree to read,

_____ minutes a day.

After I read the book,

I will finish a book report.

Student's Signature: _____

_____   _____

Parent   Teacher

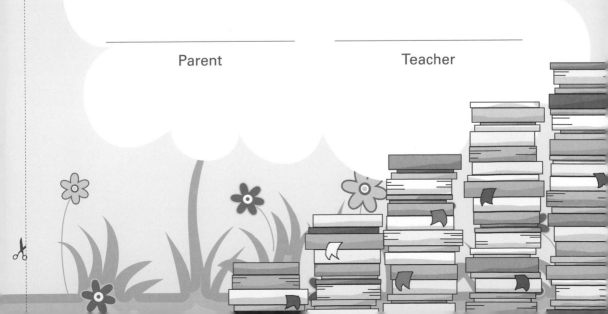

國家圖書館出版品預行編目資料

美國家庭萬用英文寫作／洪賢珠著
　--初版.-- 新北市：國際學村, 2015. 09
　　面；　　　公分

　ISBN 978-986-454-004-4(平裝)

　1.英語 2.寫作法

805.17　　　　　　　　　　104011883

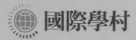

台灣廣廈 國際出版集團　　國際學村

美國家庭萬用英文寫作
從小學到大學，讓你終身受用的親子寫作書！

作者	洪賢珠
譯者	陳宥汝、陳琦超
出版者	國際學村出版社
	台灣廣廈有聲圖書有限公司
發行人／社長	江媛珍
地址	235新北市中和區中山路二段359巷7號2樓
電話	886-2-2225-5777
傳真	886-2-2225-8052
電子信箱	TaiwanMansion@booknews.com.tw
網址	http://www.booknews.com.tw
總編輯	伍峻宏
執行編輯	徐淳輔
美術編輯	毛荷馨
排版／製版／印刷／裝訂	東豪／弼聖／明和
法律顧問	第一國際法律事務所　余淑杏律師
	北辰著作權事務所　蕭雄淋律師
代理印務及圖書總經銷	知遠文化事業有限公司
地址	222新北市深坑區北深路三段155巷25號5樓
訂書電話	886-2-2664-8800
訂書傳真	886-2-2664-8801
港澳地區經銷	和平圖書有限公司
地址	香港柴灣嘉業街12號百樂門大廈17樓
電話	852-2804-6687
傳真	852-2804-6409
出版日期	2021年6月13刷
郵撥帳號	18788328
郵撥戶名	台灣廣廈有聲圖書有限公司

（購書300元以內需外加30元郵資，滿300元（含）以上免郵資）

台灣廣廈出版集團

235 新北市中和區中山路二段359巷7號2樓
2F, NO. 7, LANE 359, SEC. 2, CHUNG-SHAN RD., CHUNG-HO DIST.,
NEW TAIPEI CITY, TAIWAN, R.O.C.

 國際學村 編輯部　收

請沿虛線剪下

國際學村 讀者資料服務回函

感謝您購買這本書！
為使我們對讀者的服務能夠更加完善，
請您詳細填寫本卡各欄，
寄回本公司或傳真至（02）2225-8052，
我們將不定期寄給您我們的出版訊息。

- 您購買的書 美國家庭萬用英文寫作
- 您 的 大 名
- 購 買 書 店
- 您 的 性 別 □男 □女
- 婚　　　姻 □已婚 □單身
- 出 生 日 期 _____年_____月_____日
- 您 的 職 業 □製造業□銷售業□金融業□資訊業□學生□大眾傳播□自由業
　　　　　　　□服務業□軍警□公□教□其他
- 職　　　位 □負責人□高階主管□中級主管□一般職員□專業人員□其他
- 教 育 程 度 □高中以下（含高中）□大專□研究所□其他
- 您通常以何種方式購書？
　□逛書店□劃撥郵購□電話訂購□傳真訂購□網路訂購□銷售人員推薦□其他
- 您從何得知本書消息？
　□逛書店□報紙廣告□親友介紹□廣告信函□廣播節目□網路□書評
　□銷售人員推薦□其他
- 您想增加哪方面的知識？或對哪種類別的書籍有興趣？
　
　
- 通訊地址 □□□
　
- E-Mail
- 本公司恪守個資保護法，請問您給的 E-Mail 帳號是否願意收到本集團出版物相關
　資料 □願意 □不願意
- 聯絡電話
- 您對本書封面及內文設計的意見
　
- 您是否有興趣接受敝社新書資訊？ □沒有□有
- 給我們的建議/請列出本書的錯別字
　

請沿虛線剪下